Passion and Principle

A Sequel to Jane Austen's "Pride and Prejudice"

M. J. Felice

ISBN: 0989996808
ISBN 13: 9780989996808
Library of Congress Control Number: 2013919722
M J Felice, Midlothian, VA

Dedication

To Don

Volume I

Chapter 1

A cloaked figure stepped into the predawn darkness from the side door of Longbourn, Hertfordshire and climbed the path to the crest of her favorite hill. In only eight hours she, Elizabeth Bennet, would marry Fitzwilliam Darcy.

The expectation that a bride and groom exchange gifts on their wedding night had been a problem for a country gentleman's daughter whose groom was one of the wealthiest men in England. After much consideration, she set the parameters for her gift: it must be portable, must intrinsically represent her and must make one smile to see it since she deemed laughter important to a happy marriage. She selected a small, flat, polished oval of pink granite, the bedrock of Hertfordshire. Originality was her best hope for a gift of value.

When half-light seeped across the sky, Elizabeth held her little stone high above her head to let the first rays of sun on her wedding day sparkle the line of quartz running through its heart. Having made the commonplace unique, she wrapped her token in tissue and tied it with a white ribbon.

That evening Darcy presented his bride an exquisite garnet necklace. She watched as he read the note attached to her little gift. He smiled and kissed her stone then slipped it into the pocket nearest his heart; an act reaffirming Elizabeth's confidence in her excellent compatibility with this man.

"It *is* a problem, Mr. Darcy," twenty-two-year-old Elizabeth Darcy asserted. Wed nearly three months, she sat in a sea of rumpled blankets with nightdress buttons undone and dark tresses tumbled past her shoulders. Early light chilled her husband's bedchamber.

"You make an issue from nothing, Mrs. Darcy," he laughed. He did appreciate his wife's ability to discern and address problems except when she trained that talent on him. The master of Pemberley, six years her senior, fished for his night shirt before crossing the carpet to lay wood on the grate and bellow banked coals to a blaze. "In fact," he turned, continuing to press his point, "the Ladies of Peak Society meet today, do they not?" He counted the ladies' gathering at Braithmoor to be excellent support of his position, not that his stand required any bracing. "Your attendance at that meeting underscores our good sense to address our separate duties by day and enjoy our companionship at teatime and thereafter."

Elizabeth wondered if their delight to spar with a partner of equal intelligence and wit had evolved to value the game of debate more than it did understanding itself. Clearly, he was not addressing her request. She opted for a more direct approach as she slipped nightdress buttons into their holes. "Our marriage is less interaction and more conversation, Sir. We're wed ten weeks, but haven't shared a full day the past six."

To Darcy's mind, "interaction" and "conversation" were one and the same. He redirected her to sound logic with the first fact that came to mind. "Actually, we share every Sunday," he declared. Her silence irked him. "Well? I have the right, do I not?"

His wife met him toe to toe in the center of his carpet. "We appear to speak two languages, Fitzwilliam. You represent a day with church and guests as 'together' while I petition for a day with just us two. Conversation doesn't share life. It only reports what we separately experience."

His harrumph declared "discussion closed." Again, he modeled what disappointed her: a "harrumph" instead of compromise and the sport of argument rather than the content of the exchange.

After a last glance at broad shoulders squared against accommodation, she crossed the comfortable sitting room connecting his bedchamber to hers. A decorator from Town had caught their personalities perfectly in their respective rooms; hunter green drapes and mahogany paneling for him and sunny, silk-clad walls with curtains of garden flowers stenciled on polished chintz for her. Their sitting room in between artfully melded their opposites by infusing Darcy's deep forest with his wife's summer spirit.

Within an hour, Elizabeth's fresh curls bounced to the rhythm of her kid-clad steps descending the grand staircase. In the weeks since her marriage, she had made friends with Pemberley House, both its 127 rooms and its staff, to whom she smiled greeting en route to the morning room. The "morning room," named for its primary orientation toward the rising sun, was warmed by crimson damask walls and yellow silk upholstery with enough tables and settees between opposing fireplaces to accommodate family and friends from breakfast to tea time. Not only pleasant on its own merit, the room boasted tall windows on two sides that offered south-facing vistas of the lake encircled by emerald lawns and east-facing views of the formal gardens and the semi-detached pavilion beyond.

At their breakfast table, the mistress of Pemberley prepared her husband's cup while he turned the pages of *The Manchester Guardian*. The *Guardian* declared it was Tuesday. Wednesday would be *The Times of London*, and Thursday, *Drewry's Derby Mercury*. In deference to the hovering servants, Elizabeth forestalled her insertion of balance into marital understanding.

Shortly after ten o'clock, Darcy lagged behind Crawford, the head steward, and Evans, the steward-in-training, en route to inspect orchards along the River Wye. A hard freeze in early November had slowed the sap, but recent, warmer temperatures looked to entice premature buds. The morning was lovely, but the bright sun and cheeps of birdsong did not distract Darcy from mulling Elizabeth's petition for a shared day; his unwillingness to compromise spoke poorly of him. Arrived at the edge of the plateau, Darcy set guilt aside to guide his mount down the steep grade descending to Monsal Dale. But after reaching that verdant bowl of nature's perfect amphitheater, he found Elizabeth's "problem" still rubbed him raw. He had grasped her interest immediately when first presented, but had balked at its implication. *She wants more of me, but*

"We've got company, sir," Crawford called, nodding to where a lad had crested the escarpment and gingerly negotiated the uneven hillocks and juts of limestone. When the sharp descent nearly slipped the rider from his saddle, Darcy gave his roan rein and sped toward what looked to be impending disaster. The lad's little mare struggled to maintain its footing and began to slide downhill nearly on its rump.

"Ease up!" Darcy called to the boy, who held the reins too tight. "Lean back, not forward!" His instructions echoed across the dale and the lad responded well, though this did not mitigate Darcy's anger at the stable master; a novice ought not deliver messages in such terrain. Yet when Darcy at last intercepted the lad, it was he who nearly slid from his saddle.

"Good God, Lizzy!" he gasped as she smiled up from under the brim of the hat corralling her curls. He stared for a long minute, reliving the near catastrophe with this dearest protagonist while his heart pounded so hard it hurt. Finally, with a nod at her riding-trousers, he demanded, "What in God's name provoked you to this?"

"It is as you see it, Sir," she laughed. "My husband, who prefers to tour Pemberley by day, invites me to the same."

He stiffened, glowering that she ascribed her audacity to his support of separate days. Elizabeth looked down at the trousers that had let her sit her mount for its maximum control. The necessity to connect more closely with her husband had trumped society's requirement that a lady wear a skirt. She breathed-in the mild air of spring-in-late-autumn and admired the falls on the River Wye with eyes that sparkled like sunlight on the water.

"It is lovely. I now know why you prefer the land to me." She nodded at the stewards inspecting bare apple branches. "Please, attend your business. I shall follow at discrete distance."

Darcy left the orchards to Crawford and Evans, implying to Elizabeth she would get their day together, but her fruitless effort at interaction revealed a husband modeling more a lump of limestone, the bedrock of Derbyshire, than a partner. They paralleled the Wye downstream to the precipice of Edmund's Eyes, opposite the great landslip of Hobb's House on the far side of the river. Dismounting, they climbed a narrow path and followed it down the other side to the park where they rode manicured trails until arriving at the House. Brusquely, he motioned her to a secluded bench at lake side. Behind them, the Great House reflected unevenly on wind-ruffled water. An ankle-length, red cape from her knapsack covered her trouser indiscretion.

Scowling, Darcy dusted the autumn-littered bench with his handkerchief then invited abruptly, "Sit, please." She did, but with space between them. In a low voice, he announced, "You understand that what you did today won't happen again."

"I understand only not to interrupt your business, Mr. Darcy." He turned at the edge in her voice. "However, I shall ride when I wish." She rose. "Excuse me. I shall change clothes."

The breeze played with Darcy's dark curls while his brown eyes waxed foreboding as a summer storm. She could interpret his feelings from the color of his eyes: the more golden, the more at peace he was while the darker, the more personal turmoil he endured.

"Your stubbornness entirely misses the point, Lizzy. Sit!" That she did not accede to his demand was no surprise given their adversarial courtship. His breathing bespoke a serious effort to check his temper before he unceremoniously picked her up and set her on his lap.

Elizabeth sat stoic. Having trusted to know him well enough to think he would embrace her adventure, her mood now vied between disappointment and anger.

"Which point does my stubbornness miss, Fitzwilliam?" she asked stiffly.

"Damn it, Lizzy!" he exploded. "You saw the danger today. I'll not have a moment's peace knowing you might be off unattended when you should be…" Caution caught in his throat.

"Should be 'what'?" she bristled. "Should be serving ladies biscuits or tatting doilies?" Her soft brown eyes confronted his black ones. "I thought you knew me well enough to understand I need more than a House as entertainment for my contentment." She forced herself to calm. "I oblige my duties then fill empty hours inventing new projects until tea. I want you during some of those hours, Mr. Darcy."

"You were glad enough to accept separate days when I presented my plan in September," he rebutted. "What value is an agreement, Wife, if it's altered on a whim?"

"Is this your trouble?" she asked astonished. His charge was valid; she had agreed to that arrangement. Rather than debate, Elizabeth opted for the openness of direct words. "At first, separate days suited my needs," she began then confided her initial nerves to master her duties as mistress of one of England's Great Houses. "I know my House, Mr. Darcy. I now wish to learn my husband better."

He balked, "I think you know me as well as any person, Elizabeth."

Disappointed that he preferred to miss the point, she said, "I had hoped to learn you as well as I know myself." The admission startled her to grasp her unconscious wish.

While she watched the water, her husband studied her delicate features in profile; his wife was a beauty, both physically and in spirit. Since climbing to their wedding carriage, their union had been all he had imagined to embrace with his perfect partner. He granted that before last night's argument, which was indeed an argument, not playful sparring, he had sensed she grew discontented, yet he was uneasy to open the door completely between them. With clear evidence that his hesitation was dangerous to both her physical well-being and their mutual felicity, he reconsidered his options.

Elizabeth turned to him and said in a low voice, "I regret that you prefer 'apart' to the exclusion of even one full day together." Her disappointment pained him. She continued, "And I stand in rebuke for having waited too long to address my problem directly." With hands clasped tight in her lap, she sighed, "I bow to our differences, Mr. Darcy." Though she appeared to acquiesce when she kissed his cheek, he sensed a wall between them. "I do care deeply for you," she continued. "And I very much regret having interrupted your inspection of the orchards. It didn't happen as I'd hoped."

"What had you hoped, Lizzy?" he queried softly.

His tender tone startled her to stare, but before she could point out that she had clearly stated her hope on myriad occasions, both were distracted by Mr. Thomas as the tall, graying butler called across the lawns, "My pardon, Sir… Madam. I was just apprised of your return and thought it best to advise you that Mrs. Wittig has waited more than an hour in great distress to discuss with you, Mrs. Darcy."

Without hesitation, Darcy stood his wife firmly on her feet. "I'll entertain the lady while Mrs. Darcy dresses."

Elizabeth peered at the man who voluntarily sacrificed himself to the uninterrupted company of the emotional vicar's wife. This version of her husband was as out of character with the man she knew, as had been his recent distance from her.

Chapter 2

The ironies of life had fascinated Elizabeth Bennet since childhood when she had noted others saying and doing the opposite of their stated values and intentions. But since having made acquaintance with Mr. Darcy at a country soiree fourteen months earlier, it was the irony in her own life that invited her to shake her head. Such was her mindset when seated in the morning room watching her husband comfort the vicar's wife, who dabbed her eyes at the awful prospect of another winter ball at Braithmoor, home of the very patronizing Lady Newsome.

Elizabeth's visit to Monsal Dale had preempted her attendance at the Ladies' morning meeting. Mrs. Wittig reported that all were disappointed by Mrs. Darcy's absence, except Lady Newsome, who used the opportunity to set Braithmoor as the sole nominee to host the season's ball. When refreshments arrived, Elizabeth raised an eyebrow to hear Mrs. Wittig present the Ladies' petition that Pemberley volunteer itself to host the ball, and then she raised both brows when her husband declined said petition due to "obligations to their Christmas guests." After distracting Mrs. Wittig with a large portion of cake, a disconcerted Elizabeth discretely maneuvered Darcy to the privacy of his study at the back of the main level.

Like all of Pemberley's rooms, the study's proportions were generous. Floor-to-ceiling mahogany shelves and cupboards covered two walls, a third wall lit the chamber with tall windows and the fourth accommodated a grand fireplace and the door to Elizabeth's study. The master's retreat made room for an expansive desk, globes and map cases behind a long map table, and comfortable leather and mahogany chairs, tables and a sofa.

"Well?" he asked, leaning against a window sill, perplexed.

"I wonder why my husband believes his House cannot host both a ball and Christmas guests," she mused aloud. He turned his back and peered out a window toward sheep grazing in the distance. Elizabeth presented her issue directly, "Fitzwilliam, do you deny the ball, because my family is included among our guests?" He stood silent. She continued, "No doubt you recall last year's ball at Netherfield, at which my family distinguished themselves as center of attention. Perhaps that memory influenced your choice?" She had no doubt he protected Pemberley's reputation, not his guests' comfort.

With feigned indignation, he turned and countered, "You presume wrong, Wife. I merely lack experience hosting a ball; hence, I prefer to avoid it."

She eyed him, incredulous, and then doubtful. "Go on."

A very poor liar, Darcy took exceeding pride in his execution of the next bit. "Indeed, I've stood in receiving lines only as honored guest, not host. The responsibility doesn't entice me." With supreme effort, he delivered his next line with enough sincerity to convince. "But, Mrs. Darcy, if you can assure we will manage a successful ball, I shall bow to your confidence."

Elizabeth delivered the happy news to Mrs. Wittig, while Darcy poured a sherry and contemplated the flames dancing at his hearth. A lie, self-sacrifice, putting another's sensitivities before his own; Mr. Darcy had no doubt he had just broadened his expectation of marriage to include those of his wife.

The Darcys did share the balance of the day, but Elizabeth was less than satisfied, fact demanding that she examine her problem, not his. Since September, he had shared his House, his wealth and his excellent, though divided, company, but instead of being appreciative, Elizabeth wanted more… more than even the shared day he had just given her. For nearly an hour, she hugged her knees by the hearth in her dressing closet and analyzed the root of inconsistency fostered by muddled thoughts and feelings.

In the ten weeks since their wedding vows, she had grown to love him, not merely care deeply for him, but sincerely love him. This fact sobered a woman who had not previously loved without reservation. Having presumed that those in love felt peace and fulfillment, Elizabeth was struck that she was neither at peace, nor fulfilled; instead, she felt vulnerable, which was also not a state with which she was well-acquainted. Feeling like the captain of a ship whose rudder did not function well without the co-captain's hand on the wheel, she granted that for the first time in her life her happiness was dependent on another as much as on herself. However, dependence of the emotional sort was not part of her vocabulary, nor had life as yet acquainted her with the deep-seated trust on which such dependence relied. Love had landed her in the foreign realm of unsettling, uncontrollable emotion. *You, my dear Mrs. Darcy, have a problem.*

Having taken too long to appraise her reality, she hurried to her husband's door, but when she crossed the threshold, his bedchamber appeared lifeless but for flames on the grate.

"Fitzwilliam?" she called tentatively.

"Down here, Lizzy," he responded from the floor on the far side of the high four-poster.

Concerned, she hurried across his carpet then stopped short. Her shirt-sleeved husband relaxed on a quilt piled with cushions amid stacks of books serving as tables for two glasses of port and short, fat candles on silver salvers. After introducing their new tradition of "Elizabeth and Fitzwilliam's picnic," he knew from her look he had touched her heart.

Jokes and teases sobered with their second glasses of wine and his mea culpa. "I do regret I'm not like others, Lizzy. No, hear me out, please. I haven't admired men who wore their hearts on their sleeves, but I now see it might prove an advantage in marriage."

"I doubt 'hearts on sleeves' would suit you well, Fitzwilliam," she murmured. Certainly, she couldn't imagine him pouring his heart to others, but she did concede such might assist her to learn him more quickly.

He offered almost shyly, "You may call me 'William,' if you like."

Taken aback, she stared at him. "Is this the name I requested two months ago… the special name for you, like 'Lizzy' is for me?" He nodded. She watched him, amazed. "Do all of your deliberations require months to ponder, Mr. Darcy?"

He raised his glass, "More evidence your husband isn't like others." Then he toasted, "To history, Lizzy. Perhaps if I share a bit of mine, 'two months' will be easier to swallow." He explained that his name, 'Fitzwilliam,' had been his mother's, Lady Anne Fitzwilliam Darcy, who had made a gift of her maiden name to be his given one.

He continued, "But Fitzwilliam created confusion when the House hosted mama's family, hence on those occasions, I was called 'William.'" He chuckled and added, "Except when my grandparents visited, and then she couldn't call me 'Fitzwilliam' often enough.

"This explains 'William' but not my delay in offering it." Unaccustomed to voicing his deeper feelings, even to himself, he continued haltingly. "I shared more sympathies with mama than papa, hence my severe difficulty at twelve years when she passed, God rest her." He cleared his throat. "In his grief, papa removed reminders of her from the House and, I suppose, I imitated this in my own way. When you requested a special name, 'William' came to mind at once, but I hesitated to disturb cobwebs so thick I can barely recall my mother's face."

"Yet you offer 'William' now?" she asked softly.

"Yes. And I do so with a clear head." He reached and grazed his finger along her cheek. "Today when you said you understood why I preferred Pemberley over you, you challenged me to see our marriage from your perspective. I considered my choice for 'William' the full way home."

"Oh." What she had judged to be his distance to her had been his consideration as to how to address her need. Her look of unguarded devotion inspired the same in his golden eyes to speak a silent conversation more expressive than words. The moment stretched until his lips touched hers in a kiss whose softness belied an intensity that lost them in each other.

Afterwards still floundering for composure, Elizabeth whispered, "I wasn't expecting that."

"Nor was I," he whispered back. He had tasted the essence of love in a kiss.

"I'm all confusion," Elizabeth confessed then laughed. "It's not my strong suit."

"I echo your admissions on both counts," he admitted.

Feeling safe to test the waters between them, she hugged her knees and spoke thoughts without editing them. "I'm in awe of what you introduce in me, William. I'm both afraid and intrigued by a thing I cannot turn in my hand and inspect objectively."

"What do you fear, Lizzy?" he asked, his eyes burnished gold.

Like the rushing water of the Wye when its floodgates were opened, his invitation released the musings collected in her dressing closet. "I fear the attachment worked by love. I call it 'fear' for lack of a better word since I haven't previously felt such a bond or the deep emotion it causes me. I find things beyond my grasp disquieting. Last summer, after acknowledging I wished your good opinion of me restored, I presumed it could not be and I put my feelings in a box." A soft blush colored her cheeks; she had not shared so personally with another. His eyes encouraged her to continue. She took a breath and tested words of intimate honesty. "I now accept that 'feelings in a box' have been my habit where my deepest emotion is concerned. Yet, today the box is open, feelings tumble out, and though I'm confused by so much at once, I embrace it," Elizabeth looked into eyes of gold, "because I embrace you."

The next morning it was Mrs. Darcy who dispatched her husband to his steward, despite William's request for a second day together. Though she smiled at the irony of their changed positions, her mission was serious and required privacy. During the weeks he had left her while riding Pemberley's acres, Elizabeth's exploration of the House had recommended a project she thought would please him, but her plan required the return of some of Lady Anne's things to an empty room used as a hallway at the back of the House. After learning Darcy's troubled emotion in regard to his mother, Elizabeth would reappraise her project. Before any furniture was carried from the attics or plates removed from their packing, she would discuss the advisability of her endeavor with the Housekeeper, Mrs. Reynolds.

Mrs. Sylvia Reynolds, whose history at Pemberley stretched back decades, was a petite woman with graying hair smoothed under her ruffled cap and with bright, smoky-blue eyes focused behind little spectacles. She had liked Mrs. Darcy when that lady visited Pemberley last summer as a "Bennet" with her Aunt and Uncle Gardiner and she liked the lady even more as mistress. But upon learning the grounds for their meeting, she swallowed her smile. "I do appreciate the problem, Madam. Indeed, I've considered it since you first suggested furnishing that chamber; however, I cannot provide the guidance you request. Please, understand that a servant doesn't report the details of those who employ her." Elizabeth tempered her urge to shake the details from the woman then pondered how else she might gain insight.

That afternoon Darcy arrived early to tea with anticipation, but instead of his radiant wife awaiting him in the blue drawing room, he found a sealed note propped on the empty tea table.

Dear William,

As you see, our tea prefers a change of venue. The tray waits in my bedchamber, but before you join me, I ask you to consider a problem I can't resolve alone. I recently committed myself to an undertaking, which I believed would make you glad for my interest in our House. Once begun, my search of the attics revealed I would be including some of Lady Anne's things, which made me even happier with my endeavor until you shared your distress in her regard. Though I do very much wish to surprise you, regret would sour my happiness if my pleasure caused you pain. I ask you to guide my choice.

  Your Wife, Elizabeth

His consideration lasted so long his wife ordered fresh pots of tea twice over.

When Darcy at last opened her door, he stopped short to see Elizabeth on the same quilt spread on his carpet the night before. "Another picnic so soon?" he asked.

"Though I risk making the exceptional mundane, I couldn't resist," she declared dramatically then laughed while preparing his cup and steering conversation to the details of his ride. He understood she left it to him to broach her issue.

When she reached him his second cup, he asked, "How many pieces?"

Her nerves echoed his. "I haven't counted. They fit together in one theme."

"Will they be located in a room I frequent often?"

"You pass through it every day, but you could alter your route."

He sipped his tea in silence. She tidied the tea tray then hugged her knees and traced the colors of the quilt's separate blocks into one seamless, interconnected pattern.

The next afternoon in a corner of the high-columned, marble entrance hall, Elizabeth picked at the lace bordering her handkerchief. She anticipated her husband's return from the land at any moment. He had instructed her to proceed with her project, but required the full day to decide if he would see it. It was the fairest compromise he could offer.

When he bent to kiss her cheek, she read his choice from eyes as dark as Elizabeth had ever seen them. Darcy followed her along the main level's east hallway past high-ceilinged rooms on the right and long windows over-looking the grand, interior courtyard at left. He tensed when he noted the closed door at hall's end. Customarily left open, that door led to a broad hallway of a room, an alternate route between the back hall and the necklace of east-facing chambers.

The hallway-room also included two staircases: the "children's stairs" going up and the "garden stairs" going down.

Darcy breathed deep before grasping the knob then cracked open the door to confront the carpet he had not seen for sixteen years. Its pattern echoed the design of the Meissen chandelier which had first intrigued Elizabeth as to the room's forgotten purpose. Inside, he studied the vignettes of furniture along each wall. To his left stood the buffet topped with an open hutch resplendent with silver chargers that reflected light from the great arched window opposite. He adjusted a silver plate before proceeding to the adjacent fireplace wall where four Queen Annes in sizes from small child to papa circled the hearth fire. He gripped the backs of the two larger chairs briefly then raised his gaze to the arched window, below which a built-in walnut bench provided part of the seating around the oval table. Tentatively, he crossed to the table, lifted a porcelain cup from the breakfast service and was overcome with memories of mama preparing his plate. Turning abruptly, he glanced at the matching carpet runners from lower stairs to upper and then at the short stair wall where a sterling tea service glittered on a walnut server. He blinked, looked to the ceiling then bowed curtly before quitting his wife.

An hour later after footmen had returned all furniture but the oval table to the attics, Elizabeth still tucked china, silver and glassware into felt-lined crates when a written summons to Darcy's study interrupted. She penciled she would join him after completing the room's dismantling. Moments later, Darcy arrived in a lather.

Taken aback by the emptiness, he muttered low, "Damn it, Elizabeth. You work too fast." Then he raised his voice. "Leave that crate and come. Now, I say!" Unable to abide orders, yet loath to make a scene within earshot of staff, Elizabeth pressed her lips, raised her chin and led rather than followed.

In his study, Darcy paced. "I hadn't anticipated an entire room of my mother's things."

"You thought I begged counsel before returning a few vases to some niches?"

"Yes." He appeared as sheepish as he felt, "Yes, I did."

"Then we are each disappointed." She said curtly. "I deeply regret any contribution I made to our misunderstanding. Please excuse me. The crates await my attention." She curtsied.

"Sit, Lizzy!"

With her hand holding fast to the door knob, she turned to him. "I do not 'sit' for any person, even the man I love, Mr. Darcy. Nor do I fail to correct a mistake when I have erred and you will not deny me my right to do so."

"Yet, you'll let your stubbornness deny you understanding?"

"What is there to understand beyond your pained expression and escape?"

"Complicated emotion, Mrs. Darcy." He leaned on the mantle, struggling to share feelings. "Two days ago you said you embraced me. I… I presumed you included my frailties in that embrace. If you can only smile at a man when he entertains you with a picnic then I'm as disappointed in you as you are with me."

Humbled, Elizabeth set aside her own complicated emotion and pulled him to sit by the fire. "Forgive me, William. I was wrong to have presumed instead of discussing with you." She watched him. "I do embrace you. It's your ghosts I find hard to negotiate."

"Ghosts are part of every person, Elizabeth."

Though she was certain no issues from the past manipulated her actions, she did accept that his observation applied to many, if not most.

He cleared his throat. "I sense we've stepped from honeymoon to marriage proper." He had given this much thought while lagging behind Crawford and Evans. "Until recently, our attachment has been delightful, but superficial." She took exception. "If you consider it honestly, Wife, our first weeks couldn't get past 'superficial' since we each required adjustment to the overt details of marriage." She nodded. He continued, "Of late, you've prodded me to meet my deeper self, a person I hadn't given much conscious thought to know." And then he stepped off the cliff. "I wonder if 'learning our partner' isn't the art of marriage we each respect most."

"You've summarized our issue better than I, Fitzwilliam."

Darcy smiled and hugged her before whispering at her ear, "Of all your excellent attributes, it's your selfless honesty that encourages me to attempt the same." He held her hand and shared his recent ruminations. "You admitted to your fear on Tuesday and I admit to mine now, Elizabeth. Learning each other as you propose is like pulling on a loose thread that ultimately unravels the entire garment since sharing a little of one's deeper self will likely lead to one's entire self being exposed. One is protective of one's privacy, however, especially when one might be unaware of that which has gone unacknowledged for so long. Given this impediment to honest exchange, I wonder if the most personal aspects of sharing don't require the prodding of one's partner to entice a person's hidden-self to light."

"Your talent to analyze an issue outdoes mine, I think," Elizabeth admired.

"Thank you. It coddles a man's pride to know he contributes something of value." Despite her compliment, he did not gloat. "Be it ghosts or habit, Wife, my nature chances to irritate in future, but please know I shall work diligently to mitigate your discomfort."

Her look declared her celebration of his openness; that is until she further considered the implications of prodding. "If the necessity for marital goading is as you describe it, Husband, I perceive a problem. When I press you to share your deepest feelings, I chance your discomfort, and though I am outspoken, I don't relish causing pain to others and certainly don't wish to cause such to you."

He tensed. "Your meaning?"

"Beyond the direct issue of chancing to cause you pain, I wonder if our natures might stalemate our ability to learn the other deeply. *You* require prodding which invites conflict, yet *I* seek peace after a childhood quite the opposite." She opened her eyes wide then shook her head in disbelief. "My goodness, the joke is on me, I think. My history appears to challenge my ease with open partnership just as yours does you." And then she laughed, "I believe I've met my own ghost, William."

That evening in their sitting room warmed by wine before a flickering fire, Elizabeth tested their new marital understanding.

"I propose we invite Georgiana to remain the year with us when she comes at Christmas," she volleyed from where she sat in the circle of his arm.

Issues pertaining to his younger sister's well-being had been a point Darcy had refused to cede to discussion, as proved by his unilateral insistence that Georgiana abbreviate her holiday visit to Pemberley in order to attend the Winter Season in Town. His choice had addressed concerns voiced by the headmistress at Georgiana's former school. Mrs. Denton had confided that Georgiana's reticence to share her fine qualities at larger, social gatherings might benefit from practice in the Winter Season to better prepare for her coming-out next summer.

Elizabeth felt her husband tense before he removed his arm from her shoulders and said tightly, "A debate that insists to repeat itself until one side gets her way is referred to in some circles as 'nagging,' Mrs. Darcy."

"True," she granted with a twinkle, "but when new evidence presents itself, the person invited to prod would be remiss if she didn't abide her duty." He shifted uncomfortably. She continued, "We can provide our sister the social practice and us her extended company at Pemberley."

Certain there was a catch in her compromise, he grudgingly invited, "Go on."

"We've got our own ball in the Peak, William. By extending her stay, you will see with your own eyes how she acquits herself in a large gathering, and since our fête is celebrated at Pemberley, the assurance of home would support the courage you fear she lacks and thereby enhance her confidence at the Summer Season. If after our ball, you feel she would benefit from more practice, we can request invitations to spring affairs in Town and travel with her to make a family holiday."

Darcy made a mental note to never sell his wife's cleverness short. She pulled his arm around her shoulder and glanced up with a smile, confident her point had been made and accepted. He sipped his wine and watched the fire.

Indeed, Elizabeth's compromise solved all the problems, but one... the one he hadn't voiced. His dearest Georgiana had held him at arm's length since the previous spring, and in point of fact, she had argued particularly for four weeks at Christmas, not more. It was a preference that contravened not only the siblings' close relationship, but also Georgiana's stated desire to know her new sister better.

Chapter 3

The Earl of - - - and his son, John Fitzwilliam, enjoyed Pemberley's hospitality while hunting and fishing with George Darcy in that untamed heart of England. When the Earl's youngest daughter required a holiday from her mama, Mr. Darcy graciously accepted a third Fitzwilliam at his table.

At sixteen years, young Lady Anne Fitzwilliam made her first visit to the Great Estate and reveled in a world of private walks. At seventeen, she secreted paints and canvas in the bottom of her trunk, delighted to pursue her art while the men pursued their prey. At eighteen, she chanced upon Mr. George Darcy in his study late at night and added honest debate to her myriad reasons for loving Pemberley.

Mr. Darcy, twenty years Lady Anne's elder, was a private man accustomed to the strictures of a more staid generation in which ladies inhabited an alien world. But young Lady Anne intrigued him with her insight and her pluck, and she soon convinced him that none would guess their secret since society would not believe that a young lady and a mature gentleman could enjoy open discussion on all topics.

In early December, the coach transporting Georgiana Darcy, seventeen-year-old sister of Fitzwilliam, clattered over cobbles en route to Annapolis, the Darcy-family Townhome. Since departing Surrey that morning, her companions, Mrs. Annesley, her chaperone, and Hannah, her lady's maid, sat straight and silent like their mistress, stark contrast to four days of celebration for her cousin and half-guardian's promotion from colonel to brigadier.

A late luncheon awaited their arrival at Annapolis, but Miss Darcy waved off the footman poised to seat her, and instead collected bread and ham on a plate and ordered tea delivered upstairs. She curtsied to her pretty, copper-haired chaperone. "I've got some sorting to do, Mum."

Concerned, Mrs. Annesley watched the door close while interpreting her mistress' message: *I'm going to my studio*, her haven at the top of the house, and *Don't expect me until I've resolved my problem.* In the two years the chaperone had served her, Georgiana's "sorting" had been accomplished via the post with her cousin/guardian, Henry Fitzwilliam. But since that cousin appeared to sit at the heart of her issue at Surrey, the young lady would analyze by herself with ink on paper. The only other time she had sorted without her cousin had been last spring which had cost her a ream of paper during a fortnight.

Georgiana's studio was the space adapted by Lady Anne for her own art. Fitted with dormers in four directions and more windows in the roof, natural light brightened the space throughout the day. Awkwardly shaped, the garret was best-suited for a painter's easel which is why Henry had unlocked the door at the top of the attic stairs and introduced his ward to it four years ago after she had added watercolor painting to her talent in pen and ink portraiture. The studio was their secret since Darcy, her other guardian, could not abide unlocking doors to Lady Anne. Last year, Georgiana reorganized the studio to accommodate her newest passion, the decoration of rooms. Now, lovely fabrics shared shelves with aquarelles and ink.

Miss Darcy, tall and well-proportioned for her age, cleared her work table while awaiting the tea's delivery. Action is a good distraction, she thought as she filled her inkwell, prepared new nibs for her pen and set out a short stack of writing paper. After the footman bowed his departure, she layered woolen fabric over the tea cozy to keep the pot hot then sat by the blazing hearth and let go her emotion with nearly as many tears as when her papa died six years earlier.

Some of the tears mourned the loss of her best friend. Though the brigadier certainly didn't consider their friendship broken, she knew it was for her, despite that she couldn't specify why. Some of the tears bespoke emotional exhaustion after four days of hiding feelings she couldn't explain, and others were for physical fatigue after playing the entertaining young miss while working to learn the cousin, who she didn't know so well as she had thought. Georgiana Darcy had confronted numerous difficult adjustments since the loss of her papa, yet she sensed the issue with her cousin might be the most challenging of all.

Since her transfer to Town, the lessons served by the gossiping girls at Mrs. Denton's school and society's superficiality had not held a candle to the deception perpetrated by Mr. Wickham, whose near compromise of Georgiana had made her wary of men in general, and most particularly, of those who demonstrated an interest in her. She attributed her recovery therefrom to her guardians' gentle, steadfast encouragement; she loved them both and trusted them implicitly. Each guardian had offered differently to his ward's security: Darcy mostly as her father-figure and Henry mostly as her best friend.

Her kaleidoscope of experience had adjusted again the previous winter when her brother's attention divided among Charles Bingley, Georgiana and a niggling distraction that Georgiana thought might be Miss Elizabeth Bennet. Since last spring, Darcy's attention to his sister had been replaced by that of her cousin whose transfer to Surrey, so near to Annapolis, let one make a day's visit almost routine. Their recent months of outings to the theater, museums, symphonies, soirees and London's preeminent parks had turned the kaleidoscope again to reveal some of her happiest and most contented days… until his promotion to brigadier, that is. She dipped her pen and pressed ink on paper to put a name to her distress.

On the third day of her mistress' sequester, Hannah delivered a letter from Pemberley to the studio. She noted that the brigadier's letters, arrived since their return from Surrey, had collected in a pile with seals unbroken.

"Thank you, Hannah." Georgiana broke her brother's seal.

Half-way down the stairs, the maid heard, "Hannah, come quickly." Her mistress' soft voice had barely reached to call her back. Returned to the studio, Pemberley's letter was thrust in the maid's hands with a nervous, "Read this, please." Hannah sat by the hearth and read:

> *Pemberley, 26 November, 18- -*
> *Dearest Sister,*
> *We propose to extend your visit to Pemberley not merely to four weeks, but by twelve-fold in thanks to Elizabeth's insight. Since Pemberley will host the Peak's Winter Ball, we shall be able to provide the practice Mrs. Denton recommends, and thereafter shall enjoy your company for a full year. We hope very, very much you will embrace our invitation, dear Georgiana.*
> *Your loving brother, Fitzwilliam Darcy*

The maid studied her pretty mistress, whose blond curls bounced crisply, compliments of Hannah's curling iron, and whose extraordinary blue eyes demanded a second look. Georgiana was fetching, but in a French way, not English. Her D'Arcy heritage had conveyed high cheek bones, a petite nose, full lips, and a well-proportioned chin, now lowered in the face of crisis. The pressing nature of Darcy's proposition had distracted his sister from her issue with the brigadier.

"Tis a problem, Miss. What'll you do?" Hannah queried.

Georgiana paced the studio's polished floorboards. "I don't know" then "I must make a choice I've avoided for five years," and then "This looks to be the week I'm forced to grow up."

"Can you maintain your charade of shyness for twelve months, Miss?" Hannah asked. Georgiana had shown a meek face to all but the brigadier, chaperone and maid.

"Hardly," her mistress said as she sank into the chair opposite her friend. "After three weeks it is difficult. Four weeks is the longest my self-control can manage."

Hannah cocked her head. "Yet you want to live at Pemberley for as long as possible."

Georgiana sighed. "I want everything, Hannah dear. I want Brother to smile at my art. I want to trade Town for the Peak. And most of all, I want to be my natural self with Fitzwilliam." She sighed again. "It's too much to ask, isn't it?"

Hannah hesitated then blurted, "When something's important enough, one doesn't ask - one makes it happen." Four years her mistress' elder, Hannah had lived this lesson first-hand.

Georgiana studied the young woman with auburn curls slipping from under her cap and gray eyes lit with sensitivity and intellect. "Good advice," she agreed then added, "Please share the letter with Mrs. Annesley and say we will discuss it at tea."

Alone again, she leaned her head back on the Queen Anne and watched gray clouds jockey past a roof window. At seventeen, she had already lived two lives, and now she confronted a third. Before her twelfth birthday, she had been the happy, talented, doting daughter of George Darcy at Pemberley; shortly after that birthday, she was an orphan floundering to get her balance in London's disingenuous society; and now less than four months from her eighteenth birthday, her brother had unwittingly challenged her to choose between continuing her ruse of "shy sister" or introducing him to the artist who secretly decorated ladies' parlors. After setting aside the pages that strove to understand one guardian, she dipped her pen to sort her options in regard to the other guardian, her art, and Pemberley.

She first explored the deception with her brother apropos "shyness." It had begun as a child's misguided belief that her dependence on him supported his well-being. He had withdrawn in grief after their father's death until he had visited her at Annapolis. Shock at his sister's shy withdrawal had pulled him from his morass and dedicated him to her benefit. Her child's mind had equated his recovery with her neediness; hence, she continued playing the "shy one" after regaining her confidence. As the discrepancy between the reticent little sister and the more confident young woman grew, so did her fear to reveal her charade; her brother hated deceit.

Her art was also a lie of omission, but for her protection, not his. Her brother had been at university when she had refined her talent in pen and ink portraiture at Pemberley, but he knew she loved to draw and that papa supported her talent with tutors. On the day of papa's interment, she had shared a new portrait of her beloved father with Fitzwilliam, but he had stared at it darkly and quit her without comment. Since then, he had not queried about her art, a dagger of oversight that still pained her; he chose rather to champion her talent at the piano. It had been her cousin who coaxed her to explore aquarelle painting and who supported it with lessons; a fact her brother did not know. Neither guardian had been privy to her passion for room design until she had let slip to her cousin last September.

The chance to live in the Peak again had been her best dream and her brother's offer would likely be her last chance to do it. Next year, she would "come out" to society, after which she would likely marry and thenceforth would be only a visitor at Pemberley.

The more Georgiana wrote, the more she appreciated the far-reaching implications of her choice, hence she attempted to prioritize her issues: her brother's felicity or her art (meaning room design since it was that which was forbidden to ladies) or her desire to reconnect with Pemberley?

At five o'clock, Georgiana took tea with Mrs. Annesley who, after preparing her mistress' cup and a plate of sandwiches, insisted that the young lady eat. Since Surrey, Georgiana had been off her food; indication that her trouble was serious indeed. The chaperone laid Pemberley's letter on the table between them and got to the point. "Will you perform well at the ball, Miss?"

"It depends on whether I can pursue my art," she said between bites of cress and egg sandwich.

Georgiana's quick and certain response gave Mrs. Annesley pause. She said, "Mr. Darcy loves you, Miss, and I'm certain —"

"He loves what he knows, Mum," the young lady interrupted, "but this includes very little of me, even less of my art, and nothing at all of designing rooms. I'm sorry I've let it get so far."

The lady wondered if her mistress might purposefully sit out the ball in order to continue her work in Town. Courage and independence were laudable, but in the hands of one so young, such could be dangerous; society recalled ill-advised choices for decades after they were made.

"You can't mean you'll forfeit a year at Pemberley if he refuses the rooms, Miss!"

"No, but I can make a small studio in the storeroom off my bedchamber and work at night. I don't mean to flaunt my passion. I only want to pursue it."

"And the letters and parcels between you and Mr. Pankhurst? Your brother will guess your secret one way or another, Miss Georgiana; best to delay more projects until after your year in the Peak." Mr. Pankhurst, the owner of a fabric import business, had been the innocent conduit to Georgiana's passion for room decoration and he continued as her partner in that endeavor.

The young lady looked up, her chin raised resolutely. "I love my brother dearly, Mum, but I also love my art. If he finds me out and takes issue then I'll sit in a corner at Pemberley's ball, after which he'll dispatch me to Town and I'll continue as I have done."

Mrs. Annesley offered gently, "But when he learns your independent nature, he'll insist to keep you under his wing, no matter your performance at the ball."

Georgiana's striking eyes focused quiet determination. "I'm eighteen in March and can access my funds. If I adhere to society's expectation of a chaperone when from family, he will acquiesce to avoid a public row. I truly do not wish to cause my brother pain, Mrs. Annesley, but I believe he would be equally pained to know what it would cost me should I sacrifice my passion to his sensibilities."

The lady had no doubt Georgiana spoke her heart, but she had declared it to her chaperone not her brother. There was no way to predict the extent of her resolve face-to-face with Mr. Darcy. Her independence was in-keeping with her evolving confidence in recent years, but in many ways, she remained a protected girl in the guise of a self-assured young lady. Mrs. Annesley worried that if the young lady's courage collapsed, the girl might flounder.

An hour later, the chaperone climbed the stairs to her quarters with a heavy step. If times were different, she could counsel with the brigadier and he would talk sense to Miss Darcy, but as things stood, her mistress would not even speak her cousin's name. There was no question that Miss Darcy's youth required a guiding hand and there was no doubt that Mr. Darcy was the only guardian left to do it; his sister's tenure at Pemberley must not be left to chance.

She wiped a tear before sitting at her writing table and uncapping the ink. Feeling nearly as agonized as when her family had succumbed to diphtheria, she penned a letter to Mr. Saxon, a widower in Dover that it broke her heart to write.

Chapter 4

When Lady Anne was nineteen, a calamity nearly cost her Pemberley. While painting in the gallery, a wasp flew through an open window and stung her wrist, which sent her brush laden with zinc oxide onto the cheek of the lady in a nearby portrait. The cheek belonged to Mr. Darcy's wife, died in childbirth the previous decade. The gentleman's ire rejected his guests' apologies.

Following two months of remorse, the young lady's guilt evolved to anger at the gentleman's illogic to have taken such inordinate offense and she wrote to him.

Glenbrooke, 16 September, 17- -
Dear Mr. Darcy,
I am gratified to learn the damage to your wife's portrait is repaired.

While my family grieves for lost visits to Pemberley, I grieve for my own loss and yours as well, Sir. My loss is the freedom to put my brush to canvas. Your loss is the chance to discuss all manner of subjects with a person who does not coddle your eccentricities or acquiesce to assure her own benefit. As with our discussions in your study, the words in this letter are direct and honest and I ask you to consider them.

Our debates have caused us each to raise our voices in passion against the position of the other, after which we shared our pot of tea by the hearth-fire and laughed. I miss my discussions with the master of Pemberley even more than I do the chance to paint her loveliness. I wonder if you also remember, Mr. Darcy.

If we could indulge in debate at this moment, I would query as to how a man can deny himself honest conversation because a portrait is momentarily damaged? I would bait you to embrace the present, Sir. I would challenge you to invite my family's return, whereupon I would poke your arm and remind you that a man who cannot laugh at life misses the point.

I truly do miss our pot of tea, Mr. Darcy.
Sincerely, Lady Anne Fitzwilliam

G eneral Hiram Braxton, whose regiment quartered in Surrey, swallowed another swig of Scotch in deference to his nerves. Last March, he had feared losing his commission over a damnable misunderstanding with superiors. Two weeks thereafter, a gift from the gods in the form of a letter of inquiry had arrived on his desk when a Colonel Henry Fitzwilliam requested transfer to Braxton's regiment. Colonel Fitzwilliam, much sought after as liaison and expert negotiator, was known even to Braxton, who usually cared little for other men's successes, and he lost no time securing Henry into his fold. Thereafter, the general evolved a plan to recover his standing with higher-ups which soon expanded into a scheme that would promote him over the heads of his enemies; a scheme that required the colonel to wear a brigadier's epaulette.

Braxton was unfamiliar with the sort of man whose character required personal achievement as prerequisite for reward; hence, he was dumbfounded when the colonel balked at a promotion his tenure had not yet earned. Nor had Henry encountered the kind of man who threatened the charge of insubordination when he didn't get his way. Demotion breathed warm on Braxton's neck and only expeditious action could save him. Henry at last acceded.

To smooth the waters and recover his soon-to-be-brigadier's favor, Braxton availed himself of a private conversation overheard at a soiree in Town, during which Lady Sybille Harrington pined for her former lover, the handsome Colonel Henry Fitzwilliam. Taking the Lady aside, Braxton convinced her to attend Henry's promotion ceremony where she would surely rekindle Henry's interest since he squired no other lady in Surrey and most certainly regretted losing the attention of such a beauty as her. To Braxton's mind, a man who supported his fellows' romantic liaisons earned their gratitude and allegiance.

However to the General's dismay, his manipulation went horribly awry. While Henry was introducing Georgiana to Braxton, Lady Sybille arrived, making for icy politeness that even the General could hardly endure. During the ceremony itself, the delightful Miss Darcy lightened the mood, but only a little. The Lady pouted and Henry's anger at Braxton's meddling was barely contained; Henry had long refused the Lady's persistent petition to renew their affair.

On 10 December, a knock on Braxton's door delivered paperwork from headquarters in regard to Brigadier Fitzwilliam's new posting, the approval of which would set the general's scheme in motion. Given Henry's distaste for his unwarranted promotion, the general had deemed it best not to reveal "his surprise" until the deed was done. However a quick perusal of the attached letter bearing the Army Commandant's stamp drained the color from Braxton's ruddy cheeks, after which a detailed reading of the document sank his heart into his boots.

"You summoned me, Sir?" Brigadier Fitzwilliam saluted. His new uniform chafed at the armpit, but his extraordinary blue eyes hid any hint of discomfort.

The general indicated Henry should sit. "I like to think I take good care of my men, Brigadier," Braxton asserted leaning back in his desk chair.

"Indeed, Sir." Henry's spine stiffened imperceptibly.

"Such creates a bond of allegiance which is all-important when duty calls."

"Indeed, Sir," the brigadier repeated, sensitive to the words "allegiance" and "duty."

Of a sudden, Braxton shook the sheet bearing the Army Commandant's stamp in Henry's face. "This just arrived, Brigadier!" Braxton spat. "You, Sir, failed to mention that you're medically restricted from serving outside England. God dammit, no man earns such favor! How will you represent me at the King's negotiations in Vienna if you can't cross the Channel?"

"Vienna, Sir?" Henry did not change expression, but the grounds for his promotion to brigadier were now clear; no rank lower than brigadier served at negotiations for the King.

"Yes, dammit! I waited to announce it until approval was confirmed. Few men of thirty years get the opportunity I arranged for you and now I find you don't qualify because of bloody seasickness! It's not to be supported." Little veins showed livid on his cheeks.

Henry responded innocently. "Seasickness is an issue for most males in my family and me worst of all. Originally, I commissioned in the navy, but our first run at sea nearly killed me. The army accepted my transfer with the noted stipulation."

Braxton understood his mistake was monumental. A general could sponsor only one brigadier each decade and he had wasted his on a man whose medical exception denied the General's best hope to avoid his own demotion. His scheme had imagined Henry's exceptional skills would earn such favor that the buttons of the general who sent him would also be polished.

He eyed his officer from under bushy brows. "I see," he murmured after composing himself. "Of course, I must accede to an arrangement made with the Commandant himself. I shall count it as my good fortune that you'll remain with my regiment since there's much work to be done. Incidentally, any leave requested in future will be denied in deference to your responsibilities to me. This includes the pending leave at Christmas. You understand, of course."

"I believe I do, Sir," Henry smiled, conveying no hint of his loathing.

"Then it's good day, Sir," declared Braxton, already considering how he might pull the epaulets from Henry's shoulders and put them on a man who could at least get his tail to Vienna.

Freed from the uniform that rubbed him raw, Henry sat in shirt sleeves in his quarters with curtains drawn against distraction. He analyzed Braxton's every syllable and minute change of expression, after which he explored the weasel's possible actions against him. Certainly, the revocation of leave was but an initial slap on the wrist. Aware he was in battle for his hard-earned reputation and perhaps even his freedom, Henry faulted himself that he had not researched Braxton's character before submitting his application, a prerequisite before each of his previous requests for transfer. But his gladness for an opening advertised only an hour's ride from Annapolis had let him blindly embrace proximity.

A knock interrupted. Long-time friend, Colonel Edward Bainbridge, grinned to display two mugs of ale and a napkin of fresh-baked crusty rolls. Henry's appetite was legendary.

"Good God," Bainbridge exclaimed, "it feels like a wake here." Henry's sullen expression extinguished his friend's smile. He set out the ale and rolls before querying, "Will you tell me your problem?" Upon hearing it, Bainbridge stifled a guffaw, "Seasickness!"

"Don't make fun, Edward," Henry admonished. "My greatest wish was to explore the world, but my retching stomach nipped that wonderful adventure in the bud."

"I take it there's no way you can accommodate Braxton's plan for you in Vienna?" Then he amended, "Not that you want to play into his hand except that his hand holds the strings."

"If the Channel were calm enough and if I could endure the humiliation of vomiting for hours, I'd survive I think, but I'm loathe suffering for his benefit." He looked up and sighed, "I grant you he does hold the strings, however. Fortunately, I'm not without friends higher up and my restriction to English soil permits me time to negotiate transfer from his jurisdiction. I sense he means to cause me permanent damage, Edward."

"You can count on my support, Friend." Bainbridge rose to take his leave. "Ah, I nearly forgot. This arrived for you. It's the letter you've been hoping for, I think." He reached Henry a thin letter addressed in Georgiana's hand, collected the empty mugs and napkin and bowed.

Henry lost no time to break the seal.

> *Annapolis, 9 December, 18- -*
> *Dear Cousin,*
> *I have not written, because there was naught to report beyond that the weather is unseasonably warm. My brother has invited me to stay a year at Pemberley. The more numerous trunks required for a visit of such duration will leave no place for you to accompany us north. I notify you so you can make other arrangements.*
> *Your ward, Georgiana Darcy*

Stunned, the brigadier left her dismissive few lines on the table and stretched out on his bed, eyes closed and head reeling. His cousin was the most sincere and unpretentious person of his acquaintance, hence her words had spoken her heart; she had severed connection with him as much as a ward had the right to do.

The next morning, Brigadier Fitzwilliam arrived at Braxton's office with a freshly scribed document in hand. Henry first required the general to draft and sign a document extending his Christmas leave from two weeks to three, whereupon the brigadier signed his revocation of Exception To Sea Travel. He judged to cross the channel in April. Before returning to his men, he posted a letter to Annapolis.

> *Surrey, 11 December, 18- -*
> *Dear Princess,*
> *No worry for my comfort. I am certain I can squeeze my lanky body into a corner. I shall pack with discretion and borrow from Darcy what I can't fit into my smallest trunk.*
> *In anticipation of an illuminating journey,*
> *Your Cousin and Guardian, Henry Fitzwilliam*

Given his ward's resolve, it was incumbent on her guardian to address whatever issue she had with him sooner rather than later, and since his letters had had no effect, his only choice was to confront her in person.

Chapter 5

George Darcy tapped his fingers on the arm of the tufted leather chair as he reread young Lady Anne's letter. A man of strictest principles, his first impulse had been to feed her letter to the fire, however destroying her words would not undo her effect on him. His fury at the damage to his wife's portrait had been but a ruse to distance him from the young lady after a night of exceptional debate.

Two days after receiving her letter, he resolved his personal battle by reassuring himself that it was the discussion, not the too-young lady that he missed. On the third day, he penned an invitation to Lord Fitzwilliam and his family that they should visit Pemberley as often as they liked.

Morning sun glinted off silver chargers as Darcy turned pages of the *Guardian* while his wife sorted the early post. After reading a letter, she cried out in delight and grasped her husband's arm which nearly landed his tea in his lap.

"Good news, I take it?" he asked without changing expression.

At such moments, she called him the Prince of Understatement. After a dramatic look at the ceiling as emblem of her forbearance, she leaned over his shoulder while he read Henry's letter. "It is good news, indeed," he smiled and rubbed her sleeve, "certainly worthy of a tea stain or two." Henry's three-week leave would coincide precisely with the Bennet family's visit and there was no one who could breathe calm into familial disquiet better than Henry. After a quick curtsy, Elizabeth hurried to adjust Christmas plans with Mrs. Reynolds, leaving her husband to tap his cousin's letter beside a half-empty tea cup.

Darcy had no doubt that Henry's extended leave, and hence the chance for a less chaotic Christmas, delighted Elizabeth even more than it did him. A daughter's duty denied her open acknowledgment of her family's faults, but Darcy was certain Elizabeth suffered even more than he when her parents argued or her sisters vied for attention and especially when her mama called out the most outrageous remarks with no sense that she offended or worse, proclaimed herself a fool. Indeed, Henry would be the perfect grease to oil familial harmony.

En route to the stables, Darcy chuckled to recall this same cousin's shyness decades ago. Henry Fitzwilliam had not always been "the prince of the party." In fact, he had been a shrinking violet when, at seven years, he arrived at Pemberley as companion to five-year-old Fitzwilliam Darcy. Yet decades later, it was Henry who led festivities at the private, post-wedding party at Netherfield where, after demonstrating the waltz with Georgiana, he had taught the dance to the Darcys and Bingleys, who had wed that afternoon in a double ceremony.

Despite another spring-like morning, the air felt unsettled. Darcy again lagged behind Crawford and Evans while the elder continued his training of the younger as to a steward's responsibilities. At next year's end, Evans would assume the more active duties of steward, while the aging Crawford would continue tending the books and provide counsel to his protégé. That Darcy had attached himself to the stewards' daily forays as a matter of convenience had not been clear to him until Elizabeth's surprise in Monsal Dale. Having believed his preference for "separate days" was to replicate his parents' tradition, he was forced to admit that imitating their habit merely assured him the time to reconnect with his land after having absented himself from it too long.

Near eleven o'clock, they paused in the far west of Highfield where dry-stacked stone walls undulated in sun-bleached limestone ribbons across the tableland as far as the eye could see. Evans focused on Crawford's lesson in soil analysis that compared the root system of a clod pulled from near the stables to one just pulled from the field.

Seated in full sun, Darcy leaned against the warm stone wall and pulled two napkin-wrapped scones from his pocket. With them, Henry's letter tumbled onto the grass. He eyed the single sheet then stuffed it in his pocket. With his first bite, the scone crumbled, which was its natural tendency, but sudden

31

aggravation blamed the mess on Henry; scones were Henry's favorite. It was as if some pernicious imp had sat on Darcy's shoulder waiting to pounce. Soon after, he brushed the crumbs from his breeches and bade "Good day" to his men, who bowed and returned to their study of roots in crumbled dirt.

Darcy's ride carried him to the opposite edge of Highfield, where the lip of the plateau guarded Monsal Dale below. He followed a line of bushes to the concealed mouth of a cave, gathering sticks along the way to make a small fire in the pit just outside the cave's limestone walls. Chill tickled the air. Seated at the cave's mouth, the master relived adventuring with Henry, who had discovered this hideaway where they had spent summers defeating marauders and saving the dale from every mythical and modern enemy imaginable. *Ah, Cousin, those were good days, were they not?*

Shifting position, his hand pressed on his jacket pocket, crinkling Henry's letter inside; the sound recalled his blame of Henry for a crumbled scone. Irritation with his cousin was not something Darcy ever acknowledged, let alone worked to understand, but as a rising breeze flickered dying flames, Darcy sought the reason for his earlier antagonism.

Minutes later, he sat straight. *Dammit!* He had just inspected his feelings like a thing held in one's hand! He breathed deep before fishing in his breast pocket and studying Elizabeth's stone that he turned in his fingers. *You have the right, Lizzy. The box is open and feelings invite more feelings, but unlike you, I dread considering some of them.*

A glance at the sun disbanded thoughts of Henry. The day crept toward tea time, which he would miss if he did not make haste. After scattering the embers and dusting dirt over them, he retrieved his horse grazing on nearby Putwell Hill. Before slapping the reins, he glanced down at the Wye where the water, backed up behind a weir, smoothed to a narrow pond between Cressbrook's cliffs across the river and Pemberley's Putwell Hill. Water-cum-Jolly, as the pond was called, was where his mother loved to stand her easel on the Pemberley side. The memory pulsed through his head like a heartbeat.

A glance at Cressbrook Hall on the far side of the Wye delayed him longer. Anchored at the edge of the escarpment, the Hall commanded one of the prettiest views of the river or so Darcy had heard tell. His father's disputes with Lord Pillory, Cressbrook's owner, were legend in the region and George had forbidden his son to visi –. A thin, gray thread of smoke distracted Darcy from his thought. Only one of the Hall's twenty chimneys emitted smoke despite that the deepening chill would be felt inside all corners of the gabled, stone house. Every fireplace should be lit and their fires should be vibrant enough to produce white smoke, not grey A nerve pricked. Something was amiss. Behind the Hall and half-way up the hill called Hayfield, the stone cottages of Cressbrook Village paralleled the river; the houses evidenced no smoke or other indication of life. Darcy resolved that Evans should learn the estate's condition; stability on one's borders was almost as important as contentment within.

With his first step across Pemberley's threshold, Darcy saw Mrs. Reynolds kneading a crumpled handkerchief in distress. Tight-lipped, he led the way behind closed doors.

"Sir, it's not my place to tell it, but I believe you should know that Mrs. Darcy received an express letter just before luncheon. I was with her in her study. We were reviewing the adjustments to your guests' entertainment. She was so very pleased."

"The letter, Mrs. Reynolds?" He had not known the Housekeeper to ramble.

"Yes, Sir. It was from Longbourn. Her family won't visit us at Christmas. I tell you because it wounded her severely, I think. She has since kept to her chambers."

He touched the Housekeeper's shoulder and whispered "Thank you" before climbing the grand staircase by twos and threes then running full-out down the hallway to her door at the end.

"Lizzy? You locked the door. Open it, please." He strained to hear through the thick oak. Silence. Next he tried her door to their sitting room, but again the key had been turned and left in the lock. She did not respond to his calls which further heightened his nerves and made entry imperative, but Darcy did not summon the lock smith. Elizabeth was even keener than he to maintain personal privacy in a House full of servants. After ten minutes and a badly nicked letter opener, gouged wood, and two small wounds on his right hand, he had loosed the hinge pins and eased the door from its frame all the while cursing his awkwardness with tools.

Waning light revealed a few embers glowing beneath the grates of the opposing fireplaces in her wide chamber. A single-page letter lay on her bed.

Opening the door to her dressing closet, he breathed relief to find her curled in a Queen Anne with their picnic quilt pulled to her chin. The closet's fire had long since grown cold. After coaxing blazes at her bedchamber's hearths, he transported his wife, quilt and all, to the sofa by her corner fireplace, which shared a chimney with the sitting room. Her breathing was even and she cuddled against him. He read Mrs. Bennet's letter.

> *Longbourn, 12 December, 18- -*
> *Dear Lizzy,*
> *Awful news! Jane suffers too much from morning illness to manage the journey to Pemberley, and since I must attend her every day, we also will not travel. I told Papa you would understand, but he said "not" and has stuck himself in his study very angry and refusing to speak. He does not see the necessity that I attend Jane. He adds to my suffering a hundred-fold with his stubbornness, Lizzy, and so increases my risk to suffer the vapors that I must carry my smelling salts in my pocket. I am sure your party will be very nice, and you will not miss us one bit. Perhaps we can visit in summer after Jane delivers. Your Mama, Sally Bennet*

Mrs. Bennet had the sensitivity of a stone, which raised the question how she could produce a daughter like his Elizabeth. He mulled the mystery until his arm numbed where his wife pressed against it, whereupon he settled her on her bed, laid more wood on the fire dogs, and then pulled her be-flowered curtains closed against cold drafts. The clouds that had followed him home looked to return winter to the land. Frost stretched ice-fingers across the panes and the chilled floorboards made him glad for his mother's thick carpet that reached nearly from one fireplace to the other. The thought caught him short. He wondered why he balked to see his mama's possessions elsewhere, yet had stipulated to Mr. Pankhurst that her carpet be incorporated into Elizabeth's chamber.

When Elizabeth finally roused, she opened her eyes to a bedchamber instead of a dressing closet and the soft breathing of the napping husband stretched beside her. The mantel clock corroborated it was mid-evening and mama's letter, wadded on a table, declared William was privy to her disappointment.

She sighed to acknowledge that relations with her family were complicated, but they were not so painful as the wadded letter implied her husband to believe.

Yes, her eyes had teared to read it, but it was the unexpectedness, not the news itself, that had disconcerted her. She had long since made peace with mama's callous silliness and papa's inclination to espouse rather than to act. Among her parents and four sisters, Elizabeth was an outcast of sorts, which had been her hair-shirt until about seven years of age when she had learned the benefits of logic. Thereafter, clear thinking had reinforced her confidence as it buffered against the discrepancies between herself and most people she met.

When Darcy awoke, Elizabeth was stoking the fires. A dinner tray with polished silver domes waited on the table near the corner hearth. "Are you well?" he asked.

She turned and smiled, "Yes and very hungry." She served their dinner.

He sipped his wine, hesitant to re-open her wound, yet compelled to offer his best effort to make a bad situation right. "It's understandable that Jane can't travel and that your mama wishes to tend the mother of her first grandchild." He dug deep to infuse excitement into the next bit. "I propose we celebrate Christmas at Longbourn. It would shorten Georgiana and Henry's journey, and after Christmas, we would proceed to Pemberley for the ball. What do you think?"

"You don't understand, do you?" she asked gently. "Mama didn't invite us and she would dissuade us from coming if we proposed it. She wants Jane for herself."

Darcy's jaw set firmly against discrimination. "Forgive me for how this sounds, Wife, but you show more forbearance than I could muster given the same circumstance."

"It isn't forbearance," she stated after swallowing a bite of stew. "It's acceptance of what I can't change or comprehend." She looked up, "Nor does my family understand me. There is no fault. Our differences preclude understanding."

He leaned back to study her, his eyes becalmed and wonder-filled. "You are very good."

She buttered her bread. "I'm logical, William. It's not an attribute much prized in women, but it does support a more even temperament than evidenced by many of my sex and it lets me laugh at silliness I can't otherwise affect." She tilted her head, eyes sparkling with a tease. "Perhaps we ought be grateful for my family's delayed introduction to the Peak since we now must host our ball without them."

He stiffened. "It's no matter if they attend or not."

"At risk of presenting myself as a too disrespectful daughter, only a fool would think it 'no matter if they attend or not' and my husband is no fool." She raised her glass to him. "I have my new family at Christmas, William, for which I'm very, very happy."

Chapter 6

Lady Anne loved surprises, a characteristic her husband challenged himself to satisfy with ever greater energy. However, the day he introduced her to a great black carpet crisscrossed with green lattice entwined with mauve roses, she took the hint to actively, yet subtly, guide his taste.

As time passed, however, the Lady learned that love did not judge color combinations and proportion with the same eyes as an artist. She walked on that carpet for eleven years, and with every step, it became more dear to her. She soon gave up leading George to see beauty through her eyes; first, because it was hopeless, and second, because the most endearing aspect of his choices was his effort to please her, not whether it was something she would have selected herself.

From a studio window, Georgiana watched footmen in the alley far below as they secured trunks on the wagon and stacked bonnet boxes inside two deep-blue coaches each with a gilded P scrolled inside a gold oval on its door. Her anticipation for the journey had withered with Henry's insistence to escort her, yet she now waited and watched for him as she had since she was twelve. Habits are hard to break, she thought before forcing herself to wait in the library where no windows faced on the back garden.

During the past fortnight, she had prepared for change as best she could. As per Mrs. Annesley's advice, she dispatched a letter to her brother, in which she introduced herself, her art and her enterprise in room decoration. Mr. Pankhurst hired a young man to attend what she could not while she intended to continue as consultant from Pemberley. And she devoted long hours to the difficult meeting with her cousin. As per his method to assure advantage in negotiation, she wrote out her speech and responses to his possible rebuttals then practiced them aloud until they rolled off her tongue without stumbling.

In the back alley, Hannah, who supervised the delicate packages, was the first to see the brigadier. He waited until his trunk was tied on the wagon before crossing the garden with a confident stride.

Mrs. Annesley announced, "He's arrived, Miss. Shall I remain… for support?"

"No. Thank you. I require no support." It was confidence she did not feel, but her cousin had always counseled that if one conveys confidence, one will gain it. She received him in the library, or rather, she curtsied silent greeting and he bowed. They sat in opposite corners.

"Princess, I hope –"

She interrupted, "I prefer that you no longer call me 'Princess,' Henry."

He studied her. After a few moments, he shook his head and said, "I shan't argue that point at present" then crossed the room and laid a letter on her lap. "I didn't know the extent of our awkwardness at the start, hence, I wrote –" Mrs. Annesley knocked. The coaches waited.

Once underway, Georgiana could not recall the minutes from departing the library, to tying bonnet and cloak, to collecting the muslin-wrapped peppermint plant that sweetened her breath after a nervous stomach, to walking down the garden path, to settling across from him in the lead coach amid boxes and parcels. She was sensitive to time that passed without remembering.

As the short entourage of two coaches and a wagon threaded the streets of London and turned onto the King's Highway North, the brigadier took measure of his ward. Her silence challenged him to speak first, making clear the depth of their impasse. Not having anticipated feeling like a schoolboy, he nodded at the letter. "You might read it now, Georgiana."

"Oh… yes." She broke the seal.

> *Dear Princess,*
> *We've always been honest with one another, a habit I shan't shy from today. Your apparent curtailment of our friendship has struck me deeply, implying I took that friendship for granted. Though unintended, such is an insult to us both.*
> *Our honesty has been grounded in open discussion and I expect the same after you read this note. As I told you previously, I'm completely confused by our present*

trouble, which appeared to begin with the introduction of Lady Sybille. I've no doubt you were surprised… no, perhaps "shocked" best describes your state when General Braxton introduced her. Anyhow, I was shocked as well, as I explained that first evening. I wonder why my explanation did not calm you as you led me to believe. I will hear your feelings, Princess, and I ask that you also hear mine.

Your Cousin, Henry Fitzwilliam

Georgiana breathed deep to compose herself. She had also taken their friendship for granted, but his truth did not alter her facts. "You're an exceptional man to speak so openly."

"Your tone implies 'not exceptional enough' to warrant the renewal of our friendship," he countered with a sinking feeling.

"Henry, the trouble lies with me, not you. I am the problem. I don't judge against you. I believe you in regard to Lady Sybille."

"But…?"

She looked past her window, blinking too much. "This is more difficult that I thought."

"I want to understand, Georgiana."

She took a breath. "Our friendship died for me at Surrey, Henry."

He stared. "You have my full attention, Miss Darcy."

Her azure eyes met his, twins of her own. Nature had shared this striking shade of "Fitzwilliam blue" between cousins to let them appear more as brother and sister than they did with their own siblings. Despite the softness of her voice, she stated firmly, "Henry, reali —"

"Why 'Henry'?" he interrupted. "You haven't addressed me so before."

"Let me finish, please." She laid his letter on the seat. "Henry, reality roots our friendship in law, as guardian and ward, and in nature, as cousins. I didn't perceive the bounds of that reality until your promotion. For six years, my happiness and security counted on you and my brother through your letters or visits. More recently, however, my brother's attachment to Elizabeth and your nearer proximity in Surrey intensified my attachment to you which let me better appreciate your long-standing devotion though debates in letters, discoveries in Town, the art you encouraged me to pursue and the innumerable lessons your pressed on my impressionable self. I know now it was not your intent to convey that I was most important to you," she colored slightly, "but a person knows only the evidence put before her." Georgiana looked him in the eye. "My trust in my perception of our friendship died last month and 'Henry' reminds me of this." She focused on the fields past her window. "There is no 'Princess', only ward and cousin."

Georgiana had mastered his lessons too well. He blurted in frustration, "But Princess…"

She stiffened to hear the name she had refused him and opened her mouth in retort.

His eyes narrowed. "One moment, Miss! You've declared to live in reality and therefore must accept mine, I insist to address you as I will, without negotiation."

Her smile caught him short. "We make a good start, Brigadier. In six years you haven't once stepped past supportive guardian to 'insist' anything."

"Go on," he invited, troubled that she spoke as a peer, not his ward.

"Don't you see it?" Georgiana cried impatiently, her curls jostling at the edges of a bonnet their own shared shade of blue. "If I am to take confidence in my impression, I must trust that what I learn is the full truth and not aspects of your life selected to protect a child." To his retort that he had always been honest with her, she countered, "You taught me that conveying only part of the truth is dishonest. Certainly one doesn't report the details of one's affairs, but one can share that the holiday in Bristol was in the company of Lady A, or the study of new farm machinery was done with Lady B in tow. Even superficial knowledge invites reality."

He stared, mouth agape. "Georgiana, how on earth did you learn –"

She rolled her eyes at his obtuseness. "I had my own purpose when I entertained your friends in Surrey." Suddenly, her amiability with the other officers, several of whom had known him for much of his career, made sense. She continued, "Their memories gained clarity of detail with each mug of ale which earned me more education that I sometimes thought I could swallow." She looked past her window. "My carriage rides with Lady Sybille were also an education after she took confidence I was a friend in whom she could confide."

The elder cousin felt a hot blush rise up his neck. The younger cousin slipped his note into her reticule; their conversation had concluded. One coach now felt like two. A half-hour later, the sandwich she offered from the picnic basket tasted like one handed by a stranger.

Henry Fitzwilliam had misjudged both the issue and Georgiana. Their disconnection, however, left too big a hole in his life to accept. Gut instinct foisted him into uncharted territory. "Dammit, Georgiana!" he exclaimed in exasperation. He hunched under the low roof and methodically transferred parcels from her seat to the place where he had sat. "Make room!" She adjusted. "Now," he began, "if I share my entire history, will you trust to know me as well as any?"

Beginning with his first memories at Glenbrooke, the Fitzwilliam-family home, he proceeded through every facet of his life, editing only the inconsistency of his relationship with Darcy and the personal details between ladies and gentlemen. He responded thoughtfully to her queries as to his feelings and the motivations for his choices when life handed him a surprise. The more he shared the more she smiled until honesty renewed them to better than before.

While friendship set new seed in the first coach, confusion and despair followed in the second. Hannah cried, "You can't leave us, Mum!" Mrs. Annesley had apprised the maid that she had accepted a position in Dover to attend four children. She prepared Hannah to support her mistress when Miss Georgiana learned she would have no chaperone to permit her return to Town.

Chapter 7

Lady Anne pulled back the curtain at her boudoir window and watched her son play chase with his cousin, Henry. Though two years older, her brother's youngest was a healthy diversion for her boy, who preferred pets to playmates.

Unfortunately, a friend for Fitzwilliam opened a personal conundrum for the Lady. Her son had been her best companion while her husband rode Pemberley's acres by day; hence loss of the lad opened the mama to loneliness. Lady Anne, however, was not one to mope and within weeks she transformed the oversized closet adjoining her husband's study to make a study for herself, complete with its new public entrance of French doors opening to the back hall. When her project was completed, the gentleman took comfort to watch Anne at her desk through the door he insisted to keep open. As for Lady Anne, her eye for artistic form had not only carved a small niche in George's habits, but also blossomed her best talent, the application of her art to architecture.

Snow blanketed the Peak for five days running, to which Pemberley responded by converting three carriages to sleighs, pulling thick scarves and mittens from wardrobes and wafting white smoke from every chimney. Darcy recalled Cressbrook's smokeless chimneys and dispatched Evans to glean the condition of their neighbor as soon as the sky cleared.

While the region adjusted to the weather, the Darcys adjusted to each other's needs, the most prominent of which was more flexible schedules. Whether it was re-ordering their duties to permit time together during the day or attending their business with an open door from his study to hers, their harmony infused smiles through the entire House.

One morning near ten o'clock, Elizabeth handed several letters to the waiting footman, curtsied to her husband at the door between their studies then departed via her French doors.

Darcy caught up as she turned into the west hallway.

"You made quick work of the post this morning," he observed.

"I'm going out," she smiled. "The rest can wait until I return." She patted his sleeve and teased, "Don't trouble yourself, William. I've forsworn horse-riding for winter's duration." He did not smile. She elaborated, "I'm taking my walk early. The snow is too pretty to ignore."

"You might have invited me," he muttered, disappointed.

Noting a nearby maid, Mrs. Darcy accompanied the master to his study then clarified, "William, if I'd invited you, I would have interrupted your business, which I agreed to avoid." A knock announced the arrival of Mrs. Darcy's cloak, muff and boots.

Exhilarated by the cold, Elizabeth practically danced down the drive. She turned onto Pemberley Road where regular traffic had packed down deep snow, over which a fresh, trackless coverlet of white let her pretend she was the first to set eyes on a world sparkled with diamond dust. Of all the magical things, Elizabeth was certain that snow, as it fell in the Peak, was the best. The few proper snows at Longbourn had melted quickly in muddied messes.

She walked. She ran. She laid her muff on a snow-mounded bench, pulled mittens from her pocket then pitched snowballs at an oak; the poor results resolved her to the daily practice of snowball-pitching. She broke a small icicle from a fence and licked it like a sugar candy while reciting poems to hear them crisp and ringing in an otherwise silent landscape. Her recitation of Cowper's "A Winter Nosegay" was interrupted mid-way by the jingling of far off bells. She sat on a rock and listened. The snow-chastened world confused the bells' direction and proximity until a sleigh rounded the curve down the road. It was more seconds until she recognized her husband at the reins. He pulled to at her rock.

"Climb aboard, Mrs. Darcy!" he called as if they had arranged it.

Delighted, she asked, "How did you find me?"

"Footprints, Mrs. Darcy."

"Aha!" She laughed, poking fun at her silliness as she snuggled under the cocoon he made from the carriage blanket. He left his arm around her shoulder.

With only the conversation of tinkling of bells, they toured the west side of the park. She interpreted their silent companionship as joint appreciation of extraordinary loveliness until he turned with a too-serious look. "Next time, I expect an invitation."

Having confirmed the importance of their clear communication, she asked, "Every 'next time' or only those that suit you?"

He returned both hands to the reins and focused on the horse's rear. "Do you bait me?"

"Not at all. I protect against disappointment. If you want me to invite you every time I'd like your company, I shall do so most gladly. But if you wish an invitation only when it suits you, and at those times when it does not, you act as if I impose on you, then I'll be hurt, which usually exhibits itself with anger, which you'll then be obliged to address."

Darcy considered briefly then queried, "Will you be disappointed if I sometimes refuse your invitation despite my present request that you make it?"

"Certainly not," she answered, surprised he required reassurance, yet glad he took comfort to ask for it. "Hurt feelings and anger are responses to the surly tone delivering the refusal, not the 'No, thank you' itself," she said then loosened one hand from the reins and pulled his arm around her shoulder. "I sense our marriage grows its confidence a little, Mr. Darcy."

He smiled. "It would seem so, Wife."

The sleigh's runners cut a wide loop before returning to the shelter of the House's east portico. After agreeing to complete their respective correspondence then celebrate with a late luncheon, Elizabeth adjusted lunch time with Mr. Thomas then sat at her desk and perused the newly arrived post. Without hesitation, she opened Georgiana's letter first.

Annapolis, 19 December, 18- -
Dear Elizabeth,
I write with exceeding nerves for the letter I have just posted to my brother, hence this note to apprise you of the certain shock I have delivered him. As you have rightly noted in your letters, I am not so shy as I present myself while in my brother's company. In fact, I am not only more confident than I have led him to believe, but I also pursue a small enterprise in the decoration of rooms which brings me great pleasure. As prerequisite to my visit to Pemberley, Mrs. Annesley convinced me

to share my facts with Brother. Please forgive me the deception (it was not meant meanly) and please, please, please take note of my brother's mood that he does not become too agitated.

With sincere apology for the disquiet I fear to have delivered to you both,
Your sister, Georgiana

Elizabeth flew to the door that connected their studies and pulled it open calling, "Will-?" His name caught in her throat at first sight of his desktop where papers lay strewn amongst torn-open envelopes. She breathed deep for composure before calling to a footman in the hall. "Do you perchance know Mr. Darcy's whereabouts? I seem to have missed him." He directed her to the master's suite. She closed the door, emptied a nearby basket into which she put every paper on his desktop, then covered the lot with a concealing newspaper and carried it up the back stairs opposite his study. She knocked at his door to their sitting room.

"Not now, Wife."

She called past the crack. "Georgiana wrote to advise me of her letter to you. I'll wait in my bedchamber until you've digested her news."

Elizabeth granted that "digested" was a poor choice of words as her stomach coiled in knots for what Georgiana's letter had delivered. She did not know her husband well enough to accurately predict the extent of his ill-humor, but she was certain he suffered. The papers from his desk revealed even more than anticipated. In addition to Georgiana's letter, there were bills, correspondence and receipts from a fabric importer in Town, as well as sketches of *Renovations of the Master's Suite at Pemberley*, each one signed in the lower right-hand corner by G. D. Pems. Though his sister's letter had not declared her part in last summer's renovation of their master's suite, Darcy had surmised it and collected the evidence from his files.

Elizabeth waited through tea time and dinner for him to come to her, and then counted the chimes of Pemberley's innumerable clocks until the House retired for the night. It was her habit to address an issue head-on, but a husband gone silent for twelve hours recommended that she keep her finger on the pulse of his mood and adjust accordingly. She did not knock when she finally crossed his threshold.

Beside a hearth grown cold, Darcy slouched in an arm chair, fingertips pressed together. His eyes moved briefly to Elizabeth then looked into the distance. She unhooked the fire screen and rifled the ashes. There was not enough spark to ignite paper, but with fresh tinder, kindling and a brand from her hearth, a fire soon blazed.

"Thank you." His voice was monotone and barely audible.

"You're most welcome." Her voice was even and without particular emotion, as if they resumed a conversation about the weather. "I take it you haven't eaten?"

He shook his head. She curtsied and disappeared. After rousing kitchen to heat soup and prepare sandwiches and tea, she returned with a footman bearing a tray.

"I'm not hungry," he said after the servant quit them. "I am best left to myself,"

"Hunger isn't a requirement for eating, Sir. The clock prescribes when sustenance ought be taken and you're past due." She set the bowl of steaming soup on the table at his left. "Shall I feed you or will you do it?"

He raised his voice, "Don't be silly, Wife!"

"Excellent, we are agreed that I'll only lift the spoon if you do not." He had no doubt she would do and was certain his temper would rise past control if she did. He ate, but very slowly. With the bowl emptied, she handed him a thick meat sandwich and a fresh cup of tea. "Same agreement, Mr. Darcy." Her voice did not confront nor did her manner impose. He ate.

Except for rising to stoke the fire, Elizabeth warmed the chair across from him without indication of impatience, exasperation or judgment. Her presence focused him.

Past midnight he broke silence. "You read the letter I received?" She nodded. "And the other evidence?" She nodded. "She's a stranger to me, Elizabeth." He watched the fire. "I prefer not to see her."

Responding to his sorrowed tone, rather than his words, she said, "William, I perceive Georgiana to be honest and sensitive. She loves you and though your confusion might question this fact at present, I promise you she loves you." Then she prodded him just a little. "I only wonder how you didn't know about her art. That is, why didn't she volunteer to share it sooner?" She interpreted his silence as withdrawal and chided herself for putting too much before him.

"I am to blame," he said at last.

She looked up. "How so?"

"My father died unexpectedly, God rest him. I was twenty-two and she was twelve. I took his loss very poorly. Henry arranged for her to attend Mrs. Denton's school in Town. She didn't want to go, but there was nothing for her here. Before we buried Father, she shared a portrait she'd penned of him. She'd fixed his spirit perfectly on paper. I turned my back in emotion. I cannot fault that she protects her art after I appeared to disdain it."

"Then you knew she has talent?"

He rose up full angry. "That is the point is it not? I knew, yet I ignored it! You saw her letter. She said that she'd played to my wish for a dependent sister. What sort of brother am I to have caused her to compromise herself for my benefit?"

"William, if you fault yourself all round then why would you rather not see her?"

He collapsed in his chair. "No more, Lizzy."

She crossed to him, pressed his legs to make a lap and sat hugging his neck while she laid her cheek on the soft wool of his jacket. Gently, she asked, "You'd rather not see her because you wish to avoid the pain you believe you've caused her, is that right?"

He closed his eyes.

"Every person who loves, and then fears to have failed his love feels as you do. It's your attachment to her that makes your remorse so poignant. Are you listening?" He nodded slightly. "Just for a moment, imagine it from her side. She doesn't blame you for anything. It's her dearest wish that you accept her as she is. If you turn your back, she'll believe you turn against her rather than against yourself and your perceived failure."

Elizabeth rose, laid on another log and returned to him with a throw pulled from the settee. She smiled at his out-stretched legs - "I want my lap back, please" - then sat and pulled the throw over them together. "Much better." She snuggled close.

"Lizzy, she decorates rooms for ladies."

"I myself am impressed by that news."

"No *lady* labors for others," he stated with disgust. Elizabeth swallowed her retort. He continued, "My God, if she's found out, no man of merit will have her."

Elizabeth sat straight. "My pardon, Mr. Darcy, but does the same man who relished to rankle society without a moment's care for the import to his position, speak the words I hear?"

"It's different with ladies," he asserted. She returned to her chair.

He paced. "You know I'm right."

"I know only that you paint with too broad a brush. I recall a certain lady who disdained a gentleman's proposal because he was not gentleman enough, after which she refused his very patronizing aunt's demand that she decry interest in her nephew. Not only did that lady contradict the expectations of society, but the gentleman married her anyway." He stood stock-still before her. "I suggest that you embrace our sister as she is, William. She demonstrates a bit of your wife's independent nature and you embrace your wife very willingly." She folded the throw then asked, "Will you sleep alone or do you want company?"

Elizabeth finished her evening toilette, blew out the lamp and climbed into her own, tall four-poster. Sleep was difficult. She had not lain alone in four months.

His legs stretched to the hearth, Darcy watched flames play tag across a log. He let solitude slowly connect him with Georgiana as she had described herself in the letter. The fractured image of his little sister both taunted his pride that he had done well by her and denounced his powers of observation to have missed indications of her independence.

Dear God, he was angry, but he didn't rant, the absence of which was a striking testament to the good effect of marriage.

Yes, he blamed himself, but reason blamed her as well; two souls whose loving eyes misread each other.

He set the facts in time-perspective. Georgiana's interest in rooms would have collided with his despair to have lost Elizabeth after she had denied his first proposal; indeed, he would have refused any discussion of room decoration if she had introduced it. His eye explored the bedchamber she had made for him. He ought to have known at first look that something was amiss; no stranger could have captured his sensitivities so perfectly.

He considered the shyness that no longer plagued her; it had been his dearest wish that she would gain confidence. Yes, he was disappointed not to have shared her small steps into self-awareness, but likely they were small enough she also hadn't marked them until they had accumulated to let her fear his response.

That is the crux of it, is it not, Darcy? You believed she trusted you as confidante. The knife of failure stuck in his gut. Then he pulled it out himself. *Her letter trusts you enough to confide in you which implies a strong foundation has been laid.*

As the fire died, Darcy undid his buttons and crossed two rooms to climb into the bed his wife had warmed for him.

Chapter 8

When Lady Anne died in her thirty-third year, George did as well… in spirit. During the weeks following her interment, the family also withered; twelve-year-old Fitzwilliam retreated to the tree house with Henry while Georgiana's nanny distracted the two year old as best she could. By day, George restricted human contact to duties for Pemberley, and by night, he sat benumbed in a corner of his Annie's bedchamber.

One night he crossed Anne's threshold to find an interloper had invaded his mourning-space. Little Georgiana sat on her mother's bed caressing the pillow where her mother's head had laid. She turned at the rustling sound in the corner and saw her father, who had absented himself for days. She said, "I want mama."

"You should be asleep, Little One," he said gruffly.

"I want mama."

He took a breath. "Mama is gone."

"I want mama," she repeated, circling the pillow with little arms and holding tight. Tears glistened her cheeks.

George took a step, and then another until he stood at Annie's bed then reached his hand to push back white-blond strands stuck to Georgiana's face. The contact catapulted her into his arms. "I want mama," she screamed as loud as her little voice could do it.

With his daughter clinging tight, he escaped to his high-backed, over-stuffed chair. Together they sat; George kissing the hair he smoothed and Georgiana calling "I want mama." Her warmth and smell and her pained, four-syllable plea worked on him until his body shook and his tears started to trickle. His Little One watched him, and then she reached up and wiped his tears.

Much to staff's amazement when Mrs. Darcy challenged her husband to help decorate for Christmas, he climbed ladders to hang greens and mistletoe in the family's favorite rooms. It was a novelty for Darcy, and though he took to it well, he did require direction since an eye for artistic balance appeared to be mostly vested in his sister.

Two of the family's rooms escaped their joint endeavor: Georgiana's bedchamber, where Elizabeth had decorated it especially for her new sister, and the day room, site of the Christmas Day fête, where staff worked under a veil of high secrecy to recreate aspects of Lady Anne's last Christmas. The day room location was a compromise from Elizabeth's original plans that had intended to locate the party on the far side of the formal gardens in the semi-detached pavilion, the most modern structure in the House. But when Mrs. Reynolds advised against the pavilion, Elizabeth elected to site the party where Lady Anne had done. The pavilion, Lady Anne's design completed during her illness, had not held a stick of furniture since its completion and the Housekeeper reasoned that confronting Christmas memories in that space might be too much. Elizabeth took heed when the previously closed-lip Housekeeper gave warning.

On the eve of the coaches' arrival from Annapolis, the Darcys toured the rooms bedecked by their own hand, after which Elizabeth unveiled Georgiana's bedchamber. Crossing his sister's threshold, Darcy was amazed. In addition to the obligatory greens and red satin ribbons at the windows and mantel, Elizabeth had scattered on every surface little, jewel-colored glasses, in which small candles sparkled the chamber like a fairy forest. Leaning against the door jamb, he admired his wife with golden eyes. "You are remarkable, Mrs. Darcy."

The next afternoon delivered Georgiana and Henry to their family's arms. Darcy's greeting to his sister left Elizabeth in no doubt that her husband was more remarkable than she. He looked the shy one as he held Georgiana at arm's length then hugged her close. After admiring Henry's new uniform and greeting Mrs. Annesley, Elizabeth escorted her sister upstairs to freshen herself while Darcy invited his cousin to his study for a glass of sherry.

Though candles lit in colored glasses were not nearly so magical by day, Georgiana was genuinely delighted and hugged Elizabeth twice over. "Oh, Lizzy, this is so wonderful," she cried, and then blushed exceedingly. "Forgive me for calling you 'Lizzy,' Elizabeth. I must have visited Charles and Jane enough that I'm too comfortable with her name for you."

"Then 'Lizzy' it is!" Elizabeth struck a mock-serious pose. "But I warn you, if I'm 'Lizzy' to you, then we're sisters as if born so." After their giggles grew self-conscious, Elizabeth announced tea delayed until five o'clock to permit her sister rest after her journey.

Rest, however, was of no interest to Miss Darcy. Curled in her favorite chair, the high-backed, over-stuffed one given to her by papa, Georgiana relished the start of this "third life" in which her brother embraced her as she was. She snuggled deeper in the chair where papa had whispered her to sleep with stories of princesses and princes. In fact, papa himself had settled her in these chambers the year before his death. He had smiled at her delight in the flounces of pink ribbons supported by flying blue birds stenciled on the walls and he had pulled open every drawer of her new furnishings to show her clothes in their new home. That had been almost seven years ago. The furnishings of an eleven-year old child were inadequate for a mature young lady, but Georgiana had addressed this over time by pulling in more bureaus as necessity demanded, making her room more crowded than comfortable to all who viewed it, but herself.

She smiled when Hannah arrived to unpack the trunks already delivered to the storeroom attached to her dressing closet. Two minutes later a familiar *tap, tap-tap* rapped on Georgiana's door. Jumping up, she called Henry to enter, but her gladness collapsed to see his stormy look.

"I wish to tell you myself, Princess. Darcy and I have had words and I fear hard feelings will sour Christmas for the rest. I'm quitting Pemberley within the hour." Sympathy for her dismay tempered his anger. "It will be well, Princess. We'll write often with full honesty. Will you write two for my every one? Ah, that's my girl." He opened his arms for a hug.

At that moment, Darcy pounded on his sister's door and let himself in. "What is this?" he exploded, catching the end of a farewell embrace.

Sensing more misguided accusations on his cousin's tongue, Henry whipped around and stepped outside of his genial self to order, "In the hall, Darcy!" Then he commanded Georgiana, "Remain here!" and slammed the door.

A dull thud followed by a groan spurred Georgiana to action. Hannah emerged from the dressing closet just as her mistress opened the door to the hall. With fists raised, the two men circled each other. Her brother's left eye was very red and had begun to swell. Henry's face was smeared with blood from his nose. Darcy punched again but missed as the equally agile Henry spun and landed a right to Darcy's jaw. Darcy backed the few paces into the gallery, recovered his balance and pivoted to take advantage. Georgiana turned to Hannah. "Go quickly! Fetch Mrs. Darcy and any footmen along the way."

While the maid dashed away from the brawl, Georgiana balled her fists against the bashing and approached it. "Stop!" she cried, but her diminutive voice could not breach the din. She pushed between them. "Stop. Plea –" Her cry became a moan when her brother's fist met her shoulder instead of Henry's chin. Both men lowered their fists in horror. Elizabeth arrived with Hannah followed by two burly footmen. Reproaching himself for his sister's injury, Darcy insisted Dr. Simons be summoned.

Georgiana stepped back, watching them with a grimace for her sore shoulder and tears of disappointment for them both. Mostly she eyed Darcy. "What sort of brother welcomes a man then exchanges words causing him to quit us before trunks can be unpacked, and then accosts him when he bids farewell to his ward?"

She included Henry at the last. "And you… you hit hardest. What's wrong with you both?"

Elizabeth looked from red-eyed husband to bloodied cousin. "Will you return to civility and confine disagreement to words? Good. Do we discuss this now or after your valets have attended your wounds?"

Henry was impressed by Elizabeth's composure, though it did not surprise her husband. He sensed the distress beneath her calm. They agreed to first tend wounds.

At three o'clock the gentlemen sat in opposite corners of the Darcys' sitting room with Elizabeth as witness.

Darcy winced in pain. "You meant to leave us?" he asked, still undone by the news.

"'Mean' to leave you, Darcy. The sleigh waits as we speak."

"But you haven't been so sensitive before."

Elizabeth sat straight to hear "before." Not only did the cousins' geniality not stretch as far as she had presumed, but her husband sounded to be the historic perpetrator of ill-feeling. She studied each man carefully.

"You haven't previously accused me of duplicity," Henry responded. "I won't sleep under the roof of a man who holds me in such poor regard."

In a lowered voice, Darcy admitted, "I was angry that you kept her room design from me, despite that you learned of it in September. We are her equal guardians and by rights –"

"By rights?" Henry leaned forward. "Our ward promised me to secrecy. You were about to marry and she feared judgment against her would cloud your happiness at the wedding."

Darcy's shoulders drooped. "Oh."

All looked to the door as Georgiana entered and sat beside her sister. She had changed to an off-shoulder gown and held a cool cloth to her bruise. Both gentlemen watched the floor. Georgiana asked, "What have I missed, Lizzy?"

"Your cousin learned of your enterprise in September, to which my husband took exception since as half-guardian he ought to have been immediately apprised. It only just now came out that Henry's reticence was at your request to protect our wedding celebration."

Understanding that she sat at the heart of the fisticuffs, Georgiana looked from one to the other as she blinked against tears. "Perhaps I'm the person best advised to quit Pemberley, if my choice causes this between you." She rose, as did her brother, though stiffly.

"But –" Darcy began. He was interrupted by a sister who until that moment had always let him have his say.

"I'm sorry, Brother," she stood her ground. "The Christmas spirit goes missing, does it not?" She turned to Elizabeth gone pale. "Forgive me, Lizzy, but a family only feigning to enjoy what you've made for us would insult your efforts."

Henry rose gingerly. "Come Princess, we'll share the sleigh to Lambton where we can catch the mail coach to Town."

Darcy followed his departing sister. "Wait! Elizabeth has worked too hard."

Georgiana turned. "Can you convince Henry to remain with a happy heart, Brother?"

Darcy sat with eyes downcast. "I apologize." He looked his cousin in the eye. "I apologize that I threatened to have you removed as Georgiana's guardian."

The ladies sucked in their breath. Henry returned to his chair. "It was a stupid threat."

Darcy nodded. "It was my temper that spoke."

"Temper doesn't excuse short-sightedness, Cousin. To have me removed from your father's will, you would need show cause and that would require exposing Georgiana's enterprise, which she's worked so carefully to keep hid."

Elizabeth studied her husband whose eyes had darkened and jaw tensed at some point during Henry's rebuttal which denoted a problem beyond the issue of guardianship. She tried to determine which words had agitated him, but conversation flew too fast.

Henry continued. "In addition, the judge would have laughed you from the courtroom. Georgiana will soon be of age, and as I stated at the outset, I depart for the continent in April. You would be sore-pressed to show cause when the one you will have removed has already re –"

"You travel to the continent, Henry?" Georgiana asked. Whether due to surprise or the news itself, Elizabeth sensed her sister was in severe distress.

"Yes," he stammered, regretting he had pressed his point too far with Darcy.

"For how long?" she queried, pressing her stomach to calm the agitation inside.

"A year, perhaps longer. I'm sorry for how you learned it. I meant to present it better."

Of a sudden, Georgiana's hand flew to her mouth as she ran to Elizabeth's bedchamber. She reached the basin in time. Henry closed the door for her privacy. Elizabeth rose slowly, grasping the back of her chair for support. "It seems we are not well-suited to an elaborate Christmas celebration. I'll have staff begin its dismantling at once. Please, excuse me."

Darcy blocked the door, albeit with a limp and grimace. "Lizzy, it will be well. I promise." He looked at Henry. "I've apologized with an open heart. Do you agree to stay and accept me as if this hadn't happened?"

With a look at Elizabeth then at Darcy, Henry nodded slowly.

Elizabeth watched her husband. "What of Georgiana, William? I wonder if you can assure that she'll accept us 'as if this had not happened'."

"If Henry remains, she will as well."

Elizabeth shook her head. "The two of you have tied her in knots. If I were she, I doubt I could do more than pretend to smile no matter your agreement. I've not worked to make a fête that entertains only the pretense of happiness." With sincere regret, she looked at her husband. "I'm sorry, William. I won't chance a gilded Christmas when I'd hoped for solid gold."

Henry slipped out through Darcy's bedchamber. Marital negotiation wanted privacy.

"Come." Darcy drew her to the settee. "We'll discuss."

"To what end?" she shrugged.

"To calm our feelings before choices are taken." Then he offered, "I'm very sorry, Lizzy."

"You needn't be. You were hurt to learn you were left out and responded accordingly."

"Yes, perhaps, but you heard as well that I presumed more than was warranted." He paced. "I have a temper, Elizabeth. Perhaps you've noticed?" She hid a small smile and nodded. "I'm not proud of it and am even less proud that when it inserts itself I am less than predictable in my actions and less than careful with my words. I offer this for understanding, not to excuse my fault." In the next breath he sat across from her and reached for her hands. "I'll make it right, Wife. Henry accepted my apology and he doesn't offer his hand lightly. I've apologized to you, and though you're disappointed, I know you'll forgive me. And I'll apologize to Georgiana." He shook his head. "She seems so changed I can't say how I'll convince her, but I promise she'll embrace our family as before."

"You're very good, William." She pulled him to sit with her.

His breath was warm on her ear, "Good enough to protect our Christmas fête?"

She answered from her heart, "I want my Darcy family to be different from my Bennet, William. I shall hope you can convince our sister."

Chapter 9

Matthew Simons, eldest son of a successful merchant in Manchester, was the first in his family to graduate from university, though his choice of medicine over business did not earn his family's respect until he established a practice serving the well-to-do.

Within two years, however, Matthew was disillusioned, and on the afternoon of Michaelmas, he sat in the Old Wellington with a scotch instead of tea. His musing was interrupted by Dr. Ashworth, an elderly gentleman awaiting the connecting coach from Warmsby Heath to Lambton, who requested to sit at Matthew's table in the last empty chair in the tavern. Ashworth pursued conversation after learning Simons was a fellow physician whose drink and expression implied a problem.

Matthew confided, "I had thought medicine offered the opportunity for life-long learning in service to others, but my patients prefer leeches to common sense."

"Ah," said the old gentleman, "I take it you've met the phenomenon of mass mentality; it's a popular affliction in the city. The patient knows what was prescribed to his neighbor and demands the same for himself." Dr. Ashworth's tone implied his medical practice was not compromised by such prejudices.

"My pardon, Sir, but we were taught rural medicine is just short of medieval,"

The old man laughed, "The stereotype serves us well since by deeming us beneath them, city doctors let us be." Dr. Ashworth's coach was announced. "If you're ever near Lambton, I would welcome your visit, Sir. You can judge for yourself the independence that a country practice permits a dedicated doctor."

Mrs. Reynolds had lived most of her long life at Pemberley, first as a young girl sent to live with relatives in Pemberley Village because of too many mouths to feed at home and later as a Housemaid after her husband and son succumbed to measles in Lambton. The newly wed Lady Anne trained Sylvia Reynolds to be her lady's maid then promoted her to Housekeeper when little Fitzwilliam was three years old. Indeed, there was no more in-depth repository of knowledge about George Darcy's family than Sylvia Reynolds.

In the hours after Miss Darcy and the brigadier's arrival, Mrs. Reynolds added two new chapters to the family's story: a brother and sister who embraced as peers and cousins who stood as equals, each having drawn the other's blood. She had no doubt Lady Anne would smile to know both chapters, though only a person understanding the complicated history of the cousins would appreciate why the Lady would applaud the second one.

If Henry had had time for reflection, he would also have been impressed to have initiated fisticuffs with Darcy, but Georgiana's extreme distress at news of Vienna distracted him from everything but how to regain her trust. He had compromised his promise for open honesty with a secret that he could easily have divulged en route.

Arrived at Georgiana's door with sincere apology, he related the cold facts of Braxton's manipulation, seasickness and her distressing letter. After learning his sacrifice, she conjured a scheme to reciprocate. She would join him in Vienna. From taking a house with Hannah and Mrs. Annesley to enrolling at an art école, she evolved her plan out loud until Henry cut her short; she would be of age in March, which expected her to socialize in Town. When he refused to discuss further, she presumed he wished to meet ladies without her underfoot. He countered, "Truly, there's naught I'd like better than to learn Vienna with you, Princess, but it cannot be."

She dismissed him, claiming need to dress for tea.

In his bedchamber at the opposite end of the children's hall from his ward, Henry struggled to understand Georgiana's emotional vicissitude and his distraught responses. His analysis was interrupted by Mr. Thomas' knock. Dr. Simons had arrived and as the only family member not engaged, the brigadier was requested to entertain the guest.

Henry winced his way down the children's stairs to the newly revived breakfast room then hobbled through the necklace of east-facing chambers.

"Matthew! It has been too long." The gentlemen clapped shoulders with grins from ear to ear. Henry ordered sherry served in the morning room.

The friendship of physician and brigadier had evolved during seven years via letters mostly. Henry's disinterest in his Oxford law degree, which restricted him to work indoors and his disappointment at sea, which denied him adventure, had left the young man without direction until Dr. Simons had chanced on Mr. Darcy's dour-faced cousin at a pub in Lambton. Simons encouraged him to take the reins and make a job fit his needs, after which Henry accepted introduction to several of the doctor's friends, well-placed colonels in the army. Within a year, Lieutenant Fitzwilliam had carved out his specialty of negotiation, which supported his penchant to explore since as liaison he represented commanders at meetings across England. He repaid Matthew Simons' kindness with letters detailing new medical procedures gleaned during his travels. Henry raised a glass to his friend, a widower considered one of the treasures of the Peak for his superior medicine and his easy manner and excellent, well-read conversation.

While the two toasted in the morning room, Darcy concluded his meeting with Georgiana and summoned Elizabeth to his study to convey its good results.

"All is well, Lizzy. If I don't contravene Georgiana's work, she agrees to remain."

"She negotiated her terms? I'm impressed." Elizabeth sat back. "I didn't expect so much gumption, despite her experience with rooms. Did you learn that history too?"

"Yes. I suppose it was my interest to hear it that warmed her to another go at family." Darcy explained that Mr. Pankhurst had lectured at Mrs. Denton's School for Distinguished Young Ladies as to the types of fabrics available to decorate the homes they would someday establish. As London's premier importer of fine fabrics, he had fallen on hard times after a ship laden with the year's profit was lost at sea; hence, his lectures to eke out a small income. He had admired Georgiana's portraits hung in the school's entrance hall and requested she draw his children. While executing these, Georgiana made friends with his wife, who encouraged our sister's interest to renovate her bedchamber at Annapolis. Georgiana exchanged the portraits for the gentleman's comprehensive lessons in fabrics.

"Did she renovate her bedchamber?" Elizabeth queried, delighted to learn the details and even more to see her husband's energy to tell them.

"Yes, but she said the result represents a novice who executed all of her ideas at once, rather than select a few that harmonize into one theme." Darcy smiled. "She preserves the bedchamber as reminder that discrimination is as important as creativity and said we will either laugh when we see it or get a headache."

Considering their perfectly appointed chambers, Elizabeth noted, "She must have learned the lesson well and very quickly."

"Indeed." Darcy shook his head to think how seriously he had misunderstood Georgiana's social reticence. "Lizzy, her shyness at teas, etc. stood as cover for her game to learn the people behind their facades. She designs for the lady inside, rather than the mode of the moment and credits her success with rooms to years of absorbing personal impressions."

Elizabeth's pleasure to fit the pieces of a puzzle into their logical whole delighted to learn the details… until they defied logic when taken together.

"William, I accept she has artistic talent, that she learned fabrics and even that she might know her hostesses better than they know themselves, but it defies imagination how she got from a poorly done bedchamber to successful ladies' rooms in a matter of months."

"Ah, that was a fluke," Darcy laughed. "Mr. Pankhurst's financial woes prompted him to try his own hand at decorating since the hanging of fabric in a lady's home is where the most profit is earned. He contracted to refurbish Mrs. Geoffrey's parlor and realized too late that the famous decorating warehouses always declined her projects, because she was never satisfied with the result. Working for Mrs. Geoffrey meant losing one's investment as well as her friends as clients since she entertained often and loudly decried the decorator for her disappointment."

"Wait! Mr. Pankhurst 'tried his own hand at decorating'? I'd think he *is* a decorator, if he imports the best fabrics."

"Georgiana describes him as a business man, not a decorator; his eye knows the quality of fabrics, not how to best combine them. His talent is to predict society's taste, and then to risk sending ships farther than other importers to procure his wares." Darcy detailed Mr. Pankhurst's conundrum: he provided the best fabrics, yet was unable to establish his own design house, wherein he could retain the middle man's money. The best decorators were already employed by the best warehouses that paid a high wage, making it difficult for new firms to compete.

Elizabeth sat intrigued.

"After Pankhurst understood he had sealed his financial demise with the lady's project, Mrs. Pankhurst asked our sister to help her husband, a project that intrigued Georgiana, who was well-acquainted with Mrs. Geoffrey and considered the challenge a test of her observational prowess. To address the lady's indecisiveness, Georgiana planned the whole, then parsed it into pairs of sketched alternatives presented by Mr. Pankhurst. Delighted to believe she designed such a pretty room herself, the lady displayed the selected sketches at her many teas, which in turn grew Mr. Pankhurst's business long before Mrs. Geoffrey's parlor was completed. He credits Georgiana for his good fortune, and though he now also employs a talented young man, he counts our sister as his best asset." Darcy's expression sobered suddenly; the next part being obviously distasteful to him. "They are partners, Elizabeth. He… he pays her."

"Oh my," she looked sharply. "How is she paid?"

"He deposits directly into an account at the Bank of London in the name of G. D. Pems."

Elizabeth exhaled audibly, "Then she has protected herself from being found out." She smiled in open admiration. "I think she's done this better than I would, had I a special talent."

Her hint at self-disparagement diverted Darcy from his sister to his wife. With a touch of theater, he raised Elizabeth's chin to look at him. "Your talent is to be my wife, Mrs. Darcy, which is far more challenging than decorating rooms."

She responded with her own hint of the dramatic. "Does my husband represent his wife as having no value beyond her marriage to him?"

Their teases assured him he was forgiven. "We continue to misread the other's message, Wife. Your sensitivities and intellect are valued by all who know you, but I'm certain no one values them more than I." His lips met hers with gentle intensity. "We are made partners by more than marriage vows, My Lady," he whispered. "You not only encourage me to discover myself, but also help me derive more pleasure from that self than I thought possible."

A much revived Mrs. Darcy arrived in the morning room on her husband's arm to meet the good doctor who insisted to examine the master's now mostly purple eye. He had already declared the others' injuries to be minor. "Henry described your tussle, Mr. Darcy."

Darcy glanced sharply. Simons had referenced "Henry" by his given name, not "Brigadier Fitzwilliam." The sharing of personal names signed a deep friendship of which Darcy had no knowledge, though he had believed himself privy to all of his cousin's details. Sensitive to Darcy's changed demeanor, Dr. Simons briefly related the men's history, though he sensed Mr. Darcy cared more that he had been left out than for any particular interest in the specifics. Elizabeth also noted her husband's sensitivity. Henry and Georgiana appeared unaware from where they sat.

After judging that Darcy would recover, the physician downed his sherry amid a last bit of banter with the full company then bowed his departure. Darcy stood and encouraged him otherwise. "Your society complements our sympathies, Sir. We take tea momentarily and hope very much you'll join us."

At mention of tea, Georgiana jumped up with no care for a bruised shoulder. "My goodness, we've left out Mrs. Annesley," she cried and dashed up the grand staircase.

Henry laughed. "She recovers even more quickly than you predicted, Matthew."

Mrs. Annesley had confined herself to her quarters after hearing Hannah's report that their mistress would return to Town immediately. Collapsing into a chair, she had pressed her handkerchief to over-flowing eyes; her self-sacrifice to protect her charge having gone horribly awry. Later, Hannah arrived to announce that Mr. Darcy met with his sister and there was hope she might recant; Mrs. Annesley prayed while twisting her handkerchief into a limp swatch of linen. When Georgiana knocked and bade her chaperone join the family for tea, the lady claimed a headache which eased immediately after Hannah asked if the trunks still required packing and their mistress shook her head and smiled.

Restored enough to attend tea, but not so well to meet a handsome stranger, Mrs. Annesley rose from her curtsy to Dr. Simons and blushed exceedingly to look into the gentlest brown eyes of her acquaintance. Fearing her coloring implied more than it ought, she sat silent at the side.

The family's day of collective misunderstanding contrasted with the company's remarkable conviviality at tea time. Darcy laid it to the easy and all-inclusive conversation of Henry and the good doctor. To assure happy relations at least until morning, he invited Dr. Simons to sup with them and overnight at Pemberley since unnecessary winter travel ought be avoided. Dr. Simons hesitated to accept, however. He had not dined at Pemberley since before Lady Anne's death. Those sober memories deterred him until Mrs. Darcy and Miss Georgiana added their voices to the petition. He bowed to their supplication.

Still sensitive to her blushes when meeting the good doctor, Mrs. Annesley hastened to be the first out the door at the conclusion of tea, but Elizabeth intercepted her and whispered, "May I request a favor, Mum?" They stepped into the entrance hall where Elizabeth stated that she and her husband required fresh air, but their walk would leave no one to entertain Dr. Simons since Georgiana would rest and Henry's injuries required the same.

The lady's green eyes grew round as a cat's. "Oh, Madam, I don't think I could…" She flustered then collected herself; one did not refuse an employer's reasonable request. Dr. Simons appeared glad to sit with Mrs. Annesley in the library.

When at last outdoors on her husband's arm, Elizabeth felt like two days had been compressed into one. Conflicting emotions had been so powerful that the crunch of snow under her boot and crisp chill in the air only slowly renewed her spirit.

"We seem to have weathered a difficult series of events to good end," Darcy commented.

"No conversation, William. I'm thinking."

Darcy raised his brow then focused on a rabbit making long skips across the snow. After a half-mile he asked, "Now?"

"Not yet."

When they passed the next curve in the road, she announced, "Now."

He glanced down at her. "And what did your thoughts conclude, Mrs. Darcy" He circled his arm around her waist and drew her close.

They walked in tandem.

"I would have liked it if you had done this sooner," she stated, nodding at his arm.

He reflected, "Until we've been at this long enough for me to read your mood, I suppose I must be told." He gave her waist a squeeze.

Elizabeth slipped a gloved hand from her muff and circled his waist drawing them still closer without missing a step. They were within sight of the House. "I did it wrong just now when I held myself apart from you while I considered. You relax me more than a mile of thinking."

Her confidence fed his. "Compliment accepted, Wife. Now, might we return to the subject at hand? What have you been considering?"

"I worked to learn my ghost better." She sighed. "My family asserts that naught can rattle my composure, but today I was undone and became part of the divergent forces contributing to our trouble." She shook her head. "Logic failed me today, William. I nearly insisted to dismantle our Christmas, despite that such would have pained me severely. In fact, at one point I thought I would cry. *Me*, Mr. Darcy!"

"This is indeed serious," he teased.

"Make fun if you like, but my accumulating inconsistencies disturb me."

"If it helps at all, no one noted your emotion, Elizabeth, except me, of course, but that's to be expected."

"How so?

"Because I'm your husband," he stated as if husband-hood itself conveyed insight into one's wife. She refrained from popping his bubble of marital confidence; only moments before he had declared he must be told when to put his arm around her. He continued. "How do you do it, Lizzy? Disguising your feelings, I mean. Lord knows my expression declares my mood, whether I'd have others know it or not."

"It's not so much that I purposely hide my feelings," she said. "My calm seems to exhibit in direct proportion to the chaos around me." She waxed dramatic, "What one apprehends on the cover does not necessarily reveal the book's content."

Darcy kissed her forehead as they approached the east portico. "I wonder if my wife isn't more complicated than I am. No offense, Lizzy. I intended it as a compliment."

Before dinner, Elizabeth knocked on Mrs. Annesley's door to apologize for having requested that she entertain a guest which was the Darcys' responsibility to do. "It was poor form on my part, Mum, and I regret any awkwardness I caused you."

"I took no offense, Mrs. Darcy. I presumed you had good reason."

"Yes. The afternoon's distress had got the better of me of a sudden. The walk revived me."

"Then I am glad you asked." Mrs. Annesley next addressed the aforementioned awkwardness. "I admit to having felt more discomfort than pleasure at your request," she smiled, "but Dr. Simons is very kind and very direct which is the habit of a physician, I suppose. After perusing the library's shelves, we ascertained that we hold very few authors in like esteem."

With the last of Elizabeth's sensitivities calmed, she enjoyed dinner as much as her company. They supped in the morning room in deference to Dr. Simons' day clothes and wore their day clothes to put him further at his ease as tribute to the ease he oiled between them.

Elizabeth had only met Dr. Simons on three previous occasions: twice at church and once when he had called at Pemberley to welcome the newlyweds on their arrival in the Peak. She had thought him to be well-spoken, pleasing to the eye and very kind, but their brief encounters had not exposed his talent for delightful conversation. She deemed his effect on five people connected by marriage, birth and duty was just the ticket to assure no disappointment on Christmas Day. Before they folded their napkins, hearty "here-here's" and applause convinced the good doctor to accept Mrs. Darcy's invitation to join them for Christmas at Pemberley.

At evening's end, Georgiana, ever the night owl like her papa, declined to sleep quite yet and Henry, ever the gracious cousin, offered to sit with her. Their earlier tiff had ameliorated during the pleasant evening. By day, the library's blue-grey walls and detailed white moldings imitated Wedgewood porcelain, but at night, firelight glinted off golden accents and gold-embossed titles to feel like one sat inside a jewel.

"I'd like to hear your imaginings of Vienna," she announced softly when they were alone.

Wary of her maneuverings to join him in that city, he asked brusquely, "To what end?"

"You said you'd love nothing better than to learn it with me, but since that will not be, I should like to learn it now." She ordered tea.

Out of habit, she prepared his cup as she had insisted to do since childhood, and out of habit, he leaned back in his chair with his hands behind his head and his long legs stretched to the hearth. She curled in the chair opposite. Though he had never visited Vienna, he had read many descriptions in recent days and imagined out loud until she slept. As when she was a girl just arrived at Annapolis, he carried her to her bedchamber where Hannah settled her beneath the blankets. She did not wake when he lifted her, carried her up the grand staircase and through the gallery, nor did she wake when he paused outside her door and kissed her cheek goodnight. Henry had held Georgiana on her first day of life, and during the past six years, he had helped raise her. She was as much a sister as if she had been born so.

A man not yet recovered from a fistfight should be sorely challenged to carry a lady such a distance, but when he closed his door at the far end of her hall, his buoyed spirit soothed bruised muscles and left him full awake. Only later, as he sipped a glass of port, was he troubled by her lingering perfume. Suddenly he stood… too aware of his physical response to her and its incontrovertible truth. *Dear God, NO!* He threw the glass into the flames, quit the House and stumbled into winter's darkness with tortured tears for his company.

In her bed, Georgiana lay awake to wonder at Henry's lingering presence.

Chapter 10

During the thirteen years Lady Anne had breathed as George Darcy's wife, Christmas was a festival of candle-studded St. Lucia wreaths, bouches de noel, nesting Matreshka dolls, Dutch clogs filled with sweets and oranges, and every other tradition she could introduce to broaden her children's sense of the greater world. The innovation she introduced at her last Christmas on earth was the German tannenbaum, though she saw no sense in burning candles on a dead tree and substituted her own invention.

For ten years after the Lady's demise, George Darcy had maintained Christmas for Fitzwilliam and Georgiana, though he suffered privately for what they missed in the absence of their mother.

Following George Darcy's death, Christmas at Pemberley was a day like all the rest, except for chapel vespers on its eve.

In anticipation of his first holiday since his Abigail's death, Dr. Simons fixed a note stating his whereabouts to his cottage door on the afternoon of 24 December then steered his sleigh toward Pemberley. Though it was a Great Estate, Pemberley was laid out much differently than the rest of England's premier properties sited to impress the visitor with views of the house miles before one passed through gilded gates. Pemberley's gate, tall limestone columns supporting a scrolled P in a golden oval, opened to a quarter-mile of stone-fenced, grazing fields that gave way to an immense wooded park. Through the park, a manicured main road hugged the undulating land until the trees thinned to reveal the lawns and lake complimenting the House, which was an extraordinary construction with details from every period since late medieval times preserved so as to enhance each other. Despite its grand proportion, the House charmed the visitor like a gracious mistress inviting her guest to take his ease.

The whisper of runners on packed snow gave way to the banter and camaraderie greeting Dr. Simons' arrival, though he noted unaccustomed formality between Henry and Miss Georgiana at tea time and dinner. During the unencumbered hour before vespers, he queried Henry as to Miss Georgiana's mood, but the brigadier adroitly changed the subject.

The issue of Georgiana was not a thing Henry could discuss even with himself. Having accepted he loved her as a man made him loathe the guardian dedicated to her protection. Instinct bade him escape, but to do so before 6 January required explanation he couldn't offer; hence, he opted for his only choice: fierce attachment to Darcy, preferably away from House, and the inclusion of others when he couldn't avoid his ward. As for Georgiana, she was at first confused by Henry's distance, then hurt and most recently angry, all of which she concealed behind a smile. Town had taught her to hold feelings close, though she did confide some of her dismay to Elizabeth during an afternoon stroll. While appreciative of Georgiana's trust, Elizabeth was too preoccupied with Christmas preparations to trouble about a falling-out between cousins.

Initially, Mrs. Darcy had not thought to include Lady Anne's traditions at Christmas, but the Housekeeper's detailed archives encouraged Elizabeth to mingle past with present and Mrs. Reynolds, who rejoiced at the breakfast room's success that returned her beloved Lady to the House, now actively supported her mistress' endeavors. As vespers approached, Elizabeth reconsidered surprising her husband without any forewarning and confided to William that some of his mother's traditions were incorporated in the chapel celebration.

At nine o'clock, a beclouded night required torches to light the snow crunched under polished boots. The Darcys led the procession of guests and staff to the chapel where Elizabeth took careful measure of William's response: at the front doors, he looked past the yew wreaths tied with white ribbons, inside, his expression did not change when they passed rose scented candles on the wall sconces, and during the Bible reading, he didn't look twice at the altar cloth.

In deference to early rising on the morrow, all retired after vespers, except Darcy. He stood peering out dark windows until Elizabeth threw back the covers and hugged him from behind.

"I didn't think the memories troubled you," she said.

"Would that I had been troubled." He looked down at her with a furrowed brow. "I noticed nothing I could ascribe to my mother, Lizzy."

"Oh." She had not considered he might not remember. "They were very small additions, William," she reassured before listing them.

"Get dressed, Wife." His tone cautioned against dawdling.

The clouds had cleared to sparkle a heaven of stars so bright that the sky looked dark blue, not black. He held a lantern in one hand and his wife with the other, first pausing at the chapel's steps to inspect the wreaths, and then sniffing the air inside. Elizabeth waited in the first pew while he examined the cloth with open work on its edges, and then slowly recalled his mama stitching the red linen before his sixth Christmas. He left the lantern on the altar to light his mother's work and sat with his wife in the shadows. "I was frightened, Lizzy." She pulled his arm around her shoulders. "To not recall means that I'm losing her." He let slip a self-mocking chuckle. "For a man who works not to remember, it's a puzzle that he suffers to know the memories are fading."

His sorrow convinced Elizabeth to say nothing about the day room on the chance that he also would not remember those details.

At eight o'clock Christmas morning, a festive lot collected around a pot of tea in the morning room, after which Elizabeth directed, "To the entrance hall, all! Our Christmas will commence."

With Mrs. Annesley's help, large, white napkins folded into triangles soon blindfolded four adults to make them as dependent as children and nearly as exuberant in their exclamations at this novel beginning. Hand in hand, Elizabeth led the four along the west hall until they stood shoulder to shoulder in the wide double-doorway of the day room. The napkin points bobbing above their heads made Elizabeth and Mrs. Annesley giggle, and Hannah, as well, who was included as the party's piano accompanist.

"Before you see your Christmas, you will describe it with your noses. Breathe deep. William, you are first," Elizabeth invited.

He smiled at her excellent invention. "I smell pine, implying we celebrate in a forest."

"Excellent. Now you, Georgiana."

"I smell citrus, um, oranges! I predict we celebrate in a fruit bowl carved from pine."

"Oh, very good, Sister," Elizabeth exclaimed. "And now you, Dr. Simons."

"I smell hickory. And if I might add my ear with my nose, the crackle implies a hickory fire that will warm our celebration in a pine forest hung with oranges."

Everyone laughed. "And last but not least, you, Henry."

"I smell honey ham and roast, cinnamon buns and rye, something with apples, and –"

"Enough Cousin!" Darcy called. "You smell with your stomach as much as your nose."

"Aye, and it's well warranted," Henry called back over the others' heads, "since we ate no breakfast. I predict and sincerely hope for a buffet, Elizabeth." They all laughed.

"On the count of three," Elizabeth announced, "you will remove your blindfolds and judge your predictions." Hannah nodded she was ready. "One. Two. Three." The maid played the new *lied* from Germany, "Stille Nacht." Eyes squinted against bright sun reflected off snow beyond the diamond-paned windows. With the wonder of children, adults gasped to see the ten-foot tree hung with crystal snowflakes that sparkled like a hundred candles. Georgiana hurried to the snowflake tree to admire crimson and gold ribbons laced among branches hung with fruit, painted tin toys, and striped peppermint sticks. "Oh, Lizzy, how wonderful!" she exclaimed.

Dr. Simons admired the chamber that imitated a medieval keeping room. From a fireplace so broad to accommodate a ten-foot trunk to the leaded windows set in thick walls, and from the wide-planked floor underfoot to the massive beams supporting heavy, wrought-iron chandeliers, Dr. Simons thought he had not seen a room better suited to work a special memory.

Henry stood at the side. Despite his reputation to the contrary, he preferred to observe rather than entertain.

Elizabeth watched her husband. When he tensed at first look, she knew he remembered and she held her breath.

Darcy paused on the threshold before crossing into Christmas with a tight jaw and a hesitant step. At the buffet, he touched the red silk cloth edged with holly leaves then stared past a window as if to collect himself. Proceeding to the fireplace centered on the long wall, he leaned on the mantle bedecked with the same arrangement of greens and ribbons retrieved from sixteen-year-old memories. He studied the fire then turned to glance at the six small tables draped in green silk where they would dine. Darcy then continued to the tree, stood beside his sister and breathed deep. The set of his shoulders alerted Elizabeth when he prepared to turn and she braced herself to meet his emotion.

Fitzwilliam Darcy locked eyes with Elizabeth across the room. Her composure gave no hint of her worry she had trespassed too far. The intensity of their gazes caused the rest to pause and watch. Even Hannah lifted her fingers from the keys. "Come," he called to her. Though embarrassed for their bad manners, the guests did not avert their eyes.

She stood before him. There was no Christmas at that moment… only them.

"How did you do this, Lizzy?" She blinked to control her emotion. He had asked "how" not "why" and had said "Lizzy" not "Mrs. Darcy".

"Mrs. Reynolds keeps excellent records."

"You took an awful chance," he whispered. His eyes embraced her then his lips met hers in a married kiss that took no care for their company. With his arm remaining at his wife's waist, he turned to his guests, "I give you the most wonderful wife in all of England."

Cheers and applause filled the room, Hannah recommenced playing and Henry invited the party to the buffet to permit the Darcys the privacy not afforded them earlier.

Once settled at the small tables, Henry asked what the others could not. "Darcy, I believe we just witnessed a surprise past the Christmas we see with our eyes. May we know the secret?"

Darcy smiled at Elizabeth. "In this room you meet a good reproduction of the last Christmas designed by my mother for her family." He looked at Henry. "It was the only Christmas you didn't celebrate at Pemberley after you came to us, Cousin, and it's a thing I never thought to see again. My wife achieved the impossible and you witnessed her husband's gratitude."

"Brother?" All turned. "You said it is a reproduction. If there are any parts that differ from the original, I'd like to know them, please." Georgiana's serious tone focused her brother to report a careful list. At the last he asked, "Why, Sister?"

"I have no memory of Lady Anne, but I can read people from the details in their rooms, hence her choices introduce her to me." Her tone was academic. Henry interrupted the awkward silence to learn Elizabeth's agenda for the day while the rest digested that the daughter had no connection to her mother.

Georgiana's interest to glean bits of Lady Anne from Christmas details was, indeed, academic. Neither her father nor brother had remembered Lady Anne as more than a name to their daughter and sister, but Georgiana had not begrudged them the oversight since the hole in her life had scabbed over so completely she did not know to take an interest. To distract the others from his ward's preoccupation with Christmas details, Henry exhibited his best show of delightful, inclusive conversation while taking care to support Elizabeth's party as she had planned it.

After tea time, Georgiana stood at the tree searching out her favorite snowflake which Elizabeth had bade each to do as their token-remembrance of the day. Dr. Simons' voice startled her from behind. "It's a lovely tree, is it not, Miss Georgiana?"

"Yes, Sir. Lady Anne was very talented."

"She was a remarkable woman, your mother," he stated with open admiration.

Uncomfortable to hear praise for a mother with whom she had no connection, and therefore, no feelings, Georgiana managed only a little smile.

Dr. Simons continued. "I remember the two of you together. I attended her at the end, you know. My, she doted on you! She insisted that every visit include admiration of her precocious girl."

"Precocious, Sir?"

"Indeed, Miss Georgiana! You knew no bounds in the company of your mother. At two years, you chattered full conversations and were exceedingly inventive in your games. As her end neared, you pretended to be the doctor caring for the lady in the bed." He wiped his eyes at the memory. "I believe your medicine served her better than mine."

Georgiana smiled sincerely at mention of herself so young. She had no memory of life much before four years when Papa attended her tea parties in the playroom. Dr. Simons again imposed on her silence. "I'd be glad to share my memories of her, if you'd care to hear them. In fact, I believe I still have the volume of her medical records, if you take an interest to read them."

Out of politeness and her wish to conclude an awkward conversation, she answered, "Yes, if it were no trouble. That would be kind."

"No trouble at all, Miss Georgiana," he smiled.

Chapter 11

C hristmas stretched long into the evening past the clearing of dinner and the moving of sofas near the hearth, but after the last game of "Best Christmas Memory," the party still shied from giving up the day. Near eleven o'clock, Henry added his voice to the spit and crackle of the fire. "I believe Edmund D'Arcy smiles down at our happy company in his room."

"Who is Edmund D'Arcy, Brigadier?" Mrs. Annesley queried.

"He's the founder of Pemberley, Mum."

Dr. Simons reappraised the plaster and timber work above thick wainscoting. "Henry, are you stating that this room isn't a mere replica of the past?"

"Indeed, we sit in the original keeping room of Edmund D'Arcy's manor house built ten years before his death four centuries ago." He looked at Darcy. "I have the facts right, do I not?" Darcy nodded, confused why Henry asked corroboration when they had learned the history together.

Dr. Simons turned attention to his host. "It's an excellent tradition, Mr. Darcy. A family who preserves its past by incorporating it into the present is remarkable in this day."

Impressed by things that endure time, Mrs. Annesley wondered, "What of Pemberley's name, Mr. Darcy? Is it derived from her history like so many estates?"

Encouraged by his guests, Darcy recounted the Tale of Pemberley… a history begun with the abduction of Lord Derby's beloved, youngest daughter, who the honorable and courageous peasant, Edmund D'Arcy returned safely to her father's arms after the lord's knights had failed to do it. When Lord Derby presented the young man his reward, D'Arcy declined it, setting the stage for all the rest. Darcy smiled. "As for Pemberley, he named it for his wife, wed three years later."

Georgiana listened from near the hearth where the flames flickered light on the audience: two watched enchanted, one fitted new details with what she already knew of her new home and one leaned back with legs out-stretched studying the fire. No matter her frustration with Henry, she missed their congeniality desperately. At that moment, he glanced at her with sorrowed resignation then looked away. It was more emotion than he had shared with her for three days.

Elizabeth saw the glances between cousins. To distract others from noticing, she queried for further details of Pemberley's history, and after assurances that his company would hear more, Darcy settled back. "What would you know, Wife?"

"With the details you provided, I accept Edmund achieved what knights could not, but I can't conceive he would refuse the reward offered by his lord, not when it would benefit his family and when refusal would insult the lord."

"It was an issue of practicality. He explained he was satisfied with his shepherd's life and rued the threat to his family's well-being if robbers took an interest in buried gold. As for insult to Lord Derby, Edmund stated he imitated his lord's model of honor and obligation, hence, the young man rightly perceived no debt."

Georgiana leaned forward. "You said he 'stated' and 'explained' as if he told you himself."

"In a sense he did. Edmund D'Arcy set the precedent of scribing his history on parchment and affixing it to the back of his portrait. It hangs in the gallery as we speak."

"Precedent?" Georgiana's gasp of surprise imitated the others.' "Are you saying each portrait in our gallery is backed by its master's words?"

"Yes," Darcy said, guilty to have slighted her family education. "It's a lesson papa would have shared if he'd lived longer." He concluded the story. "The lord grasped the benefit of a liege like Edmund and imposed on him to accept land on the Wye at the frontier of his holdings."

Elizabeth studied Georgiana, who appeared to know as little of family history as she knew of Lady Anne. It was a liability Elizabeth could not imagine; she would lose some sense of self without her familial connection then noted the irony to miss those who supported her so poorly.

Dr. Simons ventured a delicate query. "If I may, Mr. Darcy, how did Pemberley's estate expand from one village to five?"

Darcy leaned forward, pride in his inheritance full evident. "Pemberley is unique in all of England, Sir. Our boundaries have grown without benefit of conquest or marital-acquisition. Instead, our reputation of fairness and honor has recommended us to those who suffer at the hands of others, including four of our villages at Pemberley and dozens of towns across England. In each case, the benefits of agriculture and mineral wealth provide the assets to transfer title to the greater estate; a fact insuring a devoted population and the resources to assure their support."

The guests nodded in admiration, but Elizabeth was distracted by a small detail gone missing. "William, I grant that Edmund was a remarkable young man, but our home's beginning counted on the abduction of a young lady to improve his fortunes."

"Your meaning?" Darcy asked, feigning confusion.

"What of the lady, Husband?"

His eyes danced golden. "Pemberley," he paused for effect, "was Lord Derby's daughter."

The ladies' eyes glistened as the party followed Darcy up the grand staircase to the gallery where they admired Edmund D'Arcy and squinted to decipher a word or two of bygone English. Given the late hour, Darcy put off recounting the story of Pemberley's missing portrait.

With a nod at the mantle clock, he announced, "It is Boxing Day and we bid you all goodnight. Come, Mrs. Darcy. You have yet to see your Christmas gift."

Neither Dr. Simons, nor Mrs. Annesley had gifts to share beyond their company, which they augmented with a pot of tea in the Library. After comparing their favorite memories of the day, he raised his cup to her. "I enjoy your company very much, Madam."

"As I do yours, Sir." Then to assure no misunderstanding, she added, "As I stated at our first meeting, I'm devoted to my husband's memory. I wouldn't wish to mislead you."

He nodded, but absent the smile she had expected. "If I may, Madam, I've lived long enough to appreciate one ought to speak forthrightly rather than demure to society's silly customs." With latent nerves as to his intent, she stood and hastened to bid goodnight. He rose as well. "I'm not proposing marriage,

Mrs. Annesley. I only wish to learn your given name, and then gain permission to speak it."

She flustered before returning to her chair in full blush. "I am Margaret."

He bowed. "As you know from conversation, I'm called Matthew. I look forward to Miss Georgiana's good performance at the ball since it will assure a year to know you better." Henry had conveyed the details of Darcy's arrangement with his sister.

Except for the awful day of their arrival, Margaret Annesley had avoided the fact of Dover, but now with Christmas past, she looked the future in the face and blanched.

"Dear lady, what is it?"

She laid out the facts while watching her lap, but looked him in the eye when she rose at the end. "I regret losing your good opinion of me, Sir." She curtsied. "Good night."

"Margaret, sit… please." His voice was very kind. Matthew Simons studied the fire for several minutes before stating, "I *am* disappointed, Margaret. Not by you or your action, but rather in its result that deprives me of the year; hence, I shall propose something unusual but not unseemly. To enjoy your company until the sixth, I ask you to assist at my practice. Please, before you decline, let me explain that the clinic is very busy. I'm good at my work and my parlor is often filled with those awaiting examination. I invite you to serve tea and otherwise distract patients from their troubles. My housekeeper attempts this, but her other duties make it difficult."

"You have thought this through in some detail, Matthew."

He laughed. "It's a physician's handicap to consider every aspect of a problem before assaying a solution."

Upstairs, Georgiana had worked a solution for how to deliver her Christmas gift to the cousin who avoided her; she leaned it unwrapped on his mantel. She had intended to present it via a game during a late party of wine and sandwiches, but after three days of distance, she accepted their habit of silly parties had passed. She sipped wine alone in a flickering fairyland.

Tap. Tap-tap. Henry stood stiffly at her door with her gift to him in his left hand and a wrapped parcel in his right. Her surprise to see him left him standing on the threshold. Past her shoulder he saw her preparation for their usual party, a thing he himself had instituted early on to let her practice entertaining. With a bow, he queried, "May I come in, Miss Darcy?"

"Forgive me. Of course, please." She poured his wine and filled his plate and they smiled to recall Elizabeth's extraordinary Christmas until Henry balanced her gift to him on his knees and admired it so sincerely that Georgiana blushed.

"It's remarkable, Princess." The oil painting depicted a bird's view of the park across the boulevard from Annapolis in which the same couple was repeated a dozen times, each devoted to a favorite diversion of guardian and ward: fishing in the pond, flying a kite, discussing on a bench, etc. The gentleman changed only in the cut of his uniform, but the girl adjusted from short skirts and long, straight hair to long skirts and upswept curls. Georgiana apologized that it was not so well executed as she would wish, but the detail required her to use oils, her least favorite medium. When she leaned close, he smelled her perfume and quickly bade her open his gift.

Her eyes showed disappointment when she glimpsed it was a music box; he had given her several such previously. But on closer inspection, this one was unique. Standing fourteen inches tall, it was porcelain topped by a gentleman and lady prepared to twirl on a gilded dance floor. "Press the button, Georgiana," he invited. Her favorite waltz tinkled for almost three minutes before trailing into silence. She had not heard any music box play so long.

She wound it again. And then again. Suddenly, she stood. "Come, Cousin, dance with me in honor of Christmas."

"But …"

"No argument," she laughed. "It belongs with your gift."

The close furnishings made a proper waltz difficult, but they managed until the music stopped in a room of dancing, colored lights. Each time she rewound it, their circle narrowed. Each time they stood closer, imperceptibly so, until her curls touched his cheek and she could smell the deliciousness of him. She felt the man beneath the shoulder of his jacket and felt his hand press on her back. She felt… he let go, retrieved the painting and bowed, all in a heartbeat that made her wonder if she had imagined the wonderful tension in his embrace.

In the mistress' bedchamber, there was no tension as Elizabeth admired William's gift across the room. Soothed by the rise and fall of his breathing and warmed by his love, she reveled in his sensitivity to her. He had surprised her with her writing table from Longbourn on which she had learned her letters and then had written years of letters to stay connected with those she cherished. Included with the refurbished table was a new companion chair upholstered to coordinate with her bedchamber. She watched her simple table in the firelight. It looked at home at Pemberley.

Chapter 12

Born to educated and talented craft folk, Hannah Miller was a fortunate girl. Her seamstress mother and musician father had each taught her their skills and their daughter doted on them and helped them in their shops that shared the main level of their row house. One summer morning, seventeen-year-old Hannah set out to do the shopping at the farmer's market. She returned to smoldering cinders. Inside of an hour, a conflagration had destroyed their entire block and with it her home, the family businesses and her beloved parents.

Being six months from legal adulthood, Hannah was consigned to an orphanage where she was assigned to clean its office. One morning after over-hearing that the orphans in her wing would be leased to a mill the following week, she stole a franked sheet from the office and stuck her letter in the out-going post addressed to her only relative, a distant cousin who worked in the kitchens at Annapolis. Colonel Fitzwilliam agreed to pay for Hannah's release, which she would reimburse with work until her eighteenth birthday, after which she would make her life in Town.

While Annapolis slept, Hannah escaped her sorrow between the covers of books in a corner of the library. One night, thirteen-year-old Georgiana's nocturnal habits discovered the maid reading Shakespeare's sonnets, a surprise that led to shy conversation, then regular discussion of favorite volumes, and then the sharing of their histories. Georgiana had not previously met another orphan and affinity for someone like herself fostered further friendship. On her eighteenth birthday, Hannah elected to remain with the girl who needed a friend.

Elizabeth Darcy could count on one hand the number of days that illness had confined her to bed, making her the exception in a family whose sensitivity to cold, wet and nerves required many a physician's visit. Nursing a stomach unsettled by too much Christmas and its weeks of preparation, she relied on her iron constitution to accomplish her morning toilette sans lady's maid. It was Boxing Day meaning that servants enjoyed their Christmas and the men enjoyed a winter hunt, which in deference to deep snow became comradeship at an inn in Buxton. Notified that Georgiana was still abed, Elizabeth emerged from her quarters with the House to herself, so to speak. Approaching the study stairs, she anticipated brewing her own pot of tea.

As she stepped down the stairs, Hannah Miller climbed up with the freshly cleaned and pressed gown from Longbourn that Mrs. Darcy had lent her to wear at the piano. The maid immediately stepped to the side and lowered her head mumbling her mission to return the gown.

"Hannah? What is it, pray?"

"No problem, Mum. Just a bit of a headache."

"A cup of tea is in order. Return the gown then join me in the kitchens."

"Oh no, Mum!" Careful to keep her face hid, she recoiled to have contradicted the mistress, "I mean I've other duties to attend if you'll forgive me to decline your kindness."

"It is Boxing Day; hence, there are no duties. I'll expect you in the kitchens, Hannah, before the tea is finished steeping."

Elizabeth counted distraction an excellent antidote to nerves as she filled the pot with boiling water and let it sit while she laid the table. After emptying the pot, she spooned tea into a strainer, refilled the pot with boiling water and covered it with a cozy. *Pleasure in a simple act is also reviving.* She had not prepared a pot of tea in four months. Her pleasure eroded, however, when Hannah failed to join her. She climbed four flights to the servants' quarters.

Mrs. Darcy sat on the sole chair in the maid's room while Hannah sat on her narrow bed, struggling to regain her composure. From Hannah's story revealed in gasps between sobs, Elizabeth gleaned that after having played the piano for hours in a proper gown rather than a servant's costume, the maid had confronted her history. So long as Hannah had felt she was more friend than servant to Georgiana, it had not troubled her to be a lady's maid instead of an independent craftsperson, but since her mistress' distraction with rooms, she felt more maid than friend. "Forgive me my impertinence, Mrs. Darcy, but I wasn't raised to be a servant."

"Your history certifies this, Miss Miller," Elizabeth affirmed. "Certainly, you're free to go whenever you like. Make your choice and we'll pay the coach fare to Town if that's what you deem best." Elizabeth thought her words were logical and generous, hence she was unprepared for the maid's sudden, incoherent sobs, from which the mistress could only make out "more complicated than 'what I deem best.'"

Mrs. Darcy pressed her lips. "This is your problem, Hannah dear, but it is my House and I insist to understand these 'complications' over a cup of tea." Her tone brooked no argument. "You have fifteen minutes to collect yourself before meeting me in my bedchamber since the tea has certainly gone cold and must be brewed afresh. No, there's no choice. I am firm that we will share a cup and will only compromise the number of stairs I must climb to do it."

A quarter-hour later, Elizabeth met a much better composed maid who insisted to relieve her mistress of the tray and set out their tea as her contribution.

The mistress raised her cup, "To understanding." The maid raised hers with awful misgiving. Mrs. Darcy continued, "I grant that open discussion is made difficult by our positions; hence, I propose that we set aside our roles for the balance of our conversation. Are you agreed?"

Hannah looked her in the eye. "Honest discussion can invite repercussions, Mum. I know you mean well, but my trouble touches more than me. I won't chance problems for others."

"The plot thickens," Elizabeth murmured.

"Pardon, Mum?"

"It's an expression." Elizabeth adjusted her tack. "I'm twenty-two, Hannah. And you?"

"Twenty-two next week, Mum."

Elizabeth nodded. "Then we've each lived long enough to know a problem insists to work itself through, whether it is now or at some point in future. I propose your choice is less whether to protect others than if I, as mistress, might be of some benefit to those involved."

A half-hour later en route to Mrs. Annesley's bedchamber, a single thought chided Elizabeth's inquisitiveness: one must take care what one insists to learn! She discovered the chaperone consoling Georgiana, who had just learned the facts of Dover, about which Mrs. Annesley would apprise Mr. Darcy on the morrow.

"Pardon my interruption, please," Elizabeth began as if naught were out of the ordinary. "Hannah will speak with you in my bedchamber, Georgiana. Yes, now. It's important."

After her sister had closed the door, Elizabeth joined the nervous chaperone on the settee. Mrs. Annesley surmised Hannah had shared the secret, but could not imagine the circumstances in which the devoted maid would do so. She learned it soon enough. "Oh my!" she exclaimed. And then again, "Oh my!" as the greater implication of Hannah's loss to her mistress took root. "I know she's been disappointed in regard to her friendship with Miss Georgiana, but I had no concept it reached so deep."

"The issue before us is both Hannah's and Miss Georgiana's well-being. If Hannah's happiness lies in Town then we must accept it, but if she's more disappointed by their failing friendship then we might help both parties to their comfort."

Together, the two women worked a plan, after which the chaperone entertained the maid while Elizabeth conferred with her sister. At the end, Georgiana hugged her sister's neck.

"Oh Lizzy, I thought I must lose Hannah after hearing her despair, but now —"

"Now, there is a small hope, Sister," she patted her sister's hand. "But if our offer to Hannah is not enough, you and I shall make the best of it together. Are you agreed?"

Summoned to Mrs. Darcy's study, Hannah arrived resolved to pursue her independence, despite Miss Georgiana's initial hardship. She was therefore nonplussed when Mrs. Darcy laid a sheet of paper on her lap and bade her to consider its contents before responding. At first, surprised and then wary, Hannah read.

Pemberley, 26 December, 18- -

Miss Hannah Miller accepts the position of Personal Secretary for Miss Georgiana Darcy commencing this day, 26 December, 18- - and continuing until Miss Miller declares this contract ended.

For her services, Miss Miller will receive a wardrobe commensurate with her position, quarters adjacent to Miss Darcy's, and a monthly stipend of £20. This position also affords her standing in the House such as enjoyed by Mrs. Annesley, including attendance at family meals and most family events.

Miss Hannah Miller (Signatory) _____

Miss Georgiana Darcy (Signatory) _____

Mrs. Elizabeth Darcy (Signatory) _____

Hannah read it a second time before asking, "Are you saying that I'm free to offer my opinion and take my own choices as regard secretarial duties?"

"In so far as Mrs. Annesley has been free to do the same within the confines of her duties, yes," Elizabeth affirmed.

"And are you happy with this, Miss?" Hannah asked her mistress.

Georgiana beamed ear to ear and nodded.

Later, while Georgiana visited with Mrs. Annesley and Hannah settled in her new quarters across the hall from Georgiana's chambers, Elizabeth soaked in a warm bath infused with fragrant oil and smiled at a very successful afternoon.

Only when she stepped from the bath, did she apprehend the possibility of an issue vis-à-vis her husband. She had trod on untested ground to have committed Pemberley to a contract without first consulting William.

Chapter 13

Returned from Buxton to a House not as he had left it, Fitzwilliam Darcy refolded Elizabeth's note. She had handed him a shock unanticipated and he stared from his desk for a half-hour before he called her to his study.

After a day of gentlemen's camaraderie, Darcy had arrived home to learn a chaperone had resigned as of 6 January and that a lady's maid was promoted to secretary. His wife's note, a technique she previously had employed to ask his opinion regarding change, now announced change as if he were a bystander in his own House. He did allow that Elizabeth had explained it well and took responsibility for her action, but he was undone that she had flaunted propriety, which he had trusted they both respected. Marriage had served him a surprise that challenged the man as well as his marriage. She arrived shortly after his summons.

"Well?" he asked after she curtsied. Though her husband did not rant, Elizabeth heard censure in his tone.

"I take it you disapprove."

He stood imposingly. "Disapprove of your solution? No. But I'm undone by your method." She nodded stiffly. "You understand that your action compromised my position."

"I apologize, Fitzwilliam." Elizabeth sat straight, her stomach knotted as tightly as the hands in her lap. Her nature had acted according to its best judgment, but that judgment had not included all of those affected. The result was an indictment of herself. She rose, "If you'll excuse me, I must prepare for tea." Her composure bespoke both awareness and acceptance of the rules she had broken and their prescribed penalty. No debate. No defense.

"Elizabeth," he looked as pained as she felt, "I wouldn't want this to come between us."

"It already has, Husband, but through no fault on your part. If I could undo my haste in settling this morning's problems, I would." She raised her chin, not against him, but against herself. "It seems you got yourself a wife whose confidence outpaced her reason." Her wound was palpable. "I need time to understand how I got it so wrong."

When tea concluded, Georgiana drew her brother to the side. "Is Lizzy ill?" she queried. "She's not herself."

Indeed, Elizabeth had performed her mistress' duty to perfection, but absent any smiles or banter. He had observed her closely at tea; she was like a box of politeness, inside of which her feelings were hid from public view. "We suffer a momentary difficulty, Georgiana. I will discuss with her." Unfortunately, his wife declined discussion since talk was only of benefit when one required more understanding, and from her view, she understood the issue clearly. Dinner was even more uncomfortable than tea.

On the Third, Fourth and Fifth Days of Christmas, Elizabeth kept to herself when not attending formal duties and, to an extent, she was not missed. Mrs. Annesley journeyed to Lambton each day to attend at Dr. Simons' clinic parlor in hope that her absence would relieve some of the unease at Pemberley. Georgiana settled into the office Hannah established for her at one end of the day room, a location her secretary intended to imply equality for the younger sister with its proximity to the master's and mistress's studies. And Darcy, sensing that his presence only intensified his wife's discomfort, continued his outings with Henry.

"Elizabeth-gone-missing" weighed severely on William not only because he missed her, but also because her transgression challenged the precepts upon which he had been raised. The rules maintained that Elizabeth's fault should cost her his trust, fully and completely. Initially, the inanity of such a censure had moderated Darcy's temper when confronting her in his study, but thereafter, reason required him to reappraise the entire system detailing who bowed to whom and the penalties for failure. In his final judgment, rules condemning a wife's considered action simply because she ranked beneath her husband were flawed. The conclusion struck him at his core.

On the Sixth Day of Christmas, Darcy awoke in an empty bed for the third morning in a row. His patience depleted, he pulled on breeches and shirt, intent to put things right. When arrived at her door, his wife looked up from her writing table where she appeared to have been sorting her thoughts for days.

"I require more time, William," she said without him asking.

"Would that I could accommodate, Elizabeth, but I miss you too much." He pulled a chair close to hers. "Explain what is so complicated to require closeting yourself for three days."

She considered then laid down her pen and traded sitting for pacing. Darcy couldn't judge if she required movement or imposed distance.

"There's nothing complicated in the problem," She began. "It's the solution that takes me in circles." With hands behind her back and periodic glances at the ceiling, she walked as if talking to herself. "I doubt I have ever done anything so reckless as with that contract. On the one hand, I am chagrined, even mortified, while on the other hand, I can't promise I won't err again; in fact, I probably will unless I can divine a solution." She paused and watched him from across the room. "I know right from wrong, William. At Longbourn, I said and did what lay within the parameters of a daughter's role, despite that I perceived realities I preferred to change. I accepted the rules without argument." She resumed pacing. "It seems I've misinterpreted my role as mistress or at least taken it too much to heart. My action in regard to Hannah demonstrates that I saw myself as your equal in the House. As disrespectful as that sounds, I cannot interpret it any other way." Her chin raised in defense of the facts while her shoulders slumped at their implication. "My former self cringes at what I have become, yet my present self doesn't know any other way to be in our House. I search for a solution that will both permit my freedom to continue as I've come to be and assure I do as the rules prescribe that I ought." She stood before him. "My problem is I don't think this is possible."

"Come." He motioned her to his lap.

She shook her head. "I can't. If I'm close to you, I'll be even more tortured to feel what this crisis threatens to take from me."

Darcy understood; their separation had had the same effect on him. He watched her. "Would it help you to know I wouldn't want a wife who couldn't act on her own initiative?"

Elizabeth eyed him, incredulous. "Not so, William. You were angry I made the contract."

"My response was to rules broken, Lizzy," he countered. "Rules I had been raised to believe were important. I have since reevaluated."

She studied him, astonished. "William, you, of all people, would not condone anyone selectively breaking the precepts of propriety."

Darcy rose and crossed with slow, resolute steps, watching her with eyes dark and emotive. "You speak of a man before he had been touched by Elizabeth Bennet, Mrs. Darcy." His finger caressed her cheek. "I've learned that marriage can alter one past recognition." With that, he lifted her in his arms and whispered low, "My God, how I love you!"

Like a magnet drawn to its counterpart, Elizabeth clung to him as if she held on to life itself. Those six words, breathed from the depths of the man, released a stubborn lady from arguments for and against her that had checkmated her ability to act. Made vulnerable by love and thereby dependent on another, she had been rescued from despair that had compromised her spirit, and in a heartbeat, he grew her seedling of trust into a deep-rooted tree.

Almost shyly, they reconnected. Each had tasted the loss of the other, making touch itself precious as if they reached beyond each other's warmth to know their partner for the first time.

Later, watching her husband's eyes as she rested in his arms, Elizabeth asked to hear in words what their bodies had spoken. "Does this mean we are returned to before as if there had been no contract?"

He responded between kisses, "No, my love. We are each changed. Your sensitivity to the rules is recalibrated while mine is numbed a bit… we have each adjusted more keenly to the other."

Chapter 14

Lady Anne took great pride in her subterfuge, as did her husband. She affected two ballrooms at opposite sides of the House: the Ballroom itself and the Grand Salon, converted to the dance by dispersing its furnishings to the far ends of both grand rooms. For those who promoted gossip as to who danced with whom, etc., the arrangement made an evening of unparalleled exertion since no one could contend to have witnessed the facts in both venues at once. Unfortunately, young Lady Newsome did not perceive the extent of Lady Anne's challenge until her dedication to know-it-all left her red-cheeked from over-exercise and white-countenanced from public censure after she had gossiped that a liaison existed when, in fact, it had not.

According to English society, a beautiful woman was graced with an aquiline profile that diminished to thin lips, a receding chin, and narrow, rounded shoulders, a combination seen as delicate and submissive. In comparison, Georgiana's more assertive French features and squared shoulders could, at best, be called "pretty," which had been of no concern to her until Pemberley's ball. She devoted hours to look like a princess, and at five o'clock on the Eighth Day of Christmas, she did. A tiara sparkled around a crown of curls and her Fitzwilliam-blue gown, studded with tiny crystals on silk tulle complemented her best assets. She turned in all directions admiring the crystals catching the light before she grimaced to force her feet into too-stiff slippers.

While Georgiana was satisfied with her result, Elizabeth's hope to host a perfect ball collapsed in her bedchamber after hearing her husband's "surprise."

"And when will this take place, Mr. Darcy?" she asked still stunned.

"At ten o'clock." The new style of long trousers and cropped jacket suited him well.

She breathed deep. "Make it eleven."

"Done!" He pulled her to her feet to step the waltz while he hummed accompaniment, but she stood immoveable as Monsal Head, the great stone cliff overlooking the Dale from the far side of the River Wye.

"Not now, William. I'm still adjusting."

Her nerves demanded that he view his scheme from her side. He had arranged for a small orchestra from Town to perform waltzes while she and he exhibited the dance. Thereafter, Georgiana, Henry, and six other couples, to whom he and Henry had taught the steps in recent days, would join them to demonstrate the magical effect of multiple couples swirling around the floor. Fitzwilliam Darcy's penchant to test society's patience had fit nicely with introducing parochial Peak society to the continental dance. But the waltz, deemed scandalous by the King's Court, was shunned by the better classes, hence Elizabeth's despair.

"I'm sorry, Lizzy," he offered after consideration. "I shall assume full responsibility."

She squared her shoulders. "Absolutely not! We are partners, Mr. Darcy."

While Elizabeth suffered to accept that the first ball she hosted would be infamous for its entertainment, Hannah inspected the changes that let a Great House appear like a palace: staff outfitted in formal livery, candle-glow and hot house flowers from every vantage, sparkling crystal – from chandeliers to vases and stemware, rooms rearranged for whist and vingt-et-un while others invited conversation and nibbling at buffets, all in addition to the impressive Ballroom and Grand Salon. After penciling her name on a card to hold a seat at the back of the ballroom, she hurried up the Grand Staircase and nearly collided with the brigadier at the top.

"You have outdone yourself, Sir" she complimented. "Every lady will hope for a dance."

He grinned, "Especially those wishing to relieve me of my bachelorhood. Such is the trial of every unattached male at these events, Miss Miller," he rolled his eyes.

"You will survive it, Sir," she laughed.

Within minutes of the first dance, the brigadier wondered if he would survive the ladies' attention; the effect of his new uniform had compounded the usual attraction to a tall, handsome, unattached male. Worse than simpering admirers, however, were his conflicted feelings in Georgiana's regard. His guardian's habit struggled to keep her in view to assure her well-being, while Henry, the man, envied those she entertained. He was not accustomed to watching her from afar since he had squired her to many of the soirees she had attended in Town; one more fact that served him the poignancy of his despair.

Darcy was well-pleased with his sister's acquittal of social responsibility, though whether she had sat or danced, he would have kept her at Pemberley. She required more than a chaperone in Town; hence he and Elizabeth would accompany her when she came out next summer.

But for sore feet and too many offers of punch from young men begging introduction, Miss Darcy took satisfaction in her effort, though the gentlemen themselves were of no consequence. She harbored no interest in a beau, had never received letters dabbed with lavender water and had not been kissed like most of the girls at her school; men's lips touched only her gloved hand.

At ten o'clock, she had managed all of the punch, dancing and discussion-of-the-weather she could tolerate and took refuge near Mr. Newsome, a bespectacled young man, who bored ladies within minutes of his introduction. With him she could smile and murmur "how interesting" while he described his bug collection and she enjoyed the ball from the side.

Georgiana was very happy for Elizabeth whose black velvet gown and splendid garnet accessories impressed even the most discriminating guests. And she was happy for her brother who looked to take his ease as host. She smiled at Dr. Simons and Mrs. Annesley at a front table and winked at Hannah who claimed an injured ankle to avoid unfamiliar dance steps, though the ruse did not deter a young man from plying her with multiple cups of punch.

Suddenly, a burst of laughter at the opposite end of the ballroom turned every head to observe a lovely, dark-haired lady pulling on the sleeve of the brigadier, who bowed to distance himself from her attention. Unfortunately for Georgiana, Mr. Newsome provided no distraction when she required it and she witnessed first-hand the history she had missed until Surrey. She had no doubt Henry could invite any of the beautiful ladies reaching to touch his arm and teasing to elicit his smile… could invite them to Bristol or to inspect farm inventions or…

"Will you excuse me for a moment, Mr. Newsome?" she smiled demurely, then bit her lip to endure stiff shoes en route to the nearest sanctuary where she could assure her privacy.

With effort, she opened a window in her brother's study and breathed in cold air, but not even winter could cool heated emotion. Her heart pounded as she struggled to understand. *I want him to look at me like he does his ladies.* Aghast at the implication, she gripped the sill until her head offered explanation. *He's your guardian, Georgiana. You're infatuated with the man who has shown you so much kindness.* Humiliated to have confused gratitude with some deeper emotion, she took solace that he was unaware of her too personal admiration until logic reckoned that his recent distance had been to protect her and him from her silliness.

"Ah, here you are, Princess," Henry called as if he had explored every room to find her. "Are you ill?" He closed the door and pushed a chair toward her.

"Thank you. I am well. I only wanted a bit of fresh air."

"Sit!" He closed the window, pulled a throw from the settee and draped it around her shoulders. "Did Newsome say something to disturb you?"

"My goodness, no! He's an entomologist and educates all who will lend an ear."

Having noted her limp, he knelt to inspect her feet. "You'll have blisters tomorrow, Princess. No, sit. I'll work circulation to relieve the pain a bit." With head bent to his task, he gently massaged the reddened flesh beneath her stockings.

Sore feet were nothing to the agony induced by confused feelings. While he showed her kindness, she wished… she wished he would hold her instead of her feet. She yearned for permission to touch his cheek and feel his lips on her hand, yearned for his scent to envelop her as it had when they danced Christmas night. Georgiana's head reeled; she wanted him to kiss her. She imagined, just for a moment, how his lips might feel against hers, but this time her imagining was a conscious thought, not the innocent longing of a person unaware of her feelings.

Glancing up, his smile sobered to see her damp cheeks. He jumped up, stuck his head past the door and ordered Miss Darcy's chamber slippers be fetched at once.

"I shan't wear them!" She stood with hands clenched against being treated like a child.

"You shall or the ball is ended for you, Miss. Any lady brought to tears by her feet can't be trusted for clear-headed choices." He smiled disarmingly and cocked his head to the side. "This is why one is appointed a guardian, Miss Darcy."

The hard reality of his legal obligation numbed Georgiana's nascent longing and she sat to let Henry slip on the comfortable slippers without further argument. But when he reached for her hand to help her stand, she refused his support. "Thank you. These are much better. You're an excellent guardian to look out for me so well. Excuse me, please."

Waiting sullenly near the ballroom's double doors, Mr. Newsome brightened immediately at Georgiana's approach. "My parents wish to make your personal acquaintance, Miss Darcy."

Georgiana thought they made an absurd pair. Bespectacled and three inches shorter, he worked his fingers in nervous agitation while she trailed in house slippers.

"Good evening, Lady Newsome, Lord Newsome. We're so glad you could attend."

"Not so glad as you are, eh, Miss?" Lord Newsome bowed and nodded toward his son.

His wife continued more tactfully after thumping her husband's shin under the tablecloth. "We look forward to entertaining you and your family at Braithmoor, Miss Darcy, though it's not so grand as Pemberley, I am sure." The Lord and his Lady had been wed long enough to imitate each other in girth, too red cheeks and rolls of fat at their necks.

"That is most kind of you, Lady Newsome."

In the background, the fiddlers stopped playing and Darcy announced the seating of an orchestra from Town. Lady Newsome lowered her voice. "We hope to make our own announcement in future, Miss Darcy," she smiled intently into the young lady's mask of politeness. Georgiana understood too late that she had paid their son too much attention.

"Indeed, Mum, Braithmoor will be proud to announce the founding of Mr. Newsome's entomology society." Georgiana curtsied. "Excuse me, please. I am to participate in my family's surprise." The irony that she traded one discomfort for another did not escape Georgiana, but she could more easily manage dance with Henry than stomach the Lord and Lady's innuendo.

Darcy concluded his introduction amid hushed murmurs and Georgiana felt sudden nerves for her brother and sister while they waited at the center of the floor with his left hand clasping her right and her left hand on his shoulder seam while her elbow rested lightly on his raised one. The issue for English society was not the touching of hands, but rather the dancers' connections at shoulder and waist, which fixed them face-to-face in a lingering, public embrace. The heresy of the waltz abjured centuries of English decorum in the reel's elaborate tease of semi-segregated men and women. Some guests sucked in their breath. Others craned to glimpse their hosts.

Whispers punctuated the silence, conveying to Darcy the censure his wife would endure in the coming weeks; some guests, the Newsomes included, quit the ballroom with noses in air. They took sanctuary in the grand salon where a minuet played as background to their collective criticism of Mrs. Darcy's social fiasco. Though Elizabeth stoically held her head high, Darcy prepared to call out and claim sole credit, but her look dissuaded him.

After the waltz's first steps, his wife's thumb tickled his palm. Darcy looked down to see her lovely eyes smiling up at him. "You appear so glum our guests might think I stepped on your foot," she said, her look declaring she could not love him more. "Our partnership balances one with the other, William."

"How so, Wife?" he asked, holding her a bit closer than a proper waltz sanctioned.

"The wife from Longbourn designed a ball to please society, but her husband, secure in his position, had the confidence to include our sensitivities in the party. I'm very glad."

Georgiana sensed Henry at her side, felt his hand at her elbow, and heard him whisper, "Now, we'll demonstrate how it is really done." He winked and flashed his most engaging smile, sweet delights that steeled her to endure heartache. She danced as if he were already in Vienna.

Miss Darcy bade good-night at midnight, despite that the majority of guests remained to practice the waltz, which required staff to hurry to prepare more bedchambers than anticipated. Hannah knocked at her door shortly after Georgiana closed it. "I am well," the mistress assured. "Too much party, that's all."

Would that it were merely too much party, Georgiana thought as she carried her writing box to the window table. She sorted her feelings toward Henry with her pen pressing black on white to isolate truth from confusion. Near dawn, she slept bent over her facts smudged with the tears of a young woman. During the next two days, she devoted herself to pen and paper, those silent friends who protected secrets as they invited open honesty.

Chapter 15

Margaret Annesley sat numb after pulling the blanket over the glazed eyes of the last of her three children strangled by diphtheria. The next day she showered the first handful of dirt on Patience's coffin before the grave diggers filled the hole. She had done the same over the boxes of Jim and Constance and her beloved husband, John, all died within a week of each other. Neighbors whispered she had gone mad with grief, but the touch of her hand via earth-on-a-coffin kept Margaret as close to them as she could henceforth be. It was the last act of love from the wife and mother who had prayed to be choked with them.

Her dreams buried, thirty-year-old Margaret tended sick beds until the epidemic passed, after which she sat in a corner of her parents' house and wept until she was wrung dry. Accepting that God intended her to continue, she applied for the work she loved best - caring for children - however, it was she who interviewed the families, not vice versa. In the end, she selected a lonely orphan whose blond locks were close in color to those of her beloved Patience.

Two years with Miss Darcy had helped the girl to more confidence, though Margaret shared credit with Georgiana's cousin. In fact, it was he who had interceded when Darcy balked against hiring Mrs. Annesley since she had no families to recommend her. Two years with Georgiana had also cracked Mrs. Annesley's shell of mourning. Though she still wore black silk, she had rejoined the living because no one could love Georgiana and feel emptiness.

On the Ninth Day of Christmas, Georgiana sat either cuddled under a throw in her favorite chair or at her writing table. Her absence did not raise concern until she declined to attend tea.

Early on the Tenth Day of Christmas, Hannah knocked on the mistress' French doors in response to Elizabeth's summons. "You wished to speak with me, Mrs. Darcy?"

"Yes, Miss Miller." Elizabeth smiled and motioned the secretary to sit. "I regret to impose on your friendship with my sister, but her family is at loss to understand her seclusion and we debate how best to support her happiness. Mr. Darcy will counsel with Dr. Simons, the brigadier will let her sort things for herself and I will force discussion. Can you help direct our choice?"

"I… I don't know, Mum. I mean, she's my friend and mistress." Hannah shifted, wishing she could offer more. "If it helps, she hasn't told me anything directly."

Elizabeth dangled a compromise. "You might guide us from your observation alone."

The secretary reflected. "I've only known her in this state once before." She described the shock at Surrey and days of cloistered writing.

"But my sister and the brigadier appeared in best spirits when they arrived!" Elizabeth exclaimed. Her sister's earlier confidences in Henry's regard had omitted mention of Surrey.

"Yes, Mum. I surmise their discussion en route repaired whatever had been damaged. She was herself again at the end of the first day's travel."

Elizabeth considered these facts in light of Georgiana's distress at Henry's recent distance. "Has she mentioned the brigadier of late?"

"Now that you mention it, no, Mum."

"And her response to Mr. Newsome's note recently arrived?"

Hannah watched her lap. This answer required her to step past observation and divulge her mistress' words. She took her choice and confided, "I'm to convey she is ill and can't receive him until 8 January."

Mistress and secretary locked eyes; here was no social excuse for Georgiana's lie. Mrs. Darcy nodded. "Be assured I shall hold our words in strictest confidence."

At nine o'clock that evening, Elizabeth arrived at her sister's door with a pot of tea and a plate of sweets neither of which loosed Georgiana's tongue. After a quarter-hour, Elizabeth lost patience.

"We will speak honestly, Sister!"

"But I do."

"Honestly of only the trivial. Your writing there," Elizabeth indicated pages peeking from beneath a throw flung in haste across the window table, "may I read it?"

"It is private."

"Precisely."

"Lizzy, please!" Georgiana caught her sister's arm. "I'm sorting thoughts and weighing choices in regard to a topic I hadn't previously considered."

"Thoughts and choices in regard to Henry?" Elizabeth asked gently. Her sister looked away. "You're very fond of him, and he's devoted to you. Do you love him, Georgiana?"

"Certainly I love him. He's my cousin and guardian,"

"And if he weren't cousin and guardian?"

"Then we would be strangers." She curled in her favorite chair and stared into the torch-lit courtyard below. "I'm not the sort of lady who turns a gentleman's head."

Whether infatuation or love, Elizabeth had no doubt as to the problem and weighed her words. "Truth can be a balm, if one owns the courage to share it. Have you told him?"

"No! He pities me as it is. Let it be. I'll recover."

"Recover with Mr. Newsome? Come Sister, it's no secret a note from that gentleman arrived this afternoon. Does disappointment with one man invite you to entertain another?"

Georgiana looked up in innocent confusion. "But that would be disingenuous."

"Indeed, unless one's disappointment overwhelms one's common sense."

That afternoon and thereafter, Georgiana's common sense presented a smiling face to her family.

On the morning of the Eleventh Day of Christmas, concern for her mistress' too quick and profound change of mood prompted Mrs. Annesley to knock on Georgiana's door.

"I would gladly forgo this last trip to Lambton, Miss, if a full day together would benefit you," she offered sincerely.

Georgiana hugged her Mrs. Annesley. "I'll miss you desperately after you quit us, Mum, but sharing today with you won't lessen my sorrow two days hence. Please, enjoy Lambton while I pray that one more day with Dr. Simons will convince you to stay." She kissed her cheek. "Failing that, I'll help pack your trunks on the morrow."

The chaperone swallowed before managing a smile; it was Miss Darcy's habit to pack her loved ones' trunks and pretend she traveled with the items she had touched.

En route to Lambton's clinic, Mrs. Annesley tried to still her unease that the young lady had conveyed two messages at once: courageous words publicly offered, and at the last, a hand-grip so tight it bruised the lady's hand.

On the Twelfth Day of Christmas, Georgiana folded petticoats and gowns with Mrs. Annesley until luncheon, which they took at the lady's tea table. Prepared for a day of her mistress' tears, the lady was dismayed by her charge's composure. "You adjust well to my pending departure, Miss. I'm glad. It relieves my worry."

Georgiana laid her fork on her plate. "Then you know me less well than I'd thought."

"Forgive me." The emotion the lady had expected from her charge welled of a sudden in her own eyes. "And forgive my tears as well. I thought I could manage without weeping." She sniffed. "I haven't known you to be so… so controlling of your feelings, Miss Georgiana." She smiled a little. "I recall when you wept to discover a nestling fallen to the ground."

The young lady looked away. "I'm growing up."

The elder lady changed subject. "Will you write me often, Miss Georgiana?"

"Only if you promise to share your thoughts with me as you would a peer. I'm finished with childhood. If you promise to share everything with me then I can share all with you."

"Well, I –"

"Promise, please. I want to keep our connection if only through the post." The yearning that slipped past her charge's lips persuaded a private woman to pledge what she wondered if she could do.

After luncheon, they folded handkerchiefs in silence until Georgiana sat on the lady's bed, and asked, "How can you quit a man who cares for you and whose company you enjoy?"

That Georgiana collected on the promise so soon set Mrs. Annesley on her heels. She hesitated before opening herself a little. "I love my husband, Miss."

"But he's dead and not to be revived while Dr. Simons is here and makes you smile."

"Facts can appear irrational where the heart is concerned, Miss. I wouldn't have accepted Matthew's attention if I'd not already committed to Dover. Since my promise is my obligation, it permitted me a few days of friendship in Derbyshire without worry it might become more." Then she revealed more personal details than she thought possible. "I felt like I lost my life when my family passed, God rest them. I won't chance such an agony again, Miss. Be it cowardly or selfish or however others might judge it, a person knows best what she can endure. Matthew understands this." She smiled, "At least he claims to." She pulled a packet from her handbag. "This is his farewell gift to me. He assured I'd correspond by purchasing franked sheets in Buxton and addressing them to himself. He said he knew I'd not waste postage already laid out."

"He knows you well, Mum," Georgiana beamed. "And what did you give him?"

Mrs. Annesley blushed. "I'd rather not say."

"But you will, I think," Georgiana teased.

"I gave him the small portrait you penned of me last summer. I hope you don't mind."

Georgiana hugged her dear Mrs. Annesley. "At first chance, I'll have Dr. Simons sit for me and will post the results to you."

That evening at the farewell party for Henry and Mrs. Annesley, Darcy smiled to see his sister fully returned to her usual self, but Henry knew otherwise. Georgiana was named for both her parents, and while Lady Anne's legacy was obvious in her art, George Darcy's gift of infernal stubbornness only showed itself when her emotion got past her. He knew from the square of her shoulders she had taken a decision and marked time until she would see it through.

When dinner concluded, Henry pressed the party to join him for a slide on the frozen lake as a sort of farewell family lark. Mrs. Annesley and Dr. Simons immediately demurred, as did Hannah, who had yet to shorten the winter cloak inherited from her mistress. Elizabeth declined since sliding might aggravate her back which let Darcy decline due to concern for his wife. When Georgiana sought her own excuse, her physician prescribed fresh air.

The party of two proceeded toward the circle of torches erected around the smoothest area of ice. Henry offered his arm which she refused, despite slipping twice en route. He shook his head at his uncle's legacy. They slid on the lake in silence then walked in silence on Pemberley Road. With no wind, winter's cold was tolerable.

Henry paused at a bench, swept it free of snow and sat. That he did not invite her rankled Georgiana to sit also, though at furthest distance from him.

"Out with it, Georgiana! What have I done that sets you against me?"

"Nothing."

"As near as I can figure, your anger began in Darcy's study the evening of the ball."

"I'm not angry!"

"Am I better advised to call it your happiness that I somehow provoked?"

"Don't bait me, Cousin."

"Aha! So now you address me as 'Cousin.' Why not 'Henry'?"

"You make my head ache with your queries."

"Then ache it will unless you tell me how I hurt you."

"You didn't hurt me. At least that wasn't your intent. I'm the problem and am addressing it."

"We make progress. I inadvertently caused you pain, which you don't own the courage to share. Do you protect yourself or me with your gallantry?"

"Stop it!" Georgiana erupted from the bench, hands balled and eyes flashing. "If you wish to humiliate me openly, you have succeeded!" She felt her cheeks flush. "I wanted to look beautiful at the ball for you. Yes, you!" She blinked against tears. "But you paid me heed only when duty called. I have accepted my reality, Cousin, and am not proud to have lived months or even years oblivious to the truth. I'm a stupid girl who knows nothing about men and a lady's response to them." Tears chapped her cheeks. "But I do know I love you. I love you and I want you to love me, not as your ward, but like your ladies." She stomped her foot. "You see! You look away, embarrassed for me."

Her raw emotion exploded his. "Never presume to know what I think and feel, Georgiana! And don't compare yourself with the shallow ladies who chase after me. You are too good."

She stomped again and would have lost her footing had he not caught her arm. She promptly freed herself. "I don't want to be 'too good'! I want you to smile at me like you smile at them. I want you to… Never mind. I shall forever be your ward. At least now you understand why there will be no letters. I can't write about the weather, when I long to write my heart. I'm sorry Henry. You've done nothing to warrant my feelings beyond being the excellent person you are. I am the problem and I find I can do nothing for it. I wish you well... no, better than well. I wish your every dream will come true. And... and I wish very much not to see you again."

"Georgiana!" He ran after her, but slipped on an icy patch and fell hard. His head crashed against the frozen road with enough force to let him appear lifeless.

"Henry! Oh, dear God." She knelt by him, but when she felt the sticky warmth of blood on his hair, she set out for the House. After several paces, she paused and returned to him, debating with every step if she could do it. Desperate longing saw its opportunity, although it was very wrong to take what was not freely given. She had never kissed a man, not on the lips, not the way the girls described in whispers at Mrs. Denton's school.

Chapter 16

Elizabeth arrived at Henry's door to wish a bandaged cousin quick recovery. "You've got a good nurse," she said, smiling at her sister. Georgiana had volunteered to assure he remained awake for the prescribed hours to protect against the ill-effects of concussion.

The brigadier lay propped on pillows with a strip of white linen tied to hold a clean patch over his wound. He appeared more like a mischievous boy than a soldier soon to represent the King. To hold his attention, Georgiana recounted memories of a child and guardian discovering together. With her soft voice as background, he relived awaking to the touch of innocence pressed against his lips; a moment's connection he treasured even while he was disgusted by what it evoked in him. His head reeled from more than a nasty bump.

Past midnight, he requested that she hold his hand.

"It's best that I don't."

"Best for you perhaps, but it would help me, Princess."

She looked down and wished her hands were more delicate; they favored her father's. She breathed deep then took his hand in both of hers. "Is that better?"

"Yes. Very much so. Thank you." He studied her. She blushed. "Georgiana, I wish to address our discussion this evening."

"You needn't. I understand."

"I doubt very much that you do since I myself denied my facts until recently." He watched her fingers circling his. "I accept the likelihood that your love for me exists more as infatuation." He held fast to her hands as she pulled away. "I do not demean your feelings, Georgiana. I merely point out what any observer would judge to be the facts." He looked up. "However, there exists no such convenient explanation for my attachment to you."

"Go on." She held her breath.

"You will always be my Princess. I do wish it could be more, but I am your guardian." His Fitzwilliam-blue eyes embraced her, but she saw only equivocation; one did not equivocate where love was concerned. "I pray someday you will understand," he said.

She withdrew her hand and watched her lap. "I understand my feeling differs from whatever attachment you're declaring. No, please, don't continue. I feel quite silly. I don't think one is supposed to feel silly when one speaks of one's love." She looked up then, but with a stranger's eyes. "I haven't yet recounted when you taught me how to clean a fish." She filled the remaining hours with more memories than he cared to recall.

The chaperone and brigadier's departure was delayed until noon to let him sleep a few hours in his bed, but now a flurry of warm handshakes and waving handkerchiefs dispatched them on their muddy journey. It was Epiphany. The air had begun to warm again.

They jostled through the Park toward Lambton, and when arrived in that busy little town, they passed the side road leading to Dr. Simon's lane without comment. With Lambton behind them, Mrs. Annesley broke silence. "She gave me a gift at the last. Did she give you one too, Brigadier?" He nodded but did not pull the bulging envelope from his attaché case. "I shall open mine, I think," she said as she loosed the ribbon and folded back the tissue. "Oh my goodness! How did she manage this?" Mrs. Annesley showed a small portrait of Dr. Simons.

"It's a good likeness," Henry said then stared past his window at the countryside melting to mud. "Georgiana can make anything happen when she sets her mind to it." He attempted a smile. "She likely sketched it while Matthew tended me, and then finished it when I slept this morning."

He waited until the privacy of his bedchamber that night before opening the envelope of heavy artist's paper wherein lay every sketch and portrait she had ever made of him.

The next weeks at Pemberley were like the world turned upside down. The evening of Epiphany, Mr. Crawford injured his back, relegating him to bed with an oak plank under his mattress. In his stead, Darcy continued Evans' training and began the quarterly visitations to the villages. Elizabeth tended the estate's correspondence and ledgers, which Darcy only accepted after she handed her mistress' duties to Georgiana, who Elizabeth reasoned would be well-served by experience. Georgiana was glad for the distraction and especially enjoyed the requisite daily meetings with Mrs. Reynolds since the Housekeeper recalled bits of Lady Anne to the daughter who didn't know her. Only Hannah noticed that Georgiana had let go room decoration and with it her spirit, both coinciding with the start of Mr. Newsome's visits.

In the weeks since the reestablishment of the breakfast room, Mrs. Reynolds had changed more than anyone at Pemberley. Her reticence to cross from servant to involved party had ebbed, but so slowly that even Elizabeth's excellent perception didn't notice when the Housekeeper hovered over her like a mother hen. Since 10 January, Mrs. Darcy had suffered daily weariness and required early afternoon naps to assure sparkling eyes when her husband arrived at tea. For her part, the Housekeeper provided pots of mild tea and delicate soda crackers throughout the day to ease the lady's unsettled stomach. Mrs. Reynolds guessed a new Darcy was in the making, but her mistress' logic explained away each symptom and spurned any hint of speculation.

The Housekeeper's attempt to support Miss Georgiana, however, met fertile ground when the young lady accepted formal meetings specifically intended to recall Lady Anne to her daughter. At nine o'clock each morning, Hannah joined them in the storerooms at the foot of the children's hall; rooms long-emptied of memories of the parents who had once habited there. Georgiana formalized their talks by pulling three chairs and two tables from Henry's nearby chambers to make a comfortable setting where Mrs. Reynolds answered the young lady's queries while Hannah scribed notes, which Georgiana then used to assist her recording of the Housekeeper's stories into a journal each night.

Hannah Miller's gladness for her mistress to learn Lady Anne was tempered by her concern at the unfolding friendship between Miss Georgiana and Mr. Newsome. That gentleman had arrived at precisely two o'clock on 8 January and every day thereafter but for Sundays. As their chaperone, Hannah witnessed the exchange of given names in the first week, followed soon after by Georgiana's support of his quest to establish a Society of Entomology first with her drafting of a formal letter to introduce him, and then with penned illustrations of the gentleman's bugs that she proposed to publish in a volume of lithographs. Each day, Hannah sensed Georgiana's increased estrangement from her former self.

Following numerous, failed attempts to discuss the issue with her mistress, Hannah suffered to know her best action. Her role both demanded the Darcys be notified and required silent allegiance to her mistress. At wits end, Hannah dispatched a full description of her fears with supporting evidence of conversations, etc. to Mrs. Annesley and begged for guidance. The former chaperone's response arrived the morning of 23 January, but Hannah's first opportunity to read it was not until that night while Georgiana recorded the day's stories. After squirreling Mrs. Annesley's response under the liner of her hat box, Hannah snuck down the children's hallway, dispatched a note to Mrs. Darcy and waited near the day room for the lady.

Elizabeth arrived with a bad stomach, but one look at the secretary's expression caused the lady to dig deep. After discussion in Darcy's study, Elizabeth hurried up the study stairs to her husband's bed. Darcy responded to her agitation half-asleep, "Mr. Newsome? You make something from nothing, Wife. Georgiana only entertains herself in our absence."

The next afternoon at five minutes past two, Elizabeth crossed the library's threshold with her needlework basket in hand; woman's instinct insisted she assure herself that Hannah's concern was unjustified.

"Good day to you both," she began as she pulled a half-embroidered doily from the basket. Georgiana went ash-white to see her sister and the fumbling gentleman attempted to reconstitute the young lady with a newspaper flapped in her face. Mrs. Darcy smiled as if such theater were commonplace in one's library of an afternoon.

"Mr. Darcy and I very much regret missing your previous visits, Mr. Newsome, but we assure you we'll attend in future." The gentleman gave up the fan after Georgiana insisted he sit. Elizabeth continued, "You take an interest in insects, do you not, Sir?"

"Yes, and I am glad to say Georgiana shares my interest and works to support my success."

Elizabeth ignored the gentleman's impertinence to address Georgiana by her given name. "Indeed, Sir, our sister takes an interest to support every acquaintance's success."

Though he appeared to be a bookish simpleton, he was no fool and responded to the intended slight with narrowed eyes while he laid out some drawings and the letter she had penned. "As you see, her support goes beyond what just anyone might expect, Madam."

Elizabeth ignored his surliness, studied the evidence, and then addressed her sister. "You're remarkable to manage both your work with Mr. Pankhurst and this too. And then she turned to Newsome. "As you are likely aware, our sister is talented in the decoration of rooms."

Georgiana watched passively as if Elizabeth's intent to drive a wedge were to no avail. Puffed up like a rooster protecting his hen, Mr. Newsome slid nearer his prize. "Madam, please! Her involvement with that man was a misguided experience due to lack of proper supervision. It is not discussed." In the next moment, the rooster became a lap dog, eyeing Georgiana with adoration.

Elizabeth shuddered to watch her sister accept his possessiveness. She eyed the interloper. "I see you're a man of judgment, Sir." He nodded, accepting the compliment. She continued, "Then you're aware that the hostess sets the topic of conversation, not the guest." He scowled at her trick that put him in his place while Elizabeth turned to Georgiana. "Sister? What of your art?"

Georgiana said matter-of-factly, "I apply it to the illustration of Percy's insects, Lizzy."

Elizabeth would have smiled at his name meaning "pierce the hedge or vale" that fit him so poorly, but the situation was too serious. "And your rooms?" Elizabeth asked.

Georgiana looked her in the eye. "I submitted my resignation to Mr. Pankhurst last week with the completion of my most recent project."

Mrs. Darcy rose abruptly, appraising Newsome with a piercing stare. "Sir, if I didn't know better, I'd think you are courting our sister. A gentleman, however, does not pursue such without first requesting permission, and since you have not done so, it is clear your influence over *Miss Darcy* stretches far past what is acceptable. Mr. Thomas will see you to the door."

"Lizzy!" Georgiana stood a tad taller than her sister and at that moment appeared equally imposing. "We'll speak in private, Elizabeth. Percy, please wait here."

Georgiana led the way to the day room where she coolly faced down Elizabeth as if she had practiced every word. "You embarrass our House and most especially me, Lizzy. Please sit with us as friend, not inquisitor."

"But I *am* your friend," Elizabeth fumbled. "You're not yourself, Georgiana. Room design is your passion, yet you cast if off to sketch bugs and accept his attention as if he were a suitor."

Changing persona in a heartbeat, Georgiana kissed her sister. "I know what I'm about, Lizzy," she reassured softly.

After Newsome departed at his usual hour, Georgiana retreated to her quarters certain Elizabeth would summon Darcy, who would then confront her in an awful row. She prepared for him with pen and paper, but when no one knocked on her door, her writing turned introspective.

> *If they could sit inside me, they would understand. It's been three weeks since Henry departed, yet I feel as if he only just rejected my feelings for him. I'm empty. He carries my heart with him. Dear God, I sound like the girls at school, but I'm not. I've explained, denounced and ignored my numbness over and over, but to no avail.*
>
> *I hate the pain of love, but I don't hate Henry. I hated myself for not being the lady he wants, but I gave that up as well. It's not my fault, just as it's not his.*
>
> *As young as I am, I know my heart is wed to him. Logic says I'll recover and vest my feelings in another, but logic can't be counted on where the heart is concerned. I know every man will forever compete with Henry for my affection.*

For Georgiana, her reality was clear and marriage to Percy Newsome addressed that reality perfectly. Loving Henry made marriage to another a mere social contract, not something she would impose on a groom who might truly care for her. At some point, she must marry to stay the harassment suffered by spinsters; Percy was her best ticket to marital anonymity since he cared only for a wife to still his mamma's nagging. Marriage sooner rather than later also dispensed with "coming-out," an insulting institution that paraded young ladies in front of young men as if at auction. As for room design, she had lost her passion for everything but escape.

Elizabeth did summon her husband from the land, and after hearing the details, Darcy did stand to address the issue with his sister. But Elizabeth dissuaded him. "There's something amiss, William… something terribly amiss. To approach her without understanding might do more harm than good."

Darcy deferred to her judgment, but was firm as to his action regarding Newsome. "He will meet *me* when he arrives tomorrow and so help me that man will not set foot at Pemberley again."

Elizabeth's description of a stubborn sister who dug in her heels in support of a cause, no matter its illogic, haunted Darcy the rest of the day. He recalled Henry's comments over the years that their ward could imitate her father's stubbornness, but Darcy's sense of the shy sister had deemed such to be impossible. He knew that if she did harbor some of their father's tendencies, he would need to seriously adjust his approach with her or he chanced an unbridgeable impasse.

Chapter 17

Mrs. Reynolds and Mr. Thomas sensed trouble after discussing the facts that evening. Miss Georgiana and Mrs. Darcy had apparently had words, though the subject was unknown. The mistress had summoned the master home and they had remained sequestered until dinner, which they had taken without Miss Georgiana, though Hannah had dined with them. Butler and Housekeeper adjusted staff's duties to maximize the family's privacy.

The next morning, Mr. Thomas delivered the note summoning Mrs. Darcy to her husband's study before breakfast. She arrived to a grim-faced William. He handed her a letter. "Read it!"

> *Braithmoor, 25 January, 18- -*
> *Dear Mr. Darcy,*
> *As befitting a suitor, I represent myself to you as an excellent candidate to maintain your sister, Georgiana, in the manner to which she is accustomed.*
> *I point out, Sir, that I am the only son and heir to my father's fortune. (A list of land and investments accompanies this petition as testament of that to which I refer.) I am educated and pursue an academic life in entomology.*
> *I shall arrive at my accustomed hour to discuss the formal arrangements for my betrothal to Miss Georgiana Darcy.*
> *Sincerely, Your future brother-in-law, Mr. Percy Newsome*

"Fetch our sister, Elizabeth."

When arrived, Georgiana was prepared for a rant; hence, she was non-plussed when her brother studied her in silence for what seemed forever. When he did speak, his voice was low and measured. "Will you explain your relationship with a man you've only just met?"

"He's of serious mind, of good character and I begin to support his study of insects."

Darcy watched her. "You believe such is a bond worthy of marriage?"

"It's better than many achieve. A partner's purpose is security, is it not?"

Darcy and Elizabeth's hearts pounded; their sister had accepted her brother's reference to marriage as if it were already part of her consideration. He reached her Newsome's petition and said, "A partner's purpose is security in love, not landholdings or bank deposits." She read it without expression, admitting privately she should have penned it for him.

Elizabeth added gently. "Your apparent choice for Mr. Newsome compromises our sense of you. We wonder what takes you from us, Sister."

"I've grown up, Lizzy."

"But growing up doesn't sacrifice all that one has been."

Georgiana's soft voice lowered to a near whisper. "I've changed, I admit it, but it's my choice. I exchange dependence for independence. I look out for myself, Lizzy."

Darcy crossed to a window, his back to her. "Your so-called independence will be to serve a pompous mother-in-law who will control your every move."

"Percy cherishes me. He'll take my side."

Darcy stood firm. "But the mother controls the son, Georgiana. You've already sacrificed room decoration. Is this not evidence enough of what you will endure?"

She laughed almost cynically. "You, yourself, wished me to give up rooms! I should think you'd be glad for Percy's good effect on me."

Elizabeth fought unaccustomed tears. "Do you love us, Sister?"

"You know I do! I love you and would do anything for you, if I could."

Darcy turned. "Then break off with Newsome and meet more young men before settling on the first one who shows attention."

She looked her brother in the eye. "I accepted Percy's proposal yesterday, Brother."

"You what!" Darcy lurched toward her. Georgiana stiffened and pressed her stomach. Darcy got control, sat at his desk and pulled a sheet of writing paper from a drawer.

"You waste the paper to deny him, Fitzwilliam," Georgiana asserted.

He did not look up. "My letter isn't addressed to Braithmoor."

She watched his pen scratch across the page. "May I ask the destination?"

"I notify Henry."

"Do not waste the franking, Brother," Georgiana countered. "Even if he received the letter today, he couldn't arrive in time."

Darcy's pen hovered over the page. "Arrive in time for what, Georgiana?"

"Custom requires a response in twenty-four hours. Since I've accepted, you must do also."

"I *must* do nothing," Darcy said, "beyond protecting you."

"Remember my age, Fitzwilliam. In six weeks, I can make my own arrangements. I suggest you spare our family the embarrassment of denying a betrothal in January that will be accepted in March."

Elizabeth stared at Georgiana's calm audacity. Darcy, however, referred to his calendar with the same composure as his sister. "I shan't respond to Mr. Newsome until the thirtieth. I stretch propriety to the limit, but it's my right and I shall take it."

She stood, of a sudden. "You're a fool, Fitzwilliam Darcy. You only embarrass us, and in the end, your evasion will be for naught. You can post your letter, but Henry won't come."

Darcy leaned across his desk. "How can you say that? He would sacrifice himself for us."

"I'm sorry for you to learn it, but there are limits to our cousin's devotion." Resigned, she shrugged and said, "Do as you will," kissed each on the cheek and quit the room.

Fearing she would be sick, Elizabeth breathed in cool air at the window that Darcy hastily opened for her. When recovered, she asked, "Did you ever think Georgiana could be so –"

"Stubborn?" He pulled the window closed. "If I did not know better, Elizabeth, I would say we have just concluded a discussion with my father." He sealed the letter, kissed his wife and quit the House on the run to dispatch Evans to Surrey.

Elizabeth retired to her bedchamber as quickly as her husband had hurried from the House. She had made best friends with her basin during the past week and had got her own peppermint plant from the gardener on the first day she had lost her stomach. She laid a leaf on her tongue before sitting at her writing table to review her personal facts.

Her calendar, with circled days each month, lacked circles in December and January. The sum of her symptoms: weariness, an unsettled stomach, gowns that fit too snugly in the bodice, a distaste for the smell of meat, a penchant to visit the privacy closet and the onset of emotions that caused her to blink against tears at the most illogical moments… all of it together fit the medical manual's description. She sat back and pressed the fine wool of her morning gown where she accepted their child grew.

Weeks of excuses to countermand these slowly exposed facts revealed how very much she was glad for a child, though it had been illogic of the highest order to deny what one wanted out of fear it might not be true. She knew without looking in the glass that her skin glowed with the magic of her condition. It *was* magic… magic of the deepest and most wondrous sort that made a new Darcy.

Her excitement to watch her husband's eyes when she handed him her calendar dimmed when she recalled his antipathy to host a ball due to lack of experience. They had not included their attitudes toward babies in their myriad discussions, an omission that might indicate his disinterest in the topic. And now with concern for Georgiana commanding his full attention, she hesitated to heap more "unexpected" on his plate. Her present pendulum of emotional unpredictability required William's unqualified happiness at her news or she chanced to weep which would definitely overwhelm him with too much. She elected to wait before announcing.

Chapter 18

The Brigadier sat on grass-tufted dunes and watched small waves foam on the rocks while he monitored his trunks sitting on the quay. The man-o-war, anchored a quarter-mile out, awaited the final runs of the skiff ferrying barrels and trunks to the bowels of that great man-made cork. God, how he dreaded the crossing, but the certain agony awaiting him did not distract him from thoughts of his ward.

Henry was certain Georgiana's love was a girl's infatuation and certain as well that she would recover, though she might not forgive him her embarrassment; in fact, the portraits she had returned to him declared the healing already began. During recent weeks, he accepted that his lack of interest in other ladies these past many months bespoke his fulfillment in Georgiana's company. She was perfect, not because she was flawless, but because she complemented him so well. He smiled when he thought of her, despite the breech-less sadness that followed soon after.

The stevedores moved to his trunks, raised each with a modicum of care then passed it from man to man. He rose as well, unnerved to eat before tomorrow's hours of vomiting. Foregoing dinner, he bedded early and slept so soundly that he was the last to hear the pounding in the darkness. Voices called for quiet. More pounding. Henry raised up on one arm to wonder and then to understand it was his door shuddering under a hearty fist.

"Your business?" he called.

"Nicholas Evans, Sir. From Pemberley."

"Come in, of course. You've traveled great distance." Henry continued innocuous conversation until certain those in nearby rooms had given up pressing their ears to the walls. A dusty, sweaty Nicholas understood and reached Henry a folded sheet bearing Darcy's seal

Pemberley, 25 January, 18- -

Dear Henry,

I write with the greatest urgency. Georgiana has accepted Mr. Newsome's hand without consulting us. I can delay my meeting with him no later than the 30ᵗʰ. It is my fervent prayer that you can return to us in time and convince her to stand down. Beyond consigning her to a nunnery, my hands are tied — she has made this a contest of wills. You have the right. She is my father revisited.

You are our last hope.

Your Cousin and "Brother," Fitzwilliam Darcy

"What day is it, Evans?"

"The wee hours of the twenty-eighth, Sir. I first travelled to Surrey where I learned of your early departure, hence my delay."

"You've done well. Go below and fetch some food while I think this through. We've serious work ahead." Henry nodded at the note. "Are you privy to its contents?" Evans shook his head. "Read it to help you concentrate your energy with mine."

Though Henry and Evans were acquainted only in passing, they complimented each other well. Time and distance, methods of transportation, finances, etc. were soon settled to permit Evans three hours' sleep and Henry two hours; he had letters to draft before his head could touch a pillow. The next morning they shook hands and set out on their respective missions.

Evans attended the less strenuous but more time-consuming aspects. He secured a wagon and team, waited for the trunks to be raised from the ship's hold, and then traveled to Surrey to deliver two sealed messages to General Braxton before transporting Henry's belongings to Pemberley. Henry had shielded Evans from the less than legal aspects of his plan, but Nicholas guessed the Brigadier had tweaked at protocol. The letter releasing his trunks was written on the General's stationery.

Upon meeting Braxton, Evans learned the brigadier had actually jeopardized himself when the saggy-jowled general read the two letters from his liaison.

"He sent you, did he?"

"Yes, Sir."

"And you'll meet him at Pemberley? It's in Derbyshire, is it not?"

"Yes, Sir. I expect he's already arrived."

"What sort of family emergency can cause a man to near blackmail?"

"Blackmail, Sir?"

"You're not privy to the contents?"

"No, Sir."

"There are two messages. If I don't accept to postpone his departure to Vienna as requested in this," he held up one sheet, "then he forfeits his rank and assignment in this." Braxton accentuated his disapprobation with several expletives. "Not one week ago, the man insisted to expedite his travel and now he reneges and makes me look the fool!" He squinted behind his spectacles. "You tell him he'd best be on the ship sailing on…," he shuffled through some papers, "on 15 March or I'll personally see to his court martial."

"I will, Sir. I'll tell him."

Evans passed a cluster of officers gathered to glean some gossip, one of whom detached himself and approached the wagon. "You're a friend of Henry Fitzwilliam?" the colonel asked.

"Aye, Sir."

"Is there trouble?"

"I wouldn't know, Sir."

"Good of you. You can't know if I'm friend or foe." The officer extended his card. "I'm Bainbridge. If there's trouble, have him contact me. My post box address is on the back. None will know we correspond. And convey to him my best wishes whatever his endeavor."

"He'll be glad to know this, Sir. I thank you."

For the Brigadier, the path was direct but imposed seriously on bone and muscle. He rode a rented horse until it required water, feed, or rest whereupon he traded it for a fresh mount. His pace was as quick as traffic would bear, and when that was not fast enough, he crossed private land, jumping fences and streams as if at the hunt.

The journey from Margate required three days, but Henry approached Lambton in two-thirds the time. His watch indicated it was half-twelve which confronted him with the irony of arriving at Pemberley while Georgiana was still awake; she kept late hours like her papa. Unwilling to compromise the advantage of surprise and requiring counsel with Darcy before he met Georgiana, Henry followed side lanes to Dr. Simons' cottage. Three hours later and returned to the living after a hot bath, a short nap, and several helpings of stew, the Brigadier set out for Pemberley in a clean suit from Dr. Simons' wardrobe.

He climbed the children's stairs at four o'clock after instructing a footman to fetch a nightshirt, wake him at seven and have his brigadier's uniform cleaned. On the verge of sleep, he turned to see Darcy burst through the door with Elizabeth close on his heels. They hugged their best hope.

"I knew you'd manage it. I knew it!" Darcy exclaimed.

Responding to Henry's gaunt look, Elizabeth said, "I believe food is in order."

"I've eaten, bathed and reconstituted myself as best possible." He pulled on Dr. Simons' jacket to cover the nightshirt for a modicum of decency. "Tell me the details, please."

While Elizabeth recounted the history, Darcy studied the man who appeared almost ill with shadowed eyes and bones pressed too prominently against the skin as if he had been off his food for weeks. Certainly even a harrowing, cross-country ride would not sap a man of so much so quickly. Elizabeth touched Darcy's sleeve. "Henry asks when Mr. Newsome might arrive."

"His habit is to come at two, but given his interest, it might be as early as eight o'clock."

"Too early to receive visitors. Put him off until ten at the earliest. She must be awakened sooner than I planned." His tone was even. "On the small chance I fail, have you an alternative?"

Elizabeth glanced at her husband then said, "We know it would be a severe imposition, but if it proves necessary, we hope you would accept Georgiana in Vienna. We would, of course, provide the house, chaperone, and any other necessity you deem suitable. Your duties are important, Henry, and it's not our intent to burden you, however we doubt Mr. Newsome would pursue her there and we know you'd keep her safe."

His silence was disconcerting following minutes of succinct and pointed questions. Henry turned his back and stood at a night-darkened window whose reflection showed a haggard man with closed eyes. He cleared his throat. "Have you informed Georgiana of your intentions?"

Darcy's stomach tightened. He had not thought Henry would refuse. "No. When she declined our offer to establish her room design in the Peak, we hesitated to show our final hand."

Elizabeth studied the brigadier. "Henry, as you stated, we must be clear. Will you accept Georgiana in Vienna if such should prove necessary?"

"It won't be necessary. Wake me at half past six." He returned to bed, pulling the blankets to his chin.

Despite exhaustion, Henry's head insisted to reconsider his best approach to help Georgiana's logic overcome her stubbornness. He felt like he hadn't slept a wink when Darcy woke him at the appointed hour.

Chapter 19

At twenty minutes before seven o'clock, Elizabeth led Hannah on tip-toe to Henry's door. The secretary clutched the brigadier's hand in her relief to see him then focused quickly to convey recent details of her mistress. Ten minutes later, she quit him with the mission to convince Georgiana to meet her cousin and left Henry to digest the secretary's insights into Georgiana's mood, including the meetings in Lady Anne's quarters. Then he said a prayer.

Georgiana blinked awake. Believing it was Percy who Hannah announced, she glanced at the early morning darkness, confused. But when she grasped it was Henry, she sat upright and firmly refused to see him. Hannah pressed her to "have it done."

While Phoebe, the new lady's maid, helped her dress, Georgiana's confidence grew; of all persons, Henry Fitzwilliam held the least sway over her. She waited in her favorite chair with fine, golden hair cascading past a blue shawl pulled close around her shoulders. There had been no time to press straight hair into curls.

Tap. Tap-tap. Her eyes narrowed to see him. Gaunt and lame, he bowed. She rose and took control. "My brother has wasted your effort."

He laughed and shook his head. "Don't think I gave any credence to Darcy's panic. We each know he responds to surprise with too much emotion." Disarmed by the unexpected, she looked down at the grey, pre-dawn courtyard. He continued, "Indeed when I read that you'd accepted Mr. Newsome, I knew at once you'd found your joy. I arrive to be the first to congratulate you and, selfishly, I will also bask in your happiness."

"Thank you. You've satisfied your mission and may leave."

"But for one small part. I will learn the details. We promised to share our details."

She stiffened. "That promise no longer applies."

He leaned against her door. "I'd accept your choice, if this weren't the most life-altering event since the death of your Papa." He shifted in pain. "Only a few minutes, please."

She studied the leaden sky now coming into focus. Since he did not confront her, she could manage a few minutes and indicated a chair across the room. "You may sit."

He made no move. "My backside shuns sitting after a two-day ride."

"Your foolishness speaks poorly for you." She sighed again. "What will you know?"

Henry stacked pillows on her bed an arm's length from her then sat gingerly. "Tell me of Mr. Newsome. I admit I misjudged him at the ball and will now learn my new cousin."

"I thought you couldn't sit." Her tone and look bespoke sudden wariness.

He chuckled sheepishly. "It's a contest between a bruised backside and legs that wobble. The legs clamor to be humored of a sudden and the backside demands as soft a seat as possible."

"You do look quite awful."

"Thank you. I promise I look better than I feel, but you can improve that for me. Tell me of Mr. Newsome." His easy manner could have been querying the topics of school lessons.

Hannah's counsel to "have it done" spurred her to comply. "He's a bit shorter than I, which you likely recall and he wears spectacles." She watched her hands in her lap.

"A man dedicated to books! An excellent recommendation!"

"Yes, I suppose, but mostly his eyes suffer from examining insects."

"Even better! I'd forgotten his devotion to bugs."

"They're insects, not bugs!"

"Merely different terms for same. You'll not deny me my own perspective, I hope."

"No. No, of course not." She added, "Percy will establish a Society of Entomology."

"Percy is it? Your attachment has grown quick and deep. I hear it in your voice. Tell me how much you love him, Princess. Your husband must be a very admirable man."

"He's not my husband! Not yet."

"Don't quibble, Georgiana. We each know your nature. Your choice makes him your husband, no matter the formal vows." He cocked his head. "You do love him, do you not?"

"Of course! That is… I'm fond of him."

"Excellent! Fondness is excellent. It will grow to an abiding love. I hear it in your voice."

His effusiveness grated on her. "You've learned what you would know. I bid you – "

"Only one more thing, Georgiana. Please. You've made no mention of your art. You will continue to decorate rooms, will you not?"

"No. It's impossible. Lady Newsome –"

"Ah, a devoted mother-in-law preserves your talent for the benefit of Braithmoor. You're a fortunate lady to be so admired."

"No. My art will illustrate Percy's insects. His mamma will tend the house."

"Gracious of her to release you from the mundane to pursue your wifely devotion." His eyes sparkled. "I'll call at Braithmoor within the week to select my bedchamber for when I visit you and your new family."

"Oh no, you mustn't! I mean, you may visit for tea, but it isn't my house to offer more."

"Then I'll wait until you have made it your house. Elizabeth made Pemberley her own in quite short order, and since you discovered your devotion to Percy more quickly than Elizabeth did hers for Darcy, I am certain you'll reign at Braithmoor in only weeks."

"You misunderstand, Henry."

"I misunderstand nothing, Princess. It's a bride's nerves which compromise your –"

A knock interrupted. Georgiana jumped visibly.

Two footmen delivered breakfast. The younger apologized, "Mrs. Reynolds was delayed, Sir. A gentleman –" A look from the elder cut him short. Henry eased himself up to inspect the breakfast under silver domes.

"The gentleman is Mr. Newsome, perhaps? Good." Then Henry ordered, "We will not be disturbed before an hour."

Georgiana sat numb. She had watched the courtyard yet had missed Percy's arrival. The walls pressed on her. She struggled to open the window.

"Permit me." He cracked it open then hobbled to lay two small tables with breakfast. "Where does Mrs. Reynolds find strawberries in winter? Ah, excellent! Have a taste, Princess."

Without conscious thought, Georgiana indulged in their old game of "Best Strawberry," designed for a girl too confused by the loss of her Papa to share with others. She tasted his, selected her own then declared his the best. "Not fair, Princess. I must taste yours to judge for myself. Ach! You have the right. Mine is much better." She swallowed a smile at his grimace.

"I expect your children to address me as Uncle Henry," he announced after a sip of tea.

"Children?" She would have spilled her cup had he not pulled a muscle to save it. "I hadn't considered children."

"Of course not. No bride considers the product of her wedding night. My pardon. It is a delicate topic, I grant you, but we're best friends and facts are facts." He appraised her. "Given your health and structure, I'd lay money to hold your little one before year's end."

Her eyes were blue saucers pasted on white porcelain. He focused on breakfast. At last she whispered the only disclaimer she could think of. "Lady Anne bore only two in ten years."

"Ah, but she bore her first in the first year and you're designed better than that Lady to bear children. Indeed, if I'm delayed much in Vienna, my arms might hold two on my return." His eyes lit at the thought. "They'll be wonderful children, Georgiana. Beautiful, happy…"

"Stop it! Stop it, now!" She exploded from her chair and turned her back to him, shoulders shaking. The image of little children inside Braithmoor's dark halls was too much. She felt a gentle touch on her shoulders. He turned her to weep against Dr. Simon's jacket. At first, she was too frightened to speak and then too despairing at the awful life she would foist on the innocent. She clung to him, sobbing. "I… I had… not… considered… children." She refused his handkerchief and wiped at her tears with trembling hands. "I'm a stupid fool."

"Forgive me. No more talk of children."

"No! You don't understand!" She screamed as much as her soft voice permitted. "I… oh dear, I've been so selfish." She was full angry. "They don't deserve such a life."

Henry asked as if they had spent the hour discussing the advisability of her marriage, "What is your choice, Georgiana?"

"Choice? You mean to marry?" She sucked in her breath. "I accepted his proposal. I have no choice. I only must discover how to protect against children." Her mind raced wondering if she could feign illness, though not being full privy to the mechanics of procreation made it difficult to know how to protect against it.

"There is always choice, Princess." Henry's voice sounded far away. "Always choice."

"My promise is my obligation." Mrs. Annesley's lesson sank her to her chair.

"Your family would rejoice if you would rescind it. What is your choice, Georgiana?"

She heard her voice, as if another spoke. "Like a child, I'd make it go away."

"Then it shall be done." His nerves prickled. She did not countermand him, but rested her head on the wing of her chair, humbled that she must depend on others… on him.

"Take no worry as to Mr. Newsome," Henry said. "His sensitivity will be humored. Tell me your preference to guide my negotiation. Do you invite his future attention?"

"He can visit as a friend." Henry leaned to hear her whisper. "He may visit after he returns from his tour, but only as a friend."

Henry's relief misjudged her mood. "I came to congratulate you, Princess," his eyes twinkled. Then he bowed, "And I'm glad to be the first to do it."

Georgiana's expression hardened as she grasped his manipulation. No matter her relief, she stomped her foot and hurled a pillow at his back before he reached the door. With her "I hate you!" ringing in his ears, Henry summoned Darcy to his bedchamber then changed into his freshly cleaned and pressed uniform.

The master arrived agitated. "Newsome ventures close to surly."

"Permit me to address him," Henry directed then added, "She recants, Darcy."

Neither Darcy nor Elizabeth had witnessed Henry, an artist with words as his palette, during delicate negotiation. Arrived at Darcy's study looking every bit the representative of the King, Henry offered his hand to Newsome with an amiable smile, ordered sherry for their guest, and then huddled with Newsome by the fire as if taking the bespectacled man into his confidence.

"Please accept my apologies, Mr. Newsome," Henry began. "Had I been aware of my ward's presumption upon you I would have come much sooner."

"Indeed, Sir. Presumption?" Newsome eyed Henry warily.

"Yes. As you know Miss Darcy has not yet come-out. It is a requirement she would avoid since she knows every young man will court her, or rather her dowry, if you take my meaning."

Newsome nodded, setting his sherry on a table. The dowry must be size-able indeed to inspire such attention.

Henry hedged, "This is delicate, Mr. Newsome. May I entrust a confi-dence?" Newsome nodded, leaning toward the brigadier as if in conspiracy. Henry continued. "I fear my ward's interest in early marriage compromises your interests, Sir. For a man of distinction who pursues more of the same through his academic work, a bride much touted in society's columns would be a coup of some merit, merit that would be lost in marriage sans her debut in society, if you take my meaning."

Newsome sat dumb, then salvaged his pride by blaming the young lady. "I am amazed, Sir," he exclaimed. "She gave no indication of an ulterior motive."

Henry shot back with equal affront. "Mr. Newsome, I am in no way impugn-ing the integrity of my ward. You offered your interest and she responded. The issue is not Miss Darcy's honesty; it is the timing of the event to which you aspire."

"Of course. Of course." Newsome said, chastened. He thought a moment. "Are you suggesting I postpone our betrothal?"

"Sir, I am proposing that you wait like all of the rest until the coming sea-son. Of course, you have serious advantage since she already knows you better than others. The point is that competition makes my ward a prize worthy of yourself, which better benefits your interests."

At the last, Newsome toasted the Darcy family, shook hands all around and departed with a smile. For good effect, the Darcys waved until his carriage was lost from view. They later discovered Henry's note on Darcy's desk:

> *Dear Darcy and Elizabeth,*
> *My regrets that I can't endure for the celebration. I'll remain abed until tomor-row. Send Georgiana a note with your love and support. She will require some time*

to recover, but she is as strong as she is stubborn. All will be well. Oh, might I impose on you for a fortnight? I have fences to mend with the army before they will offer me a bed.

Henry

Elizabeth looked up from reading. "We owe much to our cousin's sacrifice, Husband."

Darcy's celebration filled the room. "I knew he could do it! He has a way with Georgiana."

Elizabeth stared to hear William take credit for Georgiana's rescue, as if Henry were but a pawn in Darcy's grand scheme. She raised her chin, poking a euphemistic pin in his exuberance.

"What?" he asked in innocence.

"Your tone implies it is your letter to be lauded, not Henry's effort." She raised a brow at his inconsistency to praise Henry in one instance then usurp that praise for himself in the next. "One might think Henry is your 'brother' only when it serves your purpose."

"You make something from nothing, Wife," declared Darcy with a touch of hubris. "Indeed, you must grant it was my action that set the rest in motion, which by rights, affords me as much credit as any. 'Brother' is a term of camaraderie, nothing more."

"Then you define 'brother' much differently than I do 'sister'." Her tone did not judge, nor did her look condemn. "Consider it from another side, William. Though Jane's and my natures are very different, we each work to support and protect the other, including open praise for the other's success, no matter if we initiated the good results or not."

"You believe I'm self-serving?" To Darcy's surprise, he discussed rather than defended.

"Self-serving? No. But I do sense disparity in your relationship with Henry and it is inconsistency that looks to exist only on your side, my love."

His harrumph declared discussion closed, but Elizabeth knew he would mull her perspective privately.

Volume II

Chapter 20

In the fall of 18–, Henry visited Pemberley in his new Lieutenant's uniform.

"Is there nothing you can't do?" asked Darcy, impressed. Henry shrugged as he fixed the splint on the hawk's broken wing while Darcy held a handkerchief around the bird's head as a make-shift hood.

"I'm two years older, which hands me an advantage," Henry responded graciously, then added, "If you consider it, you have the capacity to master an estate while I do not, nor ever will. We each adapt to the hand we are dealt."

Darcy understood the logic, but Henry's many-faceted abilities let him taste deficiency in himself. "Ah, but you're excited by every subject while I –"

"The issue is 'interest' not 'ability,' Cousin," Henry corrected. "I command a mix of disparate facts while you focus on what is directly applicable to your needs. One mode is not better than the other. We are merely different; you are a perfectionist and I am a generalist," he offered with a smile.

"Then you don't care to master anything completely?" Darcy pressed.

Henry sobered. "I shan't have the opportunity to know that answer, Cousin. Inheritance establishes your role as master, whereas society denies me such then proscribes the choices left to me if I want to be called a gentleman." A breeze ruffled the bird's feathers. "Perhaps dabbling in every topic is my rebellion against society's restrictions on my possibilities."

On 31 January, Henry Fitzwilliam awoke to the aroma of fresh scones and ham, but his renowned appetite did not rouse him to dress. The last time he had laid his head on a pillow for a full night's rest was in Margate in anticipation

of a day of vomiting, but waking on this pillow found him between Pemberley's sweet-smelling sheets in his bedchamber. Time had disconnected from events to make reality feel like a dream. A splash of cold water established he was in Derbyshire as did the clothes in his dressing closet compliments of Darcy.

Fitzwilliam and Elizabeth received their cousin at the breakfast table with hugs and handshakes, but he didn't relax to their camaraderie until assured that Georgiana breakfasted in her quarters. In fact, to their astonishment, Henry insisted to join Darcy on his visit to Dale Village that morning, though it was clear his body did not relish another day astride a horse.

With the men set out on their mission, the mistress retired to her study to compose a letter to Mrs. Annesley. Hannah interrupted fifteen minutes later. "Miss Georgiana requests that you join her, Mum."

Elizabeth followed up the study stairs and along the back hall expecting to visit Georgiana in her bedchamber, but instead of turning down the children's hall, Hannah paused at a storeroom at the top of the children's stairs and opened it sans key.

"Welcome, Lizzy," Georgiana hugged her sister then revealed the secret meetings amid Mrs. Reynolds' tentative smile and Hannah's beaming. Elizabeth sucked in her breath to learn the true history of rooms she had not entered; William had dismissed them as "empty storerooms."

At the conclusion of Mrs. Reynolds' hour of stories, Elizabeth held her sister's hand, "I'm very glad to be included." She eyed the Housekeeper and asked, "Are the original furnishings in the attics, Mum? Good." And then she queried Georgiana, "What say you to learning Lady Anne amid the possessions that pleased her? I can't abide empty rooms."

En route to Dale Village, Darcy admired his cousin's stamina after his "great ride," though he granted that Henry's lithe build belied the endurance of an ox. On the far side of the Wye, the cousins climbed to the plateau where erosion had rippled the tableland into broad hillocks. Veering north and east, they crested the last rise and looked down on a narrow vale bisected by a stream. On the near side, pastureland descended to the water, and on the far side, mixed forest climbed steeply.

Pemberley's newest village clustered in a clearing mid-way along the stream. Three generations earlier when lead mines threatened to expand into their vale and poison their pastures, Dale villagers had petitioned Cecil Darcy to annex them to Pemberley since only a Great Estate could stand against the Crown's support of miners' rights over shepherds.' The folk of Dale Village had struck a good bargain; they would keep pace with the profit produced by Pemberley's more modern villages if the estate protected their pastoral traditions. Dale was Henry's favorite village, a place where the folk followed their hearts without compromise.

Shepherds hailed the riders as they bisected a flock feasting on tender shoots; yet another bout of balmy days teased new life from the earth. The cousins, who had unbuttoned their great coats en route, descended the long slope and forded the stream. A single lane paralleling the stream connected cottages and craft houses to the church, but that lane connected to no road. Dale Village limited its contact only to those they could watch descend the slope. The entire village welcomed the master, who led the elders to the church where they discussed present needs and plans for the next season.

While Darcy consulted, Henry set off to reconnect with this pretty place. At village end, he could make his own road to the forest at his left, to the great boulders scattered uphill at a distance or to the stream at his right. He opted for the stream until a small sound diverted his attention to the boulders. Riding toward it, he paused to listen, corrected his approach and repeated the regimen until he rounded a weathered jut of limestone a half-mile above the village. Five yards ahead, a body lay crumpled on dirt between two gray, lichen covered rocks. Low moans emitted from under the shepherd's hat; the unlucky soul had messed himself awfully. With no thought for strained muscles, Henry leapt to the ground, opened his water flask and knelt. The stench nearly overwhelmed him. He rolled the body face-up to reveal a boy drained by severe diarrhea and vomiting at once.

He raised the ashen face to drink. "Easy, lad. Easy now."

The boy, perhaps fourteen years old, looked up with glazed eyes. He worked to focus. "Br… Br …," he gasped.

Instructing him to respond with one blink for "no" and two for "yes," the brigadier collected facts before swaddling him in the great coat and securing him to the saddle. The horse recoiled against the stench, but Henry kept a firm grip while he searched for anything left behind. He collected a shoe and his water flask then led the horse downhill at the fastest pace the boy could tolerate.

Halfway to the village, peasants hurried uphill to meet them, but Henry called, "Stay back!" He nodded at a small building set apart from the rest. "Prepare that cottage with a blazing fire and blankets. Make haste! I've got a lad here and he is ill."

As if struck by lightning, villagers responded to the tenor of his orders. Some herded children into cottages at the far end of the village, others ran for Mr. Darcy and the rest prepared the cottage as instructed. Darcy met his cousin within paces of the cottage threshold.

"Stay back," Henry warned in a low voice. Darcy sucked in his breath to see the condition of the boy. "He has a brother who is also ill," Henry stated, gesturing toward the forest. "Look for a small tributary among the rocks and follow it upstream. From this lad's report, they made camp there. And Darcy, I shall insist that each who has contact with the boy or his belongings bathes when he returns." Darcy nodded full-confident his erudite cousin had sound grounds for his choices.

The villagers clustered several yards away. When the lad was loosed from the saddle a gasp rippled through them. The brigadier left the boy to his mother after instructing how to prepare the bed with blankets and the care she must take when treating him.

An hour later, three men trailed from the trees. The father carried his son, the uncle followed with two bedrolls and Darcy with two knapsacks. The single street was dotted with fires boiling water in great wash cauldrons. Henry, in peasant garb, approached the three with succinct instructions: deliver the boy to the cottage and the belongings to a nearby wagon, after which they were to bathe in a designated cottage with Darcy to go first.

Inside the "infirmary," the father found his wife soaping her hands and arms. She nodded at the empty bed. In the bed opposite, their elder son lay wrapped in thick blankets, his breath shallow and his skin very pale. Her husband watched as she undressed their younger child, dropped his soiled clothes on an old blanket on the floor then stripped away the blanket beneath him and added it to the pile. Next she washed him then peeled off that blanket as well. Lastly, she wrapped her youngest like his brother then pointed to the discards. "Deliver them to the wagon before you bathe. Ask no questions, Husband. We do as told and wait to ask later." She then held boiled and cooled water to her young son's lips and cajoled him to drink.

In a nearby cottage, Darcy stepped into his bath then stepped out again hurrying half-lathered across the floorboards to retrieve a small pink granite stone that he also lathered well. Now garbed as a tenant, he emerged to add his suit to the wagon.

A rider pulled up on Henry's horse, which had been scrubbed in the village before departure and was now cinched with a new saddle from Pemberley's stable. The man ran to the brigadier, consulted with him briefly and handed him the reins. Henry approached his cousin. "Dr. Simons is summoned." He nodded at the church and said in a low voice, "The elders await you. My precautions stoke alarm, Darcy. Calm them and assure that Pemberley will make good the loss of blankets, etc."

"Loss?"

"All is being burned on the far side of the hill. A dry dale contains contamination."

Darcy stared. "Good God, is all this necessary?"

"I truly hope not, Cousin. Reassure them so we can take our leave."

A half-hour later, two cousins on horseback forded the stream. Henry led since his detailed memory of terrain was better than any man Darcy knew. When beyond sight of village and shepherds, they twisted back to a site hid from those below, yet offering a clear view of the vale.

"Well?" Darcy had used up his limited patience. "Name the illness."

Henry studied the course of the stream from the high woods to the village. "Darcy, I have seen these symptoms only once… in York at the start of my career. It is cholera."

Darcy's look denied the possibility. "Come, Cousin," he retorted, "theory holds that cholera derives from contact with filth and these are some of the most fastidious people in England!"

"I agree. It is impossible. Not only due to their habits, but also because the disease is speculated to come from contaminated water made virulent in the heat of summer." Henry shook his head, squinting to wring the secret from the land. "But for the symptoms themselves, everything contends I have erred. And I pray that I –" He stiffened to attention, "Darcy, look!" and pointed to a thin tail of smoke above barren trees, smoke that had blended with a greying sky from other vantages. "There wasn't a village there when we explored Cressbrook as lads. This land lies too far from fields to support

131

a second village in addition to the one above the Hall. Has Pillory sold some of his property?"

The master's eyes narrowed. "According to Evans, that gentleman now employs an overseer. Two months ago, the village above the Hall appeared empty."

"Come! The smoke looks to originate above the stream where the lads camped."

Darcy understood he confronted much more than a threat to Dale Village. If this were cholera, it must be potent indeed to infect during warm winter, and if it continued into the summer months, the illness might poison the Wye itself and thereby those downstream. Darcy shivered; as serious as was the threat to the unsuspecting, even more serious would be the effect on Pemberley since she would be set in history as the site of the scourge. He pressed his mount to a gallop. They must exchange peasant shirts for jackets at the House before traveling the long route to Cressbrook.

While the mystery revealed itself at Dale Village, a hint of it arrived at the House shortly after luncheon when a rider insisted to deliver a note personally to Mrs. Darcy. The tenant, hat in hand, stared with round eyes at the high columns and grand sweep of marble stairs down which Mrs. Darcy descended. "You wished to meet with me, Mr. –?"

"Jordon, Mum." He reached in his tunic. "Brigadier Fitzwilliam told me to give this only to yerself."

One look at the folded sheet, on which Dr. Simons' name was underscored with "Urgent," advised Elizabeth's caution. She summoned Miss Darcy to join them in the library.

"Is there a problem, Mr. Jordon?"

"The brigadier found one of our lads sick and put him in a cottage with only his mother let to tend him."

"And Mr. Darcy?"

"He searches for the lad's brother with his father and uncle in the forest."

"It's all of our good fortunes that the brigadier discovered the boy and we wish him and his brother a quick recovery. Is there more you can add?"

Jordon stared at his feet, hesitating.

Elizabeth prodded, "Well, speak up!"

David Jordon had not ever spoken his mind to a lady or to a master for that matter. Georgiana arrived and sat by the hearth. Elizabeth pressed him. "Mr. Jordon, I'm glad to hear your thoughts, but you must speak if I'm to learn them."

"Yes, Mum." The thirty-year old peasant took his courage. "The brigadier, he's rattled our folk with his orders. Maybe he tells the problem there," he pointed to the note, "but he's tight-lipped to our queries. He… he even gave orders to Mr. Darcy."

"And Mr. Darcy submitted to them?"

"Yes, Mum."

"Mr. Darcy holds his cousin in high regard, Mr. Jordon. The two are like brothers. When one gives warning the other takes heed as shall we all until Dale Village is returned to its tranquility. We're glad for your honesty."

In the next hours, the sisters undertook their first collaboration. To Henry's cryptic message addressed to Dr. Simons, Elizabeth added a full recounting of the meeting with the tenant before dispatching both with Timothy on a fast mount.

The sisters pursued the clue in the note to Simons: *"The symptoms recall those I witnessed in York in the summer of 18–."* From George Darcy's basement archives, they gathered newspapers from the summer months of that year and surmised Henry's meaning after a half-hour. Elizabeth ordered tea while Georgiana collected several volumes describing the symptoms from the library. When the two cousins arrived from Dale Village on lathered horses, hot baths and a fresh change of clothes awaited them.

Chapter 21

The way to Cressbrook was contorted, despite that the two estates shared a common boundary and a raven could fly the mile separating the House and the Hall in minutes. The cousins followed Pemberley Road to the King's Highway then turned north onto Castlegate Lane, which they rode for three miles across a windswept plateau weathered to old mountains at its edges. At Wardlow Mires, they diverted west for a quarter mile then southwest at Littonfields for a long half-mile to the outskirts of Litton Village. There they turned onto Bottom Hill Road, which they nearly missed due to its derelict condition. It was another mile before the last curve around Hayfield hill exposed the magnificent Hall perched on the cliffs above Water-cum-Jolly.

Henry was glad to wait with the horses. The cousins' secret exploration of Cressbrook years earlier had not walked the settled areas of the estate and to see the Hall up close caught Henry's breath. Seventy-five feet above the River Wye, the structure stood only paces from cliff's edge. Its front door faced on the broad hill at the center of the estate where ravens circled half-way up above a line of stone cottages. The stone village looked abandoned as did the Hall, but for a single wisp of smoke. Shutters on the support houses connected to the west of the Hall were falling off their hinges while the walled garden to the east was an overgrown tangle. A stone stoop served as a humble transition from the dirt road to the front door that opened to three levels above an English basement. The edifice, studded with myriad windows and bisected by ells, looked like a miniature castle balanced on the edge of the world against the sky.

An inveterate geographer, Henry considered the lay of Cressbrook's property from its entrance in the northern grass uplands, an austere landscape of limestone jutting from balding grassland, to its predominant southern landmark of Hayfield, the twin hill to Putwell across the Wye. Hayfield was a great bosom of earth bordered by forested Cressbrook Dale to the east and stone-fenced pasturelands to the west. Amazingly, this little estate collected the full variety of Peak terrain within its boundaries and crowned it all with a prince of a Hall.

Of a sudden Henry pricked his ears. Past the corner of the farthest support building stepped a young man in rags who immediately upon espying the visitor let go the rope dragged behind him. He nodded, "Good day, Sir," then looked quickly for the rider of Darcy's horse, the reins of which Henry held while eyeing the young man with interest. A shock of tawny curls peeked from beneath the tenant's shepherd hat, his cheeks ruddy from a life lived outdoors. Gray eyes showed an active mind as they studied Henry warily.

"Good day to you, Mr. …?" Henry nodded.

"Hawkins, Sir. Daniel Hawkins."

"Mr. Hawkins, I'm Brigadier Fitzwilliam, cousin to Mr. Darcy of Pemberley who presently meets with Lord Pillory in your Hall."

"'Tis Mr. Mason he meets, Sir. Lord Pillory has not set foot at Cressbrook since August and before that not for a year."

"Mr. Mason isn't an overseer, is he?" Henry's tone conveyed mistrust of that institution.

Hawkins stepped closer. "Aye, Sir," he affirmed then asked, "yer business, Sir?"

That a shepherd asked to know a gentleman's business indicated either a courageous young man or an insolent one. Henry eased himself to the ground. "We seek information, Mr. Hawkins. There's illness at Dale Village. We're inquiring if such has also visited Cressbrook." Hawkins' blank look at the mention of Dale Village implied a very cloistered life, though he appeared to respond to "illness." Henry continued, "Dale Village is Pemberley's eastern-most settlement whose acres border Cressbrook Dale." He drew a map in the dirt including the streams and the approximate location of the smoke he had seen.

Hawkins elected to trust the man who spoke like they were peers. "What's the illness, Sir?"

"Diarrhea, vomiting, some fever. I take it from your look, Mr. Hawkins that you've seen the same at Cressbrook." During the next minutes, Hawkins revealed more than Henry expected.

When Darcy finally stormed from the Hall, he refused discussion until they were well along Castlegate Lane. At last he calmed enough to hear his cousin's report.

Several were ill and one had died among the Cressbrook tenants. Henry and Hawkins had isolated the illness to a new latrine Mr. Mason had sited on dirt too shallow to support its healthy construction. They speculated the mild temperatures had festered it and the rock beneath had let January's rains contaminate the stream downhill. At the onset of the illness, the tenants had secretly constructed a rude, second latrine in a healthy location, but fear of Mason's retribution if he knew they had circumvented his choice had kept them from dismantling the first.

Henry also reported Hawkins' recent history of Cressbrook. Two years earlier at the insistence of Lord Pillory's newest wife, Cressbrook's tenants were relocated to a makeshift village in the forest above the Cress Brook. The Lady had loathed the Hall's proximity to the stone cottages since the Hall sometimes caught the scent of barnyard. Last year, the lady's interest in society convinced her husband to London whereupon he had installed the overseer.

The lord depended on his estate for the sizeable annual check from the sale of wool while Mason augmented his regular wage by secretly felling trees, from which he produced charcoal for sale in Manchester. The most courageous of the tenants had spoken out against the villagers' poor condition and were banished by Mason last autumn. Mason restricted the tenants' felling of trees to maximize his own profit. Henry had intercepted Hawkins stealing firewood.

Darcy halted at Pemberley's gate and stared at his cousin in amazement. The history sounded like a tale from medieval times though he granted that the man he had met at the Hall gave full evidence of the evil Henry had described. "It is a problem, Cousin," Darcy stated.

Now *that* is understatement, Henry thought, but he made no comment. To his mind, Darcy had only one choice, but it was for him to conceive himself.

While the cousins inspected Cressbrook, Dr. Simons arrived at the House on his return from Dale Village. He corroborated Henry's diagnosis. At the good doctor's suggestion, Mrs. Darcy instituted a council including Mrs. Reynolds, Mr. Thomas and Mr. Crawford, recovered except to ride a horse. Together, they estimated the supplies to support Dale Village with the premise that the illness would be left nameless and the village isolated in quarantine. Cloistered with this council in Darcy's study, Hannah scribed notes and Georgiana studied maps at the long table, from whence she added considerations of distance and geography to discussion. Despite weariness and a stomach that spurned food,

Elizabeth could not be more proud of the preparation achieved before her husband stepped from his third bath of the day.

"You did well, Elizabeth. Thank you." His tone celebrated nothing.

"I take it there are more problems?"

He motioned her to the sofa. "I must to London, Lizzy. Tonight. The coach is being readied as we speak." He felt her brace herself. "I take it you understand?"

"You will meet Lord Pillory to purchase Cressbrook."

He smiled, "I presumed you would deduce it."

"Deduce it, yes, but you presume too much if you think I understand. I'm sorry for the condition of Cressbrook's tenants and I certainly support their improvement, but it makes no sense to invest our resources in a neighbor." Though Pemberley was one of England's wealthiest estates, Elizabeth's recent tending of its ledgers had reinforced her fiscal conservatism. "Lord Pillory ought to care for his own —" She stopped short to hear her selfishness. "Forgive me. Can you not convince the gentleman to tend his flock, rather than his neighbor doing it?"

"Would that I were as selfless as you assume, Wife." He settled her against him and memorized her details since it would be several days before he could touch her again. "My interest is to protect Pemberley, Lizzy. Even if Cressbrook's tenants can clear the filth or if enough cold weather returns to destroy it, the threat of more evil sits on our border in the person of Mr. Mason. If I could convince Lord Pillory to remove his overseer and make improvements, I would, but he's not the sort who accepts requests, let alone advice. My only choice is to make my best attempt to pull Cressbrook under Pemberley's wing."

"Your best attempt?" It was not her husband's habit to qualify his possibility for success. She sat at attention while Darcy described Lord Pillory's nature and the discordant history between the estates.

"And your plan to convince him?" she asked.

"I have no plan beyond requesting your Uncle Gardiner to gather information in regard to Pillory's finances. For the negotiation itself, I shall rely on luck. He despises my family enough to deny my petition even if the sale would benefit him."

Elizabeth pressed her lips in consideration then summoned her lady's maid to fetch Miss Miller who would know the wardrobe required by a lady in

London in February. Darcy argued against it even as her trunk was set on the latticed carpet in her bedchamber.

"Absolutely not! My coach will fly as fast as conditions permit. It's no journey for a lady."

She laughed, "You have no choice, Mr. Darcy. A man without a plan requires his wife!"

While Elizabeth packed, including the peppermint plant wrapped in muslin, Darcy visited his sister, recovered from her near betrothal as if it had been a month, not a day. "I shall ask Henry to manage in my absence, Sister, but you are the Darcy who remains as representative of our family. I ask that you show your face if a problem presents itself."

She sat at attention. "You anticipate a problem, Brother?"

"Not necessarily. The other villages will cooperate, but our choice to leave the illness nameless could raise nerves and compromise Henry's latitude." Darcy cleared his throat. "This evening I sensed awkwardness between you and Henry. He merely did what I rquested in regard to Newsome. Please, put aside any nerves on his account and give him your full support."

Her brother's confidence to designate her as the family's ultimate representative was a compliment Georgiana had not anticipated. She thought her chest would burst for gladness which let her accept even Henry at that moment. "You may assure our cousin that I'll set aside past differences for the benefit of Pemberley," she affirmed softly.

Darcy delayed visiting his cousin until the last. En route to Dale Village, Henry had stated his intent to depart Pemberley as soon as he had determined his general's mood. In fact, the cousins agreed to leave the majority of the belongings being transported by Evans at Pemberley until Henry sent word as to the destination of his trunks. Darcy, who balked to request a favor from any man, would now petition Henry's support twice in one week.

"I've already considered it, Darcy." Henry poured wine for them. "I can remain four weeks until the end of February at the latest. Will that do?"

They discussed contingencies until a footman announced the waiting coach. Darcy added at the last, "I nearly forgot. Georgiana sets aside past differences to support your efforts for Pemberley."

Chapter 22

The Darcys departed Pemberley at half past eight the evening of 31 January. Chilled air firmed the roadway permitting more rapid progress, though Darcy had adjusted their route to include way-stops at comfortable hostelries for Elizabeth's benefit. Despite that speed was important, Elizabeth's companionship was even more so; hence, he had not argued too forcefully against her travel. The extent of his dependence on Elizabeth's company having been made clear, Darcy accepted that marriage began to adjust his self-image from an autonomous and self-sufficient individual to partner. However after a half-hour's travel, his pleasure to feel her shoulder touching his was compromised by the uncharacteristically silent woman staring past her window.

"I expected conversation, Elizabeth. Do you regret your choice?"

"No." Her voice was wistful. "No," she repeated, "I'm considering how I'll share a bit of news, to which I can't predict your response." She turned to him. "I'd imagined to do this much differently than circumstance now requires." The mama-in-waiting could not predict how much longer she could control a stomach with a will of its own.

"Go on."

"I've nursed an uneasy stomach of late and it's quite possible we'll need add extra stops along the way to accommodate your retching wife."

His good humor collapsed to confusion then concern, and then outright anger. "Damn it, Lizzy! You're ill, yet you insisted to travel! We'll return to Pemberley at once." He reached for his cane to signal the halting of the coach by thumping on its ceiling.

"Pregnancy isn't usually considered an illness, Fitzwilliam."

The cane, hoisted in air, clattered to the floorboards.

"Pregnant? As in 'with child'?" She nodded, celebrating to hear his delight. Darcy pulled her to his lap. "I'd wondered how the Bingleys managed it before us. I mean given our passion and their shyness, I would have thought —"

"William, the Bingleys dabbled." He was so taken aback she nearly landed on the floor.

"You mean that they…? I wouldn't have guessed they had it in them." He shook his head imagining Charles and Jane behind a hay-mow. "Are you certain?"

"Yes. But it's a secret. Jane so regretted having caused my family's cancellation at Christmas she confided she is further along than publicly stated, hence her care against travel."

Stunned, Darcy continued to shake his head.

"Do you judge against them?" Elizabeth asked, concerned.

"Not at all!" He laughed. "I'm only amazed that my appraisal of them is so far from their reality." And then adjusting to his own reality, he sobered. "How late are you, Lizzy?"

"Ten weeks, lacking two days." Her smile died to see his expression.

"You waited so long to tell me?"

Elizabeth recounted her facts of wavering between hope she was pregnant and fear that she was not, and then days of waiting until conditions were right to introduce it to him.

The last bit stung him. "You waited for 'right conditions' to tell me? What do you take me for, a child who must be coddled?" He breathed deep to get control. "You must hold me in very low regard to think I require right conditions before you confide in me."

Elizabeth barely managed, "I accept your point, Husband," before tears recommended her to her handkerchief. Darcy had witnessed Elizabeth's tears only twice previously, but they had been controlled enough to let her wipe them before they reached her cheeks. The present deluge of wet already compromising her handkerchief was so out of character, he judged it was the condition of motherhood, not Lizzy herself, who wept so freely. His insight also went far to explain her recent sensitivity to jokes and teases. The accounts overheard in gentlemen's clubs suddenly made sense; fathers-to-be often bemoaned months of living with an emotionally vacillating stranger.

Darcy did not count empathy in his repertoire of natural assets, yet he reached out, held his partner's shoulders and turned her to him. "Come," he said gently, "We shall do this together."

At Pemberley, "together" sounded much different. Henry and Georgiana sparred the entire evening as to the best agenda for the tenant meeting scheduled early the next morning. While he supported that he alone address the meeting of elders from all but Dale Village, she mooted it would be best if she, a Darcy, introduced him.

At seven o'clock the next morning, Georgiana stood on the dais facing more humanity than she had ever confronted at once. She blushed to the roots of her golden hair while men of varied ages rose to honor the Darcy who introduced her cousin, despite that her voice was so soft they strained to hear. When the meeting concluded, the elders, some with jackets over their tunics and others cloaked with a blanket adapted as a coat, waited in line to shake the brigadier's hand.

Georgiana stood at the back long enough to know she had been right to stand her ground then joined Hannah and Mrs. Reynolds in her brother's study. "It's done and to good effect," she announced when they looked up from their lists of provisions. She prepared a cup of tea before sinking into the nearest Queen Anne. "They did require a Darcy to pass the baton to Henry despite that most already knew him."

Hannah laid down her pen. "And Dale Village? Will you introduce him there?"

"He says not, claiming he protects me from the illness." Georgiana crossed to a window and looked down at tenants and liveried servants stack supplies from the House in wagons.

"His reasoning is plausible, but your tone implies not. Why?"

Georgiana's expression hardened. "You hear my frustration at guardians who confuse their habits; my brother now takes confidence in my abilities while my cousin treats me like a child." Her voice tinged with anger. "I'm past patience with prejudice based on whims that presume my placid acceptance of their inconsistencies."

After Henry set out with the wagons to Dale Village, Georgiana retired to her quarters to commune with pen and paper. From love spurned to heated argument, she confronted the passion of her connection to Henry which still pulsed despite her disappointment. When she blotted the ink, she understood that concern for Pemberley brooked their divide, if only for the moment.

The Queens Head Inn at Ashby-De-La-Zouch hosted the Darcys' midday repast. While Elizabeth freshened herself in the inn's best suite, Darcy sat in the tavern and penned an express note to Aunt Gardiner inviting her to attend Elizabeth at Annapolis while the Darcys were of Town. Cheapside, the district where the Gardiner's made their comfortable home, was located some distance from the Darcy Townhouse. Uncle Gardiner, the youngest of Mrs. Bennet's siblings and an astute businessman, had not inherited the silliness of his elder sisters. Indeed, the Gardiners shared more sympathies with Elizabeth than any in her immediate family.

Resettling in their coach after lunch, they discussed Elizabeth's plan to gain Cressbrook, which Darcy thought less a plan than comic theater. "You think this will do the trick, do you?"

"It's got a better chance than arriving on Lord Pillory's doorstep with apologies for past enmity, and by the way, you wish to purchase Cressbrook."

"Indeed," he agreed. To distance himself from a role he wasn't certain he could play, Darcy changed topic. "Would you prefer a son or daughter, Wife?"

She hesitated too long. "I'd prefer not to discuss beyond the fact that we're expecting."

Surprised to meet the stranger, he proceeded delicately. "Why?"

"As happy as I am for the chance of a child, I find that the more real it becomes the more I shy from speculation about it." His expression stated he missed her point. She presented it from another angle. "If you had a lady like Jane for your wife, you would hear only happy dreams of expectation." She looked him in the eye. "But I accept what she does not; there are no promises we will hold a child at the end, William." She watched her hands in her lap. "I've known too many women who have waited nine months to hold nothing but an empty blanket. It is a fact that ladies like Jane ignore, but I cannot." She watched out her window. "I had not given much thought to a child of my own before this and am struck by the strength of my desire to hold it. Yet when I imagine kissing my baby's cheek, fear that I might have no baby to kiss sobers me. We have no control over nature's choice, William. I know this is irrational, but pregnancy seems to snuff logic with the fan of emotion."

He swallowed his frustration. "Very well, we'll discuss our preferences for names."

"No." Elizabeth's terseness hurt them both. She willed out, "It's not my intent to put us at odds. I'd do it differently if I could."

"What is your intent, Lizzy?"

She closed her eyes. "To hold my breath until September."

Darcy focused on the chilled countryside beyond his window. His wife, whose habit it was to open doors of understanding, had shut this one firmly.

Chapter 23

The trek to Dale Village had made Henry glad for colder temperatures that firmed mud to solid ground. And now after having delivered the first supplies, he held the reins of the lead wagon, relieved to have tempered the tenants' hostility following the death of the younger boy.

No, he was more than relieved. His skills at diplomacy had been sorely tested by the villagers' fear exacerbated by the child's death and quarantine. Intuition had sensed he required a partner from among their ranks and he had selected the right man in whom to confide the secret. After having pulled Jordon, the youngest and most outspoken elder, to the side and explaining both the disease and Darcy's effort to protect Dale Village, the two had worked in concert to subdue rebellion.

Henry's life had denied him ownership of anything that could be ascribed only to him except for today's success. The taste of it filled him up and glowed warm in his gut. He squared his shoulders to negotiate the delicate maneuver of an empty wagon down a steep grade behind the muscle of two Clydesdales. It was a simple matter when one knew the balance of brake and reins, but until today, he had valued his abilities more as symbol of his disdain for the narrow prerogatives society permitted him than as fulfillment of himself. The sky raced with white clouds, not grey. Tomorrow's caravan should travel in good weather and he anticipated more warm feelings of leadership and sweet success. He hoped Darcy's return might be delayed a bit.

Elizabeth's look declared her husband had once again touched her heart when she caught sight of her aunt waving at Annapolis' front door. A pretty and refined woman, Marion Gardiner's temperament complemented Elizabeth's and they set off arm-in-arm to explore the exquisite Townhouse with its housekeeper as guide.

Uncle Edward Gardiner joined Darcy in the library to discuss Lord Pillory's details. "Of necessity, Mr. Darcy, your note was circumspect, but I presumed him an adversary and hence have collected an initial summary of the man as he presents himself in Town." He handed Darcy several sheets, then waited with a sherry by the fire. His middling age had thinned his hair a little and added a bit to his waist, but neither detracted from his genial presence.

Having concluded their initial tour, the ladies took tea in the unique garden at house center. Lady Anne had considered this her best architectural invention with its glass roof pouring light into the potted garden which dispersed that light to the rest of the main level through six sets of glass-mullioned French doors.

Aunt Gardiner initiated conversation with a recounting of her recent visit to Longbourn and Netherfield, after which she revealed that Darcy's express note had made her privy to Elizabeth's secret. "Jane will be very glad to learn you share her condition, Lizzy." Aunt Gardiner proceeded carefully. "She is quite far along, I think."

Elizabeth pricked her ears. "She's not quite half-way, but in comparison to me, yes, she's quite further along."

"Her size bespeaks more than half-way, Lizzy."

Despite bosom friendship with Aunt Marion, Jane's secret was not Elizabeth's to divulge. "Yes, but appearances can be misleading. Jane wrote that she eats so much since her stomach has settled that she looks like a fat sausage." She steered conversation to the Gardiners' children.

On 2 February, Henry and his men shivered against damp cold while they drove a second entourage of wagons transporting mostly firewood to Dale Village. On arriving, Henry's happy spirit collapsed to see Jordon's expression when he motioned the brigadier to follow. Leaving the recently returned Evans to supervise the unloading, Henry hastened after Jordon to the infirmary. Inside, the young man he had met at Cressbrook rasped his breath beneath layers of blankets on the bed where the youngest had died. Henry looked sharply at Jordon then knelt close to Hawkins to feel his face and neck for fever.

"He stumbled to us three hours ago, Sir. He asked for you."

"Is this the same straw mattress as previously?"

The mother, holding a cup to the lips of her eldest, shook her head. Jordon said, "We burned it, Sir, as with all things touched by the illness."

Henry pressed an ear to Hawkins' chest then held his wrist to count heart beats. "He hails from Cressbrook. We met two days ago. Did he say why he ventured out in this cold?"

"No, Sir. He only asked for you."

Hawkins rallied under Henry's touch. "Sir! Thanks be to God."

"Your illness, Mr. Hawkins. Is it like the others?"

"I think not. It's in my chest, not my gut." He coughed. "We suffer too much from the cold, Sir. We've collected every stick of windfall, but it's not enough to heat the two sturdiest cottages." A more prolonged cough. "The strongest are felling the trees most easily hewn into logs, but even if they collect enough, we've too little food. Mr. Mason is sick. We've snuck what we could from the Hall, but it won't last us. I didn't know who else to tell."

"You've done well, Mr. Hawkins. I count on you to recover and to do it quickly."

After quitting the cottage, Jordon touched Henry's sleeve, "Come with me, Sir."

To the elders gathered in the church, the brigadier related the tenants' condition at Cressbrook and Daniel Hawkins' petition for help amid a careful dance of words that left the disease unnamed. The elders asked the brigadier to leave them to their counsel.

Henry lent his arms to the unloading while he smiled that tenant-elders had at will invited and then discharged the master's representative. Shouldering a bundle of blankets, he imagined society's discomfort if he had been the first-born son; a pragmatic man sensitive to others no matter their standing would certainly be deemed a poor specimen of an Earl.

"Brigadier?" Mr. Jordon motioned that Henry should rejoin the council.

The lead elder, Mr. Wooldridge, rose. "We're agreed, Brigadier. The folk at Cressbrook require wood and supplies more than us. With yer permission, we'll reload the wagons and then drive them to our neighbor since their illness sounds to be like ours."

Henry sat stunned both by their generosity and the possible legal trouble conveyed to Pemberley should he accept. The law held a dim view of interfering on another man's estate.

"Sir," Mr. Jordon's courage broke the silence, "is there a problem?"

The brigadier looked up with clear eyes. "No problem that can't be addressed. Your kindness is a compliment to yourselves. I speak for Mr. Hawkins to thank you most sincerely." He eyed each man. "If any should inquire, our mission is undertaken at my command. I accept your offer of drivers in deference to the illness and as tenants under my direction. You are released from fault should any choose to challenge our undertaking. Are we understood?"

"Yer fear penalties, Brigadier?" Jordon began to grasp the issue given the description of Mr. Mason's meanness.

"Perhaps, but any problem will be diverted from Pemberley."

While the wagons were loaded with food and wood, Henry dressed in thick layers topped by a blanket slitted to let his head fit through and tied with a rope around his waist. It would be a common man arrived at Cressbrook, not a representative of the King. As further precaution, Evans and his men fell back at Upperdale and returned to the House on foot. Only an erring cousin held responsibility when the wagons turned onto the public road.

While Uncle Gardiner pursued his connections with banks and warehouses and Elizabeth napped at Annapolis, Darcy's carriage arrived at Pillory's Townhouse. Before stepping into the cold rain, he reviewed Act One of Elizabeth's invention.

A butler, whose few threads of hair lay pasted to his scalp, admitted Darcy. He's a man better suited to a wig, thought Darcy who swallowed his humor and bowed acceptance of a crimson velvet chair in the formal parlor.

Lord Pillory delayed his arrival ten minutes; an insult implied but ignored. When he did enter, the wizened little man with eyes shifting constantly to glean new advantage for him barely bowed. "Mr. Darcy, to what do we owe a visit sans appointment?"

"A mission of mercy, Sir," Darcy extended his hand with an affable smile, "a mission that only you and your Lady can accommodate."

"Indeed, Sir! I'm taken aback." The lord remained standing while Darcy presumed their friendly company and returned to his uncomfortable chair.

"Given the history of our estates, I've no doubt you're surprised, Lord Pillory, however, life offers the possibility of change, especially when marriage invites one's new perspective." He made an admirable stab at a self-conscious look which convinced his host to sit and better appreciate the humiliation of a Darcy.

"I do recall rumor you had married, Mr. Darcy. This past autumn, was it not?" Darcy nodded, wringing his hands as if caught in a difficult position. The lord let his guest squirm before continuing, "Well? Describe your mission. I'm a man with many obligations!"

"Yes, well, my wife and I make our first visit to Town on business now nearly concluded. She… we would be very glad if you and Lady Pillory would dine with us on Thursday."

"Dinner?" Pillory puffed in indignation. "Sir, I've not seen you for more than a decade and we've never met your wife. Were I a shallow man, this flaunting of decorum would be an insult."

Darcy's sudden animation responded to his host's sensitivity. "Exactly as I explained it to Elizabeth, Sir." And then contritely, "But my wife insists. That is, she only just learned that you and your Lady are of Town and she so desperately wishes to make your acquaintance."

Lord Pillory nodded to the near-hairless butler to pour a sherry for his guest. "To accommodate Mrs. Darcy, we'll invite you to tea, perhaps next Tuesday?"

Elizabeth's instruction to maintain his humor prodded Darcy to find some shred of entertainment in Pillory's pretension. It was difficult. He let the glass sit on the table at his elbow as if not even libation could distract his nerves. "You've isolated our problem, Sir. We depart Town on Friday and my wife has family business but for Thursday." He gave up words, paced a bit, then stood at the front window as if there were a view past the heavy curtains. He continued, "I'll state it directly. My wife hails from Hertfordshire and longs for a friend in the Peak. You're our nearest neighbor. She has admired your Hall from Putwell Hill and longs to meet you with a passion. She freed Thursday evening to devote to you. I… I'd be in your debt if you'd accept."

Darcy turned to his host, who stroked his empty glass while the butler pulled the stopper to refill it. Pillory made no effort to cover his pleasure at his guest's discomfort. Indeed, Fitzwilliam imagined that he gloated over George Darcy's memory while the son wriggled on the point of a pin. Darcy sat and swallowed his sherry in one gulp, a nice social faux pas to complement the rest. Even the butler was impressed to see a man of Mr. Darcy's reputation so firmly under his wife's thumb that he fairly groveled. The lord nodded that Darcy's glass be refilled, then rose.

"One moment. I shall reference our social calendar."

Another few minutes and he would learn his success. Darcy calmed; he had done the best he could. He granted Elizabeth had the right to dangle the bait of humiliation with the opportunity for the gentleman's further gloating. Indeed, a man without a plan most certainly required his wife. But only if his wife is Elizabeth, he thought as he swallowed the last drop.

Chapter 24

At Pemberley House, Hannah patted Georgiana's hand to distract from what looked to be tragedy unfolding. They sat in the gallery with chairs pulled close to the windows nearest the road and peered into the darkness for any sign of wagons returning from Cressbrook. In the background, feet scurried amid worried whispers; every person feared for the fate of the men.

Two hours earlier, only dry wisps of ice had fallen when Georgiana poured tea for Hannah and herself, but before the footman removed the tray, snow hid the lake in a storm so fierce and sudden it shocked one to recall it was early February. Miss Darcy had immediately summoned Evans and they hovered over a map in her brother's study while she inquired the time for a heavily laden caravan to reach Cressbrook, unload and return to Pemberley with empty wagons.

"They might wait out the storm at Cressbrook, Miss," offered Evans.

"And if they don't?" Georgiana studied the map, lines on paper that took no consideration for weather, or day and night. "You know my cousin a little, Mr. Evans. Would he wait or return?" Evans guessed the latter. She nodded. "That's my judgment as well."

"I could gather a party to search for them, Miss."

Georgiana glanced at windows pelted by ice and strained by howling wind. She shook her head. "I won't chance putting more at risk."

Mr. Thomas and Mrs. Reynolds took it on themselves to direct the refitting of basement rooms for the dozen tenant drivers; the illness required the men's isolation and the storm demanded they be cared for in House. Kitchen prepared kettles of soup while loaves rose under linen cloths. Action distracted from worries until there was no more to be done.

Near ten o'clock, Mrs. Reynolds arrived in the gallery with tea and meat sandwiches since Miss Darcy had declined dinner. Georgiana had ordered every lamp and candelabra in the House lit to make Pemberley a beacon visible far down the Road, if the wagons could get that far. The Housekeeper passed Hannah and her mistress cups of tea. Georgiana declined.

"Drink it, Miss!" Hannah stared to hear Mrs. Reynolds' tone. "Drink it. There you go." The Housekeeper sat without invitation. "Mr. Evans and volunteers are erecting a guide above the snow to mark the roadway with lantern spikes and ropes tied between. His men will be safe. He hopes you won't blame him for contravening your orders."

Georgiana stared at her image in the window glass, which night had made into a mirror. "They'd have arrived already, if they could, Mrs. Reynolds."

"When you let go hope, Miss, you're left with naught but an empty heart." She poured herself a cup and pulled her chair close. "One night in this very gallery, Lady Anne worried so desperately it near to broke my heart. Your brother and Master Henry weren't more than seven and nine, I think. They went missing long past tea and then into the night. Your father searched for them as did every person in the House, but to no avail. I sat with my Lady and told her it would be well. She looked at me, Miss. She looked long, and said, 'We don't know what it will be, Sylvia, but until we do, we have our hope and that must be enough.'"

Hannah asked, "Where were they discovered, Mrs. Reynolds?"

"Asleep in the tree house that once sat in the great oak. They were innocents to it all. Having played themselves to exhaustion, they climbed for a rest and didn't wake to the calls all around them." Mrs. Reynolds shook her head to remember. "My goodness, what a fright we had. Lady Anne said afterwards she had thought she knew how precious her boy was to her, but that night let her feel her love to the depths of her being, a feeling so intense she could touch it as if it were a physical thing." Mrs. Reynolds told more stories of Lady Anne… stories of things gone missing and found again – stories that were interrupted by Mr. Thomas' urgent call.

"They're sighted at the bridge! Staff leaves at this moment to help them home!"

Georgiana collapsed into Mrs. Reynolds' arms. Her sobs were much as the Housekeeper remembered holding her Lady after the boys had descended the tree house ladder.

Whether it was hours or minutes before the tenants and their leader were settled in their respective quarters, Georgiana could not guess. She stood numb on the garden stairs watching staff support the half-frozen tenants to their basement quarters. But when Evans and Timothy arrived supporting the brigadier between them, Georgiana blanched and gripped the railing. Mrs. Reynolds took hold and directed her mistress upstairs. "You might supervise the maid's preparation of your cousin's room, Miss."

A short while later, the Housekeeper saw that same maid helping cook in the kitchen; Miss Darcy would prepare the room herself. Indeed, Georgiana's mission had loosed her energy to tend every detail in his quarters before Henry was half-carried from his warm bath dressed in two layers of woolen nightshirts and thick socks on his hands and feet.

His face was chapped livid red in streaks where his muffler had not covered and he shivered so violently that he trembled the blankets piled on him. Georgiana observed how Mrs. Reynolds felt his pulse and every other detail of caring for one who suffers from illness, or cold, or both. And then she pulled a chair to his bedside. "I'll do it now, Mrs. Reynolds."

The Housekeeper hesitated. "Summon me, if his symptoms concern you, Miss."

Within a half-hour of the men's arrival, the entire House knew the story. They had agreed to outrun the storm and would have come close but for a broken axle on Castlegate Lane too far past Wardlow to circle back for shelter. The delay caused by freeing the horses from their cold-hardened leather tack on the broken wagon had left them in the heart of the storm with only sheer will power to get them home. With one man driving, the second walked, connecting the wagon in front to the horses of the wagon behind. The Brigadier led the column on foot, his hand on the bridle of the lead team. He knew the way with his eyes closed, and in such a storm, one moved like a blind man. Thank the Lord for Pemberley's glow. It had fed their hope the last half-mile just when they had lost it.

Upstairs, the man praised for his courage slept as if he would not wake again.

At Annapolis, Darcy could not sing Uncle Gardiner's praises more loudly. "You have uncovered more than I'd thought possible, Uncle. I am forever indebted."

Edward Gardiner's soft brown eyes smiled. "One is not indebted to family, Mr. Darcy."

"It is 'Fitzwilliam', Uncle, or 'William,' if you prefer. I doubt Elizabeth will mind sharing her special name for me with her favorite uncle."

He laughed, "Her only uncle by birth!" and extended his hand. "Thank you, Fitzwilliam." Edward Gardiner saw himself out. He would not have a too-early arrived Lord and Lady Pillory discover him, though he was certainly unknown to them. In fact, very few were privy to his connection to Darcy which made him the perfect candidate to inquire after the Lord's accounts, particularly since Gardiner's business depended on such inquiries; as a merchant's merchant, his interest was in the solvency of men at every level of society.

Darcy hastened to dress for dinner then knocked at Elizabeth's dressing closet. She was dressed, but pale.

"I shall say you are ill," he insisted.

She rolled her eyes. "The perfect plan requires the wife, Mr. Darcy." She took a breath, pressed her stomach and pinched color to her cheeks. "There. I shall manage it," she smiled.

Late in the night, the storm passed Pemberley leaving utter stillness in its wake. While the House slept, the brigadier made his first stirrings since he had been laid to bed.

"Princess." His whisper startled Georgiana awake in her chair. The fire had burned low; the room was in full shadow. She lit a lamp. Henry's curls had matted in sweat on his brow. She laid on more wood, and then gently wiped his face before preparing a cool cloth for his forehead. He rambled, only half awake.

"So cold, Princess. I've never been so frightened. So cold and dark. A frozen hell. My feet burned so sorely I thought I couldn't take another step. One step, and then the next, and then the next. So cold, Princess."

She stroked his brow. "You're safe. All are safe, every one. You're home safe and warm." She hummed a lullaby.

When certain he slept deeply, she girded her courage and lifted the blankets to show his socks. She had never seen a man's naked feet, but his rambling had alerted her to frostbite. Socks dropped to the carpet. Henry's feet were red, uncommonly red. But several toes on each foot ominously lacked any color.

She leaned the bed-warming bricks against the screen to reheat then hastened to the library where a footman held a candle to the spines of books as she searched for her father's volume of medical conditions. Returned to Henry's bedchamber, she forced her nerves to calm. The book described red, white and black, its cure was amputation, and if one were in doubt, leeches. *Dear God!* Her first instinct was to summon Mrs. Reynolds, but since Dr. Simons would be fetched at first light and with only an hour until dawn, rousing the Housekeeper served little purpose.

Georgiana gathered evidence. Redness implied hot, but when she touched his skin, it was cold and dry as paper. She controlled her panic and touched his hands, his ears, his face. All were warm but his feet and several fingers. She fetched her pot of lip-honey, a light cream of purified wax, silver litharge, honey and myrrh combined with milk of roses. At least it would do no harm. Until Mrs. Reynolds arrived shortly after eight o'clock, Georgiana massaged lip-honey into every pore of damaged skin. The rubbing let her think some warmth returned while she learned his feet and hands as if they were her own.

Lord and Lady Pillory warmed immediately to Annapolis and their hostess' gracious welcome. It was easy for Darcy to play the deferential husband. He could not love her more for the perfect web she wove to benefit their Pemberley.

At meal's end, Elizabeth invited the Lady to the drawing room while the gentlemen retired to cognac and cigars, but Lord Pillory much preferred the Missus to the Mister and insisted to join the ladies. The Darcys took heart that their scheme might play out sooner than hoped.

While guests relaxed with an excellent port, Elizabeth opened Act II. "Lady Pillory, I so rejoice that we're neighbors." She patted the Lady's lace-gloved hand. "When you return to Cressbrook, you must visit us at once." She glanced at Darcy. "It will be a private fête, William. We'll delay the welcoming ball until they're settled."

Lord Pillory intervened fearing his wife would accept what she could not. "You're most generous, Mrs. Darcy, but we're likely to remain in Town. Our business requires it."

"Oh. Yes… yes, of course." Elizabeth's disappointment was touching, and then she brightened. "I shall volunteer myself to your benefit, Sir. While you're from house, I'll visit your Hall and report its condition. I've only seen it from atop Putwell Hill, too distant to offer a proper report, but near enough to know you must miss it very much." The lord choked on his wine. His wife thumped his back, Darcy fanned a newspaper in his face and Elizabeth patted his bony hand, exclaiming, "Oh dear, I've pained you to recall your home. I'll fetch the smelling salts."

Her sympathy exacerbated his nerves that already suffered to think the Darcys might visit a Hall that would reflect poorly on him. "No smelling salts, Madam. No need." He coughed into his handkerchief. "I'm only surprised to hear you're as attached to Cressbrook as I."

Darcy responded to his cue. "I should clarify, Lord Pillory. My Elizabeth finds a sympathy in your Hall that recalls her family home." He exhibited a husband despairing for his homesick bride. "When nostalgia grips her too severely, I drive her to the hill for a look."

"In winter?"

Elizabeth had missed the small detail of season, but her husband salvaged it with aplomb. "Our winter has been so mild of late I require only a jacket and Elizabeth a shawl. In fact, I've worried with my steward that our orchards might be made vulnerable to a sudden freeze." He leaned on the arm of his wife's chair with eyes only for her. "If I didn't know better, I'd think winter sympathizes with a wife's adjustment to the Peak and makes pretty days to let her sit on Putwell Hill."

"Indeed." The lord took no interest in doe-eyed glances between newlyweds. "So, Mrs. Darcy, your history fosters an affinity for our Hall, does it?"

"Yes. But I wouldn't have you think this is grounds for our invitation. I told Fitzwilliam that any person who lived in such a house would certainly be compatible with our sensitivities." She looked the wizened lord in the eye. "My husband has explained the history of our estates, Sir. I can do naught for the past, but your Lady and I make a good start for the future."

The little man puffed up to disclaim any possibility of future between their families, but his wife's look implied a cold bed if he put pride before her happiness. He adjusted his tack. "As I said, we're grateful and look forward to our mutual society, but we'll not be in circumstance to entertain at Cressbrook. I've considered its sale and foresee no eventuality of our return."

"Oh… my… I…" Elizabeth flustered, paused, and then as if inspired by a brilliant thought, she turned to Darcy with lashes raised in petition and a pretty pout pursed on her lips. "Please, Fitzwilliam? Please. It would bring me such happiness."

Darcy rolled his eyes to the ceiling as if to escape her theater. "Mrs. Darcy, the gentleman only seeks to ease your disappointment. No family sells its property." He petitioned the lord for support. "Tell her, Sir, if you would, please. You aren't serious to sell Cressbrook."

In predatory pose, Lord Pillory was a sudden study of beady eyes glinting, paper-thin lips glistening, and a certain glow rising from collar to cheeks. He reached his glass for another fill. "Would that I could accommodate you, Sir, but I cannot. It's yours for a price, Mr. Darcy."

Appearing undone, Darcy flustered while Pillory delighted at the prospect of sticking the son of a former foe with a sow's ear of a property. Darcy indicated that his too-delighted wife should follow him and they disappeared behind the library's doors where they continued their ruse of the lady imploring and the gentleman elucidating financial sense on the chance Pillory wandered near. Their return met a lord breathing hard. He had barely sat before they crossed the threshold.

"We regret to decline your offer, Sir." Darcy announced, while Elizabeth sat small and silent at her husband's side. "We've no use for more land." He bowed. "I appreciate your intended kindness to my wife."

Lord Pillory looked like an air bladder poked by a pin. There was no doubt he had lost his chance after having imagined enough profit to pay his creditors and assure a tidy sum in the bank. He rallied moments later. "Far be it from me to intercede in marital negotiation, but it troubles me severely to see the lady's disappointment." He patted his wife's hand for effect. "Lady Pillory and I love Cressbrook so dearly that it would count for much to know it went to those who also love her. If we can discuss further, we might agree a mutually satisfactory price."

"Again, Sir, I'm made speechless by your kindness, but negotiation with attendant attorneys requires days while my wife and I depart London on the morrow. It is unfortunate."

"Mr. Darcy, as your friend and neighbor from the Peak, I'll clear tomorrow's schedule if you'll clear yours. With our attorneys, we could reach agreement to let you depart by afternoon."

Nicholas Evans' set out for Lambton at sunrise and returned with Dr. Simons shortly after nine. "I hear you're quite the hero, my friend!" Matthew

Simons arrived at Henry's bedside after having examined the tenants, from whom he had heard a dozen versions of Henry's courage.

Miss Darcy insisted to remain. Henry explained that his ward exhibited an interest in medicine which Dr. Simons then accommodated with a running explanation of his ministering. After inspecting Henry's feet, he glanced a smile. "The sweetest smelling feet I've ever examined!"

Georgiana blushed. "It's my doing. I rubbed them with this." She passed him the little pot.

"And your grounds to do so, Miss Darcy?"

"His feet were cold and the skin too dry. It was all I could think to do."

Henry studied his cousin; he had been unaware of her night-time efforts.

"Your common sense will go far to make a good physician, Miss." Dr. Simons praised. He pulled a small vial with a cork stopper from his bag and handed it to her. "It is oil of peppermint. Potent stuff, Miss. Two drops on each foot and one on each hand, massaged into the skin in a circular motion four times each day. It stimulates circulation. But take care for yourself. Too much will leave your hands raw. Wash them well after each application."

Late that evening, Georgiana prepared for her last session of peppermint oil massage. It had been more than a day since sitting at gallery windows and worrying until she could barely breathe. She granted that so much fear does change a person, but not as she would have guessed.

She had rubbed his feet from the end of the bed, but to do his hands required her to sit on its side. As she massaged his left hand, strong and fine with long fingers and well-formed nails, she felt his eyes on her.

"I worried I wouldn't see you again, Georgiana," he said, revealing only the surface of his fear. On the road where he had accepted he might die, only one thought had planted the feet he could no longer feel in front of each other… if he succumbed, she would never know his heart.

"I troubled as well, Henry. I'm glad you're safe," she responded matter-of-factly.

"May I hold your hand when you're finished?" he invited symbolically.

"No. My hands are well and require no holding," she responded from her reality.

"Do you hate me?" He voiced the fear harbored since he had rejected her.

"Not at all. My care doesn't evidence a person who hates you."

"What does your care evidence, Princess?" he asked then held his breath to learn her heart.

She spread a clean towel on the bedcover, laid his just-massaged hand on it and looked up before dripping a drop on the other. "It speaks for itself. I care for your well-being and protect you in any way I am able."

"Spoken as a friend, not more?" He pressed the limits of love chained by obligation.

She stated firmly, "Spoken as your best friend if you like, not more," then finished his right hand, washed hers at the basin and read from his favorite book until he slept.

Herself unable to sleep, Georgiana sat at his writing table with her diary. Her fear for him had reached so deep that feelings frozen inside had warmed. She had changed profoundly in one day and scratched pen on paper to understand.

> *Pemberley, 4 February, 18- -*
>
> *I had believed to know love as I learned each new aspect of it: the feel of his arms, his scent that made me want to smell him more, jealousy that wished to possess him and the irreconcilable emptiness to know he could not love me in return. Dear God, I believed to understand it, but I understood nothing.*
>
> *Lady Anne had the right. Love is made tangible when one fears the object of one's devotion has perished.*
>
> *My happiness is that he is home and will recover. My happiness is that he will pursue his dreams no matter how far they might carry him from me. I understand better now. Love is his well-being and from that I derive my own.*

She watched him sleep curled around a pillow. His condition no longer required her nighttime vigil, but she remained at his bedside and pulled a blanket to her chin.

Chapter 25

While other lads rejoiced at summer's freedom, George Darcy required his son to transcribe the histories penned on the backs of portraits. The son complied, but with resentment and its resulting guilt. To begin, Fitzwilliam selected those with the best penmanship and easiest English, rather than transcribing them chronologically.

When Henry arrived from university, he laid out the finished stories in order and inserted the names of those still missing in the empty spaces. "Have a look, Darcy!" he called after reading those completed. "Your great-grandfather, Cecil, annexed Dale Village and his great-grandfather did the same with Priestcliffe."

Intrigued, Darcy quickly transcribed the histories of Cedric and Edward, the two remaining third generation forebears. Not only did these last two also annex lands to Pemberley, but Darcy found it even more entertaining when he noted that he, as great-grandson of Cecil, was augured to be the next master to expand the estate. The cousins studied maps to guess which neighbor might petition to attach itself; a game that interrupted Darcy's hours of transcription with good laughs. When the son had satisfied his father's expectation, the pair set off on their delayed adventure to explore the forbidden land above Dale Village.

It was only later that Darcy queried his father why he had not apprised his son of the family mythology of third generation land acquisition, to which George Darcy responded, "Had I done the telling, it might have carried the weight of expectation, whereas by learning it yourself, you can interpret our history as you will."

Henry celebrated his first dinner beyond the walls of his bedchamber with a company of three: Georgiana, Hannah, and the just-recovered Daniel Hawkins, arrived on an empty supply wagon from Dale Village to pay his respects to the brigadier. Mr. Hawkins' excellent effect on Henry's spirit prompted Georgiana's invitation that the young man should sup with them.

An express note arrived before dessert was served.

Annapolis, 6 February, 18- -

With the excellent theater invented by Elizabeth, we have concluded successful negotiation and are in possession of Cressbrook's deed. We shall set off tomorrow on a leisurely return to Pemberley. Dispatch Evans to Cressbrook to begin the support of our new tenants.

Your Brother, Fitzwilliam Darcy

Henry read Darcy's words aloud which evoked cheers from all but Daniel. "What is it, Hawkins?"

With the honesty of the land Daniel's grey eyes met Henry's blue. "If we're Pemberley's tenants then Cressbrook estate is no longer. I grant yer, it wasn't ours to keep or lose, but I'm certain none of us had bargained for this end."

No one had considered the purchase from the tenants' view since their choice was not at issue; Darcy's interest was to save Pemberley. Hawkins' dismay opened Henry's eyes to more than a point of unfairness vis-à-vis Cressbrook's tenants. While having accepted without question that a tenant's birthright granted him nothing but the possibility of survival, Henry Fitzwilliam suffered to admit that he had supported the same inequity toward tenants as society perpetrated against him, the third-born son of a Peer. In some ways, Henry had more in common with tenants than with landed aristocracy.

In a voice as sorrowed as his expression, Henry responded, "I don't know what to say, Hawkins."

"Well, I do," intervened Georgiana. "My cousin taught me that perspective is the most important aspect when confronting an issue. I suggest the two of you discuss how best to help Cressbrook's tenants adjust to their new reality, and then together, you could help them do it tomorrow. Would you mind too much staying the night at Pemberley, Mr. Hawkins?"

The brigadier and Hawkins arrived at Cressbrook as heroes to learn that Mr. Mason had succumbed to the illness. Together, the two men presented Cressbrook's transfer to Pemberley's guardianship to a stunned gathering, whose mood vacillated in waves of emotion. At the last, Henry stood with the aid of a cane. "We've laid a fact on your tongues that tastes sweet and sour at once." He looked each person in the eye. "Those of you who've lived long enough know that life sometimes hands us double-edged surprises and it's our choice whether to savor the sour or the sweet. I offer you this; each of Pemberley's villages has retained its name. You will always be 'Cressbrook' no matter who holds the deed." He focused the tenants to the sweet side by inaugurating their return to the stone village.

At Georgiana's insistence, Daniel continued as Henry's travel mate since a lone rider on the open road was an easy mark for robbers, though such attacks were now rare. To entice Hawkins to accept nights away from home, Hannah provided evening reading lessons, an enticement inspired by the young man's fascination with the library.

After two days traveling the exasperatingly long route via Castlegate Lane, the pair felled a tree across the flats of cress near where the brook met the River Wye. The makeshift bridge lay only paces from the ruins of one of Arkwright's first mills, a landmark that now belonged to Pemberley. The "bridge" reduced their travel from hours to tens of minutes, though ease of transport ironically let them stretch their work days at Cressbrook ever longer.

In the late afternoon of 9 February, Georgiana slipped her hand under the tea cozy and wondered if the pot might require a third reheat given her cousin's extended delay. Henry's devotion to Cressbrook had convinced her to present her plan.

Hannah called, "They're sighted on the Road, Miss. Mr. Hawkins' lessons await him in the day room. You'll have your privacy."

Ten minutes later, Mr. Thomas bowed. "The brigadier requires a change of clothes, Miss. He apologizes he's late."

"Is he as muddy as yesterday?"

The head butler laughed. "Much worse, Miss."

"Please ask him to bathe, Mr. Thomas and please order a fresh pot of tea as well."

Georgiana leaned back and nibbled a teacake. Love was very strange. Despite her eagerness to see him, she postponed his arrival for his benefit and soon would deprive herself to see him at all when she encouraged him to live at Cressbrook for the duration of his days in the Peak. The seed for her plan had been set by Henry himself, who had bemoaned any time on horseback with so few days before he must quit Cressbrook.

The brigadier arrived in excellent humor, which dissolved to dismay after hearing her plan. "We will speak directly, Georgiana. Your true intent is to banish me from you, is it not?"

"Why would I banish you?" she shrugged. Since his illness, their companionship had taken comfort in the other's proximity without a hint that she had once declared her love and he had refused it.

"Because…," he fumbled, "because it troubles you to see me."

"You must reevaluate the evidence, Mr. Fitzwilliam," she said tossing back another of his lessons. "We share breakfast, tea and dinner with easy conversation. If your company troubled me, I'd let you dine alone." She nodded at his chair. "Sit and enjoy your tea, silly Cousin. You make an issue from nothing."

He sat, but disdained food, his deep blue eyes probing hers. "Why, Georgiana? Why do you invite me to quit Pemberley when you know that in only weeks I shall depart England?"

She studied him to understand why he twisted her words to a different meaning. After detailing the evolution of her plan, she described the light in his eyes when he spoke of Cressbrook and its tenants. "Admit it or not, Cousin, you leave your heart with those people when you return to Pemberley." When he did not celebrate as she expected, Georgiana reached across the table and covered his hand with hers. "I want you to be happy, Henry. I want your dreams to come true. I've never seen you so committed to an endeavor or so proud of your work as you've been at Cressbrook. Your happiness is my happiness, Cousin. Sitting at Pemberley waiting until your departure would waste an opportunity to make us both happy." She reached him a plate of cakes. "If you like, Hannah and I can visit to let her continue lessons with Mr. Hawkins. She reports he makes excellent progress."

In the coach bound for Pemberley, two new realities traveled with Fitzwilliam and Elizabeth Darcy. She had publicized her pregnancy with notes to Longbourn and Netherfield and he endured the crackle of Cressbrook's deed in his pocket.

Elizabeth broke their silence on the north-bound, rain-pitted road. "I now understand the meaning of 'wrong if you do, wrong if you do not,' Fitzwilliam.

Doing right by others should make one glad, but two weeks ago I anticipated fewer obligations in February yet now I see only long months of too much."

Darcy leaned his head back on the burnished leather seat. "It was predicted in a sense." He related the history of the D'Arcy-Darcy generations gleaned while transcribing portrait stories.

"You believe in predestination?" she asked incredulous.

"I can't state precisely what I believe at this moment." He watched drops of rain play chase down his window. "I'm more conflicted as a man and master than I've ever been."

"Conflicted about what? I should think the purchase resolves the issue."

He laughed without mirth. "We've indeed exchanged places, Wife. You now see facts as ends in themselves while I perceive more problems with each solution." He felt her tense. "I meant it kindly, Lizzy. Take no umbrage."

"No umbrage, then." She put aside defensiveness, hugged his arm, and felt suddenly very smitten. "Describe the problems, Husband."

"Aside from predestination, as you put it?" he attempted a smile. "One problem is that I take no interest in an expanded Pemberley. Another is I must judge how best to help Cressbrook and incorporate her with us which invites still another, namely I am confronted with the possibility of an overseer which I don't support."

Elizabeth was surprised. "But Mr. Crawford is like an overseer and you accept him."

"Steward and overseer share many of the same attributes, yet they're intrinsically different, Lizzy. An overseer implies absence of the master, while a steward implies the direct liaison of the two. Cressbrook is too needy to recuperate with only a steward's periodic visits." And then Darcy spoke the words he had been unable to voice. "I don't accept Cressbrook in my heart, Elizabeth."

"But it's too soon!" She countered emphatically. "You expect too much from yourself." Darcy sat silent. She sensed another problem and braced herself. "Go on."

"The tenants of Cressbrook did not petition to be made part of Pemberley." He closed his eyes. "With her purchase, I've undone the tradition of four centuries."

She swallowed. "I should think one obligation outweighs the other."

He shook his head. "That was my first thought, but honesty shows it to be rationalization. Historically with each expansion of Pemberley, the old and the new have celebrated our uniqueness with two weeks of festival. You recall my explanation at Christmas; Pemberley's land acquisition has always depended on the village or town's choice, not visa-versa. We are a family grown by the folk who petition to be made our children." His voice was tight with regret. "My unilateral action has made Pemberley like all the rest in England."

The clop-clop of horses' hooves beat cadence with their hearts. Their dilemma required compromise which no matter the choice taken compromised their contentment with it.

Certain that there exists a solution for every problem if one has the wits to uncover it, she tried again. "We could sell Cressbrook." His expression confirmed a new problem.

"And when we sell her, we let go our obligation to protect all within our borders. The master of Pemberley does not serve himself, Lizzy. Cressbrook's deed commits me to her well-being. It would be an obligation abjured if I were to sell her since few would wish to purchase her even for the ludicrously low price I paid Pillory. She requires too much improvement to be home to a gentle family; hence, any buyer would install an overseer."

As they sat with a conundrum past solution, Elizabeth felt her sensitive, duty-bound husband withdraw from her in sullenness. She offered the only distraction she could think of.

"I'm sorry for it, my love, but I cannot abide 'George' for a name."

"I beg your pardon?"

"'George.' I don't care for the name. As your father's name, I presume it would be your first choice"

"Elizabeth, you insisted to hold your breath until September."

"And so I shall, but I hadn't considered names as an academic pursuit, and after some reflection, I find it would please me to learn what you like since I know only what I do not."

They laughed the entire way to Lambton, each contributing names from literature and history accompanied by outlandish justifications for their suggestions. But their silliness sobered as they neared Pemberley. Darcy insisted on "James," since it belonged both to her father as well as James D'Arcy, one of the three who had helped William of Orange to England's throne.

Both immediately agreed on "Anne," but Darcy insisted to hyphenate it with Elizabeth, making his case that Anne-by-itself was too common in his family and he could speak personally to the confusion of names. He then suggested they might employ the variation of Anne-E as a special name. It imitated his father's private "Annie" for his mother, though afterwards Darcy was surprised to have recalled that secret overheard by accident.

Their coach arrived earlier than Darcy had stated in his express note to Georgiana, hence she did not greet them in the entrance hall; she and Hannah were still at Cressbrook. With the disappointing homecoming in his craw, Darcy set off with Evans to visit Pemberley's newest acres. En route, he learned the details of the hero and then his work at Cressbrook, details that set a plan supporting Darcy's first peace in two weeks.

Chapter 26

Fitzwilliam stood straight and tall in front of his father's desk. "I should like very much to escort Henry to Pemberley, Father." George Darcy's frown hastened his son to lay out persuasive details. "There's a mail coach direct from Bakewell to Derby. He'll take the coach from Oxford and wait for me at Derby's post office. Mail coaches are very reliable."

"To what end, Son? He'll arrive no sooner if you go to him or not." George studied his son, a lanky lad, crossing quickly into manhood. The son always did as he was asked, but he did it in his own way which unsettled the father, whose independence had not taken hold until after his own father's death.

"Yes, Sir, but the intent isn't to save time, rather camaraderie." Darcy watched the floor to gather courage. "I'm old enough to travel a little on my own."

"You believe so, do you?" George shook his gray head. "I didn't travel in a mail coach until I was forty years." Fitzwilliam's disappointment encouraged George to compromise. "If you must meet Henry then you'll do it in Pemberley's coach." His tone declared discussion ended.

"Thank you, Father." The son bowed and closed the door behind him aware he should be glad, but papa's choice sat sour in his gut. No matter the path of action he laid out, his father insisted to override it as if he lacked confidence in his son. As much as he admired his father, Fitzwilliam hated the feeling of impotence George Darcy engendered in him, and worse yet, he hated that if Henry had made the same request, papa would have approved without argument.

Georgiana Darcy had never laid eyes on Cressbrook until she and Hannah crossed the footbridge, made safer with planks into which posts with a rope-rail were imbedded. Her first view of the Hall fired her artist's blood, and when she toured its rooms, she could hardly contain her sense of the possibilities therein. No sooner had she returned to the House on that first day than she dispatched a request for any projects Mr. Pankhurst could post to her.

On the afternoon of 12 February, Georgiana sat in Cressbrook's former dining room amid sketches for Mrs. Peabody's entrance hall in Town, when a hearty fist on the Hall's front door announced a visitor. With no servants at Cressbrook, Georgiana opened the door to her brother and Mr. Evans. She jumped with delight and hugged her brother's neck then dispatched Evans to fetch Henry from the village. Darcy's gladness at her welcome stilled to disquiet, however, as he watched her stoop to prepare tea at the fireplace in the parlor. She wore a pinafore over a high-necked woolen gown against the chill and looked at ease performing a servant's task. Henry apparently camped in this parlor-chamber with a worn sofa for his bed, a table for his kitchen, and a washstand. "I would have thought you'd apply your talent to make this place more appealing, Georgiana. From Evans' account, you visit daily."

She smiled, "Come. I'll show you where I pass the day."

Through a side door, she led him along a short hall to the dining room, the twin of the parlor but with windows facing south and west. "Most of the day the light is good for my art, but when it isn't I attend my correspondence." She had made a proper room with scraps of mismatched furnishings. Darcy noted evidence of Pemberley in the tea set and linens.

"Why not make Henry's side as comfortable as yours?"

"Because I take no comfort to pretend this is my Hall, Darcy!" the brigadier interrupted. With hand outstretched, he joined his cousin and laughed. "I told her she could do as she pleased with her side, but mine will remain as I found it." He eyed Georgiana, "The water boils, Princess," and then to Darcy, "She insists to do tea herself."

Accustomed to Henry's delay of teatime, Georgiana did not blink when he invited Darcy to admire progress at the village. Two cozies kept the teapot hot until they returned, at which time Darcy related the "The Taking of Cressbrook" as conceived by his wonderful wife.

Hannah had expanded her duties at Cressbrook past tutoring Mr. Hawkins to include afternoon lessons with the village children, the conclusion of which denoted the hour for the ladies' return to Pemberley. Hannah arrived at the Hall shortly before four o'clock and they departed soon after, leaving the gentlemen in amiable conversation. But the cousins' camaraderie devolved within a half-hour, after which Darcy quit the Hall in a foul mood that he silently imposed on Evans during the long trip home.

Arrived at the House, Darcy retreated to his study where he awaited Elizabeth to prod him to good humor. But it was Georgiana who knocked after having visited her sister. She hugged his neck in congratulations that he would be a papa, and then sat without invitation. "Lizzy will rest until dinner." Her eyes sparkled. "Oh Brother, I'm so happy for you both."

"Yes, it's good news," he said absently.

She sobered. "You're not happy?"

"Of course, I'm happy. I'm elated. But at present, there's more afoot than a child." He paced as if in deep contemplation to imply his sister was excused, but she sat unruffled. For five minutes, Georgiana alternated watching clouds playing chase with studying her pacing brother until Darcy sat and shared his thoughts. An hour later, he had confided his nerves apropos Cressbrook and his offer to Henry to manage it; an offer his cousin had declined. A half-hour after that, he sat across from his little sister, amazed to have discussed with her at all and even more impressed by the insight of her solution.

"Thank you, Sister," he said, bowing to conclude their meeting.

But Georgiana remained, watching him. "Are you as concerned for Lizzy as I?"

"Your meaning?"

"She appears to twist herself in knots with issues over which she has no control." Georgiana knew she ought not discuss Elizabeth without her present to defend herself, nor could she predict her brother's response when she broached a topic that was not her affair, but she proceeded anyway. "Lizzy asked that I design the nursery, but she insisted not to see it until she lays the child in its cradle as if distance protects her from disappointment."

Darcy shrugged his shoulders. "This is how she wants to do it."

"She *wants* to worry and be miserable? Not Lizzy, of all people!"

"She states she will 'hold her breath until September,' Sister. When Elizabeth takes her choice, the deed is done. I'll do my best to support her, but that's all I can do."

"And if we coddle Lizzy's choices, despite that they be poor ones, do we truly help her?"

"It's not coddling to do as one is requested, Sister." Darcy presumed his sister's silence digested his lesson in responsibility, but she was testing her next words in her head.

He was surprised to hear her challenge, "When one honors a request that will improve the other's condition, it is support, but when fulfillment of that request only exacerbates the other's suffering, I submit it to be coddling."

He gaped before inviting, "Go on."

"Brother, I don't know Lizzy as well as you, but I sincerely believe that no matter how different she might seem, our Lizzy lives inside this person who girds herself against calamity. May I give an example?" He nodded. "I refused her parameters for the nursery, but offered to show her pairs of choices about which she would comment and then select her favorite. I told her the final result would be my surprise for her. I would keep the door locked so she couldn't peek, but to do it I needed her to make choices."

"And she agreed?"

"Yes and she looked relieved. I don't think she likes herself as she is now, but she can't get around heightened emotion to be herself again. She accepted my offer with smiles and tears."

Only a short raven's flight from the House, the brigadier stared into the darkness while his dinner of stew, provided by the village women, grew cold on the parlor table. His gut churned at Darcy's offer, a proposition that had soured the success Henry had taken such pleasure to taste.

Henry Fitzwilliam accepted that every man's perspective reflected that individual's experience and he granted that Darcy's privileged opportunities had set a broad understanding of concepts such as "ownership" and "management." Nonetheless, when Darcy had asked his cousin to manage Cressbrook, Henry had declined with more energy than was warranted. In fact, Darcy had taken personal affront to be denied and had pressed for an explanation, which his cousin could not offer. Indeed, Henry was as surprised as Darcy that he did not rejoice at the chance of an excellent salary to attend the folk he loved and respected.

And therein lies the rub, Henry thought. My present view of "manage" means fulfilling another's expectations, but I have my own imaginings for Cressbrook. Having followed his own path for the first time in his life, his heart rejected working for another man, even when he was Darcy.

Honesty can be a mean thing, Henry realized. He had believed the military had offered him the best career with the chance to travel England and explore new worlds of learning while excelling as a liaison to generals. But his personal devotion to Cressbrook had exposed the ruse; he had only made do in the army after primogeniture and seasickness had closed other doors. And while making do, he had convinced himself he was personally fulfilled by accomplishing other men's missions. The truth would have been too bitter if he did not still savor the glow of a few days' success attributable to no one but himself. He closed his eyes to compose himself before swallowing cold stew and retiring early on a sofa that pretended to be a bed.

Chapter 27

During her last year, Lady Anne understood that making peace with death progressed in small steps: from clinging to everyday life, to consigning personal treasures to safe-keeping, and then scribing her thoughts in letters. Each stage marked a fork along a difficult road: first denial then mourning until, at last, acceptance. She was grateful life had lasted long enough to let her to do it right.

Today, she carefully prepared the bottom of a small, carved wooden chest raised up on lion's paws, and then she laid in bits of memories, each with a gold thread attaching a scrap of parchment to identify it.

It was much less than she wanted to leave behind, but her husband had, as yet, been unable to acknowledge the inevitable, hence she was limited to what she could accomplish by herself from bed. Requiring legs to do what she could not, she laid the responsibility on the broad shoulders of the new Head Butler, Mr. Thomas. He had procured the carved box in Buxton then hid its sealed contents in an attic.

Georgiana did not let her daily trek to Cressbrook compromise morning appointments with Mrs. Reynolds. In fact, those meetings now included Lady Anne herself with the opening of the Lady's trunks; Mrs. Reynolds recalled stories of the items as Georgiana held them to the light. After Elizabeth's suggestion to furnish Lady Anne's rooms, Mrs. Reynolds had made known her beloved mistress' trunks, which she offered as much for Lady Anne as for Miss Georgiana; the Lady had loved the child so dearly and would smile that her girl touched her precious things.

Toward the end of February, Mrs. Reynolds sat in Mr. Thomas' office confiding her regret that the last of the Lady's trunks had been emptied. The butler could not say why the word "trunk" recalled the memory of a small chest on lion's paws, but when he mentioned it, Mrs. Reynolds insisted he retrieve it at once then whispered the surprise to each lady before breakfast. Darcy's camaraderie that morning felt like eternity before he departed to the stables.

Mrs. Reynolds arrived early with the little chest in hand and sat in chambers that Miss Georgiana had returned to "before" in such detail that Sylvia Reynolds thought her former mistress might cross the threshold at any moment. She blinked back tears. The wardrobes protected the Lady's gowns in the order she preferred. The wall of shelves surrounding the French-door entrance to the dressing closet displayed every book and memento, but for the Lady's diaries gone missing at her passing. Even the interior window boxes had been reproduced and sported jaunty daffodils, Lady Anne's preference in late winter. Above the mantel, Georgiana's art had worked new portraits of her parents to stand for the originals hanging in her brother's bedchamber. And early on, she had opened the seams of the bedding and drapes before dispatching them to Mr. Pankhurst, requesting they be reproduced in their original vibrancy. These had arrived but two days ago and the Housekeeper had gasped to see them. Miss Georgiana had turned time back on itself.

The group of four collected in silence. Georgiana sat on the white linen sheet covering the carpet that she had selected to replace the great latticed one now in Elizabeth's quarters. She touched the lion's paw chest, but rather than breaking the seal, she watched her sister. "Lizzy, please know you represent my brother in addition to yourself. He should attend, but I fear he'd forbid us to continue if he were here." Elizabeth nodded, accepting this might be the case since his ghosts still sometimes caused him to balk against too many memories at once.

The young lady rubbed perspiring palms on her skirt then broke the seal and peeked inside. "There are several small items, Mrs. Reynolds." Her companions smiled. Georgiana made no effort to cover her emotion as she read the first tag penned in Lady Anne's hand. She brought to light a linen pouch containing Darcy's baby teeth, a muddy scrap of fabric identified as the tail of a wayward kite, a small, wooden boat poorly carved by Fitzwilliam, his early attempt to scribe his name, an example of his sister's scribble, the worn collar of Fitzwilliam's first dog, a yellowed daisy chain pressed and protected between two thin pieces of glass, two monogrammed sets of infants' silver forks and spoons, a sketch of Fitzwilliam, aged two, a sketch of Georgiana, aged one-and-a-half and a sketch of George Darcy and one of Lady Anne rendered the week of their marriage. She read the labels, first to herself and then aloud, before passing each to her friends.

Pressed flat on the bottom were four small envelopes each bearing the name of a family member and his age; inside each was a lock of hair secured with a white satin ribbon. At twelve-years, Fitzwilliam's hair was nearly black and very curly. At one-and-one-half-years, Georgiana's was wispy white silk and very straight. At forty-one, George Darcy's was as his son's but for a few threads of grey. Georgiana had only known her father with silver hair. And at twenty-one, cut on the day of her marriage, Anne Darcy's hair was auburn shimmered with gold highlights. Fine and thick like Georgiana's, it was nearly straight. In wonder, she looked at Mrs. Reynolds. "In the formal portrait, her hair was brown. This is nothing like that."

Georgiana did not share Lady Anne's lock, but slipped the envelope into her pocket before taking a last look in hope of another surprise. She was disappointed when she discovered it turned upside down, its corner peeking past the lining at the bottom of the box. It was a pen and ink sketch of Water-cum-Jolly, the same scene Georgiana had selected to hang above Elizabeth's corner fireplace; Elizabeth's, however, was executed in oil on full canvas. The sketch likely represented a special memory for the Lady, but no note identified its significance.

"That's the lot of it," Georgiana announced. She returned the memories to the chest, and after they disbanded, she placed it on the table in her bedchamber beside her favorite chair.

Weeks of stories had taught Georgiana more about Lady Anne than she had had any hope to know, but the more she learned the more she wished to know the Lady in her own words. It was her greatest sorrow that the Lady's diaries had been lost. Mrs. Reynolds explained that George Darcy had suffered too much at mention of his wife's name to let the Housekeeper query him as to their location. She did collect what correspondence and household documents scribed in the Lady's hand that she could locate for her young mistress, but these merely exacerbated the absence of "personal" for Georgiana. Only the messages on parchment connected the child to the mother through the confident and pretty script intended only for her family's eyes.

The longer the little chest of surprises sat in her bedchamber the more the small sketch of Water-cum-Jolly unsettled Georgiana. With its corner poked past the lining, she wondered that it was the sole item without a tag. The others presumed the sketch had got lost there, but Georgiana recalled that the trunk had been specially purchased, and more than this, she knew the Lady well enough to predict she noticed everything since an artist lives in details. Georgiana's preoccupation with the sketch wore on her friends' nerves and they pressed her to let go intuition and accept the sketch was an anomaly with no importance beyond its perfection.

On the third night after opening the chest's secrets, Georgiana slept fitfully. At three o'clock, she sat bolt upright in her bed, her covers disheveled while her head repeated emphatically: *Mother would not include a sketch in a trunk of treasures if it did not hold a special meaning.* Georgiana sat very still, her breath in gulps, her heart pounding. She had thought, *"Mother."* The moment stretched… *"Mother."*

Chapter 28

At eleven years, Georgiana more than filled her sixty-one-year-old father's lap, but he insisted not to alter their story-telling habit. One evening he asked, "What story would you like tonight, Little One?"

She challenged, "I'm growing up, Papa. I'm not a 'Little One' anymore."

Indeed, he had to concur. She was tall and looking more and more like a young lady, but he patted his lap anyway. "'Little One' isn't meant to describe you physically, Georgiana. It's my private way to say you are special to me."

"But you have no special name for Fitzwilliam," she countered innocently.

"I call him 'son.' That's very special."

She frowned. "But you call him 'son' in front of me, yet never call me 'Little One' in front of him."

"Your brother is sensitive in my regard and I fear he might think I care more for you than I do for him if I were to call you special names in his earshot."

"Then 'son' is not so special as you make it sound?"

Her queries reminded him of his Anne's probing questions. "'Son' might not be so special to him, but I see it as a father's sweetest endearment to his male child."

Georgiana looked him in the eye. "Then daughter is not as special as son?"

Dear God, George thought. "You misunderstand," he said slowly, his head racing to choose the best words. "The 'son' is raised to master Pemberley, while the 'daughter' is raised to be herself. Of the two, I should prefer the second."

"Do you mean you'd rather not master Pemberley?"

"No," he said firmly. "I mean that some are born to a narrower concept of duty and obligation than others. I merely wonder at the person I might have been if I'd been handed a different path. As daughter, you have the opportunity I did not."

Georgiana was very clear that she was glad to have been born a girl.

After long personal consideration and discussion with his wife, Darcy addressed his problem with Cressbrook on 27 February. He mounted his bay and set out on his mission while taking care to protect the several bundles attached behind his saddle: a knapsack with tinder and matches, sticks of kindling, a flask, carriage robe, and a small portrait from the Gallery protected inside a bit of quilt.

Arrived at the mouth of the cave overlooking Monsal Dale, he laid a fire. It was a good location, this. The full sun warmed the air a bit and the fire did the rest. He folded the blanket for a cushion then sat and gauged his view to the northeast… too much hedge. Methodically, he broke back branches, sat to test the view, then broke back more until he could see the line of trees delineating Cressbrook Dale from where he sat.

He opened the flask and sipped cognac, acerbic and hot against his throat. And then he carefully unwrapped the portrait and leaned Edmund D'Arcy against a stone, positioned to view both Fitzwilliam and Cressbrook from his frame. Darcy had taken his choice and would tell it to Edmund. He sipped again then focused northeast to the property just acquired.

"From the date on Cressbrook's original deed, Great-Grandfather, it wasn't organized until two centuries after your death, God rest you. I wonder if you ever walked that land." Darcy sipped again. "Likely not. There would have been no cause to explore that side of the Wye with pressing needs on this side.

"I want you to see it now. For nearly four weeks it's been titled to the heritage you began, and today I shall give it away. You lived by your obligation and set the seed for one of the Great Estates of England. And I shall live by my obligation: to preserve the spirit of what you began while I protect what is dearest to me.

"I know my choice fails my birthright and for that I've battled guilt, but ultimately, I will follow what I believe to be right. I tell you this, because I think, given the same circumstance, it would have been your choice as well."

At three o'clock, Darcy secured his horse to a bush on the Pemberley side of the Cress Brook. He crossed the log bridge and climbed to Bottom Hill Road where he dispatched a tenant to summon the brigadier to the Hall.

Darcy waited at his cousin's parlor campsite, the details of which were the same as before except that the lids of Henry's trunks sat back on their hinges. Only two days remained until his departure. For just a moment, Darcy tasted fear but gave it up. He had made his choice and Henry must accept.

"Darcy!" Henry called greeting as if their falling-out over managing Cressbrook had not occurred; his nature did not harbor hard feelings. He pulled off his gloves and extended his hand. "I was just explaining the bridge concept to the men designated to work with you from the Cressbrook side." Henry and Evans had convinced Darcy that Pemberley' newest daughter required a proper road, for which Henry's engineering skills had designed the substantial bridge to span the brook's gorge. The brigadier crossed to his leather satchel, pulled out a tidy sheaf of papers and reached them to his cousin. "Since you're here, you can take the first of my inventory of Cressbrook with you. It will assist you in its management. Would you like tea?"

"Henry, I arrive on business. Whether you wish tea before or after is your choice."

"We'll take it before, I think. My cousin who directly announces his intent invites me to a strong cup." Henry was well aware that Darcy had been raised to tip the scale to his benefit, hence stating his goal at the outset was a surprise. With the tea steeped, he set a cup on either side of the table. "Hannah delivered Georgiana's note announcing your happy event. I ought to have congratulated you at once, but I've been so involved with –"

"It's no matter, Cousin. We know you're glad for us."

"When do you expect it to arrive?"

"Late summer is her guess." Darcy added a second spoon of sugar from Pemberley's caddy. "It's in part due to our child that I come today." Darcy paused and reconsidered. "No. I'd make the same choice, child or no. Pregnancy merely coaxes me to accept it sooner."

Henry laughed. "Darcy, I require the subject to have any chance to understand."

Like a lad who hesitates to open a gift for fear it might prove to be other than he has wished for, Darcy paced to stall his announcement until he gave it up and faced his cousin head on. "I wish to be released from my obligation to Cressbrook. It sounds bad to state it so, but I speak my heart. My interest in Cressbrook's purchase was to protect Pemberley, not to acquire more acres. I want you to take her scot free. We'll transfer the deed, tomorrow if you like."

Henry did not move a muscle. The light faded from his eyes as Darcy's words sank in. "Darcy, I don't know what to say."

"Say, yes!" Darcy sat down to temper overbearing enthusiasm. "Elizabeth supports my choice and Georgiana thinks you'll do it if I make it worth your while."

"Worth my while?"

"Yes, the deed free and clear and a stipend of £5,000 for the first three years to cover initial improvements."

Henry fumbled. "Darcy, I appreciate your confidence and your generosity, but my circumstance requires me to decline with sincerest regret."

Darcy balked. "But why decline? You've invested yourself in the land and you're admired by its tenants. It's a gift. You'd owe me nothing."

"It gets worse as it gets better." Henry shook his head and crossed to the windows, his shoulders slumped. "I could accept your offer in a year or two, but not now."

Darcy had considered this possibility, but neither Cressbrook, nor he could wait. "Please, reconsider, Cousin. Today, the estate is at a good starting point, whereas months from now, it might –"

"Cousin, I…" Henry interrupted, his expression promising Darcy's disappointment. "I'm in a bit of a bind. I received a letter from a friend warning me that Braxton actively organizes to bring court martial against me. In Braxton's mind, I humiliated him by requesting early travel then postponing my departure. He has a new candidate for brigadier, who is game to leave as soon as paperwork is completed. Given Braxton's hatred, my resignation, which ought to please him, would only goad him more. Accepting Cressbrook would be my ticket to prison." He closed his eyes and inhaled deeply. "Please know, it is my fondest wish to accept, but I cannot." He smiled ironically. "Today appears to be my day for disappointment. Bainbridge's letter arrived this morning."

"You deny yourself without any effort for a solution?"

"Darcy, perhaps you haven't heard me. If I were on good terms with Braxton, I might manage resignation from a posting already accepted without his recrimination, but as it stands such will assure my incarceration. Either I see to my duties in Vienna or I languish in the goal."

"Fetch your coat."

"Are you deaf?"

"Henry, your circumstance may appear dire, but I haven't known you to capitulate in the face of trouble. You'll accompany me to Pemberley where we'll think this through." Darcy's brown eyes locked with Henry's blue. "If we can protect you, am I assured you'll accept?"

"As you described it? Free and clear? No restrictions, no expectations to fulfill?"

"As I described it."

Henry looked away, his emotion too high to share even with his cousin. "It is agreed, but I accept without the stipend."

After four hours in Darcy's study, Henry wryly noted that they had traded their usual habits. He paced while Darcy sat. He worried while Darcy reasoned calmly and logically.

When Darcy retired at ten o'clock, Henry remained in the mahogany paneled study without hope for a happy conclusion. The sea of law books, civil and military, arranged around him felt more like an ocean of words than a life raft that could gain him his dream of Cressbrook.

At eleven o'clock, Georgiana delivered a late bite, but Henry waved off food.

"It goes poorly, does it?" she asked, preparing his cup and plate anyway.

He raked his fingers through thick curls. "I feel like a drowning man, Princess."

"A man can only be determined to be drowning after he has succumbed."

He eyed her. "Your meaning?"

"If you proclaim yourself to be drowning, you had as well return to Cressbrook and pack your trunks since you already accept your effort is doomed." She nodded at the lamp. "In fact, you waste the wick and oil that burn to let you read."

He expected sympathy, not this. "And what would you do, Miss Darcy? It is a fact that I could have Cressbrook, but Braxton keeps me from it."

"Again your choice of words, Henry. Hear yourself. You don't state 'Braxton stands between me and what will be mine,' but rather you presume his victory. I think his position has trumped your superior wit." She pushed cup and plate under his nose. "There was a time when my guardian bade me to distance myself from my problem as if I were a bird looking down from a branch. He told me to sort the various parts of my issue like beads and examine each one dispassionately before reconstituting the whole. In every case, my sense of the problem was altered and appeared less formidable." She shrugged her shoulders as she patted his. "Strange that what works for one doesn't work for another."

The next morning, Henry presented Darcy a solution. "I've witnessed others released from military obligation when the first-born perishes and primogeniture promotes the son to heir."

"But you're the third born and the first two are of good health." Darcy shook his head, his buoyed spirit at his cousin's energy deflated. "Henry, we're not discussing primogeniture."

"Not directly, I grant you, but look at this." He opened a portfolio that rankled Darcy's nerves to see and required his full control to maintain a calm exterior. Henry pointed to three lines in his uncle's will. "Here he names you full heir. Here he provides for Georgiana. And here he includes me. *To my nephew, H. Fitzwilliam, I bequeath the benefits of Pemberley.*"

"Go on."

"We both know your father intended my benefit to be an open door and a bed, but if one chooses to interpret Cressbrook as a 'benefit,' it becomes an inheritance not a gift."

"But Cressbrook is the property of Pemberley, to which I am the heir."

"Are you stating this as a fact or are you possessive of Cressbrook of a sudden?"

"A fact. It is yours as I stated."

"We'll require a cooperative judge, for which I'll rely on you. You inherited Pemberley at Uncle George's death, but Cressbrook was acquired nearly seven years thereafter, therefore in a very, very loose interpretation, Cressbrook could be interpreted as a 'benefit of Pemberley.'" Henry crossed to the table strewn with open volumes. "And look here. Unless military law has been amended since this publication, it states that *"it is the right of a soldier to revert to his civilian status upon being designated heir."* It doesn't specifically name primogeniture as the circumstance, though we know that is implied. If you can produce a judge agreeable to undersigning a loose reading of both documents then Braxton can't argue it, especially if he's a judge with some standing at Court. My illustrious general hasn't the stomach to take on superiors."

The slight chance that Henry's scheme might work disarmed Darcy's initial agitation at the sight of his father's will. "We'll require an attorney as well as a judge," he said. "I'll make inquiries and we'll pursue the interviews tomorrow. Get yourself some breakfast and perhaps a nap. You look the worse for wear." And then Darcy permitted himself a modicum of hope. "Thank you for your effort. I knew if there were a solution, you would discover it."

Chapter 29

Elizabeth Darcy thought a good puzzle was the best entertainment, but the conundrum of the pen and ink sketch left no loose thread dangling to unravel its mystery. Insisting that the sketch was no accident, Georgiana had laid it beside the oil painting from Elizabeth's bedchamber, but to no avail. When Hannah added her eyes, she discovered in faded pencil on the bottom right corner of the frame's back the notation, "A.D. 31 October, 18- -", which was made significant when Mrs. Reynolds said the date corresponded to the last year of her Lady's life, not when she painted it. Presuming that an ill woman would not misdate a painting without good reason, the four examined every piece of art executed by Lady Anne. They collected eight paintings bearing a penciled date but could glean no hint as to why Lady Anne had set these apart from the others. Georgiana's preoccupation to learn her mother's meaning frustrated her fellows until, at wits end, Elizabeth persuaded her sister to accompany the gentlemen to Derby which would permit her friends a day to discuss how best to wean Georgiana from her obsession.

With a cup of weak tea, Elizabeth awaited the arrival of Housekeeper and secretary in Lady Anne's chambers. The eight paintings watched her from their place on the floor where Mrs. Reynolds recalled her mistress had leaned them in pairs during the last year of her illness. The paintings shared only superficial commonality: they all represented scenes from Pemberley, were executed by Lady Anne, measured the same dimensions, and bore a date with the letters A.D., which everyone allowed might represent "Anne Darcy."

When the three compatriots assembled, they agreed Georgiana's logic was confused by feelings for her mother, after which Elizabeth proposed they entertain the heretical. "Let's loose one of the paintings from its frame and examine every part of its components to prove there is nothing beyond the art itself." She empathized with their downcast looks. "We each regret to dash Miss Georgiana's hope, however as her friends, it's incumbent on us to hold to reality." Elizabeth pointed to the oil painting from her bedchamber. "We'll dismantle that one since its counterpart initiated my sister's interest. Mrs. Reynolds, if you would fetch a letter opener, please, we shall proceed."

With the table cleared and the painting faced down on the linen cloth, Elizabeth carefully loosed the edges of the dust cover then … "My God in Heaven!" She sat with a thud, her heart pounding while Hannah and Mrs. Reynolds moved close and drew in their breaths. On the backside of the canvas lay sheets of parchment penned in Lady Anne's hand. The mantle clock ticked and the fire crackled.

At last, Elizabeth said, "We are agreed, I think, to let my sister be the first to touch them." The others nodded. "But I very much wish to meet the Lady and Georgiana will not return from Derby until after nightfall. Are you both agreed that Hannah should read aloud only the words showing on the first sheet?" They nodded again, still in shock.

Hannah cleared her throat.

> *Pemberley, 31 October, 18- -*
> *My Dearest Children,*
> *The topic of this letter will be Family, but before I share my thoughts, I will include my general preface on the chance that my words are discovered by someone other than yourselves.*
> *I am Anne Mary Charlotte Fitzwilliam Darcy, wife to George Darcy and mother to Fitzwilliam (born 1792) and Georgiana (born 1802). I am ill, which commends me to share a mother's thoughts with the two precious children life has granted me. On the chance that hands other than my children's discover these pages, I humbly request that you search out their heirs and convey this letter to them.*
> *Fitzwilliam and Georgiana, in each of my letters I also include the following preface on the chance that you discover only one letter of the ten I have composed. I regret sincerely that I submit this communication to chance, but my difficult history with your Grandmamma requires it. With these letters I intend to preserve my deep connection to you, Fitzwilliam, and to introduce my thoughts and perspectives to you, Georgiana, since you are too young to retain any memory of me. I accept that a letter is a poor substitute for a living mother, yet it is my last resort to preserve connection with you, my wonderful children.*

I have selected the subject of Family for this letter which causes me no little consideration to assure that I present my thoughts without bias since I have known both its debilitating and exhilarating possibilities. As I see it, one both inherits and makes one's Family. The fact that each person yearns for a strong and trusted connection with others implies the importance of the institution no matter how one elects to achieve it.

You are born to a strong Family of honest and admirable character; however, the Darcy history can impose itself on its members if one permits. I say this only as a caution against presuming that your Family's precepts are the last, best judgment of an issue. From my view, they are an excellent guide, but will serve you best if maintained as suggestion rather than as dictate. I have watched your dear father struggle to discover his own preferences in light of what he has deemed to be his duty, and though I have never interfered with his choices, as your mother, I commend you to your own course. Embrace your Family as your support, not your god.

In addition to its history, I believe one's Family also exists as a living entity. Each of its members owns talents and peculiarities that, if respected, contribute to the happiness of the whole. Your father, though possessing no artistic talent in the traditional sense, supported my art without reservation. My resulting pleasure in myself increased the pleasure of our company and thereby the happiness and security of the home that has embraced you. The lesson is clear if

"It ends here, Mrs. Darcy."

Elizabeth nodded, requiring her full control not to expose more of the Lady's words. "Mrs. Reynolds, you will secure the door after us, please."

Elizabeth later queried Mrs. Reynolds why the Lady had feared her mother's interference.

The Housekeeper hesitated then spoke directly. "The Countess was opposite of her daughter in temperament, values and every other aspect. They sparred constantly when she visited Pemberley. My Lady never visited Glenbrooke after she married."

"But to think a mother might destroy her daughter's writing?"

"I don't know," Mrs. Reynolds confessed. "I've always wondered what became of my Lady's diaries. I did interrupt her sister, Lady Catherine, in Lady Anne's chambers the day of her interment, but the diaries were already missing." She shook her head. "It's a question without an answer."

In the shire seat of Derby, misgivings hung heavy over Darcy and Henry, whose success lay mostly beyond their control. Arrived in late morning, Darcy interviewed the attorneys on his list, leaving Georgiana and Henry to share a table at Ye Olde Dolphin Inn on Queen Street. She maintained an entertaining monologue to distract Henry from his nerves, an adjustment of their previous roles that Henry would have smiled at if he could.

Within the hour, Darcy introduced Mr. DeCair, an older gentleman of erudite demeanor and pleasant manners who accepted the seat offered. Mr. Darcy's reputation in the shire was beyond reproach which ought to transfer equally to his cousin, but for the delicate, legal implications of his petition; Mr. DeCair protected against connecting himself to the roguery of a man who manipulated to save his neck. Sensitive to the barrister's wariness to trust him, Henry invited him on a private stroll. Their conversation cemented their confidence in each the other.

When Mr. DeCair and Henry returned, Georgiana was missing. Darcy explained she searched out a new bonnet and thereafter would wait at the coach. Georgiana actually preferred books to bonnets, but a feminine excuse would not raise her brother's concern as she wandered in mixed company with a lagging footman as chaperone.

Mr. DeCair took charge. "Our judge of choice would be His Honor, Justice Michael. Unfortunately, he's on holiday, but I'll dispatch my man to inquire if the Justice takes that holiday locally. My connection with him will gain us audience to learn his recommendation."

By mid-afternoon four men climbed the steps of the Shire House. Flanked by Mr. DeCair and an emissary from Justice Michael, two cousins' heels clicked across the cobbled courtyard where public stocks and an iron cage, each put to regular use, greeted visitors.

Deliberation in the judge's office was confined to the second judge, Justice Chestnut, Mr. DeCair and the emissary with a letter from Justice Michael. The arrangement relieved Henry from a public interview, but increased his nerves that a meeting beyond earshot determined his fate. He glanced at Darcy leafing through a fat volume of jurisprudence as if intrigued by small print on yellowed pages.

Henry leaned to whisper. "Ought I to presume confidence from your demeanor, Darcy?"

Darcy whispered back. "I trade turning pages for pacing." The image of Darcy pacing the public hall of the Shire House hinted a small smile in Henry's otherwise too solemn eyes.

While nerves frayed on a bench in the Shire House, a dutiful footman trailed a young lady from shop to shop. Georgiana delayed at the chemist's where she searched out particular scents described in Mrs. Reynolds' stories.

"Here you are, Princess!" The former brigadier breathed hard, his tone echoing his concern after minutes of searching. The chemist looked up from his stool at the counter.

"Thank you, Mr. Hull. You may package the items I've selected." She smiled at Henry. "Calm yourself, Cousin. All is well."

Indeed, all was well. Georgiana rocked with the easy undulation of their coach while her brother and cousin celebrated their success, poking each other as they rejoiced for the potential of Cressbrook and the freedom of Pemberley.

Chapter 30

George Darcy looked down at the will whose amended terms Henry had rejected. He admitted relief that his nephew had proposed a better solution. The elderly man rubbed his temples.

George had changed his original will to name Henry as both Georgiana's sole guardian and as executor of the estate. It had not been George's intent to impugn his son's abilities, as Henry pointed out would surely be his cousin's interpretation. As for Fitzwilliam's abilities, George already knew his son would be a more capable master than his father and might even rival Edmund with his business sense and Cecil with his easy manner vis-à-vis those who depended on him.

If only we could speak without raising our voices, George thought, perhaps I could convey to Fitzwilliam my fear for Georgiana should I succumb before she is of age. She deserves a clear head to care for her, but I fear that Fitzwilliam will suffer too much at my death to make the critical choices for his sister, as well as execute the petty legal matters required to transfer property in a timely manner.

Despite difficult relations between Fitzwilliam and himself, George knew his son loved him. When Anne had died, Fitzwilliam had required nearly a year to reconnect with daily life and George feared his son would require almost as long to recover from the loss of the father.

George Darcy wadded the will Henry had shunned and dropped it in the bin beside his desk. His nephew's solution would have to do. He sat at his desk and scribed the discarded will's replacement, stipulating the cousins would share guardian and executor duties equally. George would trust Henry to negotiate Georgiana's welfare whatever Fitzwilliam's state of mind.

In the next weeks, Darcy attended his wife while Henry devoted himself to improve the lives of those now directly dependent on him. Georgiana, whose commitment to Mr. Pankhurst's projects and the Darcy nursery consumed most of her hours, stole as many private moments for herself as possible. Hannah continued her daily lessons at Cressbrook.

Georgiana's "moments for herself" immersed her in her mother while she transcribed the Lady's letters to make a set for Darcy. Georgiana was firm that she would retain the originals since she missed a living memory of the author. As her pen glided across the page, she sorrowed to copy only four-fifths of her mother's words. Lady Anne had listed ten topics, but only eight of her paintings bore the flag of her initials on the back. Included were Compassion, Family, Honesty, Children, Humor, Fear, Happiness and Death. Missing were Courage and Love.

She had dipped her pen to copy Compassion when Elizabeth interrupted with a solemn expression and delivered a letter bordered with a black band, a death notice.

"This just arrived."

"Oh my!" Georgiana read and passed it to her sister.

The family of Lord Simon Newsome
Regrets to announce
The untimely demise of their husband and father.
Commemorative services on the seventeenth day of March, 18- -
St. John's Church
Buxton, Derbyshire

Below, a personal note was scribed in a miniscule hand.

My dear Georgiana,
As you note, my family suffers under the shroud of tragedy; a slip on the stairs and injuries that precluded recovery. I look forward to visiting you at Pemberley following the requisite month of mourning.
Fondly, Lord Percy Newsome

"It is a tragedy." Elizabeth broke the silence.

"A tragedy indeed."

"Georgiana, I sense Mr. New… Lord Newsome renews interest in more than friendship?"

She capped the ink. "There is no doubt. 'Fondly' is his term of impassioned admiration."

"Will you attend the service?"

"No, he would presume too much." She kissed Elizabeth's cheek. "Let me consider how I'll manage this. I won't mislead him, but I also won't cause him pain when he's laid low."

Elizabeth rolled her eyes as she closed the door. Considering the flourish of the new Lord Newsome's signature, she wondered how low the man was laid.

That evening at dinner, Georgiana presented her plan for the gentle rejection of her resurgent suitor. At week's end, she would return to Town where her work with Mr. Pankhurst would cool Lord Newsome's romantic interest. She prodded her family to accept her plan. "It's the best on all counts. Percy will choose against me, hence sparing him my rejection and you will have unencumbered time together before you welcome your permanent addition."

Elizabeth said wistfully, "I consider you our first permanent addition."

Darcy sat silent.

Georgiana laughed, "I promise to make long visits a permanent part of my calendar." She turned to her brother, "I'd prefer Mrs. Coombes if she's available to chaperone." Mrs. Coombes, a friend of Mrs. Annesley, was known to Darcy and had excellent credentials.

That evening, master and mistress agreed that, given their sister's stubbornness, any argument against her plan would be wasted breath. Later, Darcy lay awake with sweet images of Georgiana laughing at breakfast, at her easel and playing the piano forte. After discussion with his wife, he set out the next morning for Cressbrook.

The following afternoon on another chilled and rainy day, Georgiana looked up as Elizabeth crossed Lady Anne's threshold then looked again to see Henry at her sister's heels. It had been three weeks since she had last seen him. Her work on the Darcy nursery and his at Cressbrook had distanced their friendship or at least such was Georgiana's view. She had been disappointed, but took solace in Henry's contentment.

"Close your mouth, Sister," Elizabeth laughed. "You'd catch a fly if it were in season."

Henry chuckled as well to see Georgiana non-plussed. "There was a time, Miss Darcy when you ran to greet my arrival." He tossed a wink at Elizabeth.

"Not since Surrey, Cousin." Hard words surprised each one, but most of all Georgiana, who now grasped the depth of her disappointment; he had missed her birthday the week before.

Elizabeth interrupted the awkwardness, "I'll order tea for you."

Henry groped for conversation. "Are these the letters? Elizabeth just apprised me of them."

She nodded. "You may read them, if you like."

He read while Georgiana struggled to copy Happiness.

When he finished reading, he said, "These are wonderful, Georgiana. I can hear her voice admonishing and encouraging at once." He returned them to her writing box and added, "You have a will of iron not to have shared these with Darcy. I'd have burst in on him at once."

Georgiana served tea. "You forget that my brother is more complicated than most, especially on the subject of our parents." She watched her lap, sorry for the truth. "I fear if I show these to him and he insists to keep them for himself my anger would divorce me from him. I hope he will accept these copies to let me keep both the originals and my brother."

Henry dunked his scone in the hot tea, a habit only she knew. "Each time I see you, I believe you are more grown up, Princess."

She broke her scone in half. "You missed my birthday."

He leaned back, relieved to learn the grounds for her frostiness. "So that's your trouble to see me. I told you in my note I couldn't sit a horse due to the accident at the bridge site."

Her blue met his. "You could have requested us to fetch you with a carriage."

The easy solution had not crossed his mind. "Indeed. I seem to have taken my independence from Pemberley more than I was aware. Forgive me, Georgiana." He hesitated. "If it helps at all, I've thought of you each day and most especially on 12 March." He hesitated before reaching in his inner pocket. "I wrote a poem in your honor… if you'd care to read it." He unfolded a finely scribed square of paper and reached it to her.

> *My fairy tale began with the birth*
> *Of an angel with the bluest eyes,*

Who eighteen years later shows the worth
Of honest friendship with no good-byes.
Together we learned Invent a Tease,
And Best Strawberry, and Waltz Our Dance,
And Fly a Kite, and Study the Trees
Games which our sweet friendship did advance.
For her honest words and truth's precious purse,
For the whisper of Georgiana's smile,
For the blessing to touch my deeper worth,
For the young lady who knows no guile,
I give thanks and to all decree
"My Princess" she will forever be.

Georgiana read, wiping her eyes at the last. Her recent equanimity in his regard failed her after a poem that declared in ink on paper that he did not love her as she did him. His divorce from Pemberley further poked her with the reality of their separation.

He joked, "It wasn't *that* awful! I grant I'm no Shakespeare, but –"

"Be still!" He stared at her rudeness. She took a breath. "Is there a purpose for this visit beyond a belated birthday poem?" He shifted in his chair. "Well?" Her whisper of a challenge always made him sit straighter, for which he felt silly since he was so much her elder.

"Darcy visited to announce you'll return to Town."

She nodded. Her brother's intervention explained everything. "He told you my reasons?"

"Yes. And they're well-conceived." Again he shifted. "Georgiana, I admit that Darcy petitioned my help, but I would have volunteered it had you told me the plan yourself."

"My guardians at last work in tandem."

"Your birthday released us from formal guardianship, Princess." She tidied the tea tray. "Georgiana, I arrive with a challenge that might entice you from your choice."

"My brother and cousin are each a challenge in their separate ways."

"Don't play with words! I'm serious."

She sat, his poem folded on her lap, her eyes cool in her challenge to him. "Very well."

"My Hall is in sore need of pretty rooms. You could ply your art here in the Peak and support a friend in your effort."

"My brother's suggestion?"

"Yes. But you can be sure I wouldn't broach the possibility if I didn't embrace it."

"Henry, you and my brother miss the point. I decorate to please the lady of the house that she takes pride and pleasure in her home. Your pleasure is in your land and there is no lady to guide my choices. My brother is creative and you're kind to support him, but I must decline."

He stood with a stare so intense she looked away. "Just like that? Without any consideration? Unfair, Georgiana!"

She rose to meet him, her blue rivaling his in intensity. "Not unfair! You bribe me with an undertaking that does not equate with those awaiting me in London. Besides, to do it right would require more funds than you likely could afford."

He hung his head. "Therein does lie a problem. Darcy offered to finance the renovation, but I refused. I do for myself now. I can commit no more than £500."

"You're joking, I hope."

"Don't taunt me, Georgiana!" He stood at the windows faced toward Cressbrook. "Last night, I sat with my ledgers to wring out the pittance I could offer. Albeit humble, my petition is sincere." And then full passion won out. "I sleep on a sofa in a parlor, for God's sake! I awoke this morning imagining you'd make me a proper bed chamber."

Henry declined dinner and sensed his absence troubled no one. Elizabeth was preoccupied, which focused Darcy on his wife. Georgiana's "Be still!" still rang in Henry's ear. When he crossed the footbridge, a cold drizzle dripped drops on his cheeks. He would have wagered Cressbrook itself that she would accept his open plea, a misreading of their reality that bespoke his own disjointed facts in his former ward's regard. A man of astute reasoning and sensitive perception, Henry had traded both for the emotional limbo that had written a poem to a child, who was no longer one. Face to face, he appeared to accept Georgiana as a peer, but in his head, he fixed her as a young girl in order to hold his feelings in check. His game presented him as inconsistent, a quality he abhorred, but not so much as he abjured the fact of his love for a Princess, who he denied himself the possibility of ever wooing.

It was indeed a somber group at dinner. Georgiana excused herself before dessert, leaving Darcy with a lady so disconcerted by something that she refused to discuss it.

In middle night, Darcy sat bolt upright. Elizabeth was not only missing, but her side of the bed was cold. He carried a candle from privacy closet to sitting room to her bedchamber, his heart racing faster than his legs. When he reached the door of her dressing closet, he heard weeping muffled as if to conceal itself. He held her in the cold and dark, her distress filling him with boundless patience. With her head pressed against his chest, she calmed, albeit slowly.

"Will you share it now or wait until morning?" His kisses and tone, so gentle, soothed her. She willed out the words.

"There's a problem with our child." Fresh tears clustered on her lashes. "Each day it shows itself more, William." She pulled his hand to feel her belly. "I'm grown too big too quickly. I've seen enough pregnant ladies to know my changes should show less for the weeks progressed. At this rate, it'll be born the size of a small one year old." Aunt Gardiner's efforts to confirm speculation about Jane had focused Elizabeth to note what she might have ignored a bit longer.

Darcy's concern was for his wife, not the child. A woman's most dangerous moments were during delivery and a child too large… he dug deep to keep his wits. Wrapped in a blanket, he carried her to his bedchamber and held her by the roaring fire. His pretense at confidence reassured her. "You and I are healthy and there are no aberrations in either of our families; hence, the chance for a serious problem is minimal, Lizzy. I'm certain there's another explanation." She slept at last, but Darcy could not. Even *he* knew she showed more than she ought at nearly four months. He sat holding his life in his arms until dawn's light.

The next morning, too agitated to attend Pemberley's business, Darcy paced at his lookout in the gallery. When Dr. Simons arrived, Darcy escorted him himself.

While the doctor interviewed Elizabeth, her husband sat at her corner hearth, his long torso bent forward, hands laced tight together. Concern for her had let go the infant daydreams of fatherhood; "disappointment" was too shallow to describe his sense of loss. His own pain accepted, Darcy endured the worst of all, fear for Elizabeth, who he was powerless to protect.

He sat as spectator, admiring her courage to speak personal facts so openly. And he studied Dr. Simons: the precise words of his every query, his tone and smallest change of expression. Darcy nodded approval for the doctor to examine her through the light wool of her gown and he studied the man's face when he pressed and released then pressed again. With the examination completed, Darcy held her hand. They awaited the verdict as one.

"It's too soon to judge conclusively, Mrs. Darcy, however, I can share what my experience predicts. I request to examine you in one month with an attending midwife, who is more experienced than myself in this regard." Matthew Simons' kind eyes focused on Elizabeth. "Mrs. Darcy, is there a history of multiple children in your family?"

"Multiple?"

"Likely twins. Are there incidents of twins in your family?"

Elizabeth sat dumb, shaking her head slowly back and forth as if movement settled the doctor's words in her head. "Wait, there was a distant cousin." She fixed her eyes on him. "The babies didn't survive, nor did my cousin after two weeks."

Darcy did not move, not a blink or the tiniest twitch of a muscle.

"Your cousin, Mrs. Darcy, was she a lady like yourself?"

"Her husband was a farmer with his own land and some rented property, which he also worked. She was survived by two young children who are raised by his second wife."

"A distant cousin is hardly corroboration, but I stand by my diagnosis. I can address your cousin's fate directly and with confidence however." He leaned forward, embracing both parents in his reassuring gaze. "The body is designed to carry one. When more are added, accommodation must be made. Initially this is accomplished by the body itself as you note by more size than expected. When the body reaches its limit, we accommodate with confinement to permit the children the extra weeks to grow enough to survive. I personally have never witnessed a child in a multiple birth to appear anything but normal; hence, time is our concern."

Elizabeth's voice was strained. "And my cousin, Doctor? There is a difference between a farmer's wife and myself?"

"In the case of multiple children, yes. Though your cousin likely enjoyed the luxury of a servant or two, the demands of two young children and a household to maintain would have made consistent bed rest difficult. Remember, Mrs. Darcy, the issue is time. Time off your feet to permit enough weeks for them to grow."

She kept her emotion in check until the last. The prospect of a healthy child calmed fears of the monster that had grown worry to choke her, while the idea of two at once with the chance of continued problems if she did not do it right, compounded nerves already too raw to support composure. Darcy reached her his clean handkerchief.

Matthew Simons watched Darcy slide close and embrace her shaking shoulders before kissing her cheek and whispering, "Two, Lizzy! We can do this! It is only short weeks collected to a few months. We can do this!" Mrs. Darcy laughed and hugged him.

Chapter 31

Darcy confided the surprise of twins to his sister before luncheon then announced he and Elizabeth would sequester themselves for the balance of the day. Georgiana leaned her head on the wing of her favorite chair, happy for her brother and sister, but sorry for herself. She had arisen that morning anticipating Elizabeth's counsel if she should decorate Henry's Hall.

Georgiana could sort her facts well enough; it was the final choice that stymied her. Logic demanded she forego his offer. At Cressbrook with no lady to guide her choices, she would need make the choices herself, thereby making it "her Hall," but common sense warned against vesting herself in Henry's Hall when he already owned her heart. However, against that logic pulsed her desire to attend to his comfort and her gladness to see him on a daily basis. Love pressed her to accept Henry's project, while fear stuck her feet in the muck of hesitation.

She sighed. *I require a friend to help me, Mama.* The idle thought invited action. She gathered pen and paper then shuffled the pages of her mother's letters to locate particular passages, which she copied onto one sheet.

Happiness: *"I have not met an emotion more challenging as happiness, not because it is rare, but because it requires contentment before the happiness can be embraced."*

Honesty: *"One always knows the truth inside, whether one owns the courage to admit it or not."*

Fear: *"I would not have you believe I have never feared. Fear is as natural as breathing… natural because we hesitate to cast our lot with the unknown. Fear commands us to take heed and consider our choices and then it challenges us to challenge Fear itself. Those who accept the challenge may emerge bruised from time to time, but they have stretched themselves past their parameters and thereby have earned the inevitable purse of growth and self-knowledge, no matter the success or failure of the moment."*

The next afternoon, Georgiana waved to Henry on the far side of the footbridge. He beamed, nodding at the basket on her arm. "I take it you've chosen for me, Princess." He reached his hand to help her to the Cressbrook side.

"I've chosen for myself, Henry. If it pleases you or not is your choice."

He eyed her. "I'm not prepared for riddles, Georgiana."

She laughed and poked his side. "And I'm not prepared to explain just yet!"

A half-hour later, the footfall of Henry's boots echoed off the parlor's bare floorboards. He paced. Georgiana sat straight in a shabby chair with the basket at her feet.

"I'm disappointed, Georgiana. I didn't anticipate negotiation."

"It's a necessity. I'll appoint your rooms only if I do it according to my best judgment."

"And how do you judge to do it, Miss Darcy?"

She bent to her basket and presented him a large envelope. "I've detailed it precisely. I recommend you sit while reading my proposal."

He read while she admired puffs of white clouds in shifting patterns beyond Putwell Hill. There could be no doubt when he had reached the end. "Damn it, Georgiana!" He tossed her proposal on the sofa. "I stated precisely I can't afford to do it all at once. What you have described would require at least £3,000!" He crossed to the bowed windows and looked down at the Wye; his shoulders stretched his jacket near to breaking, so personally had he vested himself in Cressbrook's improvement.

"More between £4,000 and £5,000 if it were done properly, but I think I can reduce the cost in every area to keep within our means," she said calmly.

"Our means? Are you daft and deaf at once?" He stared in disbelief. "That is nearly the extent of my entire savings and that, my dear Princess, will be invested in the land, not in a pretty place without the land improved enough to support it."

Her composure disconcerted him; he sensed his emotion tipped the scale to hand her the advantage. She remained seated, but her words lorded over him.

"I'm less deaf than you are blind, Henry Fitzwilliam. Hear me out, Sir! What good is improved land if you welcome your visitors to a Hall that is half-done and therefore humbled? This is an estate, Henry, not merely an experiment in land improvement. Your tenants take pride in the Hall as much as in fat flocks and full stomachs. A half-done house implies half-done to every man: half-done land and half-done labor. Your generous intent to put tenants before your comfort makes no difference since the success of the Hall inspires confidence in the success of all your enterprise."

He stared as if she had poured a ewer of cold water on his head then he sank onto the closest chair head in hands while the truth of her words dulled the glow of his accomplishment. His tone, low and defeated, spoke his heart. "I'm caught between two truths. I grant that you have the right, but I'm sorry to know it since the land and tenants must be put first. They must eat, Georgiana! I can only hope others won't judge our success by the sorry-ness of my Hall."

She bent to her basket and extracted several ledger sheets. "I've worked a solution." His look implied none existed. "There are nearly £2,700 from Mr. Pankhurst accrued in my account and I'll add to this with the newest projects he has petitioned me to accept. With your £500 added to my part, it's manageable, I think."

"£2,700! My God, Georgiana, every man ought to appoint rooms at that wage!"

"I shall ignore your presumption, Mr. Fitzwilliam," she said curtly.

"I apologize. You have the right. Your talents deserve what they earn you. But as to your offer, you confuse Solution with Charity. I told you that I do for myself now. No! I will not discuss it further. If you accept the challenge with a £500 purse, it is yours, otherwise not."

Calmly, Georgiana spread the ledger sheets on the tea table and motioned him to come. "You'll need examine these carefully. I've worked to include everything, but I expect there are items I missed. This is a record of six years of expenses you laid out on my behalf. I added not only the books, admissions to events and the gifts, including paint supplies and lessons, but also your visits to Annapolis. To those I've ascribed a value equal to your salary for your rank at the time, and then multiplied it by the hours encumbered in my service, including travel to and fro, of course. You see the total on the last sheet. Note, please, that my funds do not cover my debt, but I'll contribute future earnings until I've redeemed it."

"Enough!" Naked emotion echoed off grimy plaster walls. "I won't play games with words. This… this is beneath you, Georgiana Darcy! You know perfectly well that every penny I paid out was as much for my pleasure as yours."

Her sweetness had irritated him to exasperation and now she defeated him. "You speak from both sides of your mouth, Cousin and *that* is beneath you. If you offered personal funds to me out of love, then you must permit me the same privilege. But if you name my love Charity, then I must do likewise and insist to repay my debt." She took pity on a man tripped by his own lessons in logic and poked him with a disarming smile. "Actually, our negotiation is ended. No matter how you take it, your wonderful Hall will be a pretty place in not so very many weeks."

"My *wonderful* Hall? Two days ago you stated it was too needy."

"It is both, Mr. Fitzwilliam." She laughed. "My guardian taught me that one compromises his hand if he shows all his cards at once."

Georgiana curtsied and carried her basket to the front drawing room, which she immediately designated as her studio. Henry watched, frozen in place, as she climbed the two steps to the entrance hall and disappeared. An uncomfortable thought tickled the edge of his consciousness; the girl he had only superficially accepted as a peer had just forced his hand and set herself as his equal.

Chapter 32

Mrs. Darcy smiled gratitude for the cushion her lady's maid slipped in to ease her back, and then she smiled at Dr. Simons, just returned from his brief holiday in Dover and smiled at Mrs. Carroll, who the good doctor introduced as the midwife most renowned in the region for her successful delivery of twins. Mrs. Carroll, a small and energetic woman with graying hair under her cap and no frivolity on her costume, confirmed two babies, declared one was exceedingly active and estimated early September for full term.

After the examination, Darcy invited the midwife to the pavilion to gauge her opinion of his plan to make that great room the site for his wife's confinement. She explored the immense, high-ceilinged space with its opposing walls of glass then queried if it were not a bit damp. Darcy explained the fireplaces had not been lit in the seventeen years since its construction; Mrs. Darcy's confinement would inaugurate the room's use. The woman's impression of the gentleman improved to know his deep connection to his wife and her impression improved still more when he detailed changes to adapt the space to his wife's needs. In the end, she judged his choice ideal.

A man of action, Darcy made himself Elizabeth's conveyance on the stairs, escorted her during walks in the Park, monitored her naps and bedtime, etc. He was so omnipresent that her spirit recoiled under his blanket of attention, but she cloistered her discomfort behind a smile. She granted it was her challenge to accept dependence as it was his to embrace the ghosts that still pulled his strings now and then. Elizabeth thought he met his challenge with better success than she met hers. Only last week Georgiana had introduced him to Lady Anne's bedchamber and letters, and though stunned silent, he had not withdrawn.

As the babies imposed more and more on their mother, Elizabeth's spirit craved some small pretense of normality that let her depend only on herself for entertainment. Books suggested themselves at once, but without some greater purpose, even reading, which she loved, seemed more like marking time. One especially gray, dripping morning, Elizabeth wandered the main level peeking into rooms hoping for inspiration, but after an hour she found herself again in the Wedgewood library. Resigned, she sought out the shelf devoted to Derbyshire and the Peak; at least she could explore her environs if only from a chaise. After pulling out several volumes to judge which she would read first, she glimpsed a flash of gilt behind the space where they had stood and reached back to touch a row of short, thin books. One had mistakenly been returned backwards, which reflected the light from the wall sconce off the gold edges of its pages. She opened the little leather volume and read

The Personal Diary of
Reginald Darcy
October, 17- - to June, 17- -

More exploration showed two full stacks of shelves with at least two centuries of D'Arcy-Darcy diaries stored in a second row behind published titles. A footman transferred the treasure trove of her home's history to shelves in the morning room while Elizabeth designed her project: she would learn her House through the people who had made her with the goal to know the family into which her children would be born.

When Darcy arrived that afternoon, he laughed to see scores of little black-bound volumes instead of the usual vases and art. "What is this, Wife?" She explained her mission. He shook his head, "I fear my family is stale reading, Elizabeth. Reginald might appeal to you, but the rest are of less interest than *The Mirror of Graces*." It was a book detailing a lady's proper etiquette.

Surprised, she looked up from her reading, which did chance to be one of Reginald's and challenged, "But what of your father, William? I should think –"

"Unfortunately," he regretfully interrupted, "I can recommend my father's diaries least of all." Self-conscious for how it sounded, he searched to clarify. "I… I was disappointed when I read them. As a matter of fact, I couldn't get much into the first volume." Her furrowed brow demanded more detail. "In life, he was an intelligent man," Darcy continued, "serious and purposeful in his dialogue, but his diaries alternate between lists of his activities and ramblings with no discernible topic. After his death, God rest him, I had hoped to learn my father better, but soon gave up reading him since there was naught to glean."

Elizabeth let it lay, but after he bowed departure, she traded Reginald for George.

Darcy took it as providential that Elizabeth had the diaries and Georgiana had Cressbrook for entertainment while he devoted every free moment to the pavilion. Their small family did however unite at tea time and dinner, during which reports from Cressbrook were mainstays of conversation. Hannah always recounted the events of her day first since Georgiana deemed details of Mr. Hawkins's lessons and those of the village children of more interest than damask or linen for a side chair. When it was Georgiana's turn, she shared her sketches, permitting Elizabeth a peek at the Hall she would not visit until autumn.

At one point, Darcy bristled that his sister sounded possessive of Cressbrook, to which she responded calmly, "I make it mine with my decoration, Brother."

"I'd think that no matter the decoration, you'd be more attached to Pemberley," he scoffed.

Elizabeth interceded. "Your jealousy is misplaced, William. Home to a lady is the place where she makes her mark and it was you who suggested she do it at Cressbrook."

"My plan merely made a reason for her to remain with us."

"Take care, William. I hear more manipulation than interest in our sister's well-being."

"How so? She wished to appoint rooms and I got her rooms near Pemberley to do it."

Elizabeth rolled her eyes in Georgiana's direction then conveyed an expression of forbearance to a man who resisted equating a woman's world to his. She drew the parallel between Darcy's quarterly meetings with villages and Georgiana's decoration of rooms.

"Go on," he said.

"What if you were the lead elder of one of Pemberley's villages, as well as being master of all? Would you hold your village in the same light as the rest?"

Georgiana delighted in these debates that offered glimpses into her brother's nature and Elizabeth's skill to speak so he could grasp her point. He eyed his sister. "I grant you the attachment, Georgiana, but why should it be more than with other homes you have decorated?"

"There's no lady at Cressbrook, Brother. I must stand in to make the choices."

Darcy frowned. "I presumed Henry would make the choices."

Georgiana giggled and shook her head. "Lizzy, can you imagine my brother or Henry sitting for hours to select upholstery for a chair and the table best suited as its companion?"

They laughed heartily, even Darcy.

Georgiana's discussion of her day at Cressbrook left out that she and Henry exchanged long notes in regard to the rooms. And she especially did not share that they recently had begun the exchange of written teases tucked among his mail or slipped inside her paint box. She now greeted each day as much in anticipation of their shared surprises as for progress of the rooms.

In terms of the Hall, Lord and Lady Pillory had left behind only the shabbiest furnishings, which Georgiana inventoried and repurposed to better suit her cousin's needs. She was amazed at how far one could stretch a shilling with a little invention. She utilized bolt ends of every fabric Mr. Pankhurst could provide at extreme discount whether it was three yards or ten then compensated the missing yardage with a dozen bolts of heavy, cream-colored cotton in various finishes to complement the textures of the precious prints.

Her ingenuity in regard to craftsmen was particularly resourceful. A crippled tenant boy and two older girls were trained to refinish the wood pieces, a skill that earned them pride in their excellent product. She hired the upholsterer in Lambton for two weeks to educate two tenants in that craft and she hired an accomplished seamstress from Derby to live on the estate and supervise the tenant women's stitching of the drapes, etc. as per Miss Darcy's illustrations. On rainy days, the male tenants sanded the floors and woodwork, after which every square inch of plaster was repaired and painted and the wood varnished. Once the interior sparkled, they repaired the exterior.

The basics well underway, Georgiana next petitioned dear Mrs. Pankhurst to utilize her excellent taste and negotiating abilities at estate auctions in Town. With £900 in one hand and a detailed list of items missing from Cressbrook in the other, that lady outdid herself. Six weeks later, she dispatched wagonloads of high quality furnishings and housewares to Derbyshire. Even Georgiana was overwhelmed by so much at once. Henry sat with a stiff drink and stared.

While Georgiana directly addressed the Hall's challenges, Elizabeth avoided the challenge awaiting her. Her active nature so recoiled against the concept of confinement that she convinced herself a healthy body and sheer will-power would survive nine months without imposed bed rest. When Darcy proposed the pavilion as the site for her ordeal, she loved him for his generosity to offer what the House had not shared with any other, but she refused any participation in its conversion to her prison. Academically, she granted the pavilion was an excellent choice both in its dimension and its views of the Park to the east and the formal gardens to the west, each of which was accessed through opposing walls of French doors. But confinement itself fed an image of a larva locked in a cocoon of plaster and glass, and since she was not much for bugs and even less for being made to feel like one, she purposefully ignored her husband's efforts.

To meet her future needs and comfort, Darcy ordered an oversized privacy closet constructed in the area he designated to become their bedchamber, around which a dozen folding screens would provide a modicum of privacy. The rest of the grand space would accommodate areas for dining, conversation, etc. to let Elizabeth interact with the general family who would relocate their daily habits to the pavilion. Despite his disappointment that she refused to view progress first-hand, Darcy did not impose on her until one evening in April when she turned her back and announced she would manage without bed rest. His silence boded ill.

Of a sudden, he lifted her in his arms and carried her along the back hall, down the children's stairs, the garden stairs and along the colonnade, calling out as he went that the chandeliers and sconces be lit in the pavilion and that a sofa be carried there at once. Elizabeth did not squirm for release, which he presumed was to protect the children, but in fact, she felt like a child herself forced to give up her tantrum against a dose of nasty medicine. When arrived, he sat her on the sofa and stepped back.

"Look at it, Elizabeth!" he ordered. "Look at it, I say!" She looked. "It was my intent to do it all, but I now reconsider. You will do it, Wife! You will decide the furnishings to be included and where they'll be placed. If you do nothing then you will sit on this sofa with no distraction but bare walls and views through the glass when confinement begins. Tomorrow after breakfast, you'll attend your needlework, correspondence, and every other morning duty in this room until I arrive to fetch you to luncheon. Am I clear?"

She nodded.

"Good." He kissed her then added gently, "Let us to sleep. It's past your bedtime."

Chapter 33

News of Cressbrook's rebirth became a favored topic in the region given the estate's sorry condition before Mr. Fitzwilliam took the reins. When correspondence arrived from smaller landholders requesting a first-hand look at the agricultural techniques Henry had instituted, the master of Cressbrook dreamed of a future teaching-college supporting husbandry's innovations. He shared these dreams and his every other interest with Georgiana each afternoon during their newly established tea at two o'clock. The longer days of approaching summer permitted Henry this brief diversion since he could return to his labor after four o'clock when the ladies departed. Georgiana noted that his commitment to those who depended on him required him to justify every moment taken for his own pleasure.

The renovation of the Hall was also common knowledge since those who visited to inspect the land added their praise for the work inside. Mr. Hopewell, Cressbrook's former butler, heard news of the Hall while delivering firewood to customers while his wife, Cressbrook's former housekeeper/cook, heard the same from those delivering laundry to the couple's rented cottage in Lambton. The Hopewells yearned to return to their former lives and petitioned the lead elder of Cressbrook to arrange a meeting with Mr. Fitzwilliam. The elder, however, deemed Daniel best-suited to present the delicate query. Surprised by the care taken to make a simple introduction, Hawkins was dismayed when Mr. Fitzwilliam declined to meet the Hopewells. Confused, Daniel related this to Miss Hannah, who mentioned it to her mistress, who raised the issue at two o'clock tea. Henry accepted the meeting as a courtesy, but made clear he could not employ them.

Two afternoons later, Daniel introduced Mr. and Mrs. Hopewell to the master within earshot of the drawing room, which opened onto the entrance hall. Georgiana poked her head past the door. "I should like to be included if I may." The young lady's smile eased the Hopewells' nerves until they learned they met a Darcy, whereupon they tugged at their modest clothes.

Seated in the parlor, Mr. Hopewell conveyed their credentials. To Georgiana's mind, he presented much as Elizabeth's Uncle Gardiner, though Mrs. Hopewell was not so delicately formed as Aunt Marion and tried to hide her swelled and red-chafed hands.

Henry began, "I believe it best to speak directly." The Hopewells sat straight and stoic. "As you might know, I arrive at Cressbrook without the accustomed benefits of landed gentry; hence, limited resources confine my choices. Despite the elders' high recommendations and my excellent impression of you personally, I cannot consider your employment until Cressbrook's prosperity is firmly established." When Mrs. Hopewell glanced at the improvements in the parlor, Henry added gently, "The changes are beholding to Miss Darcy's talents, not my purse."

Georgiana inserted herself. "Cousin, Mr. and Mrs. Hopewell might welcome a tour of the Hall. It's two years since they last saw it." With Daniel as the Hopewells' escort, she closed the parlor door and addressed her cousin. "It *is* unfortunate, but you certainly made the right choice to deny them."

He turned his back. "I've no heart to discuss it."

"Then you're as sorry as they are for your choice?"

"I'm even sorrier since it is I who disappoint them."

"Go on." Her whisper of a voice soothed a little.

He sank into a corner chair and squinted to see Georgiana against the full sun streaming past the bowed wall of windows at her back. "I've always been conservative, Princess, despite how society prefers to perceive me." He hung his head and in a low voice shared a fact he had barely admitted to himself. "It's more than conservatism, actually. Years of following orders have made a man ill-equipped to take chances. I'll not commit to more responsibility until I'm assured the rest are well cared for." He looked up. She had moved within arm's length of his chair. He continued. "We have yet to harvest one field and it will be weeks until the sheep are sheared. I would be irresponsible to accept the luxury of servants with no promise I can support them."

"Then it truly is an issue of funds and not your judgment against them?"

"Their credentials are impeccable and they present themselves as honest and sympathetic folk so of course it's an issue of funds!"

Georgiana commiserated. "To be sure, they'd eat you into the poorhouse."

"Beg pardon?"

"I venture their interest lies less in wages than the opportunity to work in their chosen vocations. Your pocketbook must fear they'll eat too much since their pay would be a uniform, at least initially."

"You miss my point, Georgiana. They could become ill and require treatment or the harvest could go poorly letting Cressbrook support fewer rather than more. I've much to learn as master. In fact, I'm sorry for my people, who got themselves a master untrained to be one."

"I do see your point. It is incumbent on you to err on the side of care." Pausing at the door, she looked back at him. "It's the same care I mark in your choice to plant new orchards and clear new fields and add to your flocks no matter that weather might compromise your investment. It's the same conservatism that opened Cressbrook's doors to the tenants Mr. Mason banished last summer, and then filled the remaining empty houses in the village with distant cousins of your folk so that they might also know a better life." She looked him in the eye, "Your actions bespeak your talent to master, Henry, whether your head accepts you're one or not."

The addition of a butler and housekeeper/cook proved to be a good choice in terms of the Hall's upkeep and Henry's stomach, but his head continued to argue against luxury and his heart worried he might fail the confidence vested in him. Despite his personal gladness to taste success, he was a humble man who blushed to hear honest praise. The self he met at Cressbrook stood in sharp contrast to his military persona, who had slapped shoulders and accepted commendation unabashedly.

After Mrs. Hopewell cleared the stone terrace of debris and Mr. Hopewell repaired a bench, which he set at terrace-center, Henry availed himself of it every evening to sit under the heavens and wonder at the differences between the man he had been and the man he was becoming. "This is the gist of your heart's discomfort," he admitted. "You're thirty years old yet only now begin to learn yourself." He granted he had merely played a role as an officer in the King's army. Yes, he had played it well, but it was only a role and was one so clearly defined by rule and regulation that any man with half a wit could merit praise.

More nights under the stars exposed the grounds for a head and heart lacking confidence in choices taken. What Darcy had learned at his father's knee as the future master of Pemberley had gone missing in Henry's experience. His own father had taken more interest to play the role of Earl than to consciously model anything to his sons, and even if Lord John had cared to teach the art of mastering, the lessons would only have been shared with his eldest. Indeed, Henry's history had fashioned a man to make do with scraps, not one who knew how to sit at a full-course meal.

The stars were excellent guides to both heart and head. After one week, he asked if there had been others employed at the Hall and he hired back the footman and housemaid. He delegated responsibility to tenants trained to their tasks. And he educated Daniel Hawkins toward becoming steward. Then Henry stepped back and, while keeping his finger on the pulse of his little estate, he permitted his people the latitude to take pride in their own accomplishment.

Georgiana observed the changes in her cousin with mixed feelings. On the one hand, she sorrowed that he was weaning himself from her support, while on the other, she rejoiced that his confidence grew his independence since her work at the Hall would conclude in June and thereafter, Henry could no longer rely on her counsel. When the last curtain was hung and the last chair set in place, Georgiana would revert to a cousin who visited only now and then. She sensed her brother remained a bit jealous of her attentions to Cressbrook and was certain that though Darcy devoted himself to Elizabeth, such would not distract him from keeping count of his sister's full days from Pemberley without practical grounds to explain them.

Chapter 34

"You summoned me, Lizzy?" Georgiana arrived with bonnet tied and shawl folded over her arm. She had delayed the carriage to Cressbrook in response to Elizabeth's message.

With George Darcy's "Diary -Volume 1" in hand, Elizabeth explained her family project and the difficulty she had in making sense of his writing. "Please, read a few pages and tell me if it represents the papa you remember," she bade her sister.

Georgiana laughed when she reached the end of the first rambling. "Silly papa," she said. "He's playing a game though I can't imagine why since one's diary is where one conveys oneself openly. See here," she pointed to a summary of activities, "he cares nothing for this list because he doesn't discuss the items. Papa loved to expound on motivations, results and everything between. And here," she turned to a page of rambling. "This sounds much more like Papa, because the feelings and observations mix together. Only he doesn't tell the topic, hence it makes him sound a bit daft." Georgiana shook her head. "I can't explain it, Lizzy, but I'm certain he had some purpose, just as I'm certain there's some means to learn the topic. My Papa was a very rational man and valued precise written communication."

Elizabeth smiled and returned to George's excellent penmanship. She liked her father-in-law already since she loved puzzles and he presented her a very good one.

A grand coach traveling north on Castlegate Lane was a head-turning event for local folk accustomed to farm wagons and lone riders. Lord Newsome sat well positioned at the window for those who cared to crane their necks. He had postponed visiting Georgiana after the requisite month of mourning in order to introduce himself as the new representative of

Braithmoor to all who might take an interest. As circumstance increased his pomp, the lord convinced himself that Georgiana's family would press her to accept him since to count a lord among one's immediate family was an honor all strove to add to their genealogy.

He had not considered Georgiana might be from House, nor had he anticipated learning such from a pregnant woman who lacked the decorum to convey her message through a representative. Undone by Mrs. Darcy's flaunting of her condition, he wondered if the Darcys might be poorly suited to *his* genealogy, but he recovered and gave his driver directions to Cressbrook. Lord Newsome prepared to meet his lady, despite that she again appointed rooms, which affronted him personally. Attached to his new title was his supreme confidence in his perception of things.

Unfamiliar with the art of an estate that wore its agrarian dependence on its sleeve, Lord Newsome revised his appraisal of Henry Fitzwilliam as the coach negotiated Bottom Hill Road; the former brigadier was obviously a pretender to gentility. Continuing on the gentle arc toward the River Wye, Newsome realized Cressbrook sat just east of Pemberley and sensed stinking collaboration. A needy cousin and an obliging brother had connived to deprive him of his lady.

The first to apprehend his coach was Hannah en route to afternoon lessons in the village. Her stunned surprise corroborated conspiracy in the lord's eyes, as did her feigned curtsy before running along a wagon path that dipped toward the forest near Cress Brook's new bridge site.

A butler, who evidenced too much pride in his position, escorted the gentleman to the parlor and left him in a half-done chamber faced directly on Putwell Hill. Steps clattered down uncarpeted stairs; Georgiana arrived wiping her hands on her apron. He took her rush to meet him as further evidence of intrigue between cousins; the lady obviously relished his visit.

"This is an excellent surprise, Lord Newsome," she laughed as she curtsied.

He did not contradict that she addressed him by title. In fact, he smiled to hear "Lord Newsome" no matter the speaker's relation. Even his mama had taken to address him so.

"If you're surprised, Georgiana, then I am astonished. Your family appears to have consigned you to labor like a common person." He interpreted her stiffened back as defense of undeserving relations. "I cannot pretend against the lessening of my esteem for them, though I assure you your circumstance does not lessen my admiration for you."

"You've gotten quite practiced in judgment since last we met, Percy."

He winced to hear Percy, but her tone implied it was better to adjust the subject than her choice of address. "I hear you again decorate rooms. The saving grace is you do it for family."

"I would have offered you tea, but it's now my preference to offer you the door." Georgiana presented herself more like her brother than the young lady he recalled.

"Come, come, Princess," Henry entered in stocking feet, his boots too muddy to track across the maid's immaculately polished floors. "Our guest has traveled great distance." Henry bowed, "Lord Newsome, we're glad to welcome you to Cressbrook." The lord stared from the one to the other. With cool composure in the face of Newsome's haughtiness, Henry ordered tea then excused himself to change muddied breeches.

Newsome spoke with the passion of a wronged man. "*We*, Georgiana? Ought I to presume more is afoot between you two than the renovation of some rooms?"

"You're as silly as the words you speak, Percy Newsome."

"Silly?" He rose to his best height, which fell quite short of the lady's. "I'm no fool, Georgiana! It comes full clear why the then-brigadier worked to free you from your obligation to me. Indeed, a man with a poor estate would benefit exceedingly from a wealthy wife."

Henry, having descended the back stairs, arrived in the entrance hall unbeknownst to his guest. The master raised his hand to stay Mr. Hopewell's delivery of the tea tray.

"You're as insufferable as implied by your written petition for my hand, Percy Newsome. Do not feign confusion, Sir. In your letter to my brother, you presented our liaison more as a financial transaction than marriage." She raised her chin. "You mistake my cousin's and brother's interests: the latter wishes only for my happiness, while the former merely obliges my brother's request that I renovate Cressbrook Hall."

"I… forgive me, Georgiana. I only thought…"

"It is 'Miss Darcy' and I doubt very much, if you 'thought' at all. My family does not indulge in deception. Henry's 'we' refers to our connection as cousins, nothing more."

A pink-faced lord stomped past master and butler. But before his coach turned the first curve on Bottom Hill Road, Newsome's dark eyes promised retribution. His humiliation faded as he conceived the letter he would post to Mr. Darcy.

Henry arrived at the parlor with tea tray in hand. "From what I overheard, you gave him his due, Princess," he quipped with an easy smile.

"Thank you, but I don't want tea," she curtsied and hurried to her studio.

Tap, tap-tap. Henry opened the door to her studio to find Georgiana tying her bonnet. "What's wrong, Georgiana?"

"I'm going to walk." She glanced at the mantle clock. "Please ask Hannah to wait if I'm not returned when she's finished with her lessons."

"Not so fast, Miss Darcy. There is obviously a problem and I'd like to hear it."

She walked past him to the front door. "Thank you for your offer, but it is nothing you can help me with, Cousin." She stepped onto the front stoop and closed the door.

Two minutes later, Henry caught up, having noted from behind that Georgiana clenched her hands and that her shoulders slumped. "Let me walk with you, please."

"If you do, we'll only argue."

He adjusted his stride to hers. "Then we will argue, if you think we must. I've never seen you like this Georgiana which makes me too worried to turn back." They rounded the first curve on Bottom Hill Road. "Are you angry or hurt?" he asked.

"Both." She stopped on the dirt road and faced him. "I don't appreciate being queried as if I'm incapable of sorting my own issues, Henry." Her eyes looked directly into his and did not flinch. Her cheeks colored, but not with embarrassment. So high was her emotion that she did not first perceive her rudeness, and after she became aware, she did not care that she presented her beloved Henry an aspect of herself he did not know.

"I don't mean to offend, Georgiana, however, I am concerned and would appreciate to learn what troubles you so severely that you quit the Hall and upbraid me."

She turned and retraced their steps, her arms crossed against her chest, "How would you feel to learn the person you nearly married is a pompous prig? How would you feel to know that but for the sacrifice of a guardian, your life would a hell? How would you feel, Henry Fitzwilliam, to be confronted with the foolishness that nearly ruined your life and grossly affected the life of one you care for?"

Her vocabulary so distracted him, he could only respond, "I've never heard you say 'prig' or 'hell,' Princess."

"You're stuck in the past, Henry. I'm not twelve years old no matter how much you wish to preserve me as such."

That she fully grasped his game in her regard discomfited him severely. He addressed the issue that appeared to be at the heart of her despair. "I made no sacrifice when I interrupted your betrothal, Georgiana."

She stomped her foot. "You will never convince me that I don't owe you more than I could ever repay." He opened his mouth in reply. She cut him off. "*You* trained me to abide by *facts*, Henry. Fact: You compromised your career to rescue me. Fact: You would be in Vienna at this moment were it not for my stupid plan to marry Percy. Fact: You fulfilled your guardian's duty and as a result your life's path changed radically. I know you count Cressbrook a better prize than Vienna, and for that I'm glad, but this doesn't change facts that I shall live with all the days of my life. Seeing Lord Newsome this afternoon invited feelings to the fore that sit ever present in the background."

Believing that his silence affirmed his acceptance of her facts, she concluded, "You understand why I didn't invite you to walk. There is nothing you can say or do to help me out of my present feelings. I ask you to return to the Hall and let me be... please."

"There is a fact about Christmas that I've withheld, Georgiana." Their steps approached the little woods between the road and the cliff above Water-cum-Jolly. "If you'll sit with me there," he nodded at the woods, "I'll share what I ought to have done months ago."

He invited her to sit with him on a fallen log, but she declined, preferring an adjacent boulder.

"I didn't think I would ever speak to you of this, Princess, but I now feel compelled that you understand." His voice hesitated at the start, but gained confidence as he shared his burden. "I won't have you suffer from guilt you have no right to feel. I was a coward not to have explained myself at Christmas."

"You've explained yourself over and over, each time making clear my silliness and your forbearance." She had had enough of his dance around feelings he didn't share. "There are but two facts, Henry: I love you with all my heart and you don't love me likewise."

"I had no idea, Georgiana. You've appeared to be comfortable as cousins and —"

"I was raised to accept reality, Henry. I've made my peace with our facts. Attempting to put them in a different or better light only hurts me and I doubt you wish to consciously cause me pain."

She had offered him a path to escape the revelation of his feelings, an advantage any negotiator would seize on for his benefit. But her honesty and directness challenged him to the same.

"As you've stated, Princess, you are already hurt. By adding my facts, I shall hope to relieve your anguish and help you accept the lot that the Fates have handed me and thereby us." She nodded he should proceed. "First," he looked into her eyes, "I love you with all my heart, Georgiana Darcy." His words, whispered in a tone that caressed, felt like he had kissed her. His next words, however, were spoken with the resignation, to which she had grown accustomed. "But when I realized at Christmas that my love for you was more than a guardian for his ward, I confronted a second fact equally compelling."

His tone dashed hope. She braced herself to hear him. "And that fact would be?"

"You are the daughter of the man who was more a father to me than my own. My experience since the day you were born has made you my sister, Georgiana. I… I can't imagine more than holding your hand without reviling myself."

Georgiana swallowed. His words were irrational, but his tone promised he subscribed to them wholeheartedly.

"And you accept this judgment as final?" she asked.

"I have no choice."

Her heart grimaced to hear the man who had promised "there is always choice" disclaim choice when the issue was his love for her. She stood. "At best, I would judge you as confused, Henry," she said calmly and left him where he sat.

He caught up with her at the edge of the woods. "I had hoped honesty would let you understand and accept —"

"It has done both," she responded evenly. "Excuse me, please. I'll wait for Hannah at the footbridge."

That evening, Georgiana Darcy endured tea and dinner as she played her part in a happy family while picking at her food. Later, she filled sheet after crisp white sheet of paper to understand why he had insisted to share everything yet nothing with her. She wondered if she still loved a man who refused to champion his feelings because of a relationship made moot by time. She laughed at her devotion to him and then wept choking sobs of despair.

Two days later, a letter arrived for Fitzwilliam Darcy.

> *Braithmoor, 5 May, 18 - -*
> *Dear Mr. Darcy,*
> *I believe it the duty of a good neighbor to inform you of my recent visit to Cressbrook Hall. Upon arriving, I perceived Miss Georgiana's exceeding pleasure to see me; however that pleasure evaporated when your cousin, the former brigadier, arrived and showed great possessiveness of your sister. You know the man better than I, Mr. Darcy, but I took the clear impression that his interest might extend to benefit his small estate were her financial interests transferred to him.*
> *I hope this letter finds you well, Sir.*
> *Sincerely, Lord Newsome*

Chapter 35

May was a lovely time of year, which supported Elizabeth's spirits a little as she adjusted to waddling on daily walks, now restricted to a quarter mile from the House. Independent and active all of her life, she had truly convinced herself she could manage double-pregnancy better than Dr. Simons had predicted, but the waddle slowed her exceedingly and the accompanying imbalance, which required her to hold another's arm when she strolled outside, made clear that the pregnancy controlled her, not vice versa.

Breakfast was one of the few daily events that did not require change from her past habits, hence Elizabeth was always cheerful in the morning while teasing with her family and sorting the post. Gathered at the breakfast table in late April, she passed two letters to Georgiana and one to Hannah.

"Do you know someone in Warmsby Heath?" she asked her husband, passing him an envelope bordered in black. He glanced at the return address and broke the seal. From his look, he was personally touched.

Darcy cleared his throat. "Mr. and Mrs. Livesay... Holt and Marge are their given names. They were friends of my parents. She has sent news of her husband's passing, God rest him."

Elizabeth covered his hand with hers. "My condolences, William. You appear to have been quite attached to him."

"Yes, but it's been years since I've seen either of them. They visited often when I was young. Both doted on me," he smiled, "almost like grandparents."

Elizabeth glanced at Georgiana. Her expression indicated she was as surprised as Elizabeth.

"Was he landed or in business?" his wife queried.

"Neither," Darcy responded. "They were simple farmers, but took their ease in our company as if they counted themselves one of us. My parents embraced them with equal warmth. They stopped visiting after mama became ill."

"And you haven't seen them since?"

"No." He shook his head. "Perhaps papa continued correspondence. I don't know."

Georgiana slid along the bench to her brother's side and covered his other hand with hers. "If they were like grandparents, then you should write and tell Mrs. Livesay of Lizzy. It's no matter that it's been so long since you've seen her. In fact, I'll pen new portraits of you both and you can post them with your letter, if you like." She kissed his cheek and then kissed Elizabeth before setting out for Cressbrook with Hannah at her side.

Left to themselves, Elizabeth asked, "Where is Warmsby Heath, William?"

"In the far north. They had a cottage on a lake. In fact, I think Mama painted it, but I couldn't guess where the painting's got to or even if it still exists." He pushed back his chair. "I had the impression my father supported them though I don't know or why."

Georgiana arrived at Cressbrook with the completion of Henry's study on her day's agenda. It would be the first room she would declare "finished" and her energy to do it implied to Henry she had accepted the double-edged fact between them. To the contrary, Georgiana's energy was neither for the man nor his Hall; she hastened to complete her obligations to Cressbrook and the Darcys' nursery in order to expedite her departure from Derbyshire.

When Georgiana had shared these intentions with Hannah, the secretary's tepid support unsettled her mistress, who judged that living with a morose Hannah in Town would be nearly as off-putting as remaining in the Peak. Resolved to learn Hannah's heart, Georgiana interrupted their return to the House that afternoon to stroll with her along the Pemberley side of Water-cum-Jolly's sun-dappled pond.

"I shall miss this place, Hannah," she said.

"As will I, Miss Georgiana."

"Would you prefer to remain here? I mean you've vested so much of yourself in the school and I've no doubt Mr. Hawkins will miss his private lessons."

"Are you saying you don't want me to return with you?"

"No. I'm asking your preference. My own preference is that we travel together, but only if you don't leave your heart in Derbyshire."

"I don't understand, Miss Georgiana. I own nothing here. As to preferences, I would prefer to keep things as they've been, but if we must –"

"Hannah, I will not tiptoe around the issue. Do you fancy Mr. Hawkins or is it Cressbrook in general you will miss?"

"My feelings are personal and do not count in our contract, Miss Georgiana," she stated coolly, her gaze fixed on the cliffs. "Anyway, it makes no difference if I fancy him or not."

"Why?"

"Because he doesn't fancy me."

Neither had anticipated Hannah's tears.

Georgiana glanced up at the Hall whose windows would be eyes to any who chanced to look and hurried her secretary to their waiting carriage. Hanna sniffed self-consciously into her handkerchief while Georgiana regretted to have prodded her friend to tears. It was awkward. Georgiana, the younger by four years, appeared to have more experience with matters of the heart than Hannah, though she doubted her failed experience could serve as grounds for good advice. Half-way home, curiosity won out over self-doubt.

"How do you know he doesn't fancy you?" Georgiana queried of a sudden.

Hannah insisted to watch the Park rather than her mistress. "This is embarrassing, Miss. When I first met the village folk, they presumed I am a lady and I didn't correct their misperception. Daniel, um, Mr. Hawkins is very sensitive to status. I did share my history by setting London as the subject of some lessons and myself there as the daughter of craft folk, but Town can make even craft folk seem exotic in his parochial world. I think my history made it worse instead of better."

Hannah paused to consider if she would share the other issue.

"I'm twenty-two, Miss. He'll be nineteen next month. Though he's my better in intelligence and independence, he perceives himself my junior. Even if 'London' didn't separate us, *time* does and that can't be adjusted."

"Do you think he'd respond differently without these two issues?" Georgiana held Hannah's hand. "Tell me, do you sense interest from his tone or a look that he doesn't share with others? Hannah, don't be shy to acknowledge such, if it exists. A person knows when another is smitten. Tell me honestly."

Hannah blushed and nodded.

Georgiana considered briefly then submitted that Hannah should carry her classroom to the fields, weather permitting, and half of the lessons should be devoted to her learning the land from him. "Ask him to share with you. Make him your partner in learning, not just your student. Let the lesson digress when it wanders from the text you prepared. Make memories of how he looks squinting in the sunshine and how he sets his chin when he debates a topic." Hannah stared in confusion. "Listen well, Hannah Dear. It may be that he doesn't care for you as you'd have him do, but you can offer him the opportunity to know you better in the context of his life and all the while you'll be gathering precious memories to cherish if it comes to naught."

"I should think such memories would be more painful that precious, if he cannot care."

"I would have thought the same except I've learned one can't replace what one has missed. It's better to hold the memory than nothing at all." Georgiana smiled wistfully. "I've just offered you the best lesson taught me by my mother."

When arrived at the House, Hannah retired to her bedchamber to consider her friend's advice which left a solitary sister calling apology that she arrived late to tea. Georgiana stopped short on the threshold of the morning room and called to a nearby footman. "I appear to have missed tea altogether." The chamber was empty.

"No, Miss. Tea is served hereafter in the pavilion."

Dear God, Lizzy! Georgiana dropped her basket and lifted her skirts to arrive out of breath at the pavilion's doors. Dr. Simons had inaugurated Elizabeth's confinement.

From the chaise adjacent to the dining table, Elizabeth was all laughter during tea and dinner and her evening conversation was as entertaining as Georgiana's piano performance, all of which convinced the younger that the elder adapted easily to imposed restraint.

Elizabeth had complied with her husband's challenge to outfit the pavilion by making it a home within the House. On the west side, areas for dining and sleeping enjoyed garden views; a seating area clustered around the north hearth; and on the east side, areas for both a piano and a small library looked out on the Park. The space near the south hearth sat empty awaiting two cradles.

At evening's end, Georgiana kissed her sister's cheek. "Sleep well, Lizzy. Your happy adjustment makes it easier for us to adapt. Thank you." Georgiana's kindness soothed Elizabeth's knot of nerves, but that knot, deep inside, required more than kindness to untangle itself. Too many weeks of smiles that hid physical discomfort and debilitating restrictions had made an honest woman into a liar; she rebelled on the inside as sincerely as she appeared to accept.

Darcy pulled the sky blue drapes closed across the wall of French doors at either end of the great room, shrugged off his jacket and untied his neck cloth. A tear came very close to spilling, but Elizabeth blinked and dug deep for one last flash of smile. "If I may, William, I prefer to complete my adjustment alone on this first night." His disappointment pained her. She continued with apologies. "I admit I'm surprised by my request, but –"

He waved off further explanation, too stunned to discuss. With jacket and cravat in hand, he kissed her, "You must do it how it suits you, Lizzy. Sleep well, my love," he said and quit her.

After crossing the colonnade and climbing the garden stairs in a blur, Darcy paused at her breakfast table, slid along the bench and watched the pavilion's glass wall silvered by moonlight into a mirror. He had not expected to be banished.

Darcy struggled to understand. Elizabeth had changed, though he could not isolate precisely how. Since learning there would be twins, she had smiled and discussed without discovering one problem. The effect, he struggled again, the effect was amiable and delightful, as if she were the mistress entertaining a family of strangers. His eyes narrowed. No arguments. Not one! *Dammit, Lizzy!* She had not only banished him from her bed, but also from herself.

The raw emotion of a wronged man erupted; he had devoted himself to her benefit, yet did not enjoy her trust. He shoved the table aside, bounded down the stairs and dismissed the footman at the pavilion's doors.

"Elizabeth! I insist we talk!" The silence of the great room pressed on him, as if the chamber itself held its breath. The circle of screens hid the furnishings from her bedchamber arranged on her carpet of roses. "Lizzy. Are you there?" Anger ebbed. Anxiety seeped in its place. "Lizzy?"

"We'll talk tomorrow, William. You woke me from my sleep."

Darcy hesitated and nearly retraced his steps until he recalled no rustle of blankets accompanying her waking. With long strides he pushed aside the barrier of screens then stopped short. His wife, his indomitable wife, sat on their bed hugging a pillow. Her eyes were red from weeping and her expression was horrorstruck that he saw her so.

He carried her to the sofa without regard for bedclothes dragged across the floor. A hoot-owl inserted its call into the night. He held her and wondered how to open a treasure when the key was locked inside. "I've missed you, Lizzy."

"I can't see how. We're together nearly every waking moment." The knot that had loosed a little with her tears had tangled more tightly with his interruption. Her children squirmed, tickling her belly. "I'm weary, William. We'll discuss tomorrow if you still think it necessary."

"We'll do it now."

"Please, don't press the issue, Fitzwilliam. I –"

"Consider it pressed!" Her body stiffened. "In fact, Mrs. Darcy," he continued, "I believe I've done our partnership a grave disservice by catering to you too much."

"I take no interest in an argument, Mr. Darcy."

"Why ever not? We've managed some excellent ones with even more wonderful reunions afterwards. An argument might be –"

"Stop! No more!" She moved to escape, but he held fast.

"We're partners, Mrs. Darcy. Partners are committed to the same end and are bound to mutual support in its achievement." He pushed aside the curls that fell across her cheek.

She pulled away. "Please, don't. You make me feel like a child."

"If you refuse both discussion and argument, I suggest you're acting like a child, a petulant child in fact."

She stood with eyes flashing and hands clinched. "Petulant? As my partner, you should sense that the effort I make for my family's comfort is done with severe difficulty on my part."

"Elizabeth, sit please. The children," Darcy reminded.

His implication that she did not protect her children was too much. "Go! Now!"

"Why?" His even tone irked her even more.

"Because you're part of my prison!" Her words caught her short. "Forgive me. You cannot understand. Excuse me. I will to bed."

Darcy leaned back, deep-rooted to his place. "I can't understand that which you refuse to share, Elizabeth."

His steady gaze, without anger or accusation, disarmed her a little. She took a breath. "I am doing this the best I can. If it's not good enough, so be it."

She held the arm of a chair for balance to gather her blankets from the floor, but Darcy interceded and returned them to her bed. "You will note that a partner is an excellent invention, Lizzy. He can pick up errant bed clothes and …" his effort to smooth the sheet and layer two blankets on top was an exhibition in wrinkles "… he can make a lumpy bed," he smiled, "to complement your lumpy mood."

Before her pregnancy, she would have hugged him and laughed; now she only watched, sobered by the gulf between their "then" and "now."

"It's not a mood. It's who I've become." She blinked against pregnancy's tears. "This is the most difficult challenge of my life, Mr. Darcy. I regret I cannot do it better."

Darcy pulled off his boots. "Perhaps it would go better if you included me." He nodded at his side of her bed. "May I?"

Elizabeth watched him.

The blankets rustled and the ropes creaked against his weight. "Talk to me, Lizzy."

In the wee hours of the morning, Fitzwilliam Darcy stared at the prison of privacy screens long after she had relaxed against him in sleep. There had been some tears, but not so many as he had anticipated. In fact, the more he listened, the more calmly she discussed and the more composed was her demeanor. He thought they had each misjudged how to do pregnancy together. She prided herself to address her responsibilities without complaint, but in so doing her spirit had bent under the weight of protecting the well-being of three people: her babies and herself. He, a master accomplished at managing, had prided himself to support her physical well-being, unaware that her spirit required the same attention.

The nature of pregnancy connected the children to the mother, impling only she could address the burden. To encourage her to share that burden with him, he would need be inventive. In those early hours of owls' hoots and breaths of wind, Darcy devised his best plan yet: they would commit their joint efforts to a special project for their children, and in so doing, they would practice the partnership that presently eluded them.

Chapter 36

"Where are we going, Papa?"

George Darcy looked down at his little boy, a sweet and trusting child.

"We visit a special place mama has made for you." The child looked confused. George explained, "You see the tree at the edge of the lawn? Yes, the big one. Your special place sits in its leaves. Do you see mama's handkerchief waving?" He patted his son's head. "Yes, you may run to her."

A tree with mama in the leaves... little Fitzwilliam could not imagine such magic, but he soon discovered the magic was made of wood and much too high. Serious eyes followed the slats on the tree trunk that made a ladder stretching to a hole in a wood floor. His mama called him encouragement to join her, and then she called to papa, "Help him while he climbs, George," then added, "You see my point? We shelter him so much he hesitates to challenge what is foreign to him."

George Darcy nodded, as he did to all of Anne's lessons in their son's regard. George's own father had been consumed with Pemberley and his mother's health had been delicate, a combination that had not modeled the warmth required by Fitzwilliam whose temperament was more his mother's than his father's. The lad felt his papa's hands at his waist. "It's a tree house, Son. The tree is very strong and protects the house. I'll hold fast, while you climb the first time." Soon the child's sober face topped by tousled curls peered through one window, while Anne waved from the other. George laughed, "May I join you or is it a private party?"

Before George could climb the first step, Fitzwilliam's legs descended with arms working as fast as his feet could locate the next slat. "Wait, Papa! I'll help you."

The next morning after breakfast, Elizabeth quit the chaise near the pavilion's dining table and eased onto the settee facing the formal gardens. My world is a chaise or a bed or a settee, she observed. Thank goodness for the settee or I could not pretend to normality! She amended "pretend" to "take comfort in." After having untangled a good part of her trouble in William's arms, she felt more herself than she had in months and vowed to keep martyrdom to a minimum.

"Mrs. Darcy, see this!" Darcy rushed past the doors to exhibit a diagram. "What say you?"

"If I knew what it represents, I could better share my opinion." She turned it this way and that, but without improved effect.

"It's a tree house! I added several embellishments to the original."

The subject of "tree house" helped since she could connect it with Mrs. Reynolds' stories, though she was no closer to deciphering his lines. "I haven't seen the original. Describe what I ought to be appreciating." After grasping the intent of his project, she laughed until she wiped her eyes. "Fitzwilliam Darcy, your poor letter opener is full evidence that of all of the projects to undertake for your children's benefit, constructing a tree house ought not be one of them!"

He laughed with her. "I accept your skepticism and admit I shall have help."

"Much better, William. The carpenters can saw and nail and you can supervise. You are excellent at supervising."

He watched her intently while emphasizing in a low voice, "As are you, Mrs. Darcy."

After a moment, her eyes opened wide. "You can't be serious!"

"Fully and completely!"

"William, I appreciate you will distract me from tedium, but this would be a farce!"

He was not discouraged; by his hand and with her direction, they would build a tree house.

Within the hour, his horse followed Castlegate Lane to Cressbrook since the Wye was at high water and the New Road and its bridge were weeks from completion. It would be a simple thing for Henry to draft the plans, from which Elizabeth would interpret the measurement and placement of each plank to her husband, who unfortunately read schematic plans with the same talent as he drew diagrams. For his part, he vowed to master the use of carpentry tools.

After tying his horse, Darcy stood on Cressbrook's stone stoop anticipating not only plans for the tree house, but also the opportunity to see the fruit of Georgiana's sketches. However, his pleasure was distracted when a footman opened the door. Having been sensitive to her brother's raised eyebrow when she included Mr. Hopewell and his wife in dinner stories, Georgiana had omitted mention of the maid and footman. Darcy's surprise slowly seeped to unease fed by Lord Newsome's assertion that secrets were at play at Cressbrook.

Darcy waved off the footman's offer to fetch Miss Darcy, preferring to explore on his own while awaiting Henry's arrival from the bridge site. His tour settled his disquiet after discovering the tenant ladies stitching under the direction of the seamstress, and then meeting two tenants carrying a beautifully refinished table, which they placed between two chairs in the parlor. Darcy relaxed in one of those chairs and admired the transformation wrought by his sister's talent until he considered all of it together. Henry had offered only £500, but even a sorcerer's magic could not stretch £500 so far. Deeply disturbed, Darcy resolved to learn the state of Georgiana's dowry.

"Ah, Darcy, an excellent surprise!" Henry bowed then reached his hand. "Have you seen Georgiana? She's likely upstairs. I'll summon her straight away."

"No need. I arrive with a request for you, Cousin."

Intrigued, Henry led Darcy to his newly completed study, and with great pride, he held the door for his guest. The grey sky roiling outside the long windows could not dampen the serenity of the master's study. "How does it please you? Your sister is amazing, is she not?"

Taken aback by the full effect of the finished room, Darcy admired light blue walls and white woodwork with bookshelves made to look built-in through the clever use of molding. Fabric at the windows and on the furnishings combined patterns and solids to excellent effect. From the large desk backed to the oversized garden window, to a sofa between the front windows, to the tea table flanked by two Queen Annes flanking a tea table near the hearth, the room met every requirement of a gentleman's study.

"Choose your seat, Darcy," he invited.

Henry's pleasure to entertain his cousin in his proper study turned to mirth when he learned Darcy's project. "You must be playing. You and Elizabeth are better advised to scribe odes to your children. You can't hammer a nail!"

"You miss the point. It's precisely our individual limitations that recommend the project. If we can achieve the impossible by constructing a tree house then we can manage anything."

Henry studied Darcy's diagram, after which he opted to make a new sketch according to his cousin's verbal description. He was impressed with Darcy's vision. "I see all of the aspects of the old tree house, yet this is much improved," he exclaimed, and then chuckled, "Are you sure you're not building this for yourself, Cousin?"

Darcy's expression darkened briefly. "Perhaps, in a way," he admitted, "but mostly I knew such joy there that I want the same for my children." Then he confided, "Honestly, my first thought is for Lizzy. I hope to connect her to the children for whom she fears to hope. If it were one child, I doubt this would be an issue, but two at once combined with the sad demise of her cousin compromises her confidence a bit."

Impressed by Darcy's deeper motive and his unaccustomed sharing of feelings, Henry accepted. "I'll take my measurement of the old oak tomorrow and should complete the plans by week's end. Let us toast the impossible."

Mr. Hopewell delivered a decanter and stemware in delicately etched ruby crystal, to which Darcy paid inordinate attention.

"Is there a problem?"

"Where did you procure this set?

Darcy's tone declared Henry's mistake. He had presumed too much ease with his cousin and had not thought to order sherry served in the simple glass service.

"It's a gift from Georgiana... a house warming gift since it warms my heart to see it and remember my aunt."

Darcy tossed back the sherry in one swallow then glared. "You'll pack it immediately and I'll return it to the House. She has no right to disperse Mother's things across the land. I don't fault you. It's Georgiana who has erred."

The fire popped in a room turned cold. "We have a problem, Darcy. I'll only return them to Georgiana and will do so only at her request."

"Do not bait me. I have the right!"

Henry summoned Mr. Hopewell, whispered at the butler's ear, passed him the tray then turned and said, "Sorry, Cousin."

Infuriated, Darcy called after the butler to fetch Miss Darcy to them.

Georgiana's happy greeting to Darcy withered to see cousin and brother standing stiff and apart. And then she stiffened to hear her brother's demand. "Our mother would have given them herself if she were here, Fitzwilliam," she asserted.

"Don't pretend to know her, Sister! I've had quite enough of your presumption and secrecy. You'll request that Henry returns them then you'll accompany me home."

She eyed her cousin. "The set is my gift to Cressbrook. Put it to good use." And to her brother, "You disappoint me, Fitzwilliam."

"I disappoint you?" Darcy raged. "My God, but you have outgrown your place!"

The long ride home was a hell-storm of accusations and demands imposed by a self-righteous temper on a silent young lady who stared straight ahead. Hannah pressed her nails into her palms to keep from defending what her mistress did not.

The full way home, Georgiana considered her response to Darcy. His anger was what she had anticipated at Christmas; hence, she was not so undone as Hannah. After consideration, she was very clear; once arrived at the House, they would discuss on her terms, not his.

Chapter 37

With the basket of flowers on her arm, Mrs. Reynolds knocked on Lady Anne's door as she did each morning. "It's a disparate mix today, Mum," she announced showing the collection of forget-me-nots, yellow tea roses, baby's breath and assorted greens; Lady Anne wanted only perfect blooms no matter their combination. The ivory-colored porcelain vase from Glenbrooke stood ready on the Lady's table.

Six-month-old Georgiana reached for the forget-me-nots as her mother sorted the blossoms with one hand and held her baby with the other. "Yes, those are very pretty, my darling," she kissed her daughter's head, "but we'll set the greens first then the roses, and then the rest."

While Georgiana sat on her lap and played with the petals from the extra rose, Lady Anne took her moment to privately commemorate her freedom. She granted that her triumph to see Glenbrooke's vase displaying Pemberley's beauty represented a grudge she ought to have long since let go of, but when one escapes from hell to heaven, she is permitted to celebrate her deliverance as long as it pleases her.

Georgiana marched a direct path to Lady Anne's chambers despite that Darcy had ordered her to his study. When he crossed their mother's threshold in pursuit, she confronted him.

"You humiliated me."

"Your behavior justifies my response," he countered. "Your secrecy with this room should have undermined my trust, but I forgave you and this is my reward! I insist the decanter set be returned and all of this," his arm made a grand sweep of the room, "be returned to the attics."

"You think our mother is your property alone?"

"I state with assurance that each of the books on these shelves and the gowns in those wardrobes hold real memories for me and only for me."

"Our cousin also loved her, Brother."

"Son and nephew are not the same. Henry knows this, as should you."

Georgiana's eyes flashed. "This is what I know. You're selfish in the worst sense of the word. I deserve her as much as you, whether I own the memories or not."

"What we deserve and what we receive are not ours to control, Georgiana. I ought not be blamed that I was twelve years and you were but two. You cannot know the agony to have known her and then lose her."

"You're more arrogant than I believed possible! Hear me out! While you protect your pain, she weeps for you. You may remember events, but you don't remember her. You left her locked in a dark attic away from the House she loved, untouched by those who loved her."

"The decanter set will be returned, as will her belongings to her trunks."

"Then you'll need crush me to do it."

"You're acting the fool, Georgiana."

"It's not foolish to stand for my mother. It's admiration for a woman I know better than you." She raised her chin. "Do as you will, but know you will fight me to do it."

Darcy paced his study before presenting his case to a sorrowed wife, who Hannah had already apprised of the trouble. Elizabeth did not conceal her sorrow.

"You blame me!" he defended.

"Blame you for loving your mother? No, I do not."

"But in regard to Georgiana, you blame me."

"There's no reason to blame you, my love. You already blame yourself."

"I merely ask that she understands."

Elizabeth shook her head. "You insist that she acquiesces to your orders. It matters not if she understands."

"Do you understand, Lizzy?"

"I understand you were blessed with a mother so dear that her loss remains too much to confront completely." She reached her hand to him. "I also understand that Georgiana has learned her mother through the things you preserved. You each protect the same mother, but you have opposite prescriptions to do it."

"It's an issue of respect that she refuses me."

"Hear yourself, William. You require her both to understand and obey, conflicting demands that bode ill for a positive resolution of your equally passionate positions."

That night, Hannah assisted her mistress to transfer Georgiana's most precious things from her bedchamber to mingle with those in Lady Anne's, and then Georgiana slipped between the sheets of her new quarters.

The next morning, Darcy arrived at his bedchamber to dress and discovered a note leaned on his mantle between the portraits of his parents.

> *My dearest William,*
> *I suggest you read your mother's letters in one sitting, and then consider if your method of "protection" or Georgiana's would please her more.*
> *I love you, Lizzy*

Darcy reread the letters then strolled the Park before knocking at his sister's door. Hannah peeked out from her door across the hall and directed him to Georgiana's new quarters. He had come in conciliation, but his sister's usurpation of their mother's chambers was past forgiveness.

With his first step across Lady Anne's threshold, his criticism crumbled in confusion. Georgiana sat huddled in her favorite chair pulled close to the bank of windows, its flower boxes filled with early primroses. Her eyes, pink-rimmed, stared at nothing. He stopped short to put a name to the floral-scent permeating the room, a scent with a presence that made him sit before querying, "It's Mother's perfume, is it not?"

Georgiana nodded, fresh tears overflowing.

A knock announced Mrs. Reynolds delivering a tray. "My pardon, Sir. I discovered Miss Georgiana as you see her and hoped tea and toast might support her recovery. I take full responsibility, Sir. I so rejoiced to have finally got it right I didn't think what it might cause."

"You refer to the perfume, Mrs. Reynolds?" he asked, trying to make sense of the scene.

"Yes, Sir. She purchased the ingredients in Derby. My Lady had kept the proportions private and I've worked weeks to get it right." Darcy struggled to connect perfume with tears while the Housekeeper cajoled her mistress to one sip and then another.

"She weeps because of a scent, Mrs. Reynolds?" he queried, still confounded.

"She weeps for her mother, Sir. The scent connects her to Lady Anne. I wouldn't have thought a scent could pull a young child's memory from the mists of the forgotten, but it is so."

Mrs. Reynolds curtsied and departed.

Georgiana's voice was so soft it was nearly lost in the sound of the door closing. "Forgive me, Brother. I didn't understand."

"Understand what, Sister?"

"The pain of losing her. I'd so rejoiced to learn her that I saw nothing beyond it." Her words were halting as if she mourned her mother only just deceased.

Her state squeezed Darcy's heart. He sat at her feet and reached to hold her hand. "What else was there for you to see, Georgiana? Is this all the result of perfume?"

She nodded, watching him with eyes made bluer for their pain. "I celebrated when Mrs. Reynolds brought the vial to me this morning. I knew she'd got it right, knew it at once, just as I had known her previous attempts missed the mark. I insisted to dab it everywhere and fill the room with another piece of my mother gone missing." Her eyes watched the details of the room, not him. "I remember, Brother. I remember feelings. I remember happiness to hear her laugh and safeness to feel her arms hug soft and warm around me. I remember the pure feelings of a small child who knew no names for them." And then her eyes embraced him with her pain. "I feel what I've lost and I can't bear it."

Of a sudden, Darcy's pain released and mingled with his sister's. She bent to touch his curls. "I can't conceive how deeply you must feel your loss. All that I have of her floats in the air around us. Her scent alone makes me so sorry that I struggle to breathe." Her tears fell with his. "I want mama. I want her so desperately." Their despair echoed off their mother's walls.

"You may do with her belongings as you wish, Brother. I thought that resettling myself in her bedchamber protected her. I was naïve. These are only things. There's nothing left of her to protect." She rose. Her brother watched Georgiana collect her own things on the bed in the slowed motion of a mourner's disconnection.

At nine o'clock that evening, Darcy arrived at the door of his sister's crowded, blue bird beribboned bedchamber leading a small procession of footmen. The first transported the tea table from Lady Anne's bedchamber and the next three carried a candelabrum, a small clock and a gold-rimmed ivory vase brimming with red roses. The last footman delivered a dinner tray. She stared as Darcy laid the table then held a chair for her to join him at a dinner served on mismatched porcelain. He raised his glass. "To our mother, may she always be remembered."

"I don't understand."

"Understanding can wait. The toast Georgiana - say the words as I spoke them."

While they dined on Lady Anne's favorite menu: roast, Yorkshire pudding and Brussels sprouts, Darcy explained. Their mother especially admired the candelabrum; its elegantly simple design made it comfortable at both a fête and a private meal. She treasured the clock because it made no tic-tock sound; the chimes and gongs of Pemberley's myriad timepieces had sometimes irritated her and she said the silent clock was their secret, son and mother, since papa might sense criticism. The vase had been their mother's mother's; the only item Lady Anne had gotten from Glenbrooke. She had prized it, though she had not elaborated on its significance. The tableware represented her favorite patterns, less elegant in their eclectic combination, but very happy. Darcy paused before confiding, "I had forgotten the vase until planning this dinner. She had asked me to fill it each day with fresh flowers; a promise I didn't keep until this evening."

Georgiana listened then ate because he ate and smiled because he smiled. At the last, she wept again, this time in her brother's arms when he thanked her for returning his mother to him. And when he wept still more memories of Mother, he let her wipe his tears.

Arrived at the pavilion after eleven, Darcy crossed the parquet floor in his stocking feet.

"Did it go well, William?" Elizabeth called from behind the screen.

"I'd hoped not to wake you," he responded, pulling off his jacket and unbuttoning his breeches. He creaked the bed's ropes. "Yes, it went well." Darcy groped for her hand and lifted it to touch his eyes. "I haven't wept so much since father passed, God rest him."

She struggled to sit. "Light a lamp. I will know every detail."

He adjusted the screens, lit the lamp and fluffed the pillows for her comfort before describing the dinner and the discussion thereafter. "It's incongruous and sounds selfish to admit, but I sense that Georgiana's pain helps to heal my own."

"Not so incongruous and certainly not selfish, William. It makes perfect sense that your sibling is best suited to acknowledge and commiserate with your loss."

"Is that what happened?" he asked in amazement. "You slip pieces so easily in place, Wife." He focused on the screen at the foot of her bed. "Georgiana is remarkable."

"As are you, William. There are few men so strong and good to reevaluate their position in light of new facts and then to adjust their understanding without hubris."

"You make me sound the hero," he scoffed.

She smiled the smile that lit her eyes and wrapped him in her warmth. "Perhaps not the art of hero as lauded in histories, but your nature is heroic to me because you consider new points of view despite that they could threaten your comfort." She shifted of a sudden and tugged at her nightdress. "Help me, please." With her great abdomen exposed, she reached for his hands and held them against her warm skin. "Can you feel them move a little?" He nodded. "Would that they will inherit their father's nature since with it they'll be assured a contented life."

His fingers felt a kick and little tickles. "Pardon to disagree, Lizzy, but I don't see that following my path would lead any person to a contented life." He grimaced to recall the arrogance he had so easily and often dispensed "before Elizabeth."

She held his face to look at her. "The issue is not that you are perfect, William, but that you have the courage to perfect what is not. It's a precious quality and will serve our babies better than any inheritance we could pass to them."

Chapter 38

From the library window, the Housekeeper looked across the lawns to where her master waited in shirt sleeves beside sawhorses supporting boards, a hammer and a saw. Soon, Mrs. Darcy would arrive borne on an upholstered wagon pulled across a specially constructed path to get her smoothly from the pavilion to a chaise waiting under the great oak. Mr. Darcy's awkwardness with tools aside, Mrs. Reynolds thought his plan was just the ticket to help his wife bear the boredom that weighed on her spirit. She glanced at a clock, gave a final look at the great oak then hurried to meet the tea tray being delivered to Miss Georgiana in the nursery.

Her young mistress sat in a Queen Anne near the hearth though the day required no fire. Georgiana could be found in this spot most times of the day, a choice that wouldn't raise an eyebrow except that she only sat. The young lady with the energy of three had lost all motivation since experiencing her mama, a thing that would have pained the mama past bearing.

"Ah, here you are Miss and here is tea. I know you didn't order it, but I had a hankering for a cup and thought we might share some together."

"You're very kind, Mrs. Reynolds," Georgiana answered absently.

"Hannah told me yesterday that the last of the furnishings in Cressbrook's drawing room were set in place. Did she tell you as well, Miss? Of course she did. Silly of me to ask. Anyhow, I should like very much to see the room completed and thought we might visit there this afternoon."

"Not today, Mum. Maybe another day, but not today."

Under the great oak, Darcy awaited his wife in his new world of mended fences that he had not known were broken: he smiled to remember his mama and he treasured the sister, who had become his peer. Extraordinary, how small adjustments to one's perspective can alter a person's view to the good, he mused until he sobered to think of Georgiana's persistent unhappiness. She clung to mourning. Together, the Darcys cajoled her to sit with them at mealtime and to join her brother on daily walks. Superficially, she did appear improved, but on closer look, her spirit had gone missing.

Darcy looked up at the sound of Elizabeth's wagon crunching on the gravel path as footmen pushed from behind and another pulled its tongue to steer. Gripping the wagon's padded sides, Elizabeth made a valiant attempt to look more like a mistress than a turnip being borne to market. After Mrs. Darcy settled on the chaise under the great oak with her lemonade in easy reach on a low table, the Darcys had at it.

The new design for the tree house differed from the old in deference to storm damage to the original's supporting limb. The new house on the opposite side of the tree would balance on sturdy limbs that required a separate ladder for access rather than slats nailed to the trunk. While a ladder could easily be had, Darcy deemed it part of the house and would construct it.

Despite judging their project as silly, Elizabeth granted that a day of sun filtering through the leaves delighted her beyond words. *If only I attended a picnic rather than William's humiliation,* she thought. Sipping lemonade, she pretended not to see the third time he hammered his thumb instead of the nail on the first tread to be affixed to the rails.

"Damn it, Lizzy! No man should be born with such limited dexterity!"

"Your talent is in the saddle, William." He ignored her. She admired his tenacity. "Mark where the nails should go then bring it here and let me start them."

"Certainly not! You can't heft a hammer in your condition."

"My condition restricts me to my bottom, not the use of my arms. Mark the places and bring me the board."

With three slats in place, she noted their mistake. "William, come. Look at our ladder."

"It's askew."

"Agreed. Your wife misled you as to the placement of the steps. We must start over."

"But, Lizzy —"

"William, if you expect children to play on this thing, whatever it shows itself to be at the end, it must be safe. Pull it apart. We'll begin again tomorrow."

Darcy took heart. If nothing else, his wife had engaged with their project.

The next morning, Elizabeth opened her eyes to judge the weather past the French doors. Anticipation for another day under the great oak had dissolved all antipathy to their silly project.

Returned to her sun-dappled chaise, she insisted her husband summon Mr. Blake, the master carpenter, to the mess of boards that was William's self-imposed purgatory. The carpenter augmented Darcy's clutch of tools with a plumb bob, a rudimentary level, an awl to punch the board so it would more easily accept the nail, a chisel, a pry-bar to undo mistakes and a device of Mr. Blake's own design that looked much like an oversized pincer to distance one's finger and thumb from the nail, and hence, the hammer. Though Darcy would have at it directly, Elizabeth insisted he practice with each tool, particularly the pincer.

Darcy took his confidence after luncheon and decreed construction would begin. She looked up from her embroidery and insisted, "Keep at your practice, William."

"Unnecessary!" Arrogant both in tone and look, Darcy reached for the level and the first board. "I can do it well enough, Elizabeth."

She snipped at threads to remove several sorry stitches. "Nearly the same words I spoke to my mama when I disdained more practice at needlework and look what it got me."

She poked a needle into linen and he nailed a practice board until tea time.

To Elizabeth's mind, tea at the low table at four o'clock was the sweetest aspect of their day. With a soft breeze fluttering the linen cloth and birdsong as backdrop to their conversation, this small corner of confinement came closest to letting her forget it.

She did not state her contentment directly, but Darcy saw it in her eyes and heard it in her laughter. She even joked a little, and though he was sometimes the butt of it, he bore it well. On the third day, he chanced a tease, which she returned with a laugh and repartee. He had conceived his grand project to supplant fear with happy expectations for her children, but he realized it also set the foundation for their new family.

While the Darcys managed a few straight treads, their sister sat in the nursery she would not complete, nor would she return to Cressbrook. Both were far enough advanced they could be done by others. She would return to Town as soon as Mrs. Coombes could free her schedule.

Georgiana's trouble was not mourning mama, though it was convenient that her family believed so. Instead, she had mulled her feelings regarding Henry's choice and the result left her numb. The memory of his "I love you with all my heart, Georgiana Darcy" promised he felt for her as she had dreamed he might, but his willingness to disdain his feelings spoke poorly for him. She questioned if the love each felt for the other were different since her love would fight against all odds to win him if she thought there were a chance. Perhaps his powers of reasoning were a myth; a rational mind would not hold their love hostage to a childhood relationship. Either way, he missed the mark as a person, in whom she would vest her life. She would always admire him for his worthy aspects, but she no longer blindly loved him. And so she sat, hardened by disappointment that she would never have believed could be delivered by Henry's hand.

Chapter 39

George Darcy wandered Fin Cop, the ancient grassland where with one unin-terrupted sweep of the eye a man knew from whence he had come and where he was going. The autumn grass, brittle in the wind, scraped his boots and studded his breeches with its seed. With tears streaming down his cheeks, he considered Anne's choice that would tear his life from him.

She was five months pregnant with their son's sibling: a child denied them by nine years of miscarriages. However, the granting of their greatest wish presented George the agony of one joy traded for another. He would bury his beloved wife, if she kept the child or would lose the child if she accepted the surgery to remove her cancer. Given, there was no assurance she would survive the surgery, but Dr. Ashworth believed there was a chance and George held to chance as promise. The mighty wills of master and mistress had collided over the meaning of happiness. In the absolute reality of life and death, his Anne had chosen for the life that had the best chance to survive.

Henry did not know the crux of Georgiana's trouble, but he was certain it was not the mourning of her mother. When he had delivered the tree house plans to Darcy, Georgiana had been summoned to tea, at which she selected three iced petit fours and a chocolate bon-bon for her plate. People in mourning tended to prefer bread, the more fresh the better, not sugar confec-tions. More importantly, she did not wince once to hear her mother's name in conversation; a point tested multiple times from different vantages by Henry. Physical evidence made clear she was in severe distress, but she did not sit with stiffly squared shoulders; hence, her issue was not stubborn support of some cause. She did, however, appear benumbed. The light had left her eyes and he thought they dimmed a bit more when he spoke or a reference was made to him. Her monotone voice revealed no clues beyond echoing the obvious; Georgiana, the person and personality, had been compromised.

Returned to Cressbrook that evening, Henry made preparation: Hawkins would tend Cressbrook's ledgers while Broadstone was made foreman at the bridge site. The master of Cressbrook would devote himself without interruption to isolating the cause of his Princess' trouble, and then attempt to relieve her of it.

Henry was confident he knew Georgiana as well as he knew himself. Honesty, however, required him to amend that observation. Since he had not begun to learn much about himself before Cressbrook, he likely knew Georgiana better than himself. To him, she had made herself an open book, from which he now methodically gathered his evidence. Her humor differentiated between important and less so; hence, her trouble was so serious she could not laugh at it. Her logic and analytical skills were excellent; hence, she had inspected her problem from all sides and her conclusion was irrefutable. Her values were deep-set; hence, a serious and irrefutable issue challenged the essence of what she held dearest, meaning the trouble centered on Darcy, Elizabeth, Henry or her art.

Late in his first day of deliberation, Henry Fitzwilliam quit his Hall to wander Cressbrook's paths. He had deduced he might be the cause of his Georgiana's trouble. After two hours, he had come full circle and found himself in the little woods between the road and the cliff. The wind rustled the leaves in a night with only stars for light. He first sat on his log then stood and crossed to the stone where Georgiana had sat, metaphorically stepping in her shoes and reliving events since Christmas from her view. From confusion at being shunned without explanation, to admitting her love for him in the face of his disdain… from hearing explanations of his feelings that exhibited no feeling of substance to listening to him openly declare his love then deny it to her. Henry sat accused and found guilty. He had done this to her.

Though Henry thought he had deduced the riddle of his Princess' problem in less than twenty-four hours, he required a fortnight to accept how he would address it. At the end of two weeks, he arrived at the pavilion at tea time gratified by the Darcys' delight to see him; however, the same could not be said for Georgiana. Miss Darcy's soft voice contributed very little to the several hours of conversation. When Henry took his leave near eight o'clock, he glanced at Georgiana and invited her into the pretty evening beyond the French doors. Darcy pressed his sister to accept their cousin's invitation to hear the progress at Cressbrook.

Their feet made better conversation with the gravel than did the couple with each other. He knew she would neither accept discussion on a topic she had declared closed, nor believe the renewed pledge of his feelings after too much disappointment. He had but one hope to reach her.

After a half-mile, he broke silence. "I've missed you, Princess."

"It's my teases, not me that you miss," she discounted softly.

After another half-mile he said, "Much has changed at Cressbrook, Georgiana."

She responded dispassionately, "I'm glad for you Henry."

More minutes. They had returned to the hedge separating the lawn and the formal garden.

With trepidation, he reached inside his jacket. "I wrote you a poem."

Georgiana balked against accepting the watermarked sheet folded like a kite and sealed with red wax. The last poem, as sweet as it had been, had hurt more than it had satisfied.

As if in conversation with an acquaintance, she commented, "I hadn't guessed during our years of correspondence that you were partial to rhyming. Do you write much poetry, Cousin?"

"Only to you, Princess," he said honestly.

She raised her brow, distancing herself from the emotion he implied. "Then I should like to read it." She took the kite-poem and slipped her finger under the flap to break the seal.

"No. Please. Wait until you're alone, Georgiana." He reached to stop her then stuffed his hands in his pockets, too aware that he again offered to her, and then qualified how he offered it.

"You make it seem more personal than I'm prepared to read," she said coolly. Only the natural softness of her voice declared it was Georgiana who spoke. She had, indeed, cut him off completely.

He escorted her in silence along the gravel drive and under the east portico where they passed through the arched entrance to the House's interior courtyard. He paused at the steps leading to Pemberley's front doors. "I am sincere that I miss you, Georgiana. Whether it's your talent to square me to reality or my pleasure to know you're in my Hall, a man is stuck with his deepest thoughts when his Princess goes missing."

"You are a remarkable man to be so open with your feelings." Her tone promised she did not celebrate him to be very open or remarkable. She curtsied and quit him.

While Georgiana prepared for bed, a kite-poem watched her from the window table. She would have left it lying there, but for Hannah's long ago admonition "have it done." She broke the seal and read the perfectly scribed lines inside.

Following a very slow read, she leaned back in her favorite chair and closed her eyes. The breeze from the courtyard played with a tendril at her ear.

I stand at my window teared by the rain
In my study made lovely by your hand,
And am caught by the truth of love's refrain
That without you, I'm but half a man.
Yes, it is difficult to hold the child
I protected as sister all her life,
But harder still is the terrible trial
To face life without you as my dear wife.
I have made my choice, though perhaps too late
To entice your trust and your devotion.
If you can but forgive this pitiful mate,
For your hand I will cross any ocean.
That I write rather than speak shows my fear
I no longer have my Princess' ear.

I love you, Georgiana. I humbly request to court you in the hope you might accept
to be my wife and partner as you already are and forever will be in my heart.
In deepest devotion, Henry

Georgiana sat impassive while hope and despair waged battle inside her.

Henry paced his master's suite across the Wye. His fear that he might fail to overcome his self-loathing to touch her mocked that he had any chance to win her And equally as sobering, he feared just as much that she would not give him the opportunity to try to touch her.

He slept fitfully.

Chapter 40

The door latch of Cressbrook's master suite clicked Henry awake. "Name yourself!"

"It's me." The soft voice of hope had conquered trudging in the night, clambering through a study window and feeling her way in darkness up the Hall's backstairs in stocking feet.

"My God, Georgiana!" He glanced at the clock as she laid her cloak across a chair. "It's four in the morning!"

The moon lit the way to his bedside. She tossed the kite poem on his bedcover then creaked the bed ropes to sit beside it. "I walked with a lantern." She had practiced her words as diversion from night noises. "I left a note. Hannah will say I came early to see the progress here." Georgiana looked him in the eye. "I will understand your message, Henry."

If it had been anyone else, he would have opened his arms and invited, "Come," but she was Georgiana. After too long, he said, "Let me dress" and motioned her leave.

With his poem in hand, Georgiana sat on a slipper chair in the upper hall where the balustrade overlooked the foyer. She waited full aware that his voice had sounded of fear, not love. She committed the sight of him in his bed to memory: the blanket clasped to his chin to cover his nakedness, his bare shoulders rippling muscles grown to meet the needs of his estate, and the shadow of his beard making him even more handsome than his day-self. He arrived after more minutes than were required to dress formally though he had only pulled on breeches, shirt, and jacket. She knew that a lover ought not require extra time to compose himself.

They walked in silence along Bottom Hill Road to where it split and dipped to the bridge site. He offered his arm. She declined. Enough trees had been cleared to let the moonlight finger through. Standing near the edge of the ravine, he pointed out the progress on either side where thick cedar logs had been wedged into holes chiseled in the rock then he described the stages that would follow. He felt her eyes on him throughout.

He turned and let honesty speak. "As I stated in the poem, Georgiana, I've made my choice for us, but shall proceed slowly to allow me to adjust."

"Adjust to touching your sister?"

He nodded, discomfited by how she said it, and then disquieted that she watched him as if learning him for the first time.

"You are a beloved friend, Henry; a friend who would make all right in the world if he could." Her expression conveyed more than sadness… pity. "I doubt there exists a man as wonderful as the man I loved." She laughed at herself for what loving him had cost her. "You've set the mark so high I chance to be a spinster."

He opened his mouth to speak. She shook her head.

"No more, dear Henry. The distance is too great between what you offer and what I want. It's a distance that words can't bridge." She handed him his poem and ran the path that would carry her home to sit at breakfast before Darcy learned she had been missing.

Henry Fitzwilliam stood transfixed. The looking glass Georgiana had held to him reflected a spineless man… a man he didn't recognize as himself until he looked down to see the kite-poem in his hand. Of all the shackles he'd thrown off during the past three months, this one gloated to have succeeded in binding him to a history of second best. He wadded his words, threw them to the ground and tore after her.

He ran… ran through tall grass damp with dew, slipping down a steep slope to catch up via a short cut. Despite his speed, he could not see her until finally he glimpsed her cape nearing the footbridge. "Georgiana," he called. "Georgiana, wait!"

"No more, Henry." She called over her shoulder. "I don't want you."

He caught her at the footbridge in the half-light of dawn. She pulled away. He held fast, out of breath. "But I want you … for my wife… the mother of my children."

She turned her back to him, but did not step to cross the bridge.

"Kiss me, Georgiana."

She stood her ground. "A man who wants a kiss does it himself."

He followed orders and turned her to him, held her face with trembling hands and closed his eyes. His lips touched his love in a symphony that swooned his head and made him gasp to know the taste of such emotion.

If Georgiana had had confidence in the art of kissing, she would have appreciated his effort to overcome the bounds of sibling-like attachment, but she was too nervous. When he bent to her, she recalled the Darcys' kiss at Christmas. When his lips touched hers, she was lost in him, but when they parted, nerves returned to let her worry she had done her part poorly.

They shared a boulder at the edge of the Cress Brook, where its waters tumbled white past the green cushion of cress. He breathed hard.

"Was it so awful?" she asked, staring straight ahead. Her voice trembled at her failure. "I hadn't thought my kiss would make a man draw away." He did not respond. She continued, mortified. "Perhaps my inexperience makes you reconsider. I know that I'm not so –"

"Be still, Georgiana!"

She turned, "Pardon?"

Naked in his emotion, he said, "You presume wrong. Give me a moment and I'll explain." The inveterate teacher blushed exceedingly as he stumbled to relate the physical facts of a man who had been without a woman for a year; her lips had aroused him nearly past control.

He did not anticipate her laugh and declaration, "But this is excellent!"

"Dear God, what can be excellent about a man who lusts with his first kiss?"

She sobered. "If the body lusts, then you've given up the child and accept me as a woman." The term "woman" caught in her throat, but she swallowed to accept this was what she offered... what she wanted to be to him. Best Friend was not enough; woman was all that was left. Shyly, she took her courage and leaned to brush her lips across his. Again, he pulled away.

Still tuned more to her nerves than his facts, she withdrew. "I'll do it better with practice. I regret I compare poorly to the others who –"

The invocation of "others" fired his anger, which conveniently cooled his passion. "If you mention 'others' again, I'll lose my temper, Georgiana Darcy! There *are* no others or are you too stubborn to see it?" He calmed to see her innocence warmed by the blush of dawn, and then added softly, "I've never kissed a lady I love, Georgiana... not until now. You are the first."

She controlled her curiosity to hear every detail of his admiration. Though their bodies did not touch, his scent embraced her and drew her nearer. Indeed, when she put her mind to it, she could make anything happen. Slowly, she pulled his arm around her. He did not recoil. She laid her head on his shoulder. He kissed her forehead, her cheek, her lips… softly, shyly… kisses that suddenly ignited her deep-inside with the mystery of passion. She pressed herself against his chest, her arms locked around his neck, her lips, now not so shy, caressing his face until he echoed her intensity, briefly.

Bubbles in the brook merged with the Wye. He shook his head. "My God, but you test me Georgiana. Who'd have thought…"

She sensed he prattled to temper desire, to change the subject, so to speak, but once aroused, she took no interest in diversions. She let him converse with himself, while she considered their reality: a man who offered himself in a poem, then hedged his offer, then embraced her… and then what? She worried new fears might consume him and old illogic might compromise resolve, a possibility she would forestall with a connection he could not break, though she had no concept how to do it. *If one presents oneself as confident, so one will be perceived.*

"Come, we'll stroll Cressbrook." She stood and offered him her hand.

"A stroll? But I just invited you to breakfast. I presumed we'd take it on the terrace."

"Another morning." She laughed. "At present I'm not hungry and would rather walk. You may fetch a loaf from Mrs. Hopewell, if you like."

With a basket swinging on his left arm and Georgiana attached to his right, they smiled morning greetings to tenants along the way. She led him uphill along Bottom Hill Road toward Village Lane. Once past the lane, the road dwindled to a wagon rut nearly overgrown. Dew collected on her hem. She invited him to a porch in the abandoned clutch of old stone houses overlooking Ravensdale then coaxed him to lean back and feel the sun as it tipped onto the grassy, upper reaches of the brook. Ravens circled overhead, cawing conversation as they swooped to find their breakfast. Georgiana broke the loaf while Henry uncorked the wine, a quick substitute for more difficult-to-transport hot tea. They made their breakfast under gently swaying branches.

He daydreamed their future aloud while she reassured herself that nature would guide the uninitiated. Slowly, she invited them to kisses that teased without words, of touches that caught one's breath, of gasps that bespoke passion whose surface they only grazed. He pushed her at arm's length, insisting they return to the Hall. But she distracted him with her own dreams of the future, her head resting on his chest. He calmed and played with the remnants of her curls. She could hear his heart thump and his breath, a gentle whoosh of air, as if both his heart and breath belonged to her.

"I love you, Henry Fitzwilliam," she declared, stroking his hair and looking long into his eyes. She had gleaned enough about kisses to tingle his every nerve before he pulled away. The woman he had awakened breathed in short breaths. "Please, kiss me as if I'm your wife." Her look promised she had taken her choice. "Kiss me, husband."

He blamed himself that he could have, should have taken control, but her hand, slipped inside his shirt, distracted him until pulling away would have humiliated her. Better stated, he wanted her too much. Time suspended… he loosed pins and tumbled her hair past her shoulders. Time suspended… she loosed buttons and slipped his hand inside her bodice. Time suspended …

Dear God in Heaven.

Later, he settled her to lie on him as a cushion against stiff floorboards. The sun glinted off the perfumed gold of fine hair cascaded around his face. He worried he had hurt her too much. Her kisses convinced him otherwise.

Reality required action. "We'll marry straight away. I'll visit Darcy this morning."

She recalled the Christmas fisticuffs. "And my brother's response?"

"You're of age. If he refuses, we'll elope."

She shook her head. "I want a proper wedding with my family in attendance."

He replied slowly, "There's an even chance you'll not get a proper wedding with me."

The prospect of elopement sobered Georgiana. She pressed her ear to his heart until she was certain of her own. "I want to marry with my family as witness, Henry."

Knowing Georgiana, he would have predicted this would be her choice. He tried to connect the lady in his arms with the princess he had been loath to touch, but try as he might, he could no longer meet that girl; her memory sat in history as if another part of him had lived it.

"Help me understand the problem with my brother."

"I know Darcy loves me, but his love is tangled in competition I don't understand. I am certain, however, that on the point of our marriage, he'll be ill-disposed to give his blessing.

Volume III

Chapter 41

Shortly before luncheon, Mr. Fitzwilliam and Miss Darcy descended Hayfield with proper distance separating them. Georgiana wondered if Henry only wished to convey the innocence of their morning picnic or if he felt the same shyness as she. Their passion on the porch in Ravensdale seemed far away as they followed the overgrown path into everyday life.

Henry ordered luncheon served in his study then fetched a small looking glass and comb with which his lady could tidy the disheveled locks hid beneath her bonnet. While she waited, Georgiana read the note Hannah had left for her on the hall table.

> *Dear Miss Georgiana,*
>
> *I cannot tell you my relief to learn you arrived safely at Cressbrook. I did as you instructed and, as best I could, deflected concern about your choice to set out alone. Your brother had a dark look and quit the breakfast table early. Mrs. Darcy apologized, referring to a recent letter that had made him too sensitive.*
>
> *The day is so pretty that Mr. Hawkins asked to take his lessons in the field nearest the woods past the stables, which is where I shall be if you need me.*
>
> *Sincerely, Hannah Miller*

Georgiana slipped the note in her pocket; the last of her ebullience had collapsed to read it. Her brother's issues with Henry aside, she had likely compromised his acceptance of their marriage by hiding her feelings for Henry from all but Elizabeth. Inadvertently, she had repeated her childhood mistake of revealing only part of herself to her brother, a mistake that boded ill if the news of her early trek to Cressbrook had caused her brother to quit his breakfast.

Returned with comb and mirror, Henry was discomfited by her changed demeanor and worried she regretted their morning tryst. Despite his connection with the woman, his guardian's habit pressed him to protect her from events that proceeded more quickly than her youth might wholly embrace. It did not occur to him it was she who had initiated their union. Mr. Hopewell served luncheon to uncommonly quiet cousins.

When she focused on her plate, not him, Henry took it as corroboration of her regret. "You're very quiet, Princess. Are you… are you sorry for this morning?"

She looked up, confused. "Sorry? About what?"

He had not thought he would need detail the topic and was ill-prepared to explain. "I only wonder whether you require time to consider –" He avoided her eyes as he groped for words. "I mean, I don't want to presume too much if you're not ready."

She scraped back her chair, tossed her napkin on the table and crossed to the large window faced on the walled garden, the neglected corner of Cressbrook now cleared of its tangled undergrowth and awaiting proper landscaping. With her back squared, she snuffed whatever discussion Henry had tried to begin. He stood behind her, hands in his pockets.

"Forgive me. My query was meant to support, not challenge you."

"Is this how it will be when we're married?" she queried. "You accept me as your peer one minute then question my maturity in the next?" Georgiana turned and looked him in the eye. "I have so much to prove to my brother in regard to my feelings for you, I don't have the energy to also need prove them to you." She raised her chin. "I shall only marry a man who trusts me as well as he trusts himself. Do you require time to consider *your* choice, Sir?"

He smiled, shook his head and embraced her all at once. "There is no choice, Georgiana," he whispered. "You are the love of my life."

Later as they sat close on the sofa discussing her brother's inconsistency in Henry's regard, Georgiana understood that she and Henry would require many more "moments of adjustment" like their misunderstanding at breakfast. Years of accumulated habit on both sides demanded that each habit be confronted before they settled firmly into their partnership.

She lay her head on his shoulder. "Do you feel it?" she asked. "We conversed just now like we did this morning, speaking our hearts without interference of age or obligation." She looked up at him. "Is it silly to wonder if our hearts have been talking for years only we couldn't hear them, because I was too young and you were too protective?" His kiss answered for him.

Appreciation of their own history, however, did not better her understanding of her brother's inconsistency toward Henry. When she asked for specific examples, he offered the fisticuffs at Christmas. "My response to his off-handed query about your room decoration provoked him, which hindsight declares to be understandable. The problem is that he didn't trouble to query for background as he would do of any other who raised his ire. And more troubling still is that he not only blamed me, but he also judged me, me who when he's in a different frame of mind he calls 'brother.' His animosity is unpredictable, but when it shows itself, it is heartfelt."

"Why do you accept from him what you wouldn't do from others?"

Henry watched the fire. "I promised your parents I'd stand by him. He apologizes for his anger, Georgiana, but never for his love. I like to think this means he loves me more than not."

"Do you fear his eruptions?"

He chuckled, "Fear? No, I'm not afraid of him." His smile slipped into sadness. "I suppose I prefer to think love is all he feels for me and am disappointed when he shows the opposite."

"Henry," Georgiana sat up and watched him, "do you think you might have hesitated to acknowledge your feelings for me to avoid confrontation with him?"

Disconcerted, he crossed to stare at the empty garden beds then turned, crestfallen. "I hate to think he could influence me so, but, yes, it's possible. Forgive me, Georgiana."

She hurried to him and hugged his chest. "There's naught to forgive. We each have catered to him, I even more than you. It's another habit we must work to let go of."

Before their last kiss of the afternoon, they shared one more animated discussion, this in regard to the necessity of a carriage, in which Mr. Fitzwilliam would transport his bride. She argued against unneeded expense, but he won out. They agreed to ask Darcy's blessing before Henry departed for Town to make his purchase of a used conveyance.

Under the shade of the great oak, Elizabeth watched her husband stand back to admire the few slats on the ladder and glow his pride in a job well done. Straight, square and firmly fixed, they were the preeminent achievement of a man who privately had begun to wonder if he could do it. He patted himself on the back since Elizabeth did not. "What say you, Wife? A very professional result, I think."

She tossed him the gauntlet as gently as possible. "It is indeed excellent, but it's only three steps that required two days. We've mastered the art, but fail in the alacrity."

Deflated by her poke of reality, he sank to a squat, focusing on the limbs where his ladder must reach before he could hoist the floor joists and begin the actual house. "I can't do it, can I?"

"Sit with me, William." He sat on the edge of her chaise. She held his hand. "We *can* do it. You've proven your skill with tools and I've proven mine to interpret the plans to you, but *we* are limited by inexperience and most especially because I can't hold the boards while you have at them with your hammer. I submit we are best advised to add an extra pair of arms."

"No!" He turned sharply. "The value is lost if it's done with hands other than our own."

She studied the ladder, admiring the success she had wrongly doubted they could achieve. "I'll leave it to you to resolve our dilemma, Husband. But keep in mind that your wife and children will be disappointed if you forfeit our dream to the small problem of a pair of hands."

At tea time, the ladder boasted one more step: perfectly spaced, perfectly square, yet too slowly done when considering the entire project. But Darcy celebrated nonetheless since Elizabeth had included their children among those who looked forward to its completion.

Flushed with success to have coaxed her acceptance that their babies would live to play among the leaves of the old oak, Darcy privately admitted the reason for his snail's pace. He lacked the confidence to secure the frame and lay the floor joists when the ladder was completed; hence, he stalled the ladder's progress. Indeed, his issue was inexperience, a hurdle he granted he could master with trial and error, but they lacked the luxury of years for him to do it.

Darcy's personal debate was interrupted by Georgiana, who arrived behind the footman bearing the tea tray. She kissed their cheeks then sat contritely on the end of Elizabeth's chaise.

"I wish to apologize. Hannah said you were upset that I traveled without her this morning."

Darcy scowled. Elizabeth interceded, "We hope this doesn't set a precedent that will be oft repeated, Sister. We were concerned."

"Yes. I mean I understand you worried and I'm sorry for it, and no, it will not set a precedent." Georgiana opened a folder, "If you're not too angry, I'll share what lured me there so early." Her design for that estate's annual well dressing plaque was only partially done, but to an inartistic person, it did look to represent a day's work.

"You could have as well drawn this at Pemberley," Darcy said, curtly.

"That was my intention," she replied, "until I realized I must know which blooms are in season. It's been weeks since I was there and the plaque must be decorated with what is available on the grounds of the estate it represents."

Though she had successfully ameliorated her family's disapprobation, Georgiana's stomach churned. She had consciously lied with the goal to deceive. It felt very different from a child protecting her brother with the pretense of a dependent sister.

The next morning, Elizabeth settled back on her chaise under the great oak with her embroidery in hand when a stranger's voice startled her needle to miss a stitch.

"Good day, Sir." A lad in his mid-teens, garbed in tunic and trousers, bowed first to Mr. Darcy and then to Missus.

"Mrs. Darcy, may I introduce Christopher. He'll be the extra arms you recommended."

Darcy basked in her looks of admiration when he detailed his arrangement at luncheon. Christopher, a novice apprenticed to Mr. Blake, understood the rudiments of construction without the confidence to usurp the project from the Darcys. He would add his hands when bade to do so, and when they confronted a conundrum they could not untangle, they would invite his suggestion for consideration. At the end of the lad's first day, a perfect ladder supported Darcy's climb into the leaves of the old oak without a squeak.

The afternoon tea tray arrived, and shortly thereafter, so did Georgina and Henry, which Darcy counted as fortuitous and presented his ladder with exceeding pride. Elizabeth, however, studied her sister and cousin soberly. She perceived their connection before Henry announced it with the second cup of tea.

"Darcy, I arrive on a serious mission that custom would have me address in private, but since we're family, I'll do it now," he began.

Darcy sobered, sensing a challenge. "Go on."

Elizabeth returned her cup to the tray. Georgiana slid nearer Henry on the blanket.

"It's a matter of the heart to which you've not been privy. I myself wasn't unaware of my deepest attachment until this past Christmas. I rejoice to announce my feelings are reciprocated."

Elizabeth watched Georgiana, who blushed a little and looked very happy. But Darcy, too relieved that a betrothal not a challenge was Henry's topic, focused only on him. "We celebrate with you and extend our congratulations." He slapped Henry's shoulder with a laugh, "Honestly, I'd wondered if you'd ever settle on just one. We're glad to welcome another to our little family. Who is the lady?"

"That's the point, Darcy. We won't be adding another to our number."

Darcy looked confused. His wife braced herself.

Georgiana's soft voice continued for them both. "I'm the lady, Fitzwilliam."

"We ask your blessing on our union, Darcy," Henry said with hand outstretched.

Fitzwilliam Darcy sat stiff on the edge of Elizabeth's chaise. The breeze jostled his curls around a face turned to stone. He ignored his cousin's hand, bowed, and made haste toward the House. Elizabeth watched her lap to afford the couple privacy.

No matter Henry's description of what might lie in store, Georgiana had not believed her brother would include her in the spurning of "his brother." She panicked, "Do something, Henry!" Then pleaded, "Please, do something to make it right."

"I explained our history, Princess." He rose. "I'll do my best, but understand that he might make you choose between us." He crossed the lawns to meet the master in his study.

Georgiana's happiness puddled in drips on her gown. Elizabeth called softly for her sister to join to her. "It will be well," Elizabeth soothed. "William requires time to adjust. I fear he was blind to the hints of your attachment which makes this more a shock than cause for celebration."

"It's more than that, Lizzy." Georgiana described the imbalanced relationship of two brothers-who-were-not until Henry stormed across the lawns, nodded to Elizabeth, and summoned Georgiana to him. He spoke in low tones, kissed her cheek, and galloped off.

Georgiana returned to her sister. "He departs for Town to purchase a carriage for his bride's transport. On his return, he'll settle the issue with my brother," and then she cloistered herself in her bedchamber on a threadbare, overstuffed chair.

Chapter 42

Young Darcy indulged his mama with a smile when she spoke of his cousin's impending arrival, but at five years of age, the child was content with his rabbits and dogs. Mostly however, he loved his mama: her smell, her smile, her way of making something foreign understandable, like why a big frog sat on the back of a little one and her singular way to make him feel like the most loved little boy in the world.

Despite his parents' efforts to prepare him, Darcy did not fully comprehend the meaning of "having your cousin live with us" until the second month when Darcy's favorite dog followed Henry instead of him and wild emotion sank little teeth into the cousin's arm. Darcy had never seen his mother angry, at least not with him, and he shrank inside when she scolded with a furious look. Shortly thereafter, mama bandaged Henry's arm and kissed him, and papa tousled Henry's tight, sandy curls. Their son, momentarily left out, filled with a foreign feeling.

As much as he loved Henry, as much as he cherished their secrets and their giggles long past bedtime, little Darcy hated to see his parents love his cousin and he took pleasure when Henry fell from grace. On the odd occasion when a particularly peevish mood let the younger stick out his foot to help the elder fall, Darcy suffered awful guilt made worse because Henry never told on him.

For three days, the Darcys' tree house remained a ladder climbing into leaves while the Darcy siblings negotiated Georgiana's future. Elizabeth offered reason to balance her husband's passion, but mostly she sat at the side sorting her family's confusion in her diary.

Pemberley, 25 May, 18- -

My gladness for Henry and Georgiana is compromised by hints that they place William's feelings above their own; a choice that bodes ill for a happy union.

My greater concern, however, is for William's response to their betrothal. His illogical attacks on our cousin frighten me for our family's future. My husband awaits confirmation from the Bank of London as to Henry's interest in Georgiana's dowry; a silly thing since Henry refused William's offer of a stipend to improve Cressbrook. That Lord Newsome's allegation of Henry's duplicity sits at the root of William's sensitivity is even more illogical since that man expressed his passion for Georgiana as a union of land holdings. Most recently, William confronts our sister with detailed evidence of Henry's flirtations to raise doubt about his character which-

She closed her diary as Darcy burst through the pavilion's doors in agitation.

"I entertained Georgiana for the past hour." He drew a chair close to the settee. "She proposes a compromise, Lizzy! As if one compromises when one truly loves another!"

"Calm yourself, William. Describe the compromise."

"She'll attend the Summer Season in Town to demonstrate that time and distance do not diminish her feelings for him. In return, I must convey my blessing."

"And …? William, your tone implies you find your part difficult."

"Consider the facts, Wife! This isn't how a betrothal rooted in love unfolds. There's been no courtship, no sign they share any feelings beyond guardian and ward. It's not right."

She dispatched her husband to inspect progress at the New Road then organized her thoughts and invited her sister to a private tête-à-tête. Georgiana corroborated the details of the compromise, after which Elizabeth did not mince words. "You divide your allegiance, Sister."

"You miss the point, Lizzy. I'm assured of Henry's devotion and commitment. If three weeks at the summer season will convince my brother then they are weeks well spent."

Elizabeth's talent to view an issue from each party's perspective made her heart pound for the honest emotion on all sides, despite that William's was irrational. "If I were in your place, I wouldn't accept the disparagement of my love no matter the person arguing against him."

"It's more complicated for me, Lizzy. It's been only a few months since I discovered my mother and but three weeks since my brother and I have connected as never before. I've only just got my family, and if a compromise preserves it, then the social season is a small price. My family is too precious, Lizzy."

"Henry is your first family, if you love him."

"I do love him! Why is it no one trusts my words?"

"Because words are easy and actions are not."

"Do you suggest I marry Henry without my brother's blessing?" Georgiana looked her sister in the eye. "It would end my connection to Pemberley, Lizzy. Brother has implied as much. He believes my child's admiration has become infatuation and he blames Henry for taking advantage of it. Elopement would imply to my brother that Henry is so desperate to control my dowry that he scoffs at the tradition of a family's blessing to do it." Elizabeth accepted this might be Darcy's reasoning, a point of honesty that muddled her argument and let Georgiana take her own counsel.

Each morning, the younger Darcy escaped to Cressbrook under the pretense to supervise the preparation of the well dressing plaque and every afternoon she returned pretending to the camaraderie she hoped to preserve with her brother.

Her daily absence permitted the Darcys their own escape under the great oak, their respite from the strain of family meals that too carefully avoided an opinion on any topic for fear of compromising the brother and sister's truce. Darcy had agreed: if she promised an honest go at the summer season and still wanted Henry on her return, he would announce their betrothal at Christmas. In deference to Cressbrook's well dressing fête, her departure was set for 8 June.

On the first day of June, a fine, plum-colored conveyance emblazoned with a gold "C," scrolled inside a golden oval, pulled-to under the east portico shortly after tea. It was clear by the dust on both carriage and driver that Henry had traveled directly to Pemberley on the last leg of his journey. Darcy set his jaw to see his cousin. Elizabeth held her breath. And Georgiana made to go to him, but of a sudden her world moved in slowed motion. Henry jumped from the driver's seat and dusted his breeches as he negotiated the garden paths to arrive at the French doors before she could warn him. She knew her mistake before one word was uttered.

"Darcy, I request our private consultation in your study," Henry began, as if continuing discussion from the previous week.

"No need, Cousin. Georgiana has resolved the issue." Darcy's surly tone conveyed control of what ought to have been Henry's. Georgiana stared. Elizabeth's eyes narrowed.

Henry glanced at Georgiana then focused on Darcy. "Proceed."

"My sister acknowledges the worthiness of my concern in regard to your proposed nuptials and agrees to…" Darcy delineated the details with special emphasis on the test of his sister's devotion and only fleeting mention of a wedding announcement at Christmas. Georgiana had let Henry discover his part in a play already scripted while she watched her lap, too undone to confront her brother's twisting of the facts. From her chaise propped with pillows, Elizabeth hid her eyes and bit her tongue, too angry to let William see her look and too fearful she might intercede; she would not contribute to Henry's humiliation. Privately, Darcy granted the arrogance of his tone, but control of a potential problem far out-weighed any conscience for manners. At the last, he challenged his cousin to accept the conditions.

Without a word or backward glance, Henry turned on his heel and quit them. The silence was interrupted only by his footfall on the colonnade's stone walkway. Georgiana scraped back her chair and lifted her skirts to chase after him. For his part, Darcy took refuge in innocence against his wife's accusatory look. "What? It was my right to present her compromise," he defended.

"I didn't know you hated him, Mr. Darcy."

Georgiana did not catch up until Henry reached to climb to the driver's bench of the vehicle he no longer cared for. His pride in his carriage had collapsed with the rest of the celebration he had brought to Pemberley.

"Henry, please!" Georgiana pulled on his sleeve.

He glanced expressionless and took the first step to the bench and his escape.

"Please!" She made to climb after him.

"Please what?" he erupted. "I'm too undone at present to please anyone. Let me be until I've collected myself."

"No, please, we must discuss!"

His eyes bore into her. "Discuss? You discussed with Darcy, who announced the fruit of it to me. I didn't anticipate nor do I accept a wife who announces to her husband."

Those few moments in the sun away from Darcy and confronted with a Princess whose sorrow evolved to grief before his eyes, those moments invited insight where there had been only despair. He understood her interest in compromise. He understood that he railed against her instead of Darcy. And he even understood it had been Darcy's history to trump his cousin by controlling the last word, a circumstance Henry would no longer tolerate.

"Come, we'll walk a bit," he offered.

Georgiana's stomach required their detour from the path shaded by towering lymes. He held her shoulders, and after she calmed, he plucked the most delicate leaves from the wild mint they had passed and laid them on her tongue. They proceeded in silence until he took his stand. "You must accept one thing, Georgiana. My wife will discuss with me and announce to others. Before you agree to my condition, I ask you to consider carefully."

"Do you forgive me?"

"Yes, if it eases your heart, but truly there's naught to forgive. We hadn't discussed this; hence, neither of us grasped its significance. We understand now, however. I'll not press you to choose for me, nor do I require a hasty response. It's too important." She honored his request to seriously consider, honored it for a full five paces before she faced him with a raised chin.

"I'll fetch my cloak and bonnet. We'll elope today."

"And Darcy?"

"Let him respond as he will. I'll not lose you."

Her words undid his heartache. "Georgiana, do you truly believe your compromise would earn Darcy's unreserved blessing?"

Hearing Henry state it so, Georgiana understood Elizabeth's message. "I can believe very little in regard to my brother at present. I had hoped my offer would calm whatever goads him to turn on you. He continues to treat me as a child and you as his lackey."

Henry chuckled. "Lackey?"

"Can you think of a better term? He insisted that you take Cressbrook, but denies you his sister, as if... as if, you're a puppet he can manipulate according to his interest." The last whiffs of Georgiana's confusion cleared. "To be full honest, I care so little for him at present," she looked up, "I'd welcome elopement if Lizzy's condition didn't preclude her standing with me."

A man confident in his position can be magnanimous. He held her close and stroked her hair. "I want our wedding to be the memory you wish for, Princess. We'll endure the summer season, marry at Christmas, and then, my precious Georgiana," he kissed her, "I'll have my Princess for my wife." On their return to the pavilion, Henry reported their choice to Elizabeth not Darcy, after which Georgiana quit them all and retreated hastily to her mother's chambers to again lose her stomach.

Chapter 43

Henry Fitzwilliam endured Cressbrook's admiration of the fine, enclosed carriage, but as soon as it was seemly, he hastened to the seclusion of his master's suite. Seated at the bowed windows overlooking the Wye far below, he granted to have learned another lesson. He had lied to himself about not caring if he had Darcy's approval and now Darcy had cleared the air between them. As bitter a memory as the afternoon's events remained, Darcy had released Henry from his pledges to Uncle George and Aunt Anne.

He watched the evening sun sparkle the ribbon of water into a golden, eternal thread that at once divided and connected this corner of White Peak. *Life is naught but a strand connecting choices. I'm sorry for you, Darcy. You'll lose us both, if you don't take care.*

At Pemberley, the Darcys waited dinner until a servant announced Georgiana would sup alone. Guilt cost Darcy his appetite. He climbed the children's stairs at eight o'clock and tapped on their mother's door. "I thought I'd find you here. We missed you at dinner."

Georgiana sat tense at her mother's writing table, having quickly slipped worn calendar pages under her diary at his knock. "I ordered a tray."

"Yes, we received your message. We did miss you, however."

She studied her hands. Darcy sat. "We supped on chops and potatoes with bread pudding for dessert. Did you eat the same?" She shook her head still watching her lap. "Georgiana, I'm making every effort at conversation. The least you could do is help me."

"I ate soup and soda bread."

Darcy looked to the ceiling for the patience to which Elizabeth had sworn him. "Your light fare was in deference to your agitation, perhaps?" Darcy leaned forward. "Well?"

"I had no appetite."

"A common consequence of nerves."

"Yes, but not for me."

"Go on."

"I have been sorting my obligations before my coach departs." She looked up. "My solution for one problem invites others I hadn't considered."

"You refer to your work at the Hall?"

"That and your children's nursery."

"We could delay your departure, if you like."

"No. I'll not compromise our agreement and chance your claim that you ought not be held to your side of it."

Darcy's demeanor blackened. "I take exception to your implication, though I'm certain it wasn't your intent to impugn my honor."

"Your honor represents itself by your contradictions, Brother."

He turned his back and clenched his hands for control. "Your meaning?"

"A man compromising friendship with the one he calls 'brother' calls 'trust' to question."

"You're angry with me. Lord knows, Elizabeth shares your feeling!"

"Less anger than disappointment and less with you than with myself. But I do sense deepest anger inside me and I worry it will show itself."

Her tone unsettled him exceedingly. He stood at their mother's windows near flower boxes of purple and white iris. "Every person feels anger now and then."

Georgiana stood beside him. Late evening shadowed their faces. "I agree. Every person does feel anger now and then." She looked up at him, not to him, but at him. "But I sense my anger will be absolute and I shy from an emotion that precludes forgiveness."

"I am your brother, Georgiana!"

"And Henry is your best friend."

Darcy quit her shortly thereafter to walk the nearer paths of the Park under a waning moon. Georgiana had shared an embrace and "I love you" with the aura of one paying farewell.

When he returned to the pavilion, Elizabeth set aside George Darcy's first volume that she still struggled to decode. Her husband recounted everything and waited for her to show him a happier view of what he sensed had been a mistake of extraordinary proportion.

"She didn't want to choose between you and Henry."

"But why choose? I am her brother and he is her …'"

"Her what, William? You're clearly opposed to Henry as Georgiana's husband." She pulled his hand onto her lap. "Explain your antipathy and leave out the ruse of dowry."

"I couldn't bear it if Georgiana is hurt."

"You refer to his history with ladies?" Darcy nodded. Elizabeth shook her head. "But she's full aware of that history. She trusts his devotion and for my part, I do as well."

Darcy closed his eyes. "If he causes Georgiana any pain, I'll be forced to severe my ties with him." He looked up. "I protect against losing my best friend."

"You have so little faith in him?"

"I know him, Lizzy. He thrives on adventure and new endeavors. I love him despite his exigencies, but now they threaten Georgiana. If they touch her, they'll compromise him and me."

"But he chose to root himself at Cressbrook," she pointed out. "He forfeited far-flung adventure of his own accord and he's protected Georgiana too long to abuse her feelings." Elizabeth sighed, "Whether you accept it or not, she makes clear that your continued interference will cost you your sister." She reached for him. "Come to bed, William. You must accept what is and trust for the best."

Georgiana hoped for the best as she lit a lamp and cuddled under a throw in her favorite chair beside her mother's window boxes. Unfortunately, fear of irreconcilable anger against her brother was the least of her urgent worries. She was two weeks late, a fact which the worn pages of her personal calendar attested had not previously occurred. While the House slept, she sat with her mother's letters, but mama had not anticipated a daughter with a child-too-soon and offered nothing. Georgiana pulled a sheet from her writing box and dipped her pen to apprise Mrs. Annesley of her facts, praying all the while that her issue lay in tangled nerves, which would soon loose themselves enough to return her to her former self and let her mark her calendar again.

Chapter 44

Though prudence arrived too late to Darcy, the family's habits did super-ficially return to before; Georgiana visited Cressbrook and prepared for the well dressing fête while the Darcys attended their tree house. William and Elizabeth's sanctuary from familial dissension remained less a house than a lad-der reaching to a platform of eight feet by ten, but it was more than they had imagined possible. When Darcy nearly fell from the platform while construct-ing the first wall, young Christopher suggested they assemble the walls on the ground and hoist them into position. With the first wall in place, Elizabeth regretted her insistence for extra hands. At this rate, the house would be com-pleted before August, leaving her long weeks without distraction.

While Darcy measured boards, she considered their stilted family evenings. William struggled to make amends by sharing childhood stories of Henry and him. Though appreciative, Georgiana was preoccupied, which Darcy inter-preted as censure, and against which, he made still more strenuous attempts to mollify her. Elizabeth attributed their sister's waning energy to disappointment for uncompleted projects as her departure neared, an insight that prompted Darcy to cancel Georgiana's compromise; instead, he proposed she remain at Pemberley, complete her projects, and organize an October wedding with Henry. But Georgiana declined his kindness since only a wedding before August would address the issue of her unmarked calendar. Darcy took her rejection as continued punishment which sat heavy in his gut. He began to withdraw into himself and only the shade of the great oak drew back the curtain to show his wife all of the happy facets of the man she loved.

With the second wall nearly completed, Darcy welcomed tea after another day of excellent accomplishment. Before they sipped their first cup dry, a foot-man loped across the lawn with an express letter from Jane announcing "Marion

Elizabeth's" arrival three days earlier. Intensely serious, Elizabeth stroked the wisp of blond hair attached with sealing wax.

Misinterpreting his wife's demeanor, Darcy reassured, "Unless one knew she arrived late by two weeks, no one would guess that Baby Marion is a child too soon, Lizzy. No worry, my love. Few take notice about the alignment of dates nowadays. My father's generation was raised to condemn, but today it's of little concern."

"My concern is not for Jane and Charles." She tilted her head hinting at a smile, "I only would have laid money we have more passion in our toes than the Bingleys have between them, yet it's they who dabbled, while we sat demurely awaiting the vicar's permission. These facts compromise my sense of things and you know I hold my sense of things in very high regard."

He laughed. "If you'd been privy to the Bingleys' dabbling, would you have let us do it?"

She kissed him with her eyes. "No. Every person would have guessed what we were about. After you awakened me inside, I couldn't conceal my attachment to you."

With no regard for their public location, Darcy shared a married kiss that left them panting; a problem since on her last visit Mrs. Carroll had forbade them further passion until after their children's delivery. Elizabeth refocused their attention. "It would seem every couple proceeds according to their own design. I doubt either of us could have managed pregnancy much earlier than it arrived to us and I know for a fact I wouldn't have survived confinement in winter with no tree house to distract me." She gazed up into the great oak. "It's a lovely thing, Mr. Darcy." It warmed Darcy's heart to hear her admiration.

He could not have managed celibacy were it not for their deep connection. Their bond, when combined with Mrs. Carroll's recommendation for twice-daily horse riding and labor at the tree house dissipated enough energy to let him survive their physical distance.

Darcy's afternoon ride set off through the Park, crossed the Wye below the falls, and carried him to Monsal Head where the New Road connected with the old. Initially, a road joining Cressbrook to its mother estate made economic sense, but with the transfer of the deed, the road represented the bond between cousins. Darcy troubled that he left out "brother" from that bond.

The New Road was well-advanced in its construction. The roadway had been cleared of trees before the sap had begun to flow. Three arched stone bridges stood nearly completed over the streams crossing the road. Forest left standing on both sides of the single-lane protected riders from the near constant wind across this edge of Fin Cop.

The New Road stretched a quarter-mile past Pemberley's border and ended at the deep chasm of the Cress Brook where Darcy sat on a boulder admiring Henry's bridge. Its design imitated the new style of trestles used in railroad construction, sturdy but lacking the ambiance of Pemberley's arched stone. Sunk into holes in the rock gorge, thick beams criss-crossed to support the spans that had just been secured in place. Soon planks would be bolted to the spans and then railings on either side.

Voices from the Cressbrook side distracted Darcy. Through the leaves, he glimpsed Henry escorting Georgiana along Bottom Hill Road where it merged with the path to the footbridge. He carried Georgiana's basket and held her firmly at the waist, an aspect of personal that Darcy had not witnessed between them. When she looked up at him, Darcy was certain that Henry kissed her on the lips with the duration of a married kiss though her bonnet hid the details.

A protective brother galloped hard across the greater expanse of Pemberley, but exertion did not settle his agitation. He shared no stories at dinner. Before kissing her family good-night, Georgiana invited Darcy to attend Cressbrook's well dressing celebration two days hence.

After the blue silk drapes were drawn across the pavilion's glass and light was snuffed to only golden flickers on the grate, Elizabeth asked from her place by the fire, "Will you tell me your problem?" Darcy recounted another couple's privacy, to which she responded, "I'd think such a demonstration would nullify concern about their mutual attachment."

He sighed. "I presumed you wouldn't understand."

"What else is there to understand? Their devotion should allay your fears." She fixed him with a firm look. "William, if there's a further aspect to your worry, I will hear it."

Haltingly, he described the ladies Henry Fitzwilliam had previously escorted, each so beautiful that heads turned to look when they passed. As dearly as he loved and admired his sister, an objective eye could not pay her the same compliment. For Darcy, this inconsistency cast doubt on his cousin's motivation.

Elizabeth could not say if she were more taken aback by the subject of his concern or by her sense that he groped for grounds of criticism. She watched her hands. Darcy shifted uncomfortably. Finally, Elizabeth observed, "The consistent thread connecting your appraisal of Henry's various faults points to his integrity. On what grounds do you believe him to be dishonest?"

Darcy raked fingers through his curls. "It's not dishonesty…" He could not finish it.

"William, I begin to believe that no matter the evidence to the contrary, you will search out some reason to refuse acceptance of Henry as Georgiana's husband." She rose with difficulty and stood by the sofa. "If this is the case, my love, we stand to endure very awkward family relations for the balance of our days."

Chapter 45

With a lamp at her elbow, Georgiana Darcy sat in her favorite chair pulled close to her mother's hearth and read Mrs. Annesley's letter, which listed pregnancy's symptoms and concluded with unsolicited advice, all offered without judgment. Georgiana required several readings to digest the facts then watched the flames on the grate. Mrs. Annesley had pointed out a problem past solution: Georgiana's insistence to adhere to the agreement with her brother set her departure before her second missing could corroborate her condition.

That night she slept in her mother's bed and the next morning she sat at her child's dressing table in her former quarters, each venue conveying an equal sense of borrowing another person's rooms. If she had not nursed far more pressing concerns, she might have troubled that she no longer belonged. As it was, she accepted this as fact.

While the tree house distracted Darcy from his turmoil, Cressbrook's intense activity that readied it for the well dressing distracted his sister. From trimmed hedges to groomed flower boxes beneath every cottage window, Georgiana helped the tenants primp and polish to show Cressbrook's best face to the morrow's visitors; an estate that had survived tainted water vested deep reverence in the celebration of healthy wells. Five feet by six feet, the well dressing plaque was covered with a skim of damp clay into which tenants pressed petals, seeds and other bits of nature making a pictorial tribute to healthy water. Sprinkled with water to keep it fresh and waiting in the shade to keep it cool, the well dressing plaque witnessed the village's final preparations of the church and the food to be served: caldrons of stew, a sheep and a pig being prepared for the spit and dozens of loaves rising under white linen napkins lent by the Hall.

Mr. Hawkins arrived with fiddle in hand to practice with the other musicians following his abbreviated lessons. This was Georgiana's signal to join Mrs. Hopewell and Hannah in the walled garden where all three bent to set the last blossoms in beds resurrected from neglect. Reconstitution of this garden was their gift to complete the tenants' pride in their Cressbrook.

The next morning, Darcy's preparation to attend the fête was distracted by Elizabeth's preoccupation with a diary-page. When he drew close to tease her, he was surprised to see it was the first volume of George Darcy's. "Are you memorizing the passage?" he asked, amused.

"Not at all," she smiled up at him, nibbling a currant biscuit. "I'm looking for a clue."

"To what?"

"To the context of his rambling. Your father must have been very clever, because I've worked to unravel the mystery for more than three weeks, but it still eludes me."

"There *is* no context, Mrs. Darcy. I searched for the same myself and found nothing after a month of diligent effort."

Her eyes sparkled. "Then I have one more week to sort the puzzle if I am to beat you."

Darcy arrived an hour before the dedication of the plaque on a visit fraught with discomfort; he hadn't spoken to Henry since humiliating him in the pavilion. Tethering his horse to graze near the footbridge, he crossed as "family" rather than representative of a Great Estate, a choice made for his comfort since the day was too warm to endure sun-baked exposure on Castlegate Lane. His appraisal of the improvements at Cressbrook declared he had visited too rarely. Challenged to explain his distance from his neighbor, he accepted that each of his visits had been predicated on some benefit to himself, not Henry.

Darcy climbed to the stone village with other visitors, though his station set him apart and he effectively walked alone. Arrived at the village, his isolation compounded when Cressbrook's tenants embraced friends and distant relatives, leaving Darcy to himself. It was Henry who found him and escorted Darcy under a shade tree before extending him a proper welcome.

"We're glad you are come. Georgiana will be especially happy. I thank you."

"I'm impressed by the numbers your well-dressing attracts, Cousin."

"Georgiana deserves the credit, as she does for all of this. She and Hannah lettered invitations that were read to every congregation in the region at Sunday services. She'd be here to greet you herself, but is ill-disposed, a combination of nerves and excitement, I wager."

Darcy nodded then addressed his cousin self-consciously. "I admit I didn't know how you'd receive me, Henry."

"The occasion invites us to a show of civility, Darcy. To my mind, personal issues aren't for public consumption."

Disappointed, Darcy studied the close-trimmed grass underfoot. In all of their years, Henry had always forgiven his cousin's irascible moments; it seemed those years had passed.

Georgiana arrived in short order sucking on a mint leaf. Her porcelain complexion set off the blue of her eyes. She smiled at Henry then looped her arm through her brother's and escorted him to admire the plaque before the pageantry began.

It was a work of love. The tenants had pressed nature's bounty to make a ribbon of water dancing over stones. The Cress Brook laced together symbols of the small estate: at the top stood the Hall and two-thirds down rose the sentinel cliffs beside Water-cum-Jolly, on the left, green fields dotted with white sheep, and on the right, a representation of the hillside village. Above it all, two ravens flew against the sky. And at the bottom, the brook flowed into the River Wye with the words 'Cressbrook 18- -' spelled out in dried cress. The day was as lovely as Georgiana's design.

Darcy waited until late afternoon before requesting to see the bridge from Cressbrook's side. From the village lane down to the spur that would soon be connected to Pemberley, Henry led his cousin in silence. When arrived at the nearly completed bridge, he pricked his ears to hear Darcy's magnanimous tribute to a project well done. "For what are you preparing me, Darcy?"

"I beg your pardon?"

"It's your custom to compliment before you pounce."

"I don't pounce, Cousin!"

"We won't quibble over words, Darcy. You get my meaning. What will you discuss?"

"To the point, I take it?"

Henry nodded, leaning against an oak tree.

"I will clarify an issue that continues to trouble me, Cousin. I present it not for argument, but to pursue its resolution and then return to our previous good humor."

"Go on."

"It's been your custom for as long as you have escorted ladies to select the daintiest and most beautiful for your companions, yet you have proposed to Georgiana. As dearly as I love my sister, she doesn't embody what you previously admired. I ask you, 'why Georgiana'?"

Fury balled Henry's hands. He threatened in a low voice, "If you demean my bride again, you'll get more than a black eye." His own eyes shot daggers. "Ye gods, you are superficial!"

"Superficial or not, I speak to facts. Why do you woo a young lady twelve years your junior who evidences none of the attributes you previously prized… a young lady who already loves you as a brother and could be easily convinced to misinterpret that love as more?"

"This is what you think?" Henry breathed deep for control. "All these years I've forgiven you your moods believing them to be only that." Then cynically, "The joke is on me, is it not?"

"Henry, I …"

"Enough! Whether you'll soften your implication or lay on more insult, you've said enough." He slumped against the tree trunk, his usually lilting voice colorless. "I'll provide some details, but in deference to Georgiana, not you. You deserve none of our details, Darcy.

"She is my best partner. When she understood our fact, I put her off. Her despair explains her choice for Newsome. She's grown up, Darcy, whether you accept her as a woman or not. We are equals, she and I, though I shrank against accepting it, and even after I did, I couldn't get past the challenge to embrace the woman I'd raised like a sister. She refused to accept a man offering her only half a life – a man who acknowledged his love, but wouldn't demonstrate it."

Darcy winced. "I appear to have misjudged …"

Henry rose. "You've more than misjudged. You're as Janus-faced as they come! You took a country lady for your wife, a lady who represented none of the aspects of the ladies you'd previously entertained, yet you deny me the same. And beyond this, you ascribe to me the basest of motivations. I suppose you imagine I seek Georgiana's dowry for my benefit?"

Darcy hung his head and nodded.

"If Georgiana learns of this talk, she might not speak to you again. It will go no further."

Again Darcy nodded. He was left to find his own path to his horse.

Neither Darcy nor Elizabeth had much appetite for dinner after he had confided to her. Near bedtime, he recovered enough to ascribe some blame to Henry who could have accepted Darcy's good intentions. To this, his wife picked at imaginary lint on her nightdress.

Chapter 46

Rather than supervise the packing of her trunks to attend the Summer Season, Georgiana jostled in a carriage bound for Lambton. Mrs. Annesley's express note had arrived that morning with a plan to gain Georgiana a fortnight at Pemberley; time enough to know for certain. She arrived at Dr. Simons' cottage a mess of nerves though she presented a composed young woman to those waiting in his parlor.

Mrs. Annesley had assured that Dr. Simons would neither judge Georgiana, nor break a confidence, and as he studied the little sheets of her personal calendar, she sensed this was so. He leaned back in his chair. "You know your calendar speaks to the fact, do you not? You haven't been more than two days late in your entire history." She nodded, her hands clasped tight in her lap. He spoke to her nerves. "Nature can be unpredictable, however. It's best to corroborate before announcing." They sipped tea while he laid out a plan abetted by a letter from Mrs. Annesley, in which she had confided all she knew of the couple's deep and mutual connection, details that reinforced Simons' confidence in Henry, whose action had raised delicate questions of integrity.

The next morning a rider arrived in a lather to summon Dr. Simons to Pemberley. The good doctor was prepared. With furrowed brow and an envelope of sugar tablets pressed the night before, he discussed his diagnosis with the Darcys while a hive-splotched young lady lay in her mother's bed; the hives being a controlled allergic reaction of Dr. Simons' invention. After muttering an impressively long Latin name, he assured them she would recover with a fortnight of bed rest and one tablet three times a day taken with hot tea.

Elizabeth turned to Darcy. "You must notify Annapolis and the new chaperone at once."

He nodded, bowed to Dr. Simons and set off for his study, but at the children's stairs, he detoured to his mother's chambers to hold Georgiana's hand.

Elizabeth dispatched word to Henry, who came at once and every day thereafter, despite the open wound with Darcy.

Concern for their sister postponed work on the tree house. William read to Georgiana morning and evening while her afternoons belonged to Henry. He was all civility when he paid respects to the Darcys before visiting Georgiana, but public politeness was salt in the wound for William, who accepted he had erred with no way to make it right. The Bank of London had reported two inquiries in regard to Miss Darcy's dowry: the first, by Lord Simon Newsome in late January as to the account's balance, and the second, by Mr. Henry Fitzwilliam for arrangements to permit only Miss Darcy access to the account after their marriage; the funds were intended for her support if he met an early demise.

For Georgiana, a fortnight of reflection produced as much discomfort as would an honest illness. She accepted she would be a mother though such did not frighten her so much as she would have thought after having learned her own mama. She conceived several plans to protect Henry from censure and settled on the scheme that required a year's separation from him to support the ruse that a different gentleman had fathered their child.

Until Georgiana regained her health, Hannah refused to leave her mistress' side, despite stories of despairing children and a very out-of-sorts Mr. Hawkins at Cressbrook. On the Monday of Georgiana's second week, Daniel accompanied Henry to Pemberley. Mr. Hawkins met first with Miss Hannah Miller, and then with Mr. Fitzwilliam Darcy. A glowing Hannah fed her mistress soup and toast that evening. Mr. Darcy, the male of responsibility, had given his blessing to her union with Daniel. That night, Georgiana added another piece to her consideration; her brother had not been so forthcoming in her regard.

After two weeks of deliberation as if she were a bird perched on a branch, Georgiana was declared recovered and ventured from Pemberley in Henry's carriage to test the new bridge that lacked but one of its railings. It was 23 June.

She was overwhelmed by her welcome. The staff of four queued in the entrance hall curtsying and bowing as if she were a queen. Henry made to escort her to the parlor, but she preferred his study, to which staff quickly adjusted the sumptuous mid-morning repast near the master's hearth. He covered her lap with a quilt sewn by the tenant women with scraps from the Hall's projects. Savoring the moment, Georgiana postponed serious discussion until tea's conclusion, after which she spoke directly.

"Henry, we confront a trouble which the past fortnight has confirmed, and for which I have worked a solution described in this note."

He slowly lowered his cup to its saucer. "Go on."

"I'm pregnant."

Expressionless, he sat as if knocked on the head. When his heart stopped pounding in his ears, he requested her calendar sheets, which she reached to him along with the note detailing her plan to protect him. She excused herself to visit the basin across the hall.

On her return, he reached her a mint leaf without looking up. "I've ordered the carriage. We'll reach Buxton before the magistrate's office closes. The vicar will marry us this evening."

"No."

"Don't argue with me, Georgiana! I read your pretense of a plan. Do you take me for a fool and a coward at once? It's an absurdity unworthy of discussion that I should relinquish claim to the parentage of my child! We'll marry at once and let the rest respond as they will."

"No."

He rose, full angry. "Georgiana …"

She rose as well. "Hear me out. I won't wed in the company of strangers. When we marry it will be a proper ceremony. I want the memory."

"And if he denies the ceremony?"

"Then we will host it at Cressbrook. I won't miss a proper wedding. I'm firm on that."

He watched her while imaginings of Darcy's assured response sank a boulder in his gut. His head raced to discover some means to protect her from a family-divided, but granted that the hour to safeguard his princess had been on the porch in Ravensdale.

Henry reached into his bottom desk drawer and pulled out a velvet bag secured by golden cords. "I intended to give you this on our wedding day, but since we're already joined in our hearts, formality is made moot. I request that you wear it when we meet the Darcys this afternoon." He pressed the bag in her hands. "It's a family piece retrieved when I visited my parents after purchasing the carriage. It was promised to my bride. I hope it pleases you, Princess." Georgiana loosened the gold cords and reached two fingers inside to touch the cool smoothness of gem stones. "Go on. You'll see it was meant for you and you alone."

Georgiana stared at her reflection in the looking glass where a circle of perfectly matched, round, Fitzwilliam blue sapphires sparkled intensely with her slightest movement. He kissed her neck where the clasp lay. "You're my wife, Princess."

The master of Cressbrook held the reins in one hand and his bride's hand with the other. They had gone half the distance to the House without a word passed between them when he sensed a problem. He halted their carriage near the Great Bridge that crossed the River Wye.

"Your thoughts?"

She watched the water. "I wonder if our accident has made you sorry, if only a little."

His eyes bespoke his heart. "Hear me, Georgiana! After thirty years I had naught but a few trunks to my name until these last months, that is. Imagine my joy: I've got a Hall made lovely by your hand, soon your hand itself and then a child." He touched the place where his son or daughter grew. "So much good fortune makes me speechless." The warmth of his embrace loosed her tears of worry and relief. "We're a family, Princess," he whispered. "We will celebrate no matter others' sensitivities. Our child is cherished no matter the date of its arrival."

When Cressbrook's carriage trotted into view at tea time, Darcy smiled under the great oak in innocent anticipation of a happy reunion, but Elizabeth held her breath. Even at a distance, Georgiana's necklace could not be missed and it could have but one meaning. When the couple approached, Darcy stared as well. The jewels would be valued at more than half of Georgiana's dowry. He let go any hope for rapprochement when Henry abruptly insisted to discuss in the master's study.

Once arrived, Henry refused a chair.

Darcy stood as well. "I sense you'll announce rather than discuss, Cousin. Out with it."

"Georgiana and I will expedite our marriage to the end of July at the latest."

"Expedite?"

"She wishes a proper wedding at Pemberley attended by as many of our small family as possible. She's pregnant, Darcy."

Darcy blanched and sank into the nearest chair as if taken ill.

"I regret the shock, Cousin."

Like the mighty forces of the earth let loose, Darcy erupted and pressed his cousin against shelves of books whose pages they had turned together. He ringed a passive Henry's neck with an iron grip. "You did this to her? Dear God in Heaven! You did this to her!" A wave of sickness loosed his hands. Darcy breathed deep at the nearest open window and then wept.

Georgiana sat with her sister under the great oak where she conveyed the facts. Elizabeth's expression was a small window to the pain she imagined her husband suffered.

"I'd hoped you wouldn't condemn us, Lizzy," Georgiana said.

"It's less condemnation than sorrow. I wish you had done it differently, that's all."

Georgiana sat straighter. "The choice to abstain would have likely denied us our happiness. I enticed Henry full aware where it would lead. I did it to bind him to me and quash his guardian's hesitation." Elizabeth struggled to see it from her sister's side. Georgiana continued. "You know I've loved him since, my goodness, I don't know when and you know he rejected me. We didn't speak again of feelings until two months ago. But when he did acknowledge his love for me, he couldn't touch me, Lizzy. Our first kiss cost him much personal struggle," Georgiana blushed exceedingly, "but when our lips touched, it was one soul to the other. I would not lose my chance for happiness, Lizzy. I... I seduced him. Consciously seduced him. He accepts his connection is to the woman not the ward."

Such personal details pained Elizabeth as much to hear as it did Georgiana to share, but she pressed for one more fact. "My pardon to inquire, but since that first time —"

"Since that time, there's been naught but our precious memory. Henry said we wouldn't press our luck unaware we'd already pressed it too far. He is innocent, Lizzy, though it is he who will be blamed." Georgiana sat on the edge of the chaise and took Elizabeth's hands in hers. "I want a proper wedding, Lizzy. If possible, we'll celebrate at Pemberley, if not, then at Cressbrook. We leave it to you and Brother."

Elizabeth asked Georgiana to join her in the pavilion, but the lady, now not so young as her years implied, declined with a kiss and waited in the plum-colored carriage.

In the master's study, Darcy sat expressionless for so long that Henry feared for him, but he knew there was no balm to salve the pain he had served. A strained voice broke the silence.

"You must marry, of course. And it will be at Pemberley in deference to Georgiana's wishes. We will comply with the guest list she provides. As for you and me, we are strangers." Henry nodded, his heart breaking with Darcy's. The master of Pemberley continued. "My only solace is to believe you care for her and I hope she cares for you more than her worship of a beloved guardian." Darcy paused and fixed his cousin with contempt. "Beyond this, I am left to loathe the friendship I have loved. You have disgraced my sister. I shan't forgive you."

His empathy evaporated, Henry fixed Darcy with his own cold glare of disdain. "I expected your derision and even your hatred, but never, hear me, NEVER demean my wife and child by implying they are compromised by the lapse of a few weeks until a formal ceremony." His voice cut the air. "I regret to have disappointed you, but beyond that, I hold my head high and revel in our happiness. We accept your generosity of a wedding. Good day."

Before reins were slapped on horses rumps, the whispers among staff began. No details were required to know the family suffered. All waited, holding their combined breaths.

Elizabeth was surprised that her husband did not escape to sort his feelings; instead, he sat with her, their hands entwined in silence. No words could express the loss of a loved one.

At last he spoke, "I promised a proper wedding, a thing I'll leave to you."

"Mrs. Reynolds and I shall manage it."

"I hate him for denying me my brother, Elizabeth."

Respect for Darcy's sincerity silenced his wife's insight. Clearly, it was William who denied himself Henry's friendship, not vice versa. Clearly, if it were anyone but Georgiana, he would overlook the lapse of a few weeks. Technically, Elizabeth appreciated that it was a shock and she even accepted that a brother might feel differently than a sister at such news, but since all wished to preserve their friendships, and William likely most of all, it made no sense that he jeopardized the family he loved in support of a principle he did not otherwise hold in high regard.

That night behind the wall of screens, she asked him to explain his condemnation of Henry in light of Georgiana's declaration that it was she who had seduced him. Darcy balked. Elizabeth prodded. He relented, his voice tired and halting as he spoke the facts.

"Even if she were a seductress, which we both agree she is not, the design of a man provides him full warning of what will ensue if he does not get control. Henry proceeded full aware where her overtures would lead and thereby he owns the responsibility." Despite his pain, Darcy forced out the next words. "My father, who championed self-control and obligation to one's duty, loved my cousin as a son, a son to whom my father had entrusted the care and protection of his daughter. It is not merely the act itself that compromises love for my Cousin, but even more damning is the pain such an act would have caused my father. I thank God he's not alive to know this man's defilement of his trust and confidence."

The next morning after breakfast, Elizabeth was glad rain forestalled work on the tree house. Two days earlier, she had discovered the key to decoding George Darcy's ramblings. A lady on a mission now settled near the fireplace to begin the interpretation of forty volumes, praying all the while that the father would shed light on the history of brothers who were not.

Chapter 47

"You draw and paint this place again and again!" Lady Catherine's scorn echoed off the limestone walls of Water-cum-Jolly.

"Ah, but I have the talent to wrest new insights from an old friend." Lady Anne had not invited her elder sister to accompany her.

Catherine's small eyes narrowed. "New insights, indeed! You disdain us so consistently, I wonder if mama isn't right that you aren't to be trusted." Catherine bit her lip, angry that Anne had provoked her to voice what she had promised their mother she would not.

Having alienated herself from her family with her marriage to George, Anne already expected the worst from her mama, who at this moment was likely searching Anne's letters for any words that might diminish the Fitzwilliam family were they to be made public. She cleaned the nib of her pen and tucked away the perfect sketch of Water-cum-Jolly. "Trust is a thing you and mama contort to a new meaning, Sister," she said, folding her easel.

In deference to the Darcys' social standing, two ceremonies would be celebrated: the first at the church in Lambton with the multitude from the region in attendance, and the second, in Pemberley's formal garden with family and invitees where Elizabeth would sit as witness from her chaise. Several weeks of preparation as well as the arrival of guests were required before festivities could begin. Mrs. Wittig was honored to organize the service in town, while at Pemberley, Georgiana consulted with Elizabeth, who managed the invitations, ceremony and reception, and Mrs. Reynolds, who coordinated preparation of guest rooms and menus. Local musicians were hired and the tenants of both estates were invited to sit on the lawns and celebrate at their own party afterward.

Lady Catherine de Bourgh arrived with her daughter, Anne, who trailed as the petite shadow of her mama. Anne's most distinguishing characteristic was to sneeze into more handkerchiefs in one day than most ladies sullied in a week. Elizabeth studied Anne at tea, surprised by a moment of pity for her watery-eyed cousin.

"You add staring to the insolence that requires us take tea in the company of your belly, Eliza," Aunt Catherine berated. "I would have thought these months at Pemberley would have seeped some refinement into your country ways!"

Darcy moved to defend, but Georgiana interceded. "It is I who insist my sister shares our events, Aunt. I'm sure you don't imply I'm without manners." Her sweet voice disarmed the grand dame momentarily. "And as for staring, I'm also drawn to Anne's attire that replicates your own so precisely. When one sets oneself apart, one cannot decry an admirer's second look."

One did not contradict Lady Catherine! The Lady's head barely turned in Georgiana's direction as she oozed her judgment. "Well, well. I hear the sound of my dear, dead sister from the lips of her youngest. You are well advised, Georgiana, to consider to whom you speak. My magnanimity begins to stretch thin, despite that it is you we've come to honor."

"Then, dear Aunt, we are agreed to set aside any words not conducive to a pleasant enterprise." Georgiana turned to Anne. "Did you enjoy good weather on your journey, Cousin?"

The Darcys exchanged astonished glances. Georgiana had managed without them.

The next afternoon, Henry arrived an hour before the four coaches conveying his family. His bride ran to meet him and the two strolled the Park while Lady Catherine glowered that her nephew had not first attended her. When Darcy's eyes darkened and he raised a brow, she swallowed her invective.

Within the hour, the Fitzwilliam family clambered from too many coaches followed by wagons bearing an embarrassing number of trunks. *I think they even impress themselves*, Elizabeth mused. She, however, was not entertained by the Earl of - - -, or his wife, their two sons and their wives and children. All were handsome in face and manners and none derided Georgiana's choice of the pavilion for their assembly, but as libation flowed, the Fitzwilliams from Glenbrooke peeled masks from first impressions to show a shallow, bickering lot.

Elizabeth better understood Henry's history the next day when Lord John and Lady Mary omitted their youngest son from conversation. Robert, their eldest, commanded full attention while the middle son lapped at the heels of the first. Their wives vied with each other for center stage and made no effort to include Georgiana. Darcy bridged the chasm of inequity by inserting the respect afforded Pemberley to place the bridal couple at the fore.

That evening, Georgiana managed some private minutes with Henry. Their guests would visit Cressbrook on the morrow and Darcy had astonished his sister by announcing he would also attend. She hugged Henry's arm. "I think it goes better with my brother."

"Because he intercedes? No, he supports against injustice in general, not me in particular."

"But his choice to accompany them to Cressbrook! I'm certain he means to assure your support. I'd think you would appreciate his efforts, not dismiss them."

"He knows I'm appreciative, just as I know naught has changed between us. It's the nature of the man, Georgiana. He doesn't forgive transgression after he judges it to exist. 'Once his good opinion is lost, it is lost forever,' as the protagonist of a great writer once said."

That night Elizabeth also probed if her husband's actions intimated a change of heart.

"No. As much as I sincerely wish it could be so." He propped his pillows, indicating he would discuss. "I hadn't anticipated defending him, but you saw how they were."

"The entire evening I tried to understand their behavior, but could not." She reflected, "They themselves appear blind to their callousness. Can you explain it?"

"Their grounds adjust with each person." Darcy described a father whose interest lay only in his first born, which supported the primogeniture-engendered competition between Henry's brothers." And as for Lady Mary," he continued, "she is better equipped to bear children than to nurture them."

Elizabeth sighed. "It seems our Henry is a poor fit with his family."

"Indeed, he is a poor fit. Mother once said it hadn't been father's and her intent to take Henry on permanently. But when they saw he wasn't missed at home and noted our camaraderie, they deemed it best on all counts."

"Then it was happenstance rather than his choice that placed him here?"

"Happenstance that placed him, but his choice to remain; he loved us like his own. You have the right. He doesn't fit with them: he leads while they follow, explores while they sit, and makes his own way while they depend on others. He's the only man of merit among them."

Elizabeth proceeded carefully. "Knowing his background makes one sympathetic to him."

Darcy settled back on his pillows to sleep, and said in closure, "His bad luck only instructs me to be glad my sibling was born female."

At that moment, the twins squirmed, alerting their mother to an issue she had not considered. "What if our babies are both sons?" She nudged her husband's back. "William, I can't bear to think that but for a few minutes, one would be favored over the other!"

"Whether it's minutes or years, Lizzy, such is the effect of an inequitable law." He reached to stroke her belly. "You may join me to hope that the Bennet tradition of daughters will spare us the legal difficulties to impose fairness on an unfair world."

"Do you mean you'll divide Pemberley, if they're both sons?"

"I hope for girls, Lizzy, or better yet one of each and then pray the rest are daughters. Beyond that, I promise our children won't be slighted by the law."

The next day, Cressbrook hosted its guests: first, with a tour of the land escorted by Henry, and then a tour of the Hall guided by Georgiana, followed by luncheon on the terrace hosted by both together. Left at Pemberley, Elizabeth divided her time between glances at the mantel clock and the east portico on the far side of the gardens where the special gift for Georgiana ought to have long since arrived. It was another half-hour before Dr. Simons' carriage relieved her anxiety and Mrs. Annesley crossed the garden, her copper curls glinting in the sun against a leaf green bonnet.

Dr. Simons remained only long enough to ask after Elizabeth's comfort, count her pulse and hear her heart, the latter improved by Darcy's gift of the new invention of a stethoscope designed for both ears to listen at once. Elizabeth presumed it was a physician's habit to listen and count at every opportunity, herself unaware of the doctor and midwife's concern that their patient would not manage the full term.

Dogs barked greeting on the road to announce carriages returning from Cressbrook. Mrs. Annesley stepped behind a yew bush while the guests retired to change for tea and bride, groom, and brother followed the garden paths to Elizabeth. When Georgiana caught sight of the lady, she lifted her skirts and dashed into Mrs. Annesley's arms. "Oh my goodness! You said you couldn't come." She kissed the lady's cheek. "My goodness, how did you manage it?"

With the party clustered in chairs near the open French doors, Mrs. Annesley explained that Georgiana must thank Mrs. Darcy for the release from her contract after a replacement was located.

"You are released, Mum?" Georgiana's eyes sparkled at the prospect of a long visit then clouded to realize that her wedding had cost Mrs. Annesley her employment.

She turned to her sister. "How did this happen, Lizzy?"

The query interrupted Elizabeth's repositioning of the cushions at her back. She found it increasingly difficult to maintain her comfort for tens of minutes before aches required another adjustment. "When you confided Mrs. Annesley couldn't attend, I wrote her immediately."

She held her sister's hand. "She is our wedding gift, including her salary, until you no longer require her support as the nanny to your child… that is, if you and Henry accept."

Georgiana looked at Henry, who nodded. She burst into giggles, wiped at tears of happiness and ecstatically hugged each person, inviting hearty smiles all round.

Chapter 48

Lady Anne submitted to a second, public wedding following her elopement. The wedding in Pemberley's ballroom was her last concession to the family that shunned her in one breath and, for appearances' sake, embraced her in the next. It was her husband's strength that got her through. For all of her independence, she required him at her side to confront the world.

The bridal couple arrived at Lambton Church in separate carriages on the morning of 25 July. They exited the church a half-hour later to the cheers of hundreds of strangers. Wedding arches wrapped with white ribbons and flower garlands waggled above the bride and groom as they ran hand-in-hand along the gravel path toward the plum-colored carriage festooned with flowers and billows of white tulle. Children laughed as they tossed rose petals at the couple's feet while their mothers tossed petals high into the air to rain a sweet beginning on the union.

The vicar's carriage led the procession to Pemberley. En route, landsmen and their families waved and called greeting from the roadside to make a party nearly two miles long. Mr. and Mrs. Fitzwilliam waved greeting like a newly coroneted prince and his princess. "I shan't forget this, Henry. Thank you," Georgiana whispered as they passed Pemberley's gates.

The garden nuptials would begin an hour after the arrival of bride and groom. While Georgiana described the church wedding to Elizabeth in the pavilion, the groom attended the gentlemen in the morning room with a glass of sherry in hand. Conversation was dominated by those with some stature at Court who worked to impress those with less. Henry stood at the back glad for a moment to recall happy memories in the House that no longer welcomed him.

Musicians played local tunes for the multitude of tenants waiting on blankets spread on the lawns until a horn announced the formal guests should seat themselves. Henry's gift to his bride was a delicate, double-wide arbor designed and constructed by his hand, under which they would promise their vows in Pemberley's garden and then make it the entrance to Cressbrook's new terrace garden. At either side of the arbor, Mrs. Annesley and Dr. Simons waited as matron and groomsman. Henry took his place, the musicians paused and the company hushed.

A violin's melody escorted Georgiana on her brother's arm past the pavilion's glass façade to where the garden met the lawns. They proceeded slowly along the hedge to assure the tenants' good view of the bride before Darcy and his sister reached the sculpted break in the hedge-row and began their march through the center of the garden. Darcy leaned to her, "I love you, Georgiana." And she whispered back, "As I do you, Fitzwilliam." Mr. Darcy escorted his sister past invited guests until he passed her to the man who had been his brother. He noted with irony that the brother lost to his heart would be his brother-in-law.

Standing near the French doors, Darcy bent to Elizabeth's ear. "I admired Georgiana's necklace to my uncle en route to the church. It's a family piece."

"I like the Earl better that he didn't leave Henry without inheritance."

"It's not as it appears. The necklace was passed to the Lord by his mama, but my Aunt thought it too plain and promised it to Henry since the stones match the color of his eyes."

"Oh." Elizabeth held fast to her husband's hand and sat as straight as nature permitted to best represent the precious part of Georgiana's family.

The groom stood tall, his eyes only for the lady who wore her family as witness. Lady Anne's wedding gown, adjusted to Georgiana's form, suited her daughter. Elizabeth's wedding bonnet billowed tulle in the gentle breeze. Forget-me-nots and yellow roses from Pemberley and ivy from Cressbrook completed the simple bouquet, beneath which she held her father's New Testament, wherein lay the envelope containing her brother's lock of hair.

Afterwards, the family, the vicar and his wife, and designated guests attended the fête in the pavilion, its furnishings adjusted to accommodate the buffet and a large area for dance. Near eight o'clock, Henry toasted the Darcys' generosity. The guests then proceeded with toasts meant more to hear their own voices than sincere connection with the bride and groom. Elizabeth grimaced at the superficiality and hoped Georgiana's happiness shielded her from it.

Lord John, his cheeks flushed with too much liquid celebration, argued in low tones with his Lady before he stood and raised his glass to the bridal couple. "My wife thinks I ought not share a bit of family history, but I shall disclose a small fact we'd forgotten until en route here."

Lady Catherine pressed her lips. The rest tittered at a toast turned into a history lesson.

"Each has admired the necklace our son presented his bride; as well you should since it is remarkable both in the cut and color of the stones." He tipped his glass to Georgiana, himself a bit off-balance. "It wasn't intended for my branch of the family tree, rather it had been promised to my now deceased sister, who after losing favor with her mama also lost the necklace. What should be a sad tale, however, is made joyous since the lady now wearing it is the daughter of that sister, Lady Anne." His audience gasped and stared at Georgiana's neck. He raised his glass to Georgiana's portrait of Anne Darcy above the mantel. "It's right to include you in our party Anne. I bow to powers-unknown that your necklace has come home, so to speak."

Elizabeth touched the garnet garden at her throat; George's replacement for sapphires lost.

The guests' tittering looked to make a spectacle of Georgiana, against which Darcy moved to protect his sister until he felt Elizabeth's hand on his sleeve. Such was now Henry's duty, which he attended adeptly with a final toast and the announcement that their carriage waited.

In deference to Elizabeth's weariness, the party disbanded shortly thereafter.

Chapter 49

Lady Anne's final days were Pemberley's deepest agony. Three nights before the Lady's last breath, Mrs. Reynolds woke fourteen-year-old Master Henry. His aunt requested a meeting. Mrs. Reynolds prepared him to see her condition; a kindness that braced the lad to forfeit the memory of his vibrant aunt.

He knocked. "Aunt?"

"Come." Her voice strained to force words past the morphine cloud that sedated her. She moved her hand slightly, indicating he should approach, but his feet balked to embrace death. "Come, I'm the same person."

He sat, watching her hand, limp on the covers then reached out and covered it with his. Tears slipped down his cheeks. "I don't want you to die."

"As you see, in some things there is no choice."

"There's no family without you," he choked.

"Henry, look at me." Flickers of Lady Anne escaped past the glaze of morphine. He felt her bones press his hand slightly. "A family is a living thing... like a garden. While the seasons shrivel some stems, they coax new shoots nearby. It's the natural way of things. The family endures, my dear. It is each member's choice how he'll tend it in the new season."

She coughed for too long. He rose to leave. "Sit." She coughed some more.

"As I've done with Fitzwilliam, I invite you to see the facts as they lie before you and let you speak your heart so that you can hear the truth from my lips. These are our last moments. It is your choice if you fill them with tears or words."

She met his denial with reality. She met his pain with gentle reassurance. And she met his fear of missing her too much with a gift.

"There are two kinds of death, Henry. The first is when one no longer breathes, and the second when those who live no longer remember. I want you to

291

recall me as a comfort that continues my joy in life in your own. When you miss me, go to the place I love best to stand my easel. Sit among the wildflowers and hear the water. I'll be with you, my dear. I'll be the breeze that whispers past your cheek and the dappled sun that plays on your breeches. Go to Water-cum-Jolly and sit with me. I will be there."

A carriage emblazoned with a golden "C" pulled-to on a wagon path off Pemberley Road.

Henry sensed his bride's rising emotion and apologized, "I'm sorry, my love. Papa loses his wits when he tips the glass too much."

His wife breathed deep to stave off tears. "It's not that. I'm glad to know the history. I'm only so disappointed in myself. I thought a wedding with family was the memory I'd cherish, but it's the strangers at the church I'll recall with a smile. Tonight, I felt... I can't explain it." She wiped a tear and looked at him. "I misjudged what was important and chose a bad memory for our beginning. I'm so very, very sorry."

He creaked the seat leather as he leaned back with his wife in his arms. The night was good company. "We're our own family, Mrs. Fitzwilliam."

She sniffed.

"Sweet Georgiana, a memory is but a fact. It is how one elects to embrace it that makes it good or bad." He considered for a moment. "If you're not too tired when we arrive home, I'll share a precious memory. Most would judge it to be sad, but to me it's been a blessing."

Arrived at Cress Brook's bridge, the Fitzwilliams' caught their breath to see every lantern on the estate queued from the bridge to the Hall's front stoop. Their tenants had planted a ribbon of fairy-light to welcome the bride and groom. He kissed her a married kiss before they slowly rolled by the path of fairies. "Cressbrook makes a memory dimming all the rest, Mrs. Fitzwilliam."

They proceeded past the lanterns to where the woods stood between the road and the cliff. Near the lip of the precipice above Water-cum-Jolly, Henry made a nest from the carriage robe and they sat, she in her mother's white satin gown and he more in love than he thought one man's heart could hold.

Georgiana studied the woods below where the moon glowed ghosts of light on the far side of the water. Her husband had recounted his last meeting with his Aunt Anne. "You got Cressbrook and I got her necklace," she mused. "Do you think she had a hand in it?"

"Do you?"

"I'd like to believe she knows everything and that she approves. It would be the blessing my brother begrudges us." The Wye roared its water over the weir. "What did she give brother?"

"The tree house she had built for him. It was his favorite place in all of Pemberley. He sat up there for months after her death, God rest her."

"But why did she give you something permanent and brother something not?"

He laughed and stroked her cheek. "You inject symbolism where there's none, Mrs. Fitzwilliam." He settled her against him and watched where the moon kissed Water-cum-Jolly with silver. "The tree house was her perfect gift to Darcy. It was a place that embodied their deep connection and a place, I have no doubt, she believed would endure as long as the great oak itself. Since there was no tree house connecting me to her, she gave me this as an excellent and generous second-best. When Darcy returned from his first year at university the tree house was missing. Uncle's choice to have it dismantled after it was damaged by a winter storm nearly brought Darcy and your father to blows. I stepped between them when I arrived two days later."

"I do recall the bad blood, though I didn't know its cause. Those days before you arrived were the only nights papa didn't read to me," she remembered. "Knowing papa, he suffered every bit as much as my brother. I wonder he didn't offer to have another tree house constructed."

"Ah, but he did, however, that only infuriated Darcy more. As solace to my cousin, I shared my gift of this place where he could meet his mother. I didn't think to view it from his perspective, a stupid thing on my part. He was jealous and angry, perhaps that she had given me a gift at all, or perhaps, as you noted, that mine endured while his had not." He pointed to two boulders at waters' edge. "We sat there while I reasoned with him and," he pointed to the water, "we landed there after heroic fisticuffs. I hit my head, went under, and awoke to an ashen-faced Darcy weeping that he couldn't bear to lose both me and his mama."

"He saved you!"

"Aye, after he nearly killed me."

"Husband?" she liked to say husband and watch Henry's gladness to hear it, "have you ever considered that my brother is a mix of opposites? He evokes one's love and then one's ire to make it impossible to completely despair of him or wholly embrace him."

Henry chuckled. "I once likened Darcy to an onion of indeterminate size… an onion that makes one weep as he peels away one layer only to discover another layer beneath. The difficulty with my brother-in-law is that one doesn't know when there are no more layers and one holds the heart of the man."

Chapter 50

Rain delayed its pummeling of Pemberley until the last of its guests waved their handkerchiefs from coach windows, but not long enough to let the Darcys' resume work on their tree house. Neither spoke of the past week's events. The master settled at the pavilion's dining table with his correspondence and the mistress fluffed a pillow at her back before opening a shabby, little leather volume. It was a gift from Dr. Simons to Georgiana, who had rediscovered it while packing for her move to Cressbrook. She had loaned it to Elizabeth, in part as distraction from confinement, and in part, as a footnote to Elizabeth's Darcy Family Research.

William glanced at his wife when she sat up in the midst of reading, then sat back and appeared to reread a passage. He queried if she had found another puzzle, to which she responded "Perhaps" and continued reading the little book to the end.

That evening she nodded with a tease at the time-worn volume on her night table. "It's intriguing what one can learn about one's husband from his mama's medical records."

"Medical records?" Perplexed, he looked from little book to wife.

After explaining the path from Dr. Simons via Georgiana to her hands, she said, "Until reading her records, I hadn't guessed your family was so religious."

"I wouldn't judge that we're more religious than others," he countered.

"Not 'us,' *your parents*," she clarified. "Only the truly devout would celebrate their son's birth on the day of his christening."

"Beg pardon?"

"Your mother delivered you on 16 September yet we mark your birthday on 20 December coinciding with your christening." Elizabeth's head had so quickly reconciled disparate facts with the christening date she hadn't considered possible implications. Her husband's confusion-turned-to-agitation made clear she'd erred awfully. "I must have misinterpreted," she offered hastily, then added, "in fact, the attending physician had such poor handwriting that I –"

"Give me the book, Elizabeth," he ordered.

After reading the designated page and its sister-pages before and after, Darcy declared the elderly Ashworth, who had preceded Dr. Simons, must have been so overworked that he not only erred as to the birth date, but the birth site as well. Darcy was born at Pemberley not Warmsby Heath, though afterward the unique place name unsettled him.

The next morning, Darcy's preoccupation with estate correspondence assured his wife that her too glib poke into the past had not bothered so much as she had feared. She turned a page in Prudence Darcy's diary which, when combined with her husband's, Hastings, presented a real mystery as to how their self-possession could have sired their introspective and sympathetic son, George.

"Did you know your grandmamma tended toward hypochondria?" she asked a half-hour later. "She seems to have left your father's care to tutors while caring for herself with diligence."

"No. No, I didn't," Darcy answered, self-conscious that he had only transcribed the formal histories on the backs of paintings without further interest to learn more. "In fact, I don't recall my father saying much of anything about life before my birth."

"Not even his father's austere view of the world? I'm sure I couldn't have endured a full meal with that man let alone have survived with him as my parent."

Darcy resolved to read some diaries to let him participate in a conversation on the topic of deceased Darcys. And he did, but he chose his mother's medical records to begin. When he could discover no apparent mistakes beyond his birth date and place, he inspected his baptismal record to verify his facts. Two days later, he probed Mrs. Reynolds' memory to substantiate the old doctor's failing faculties.

"I'm sorry, Sir," the Housekeeper responded innocently. "Dr. Ashworth was elderly, but his mind was clear. Your father trusted him implicitly."

"I see."

Mrs. Reynolds could see that he did not. "If I may, Sir, is there a particular problem your query addresses? Perhaps if I knew it, I could answer more precisely."

Darcy weighed the issue of confiding a personal matter to staff and shook his head.

Several days later, he summoned the Housekeeper to his study.

"Do you recall our recent conversation in regard to Dr. Ashworth?" he began. "I should like to pursue it further after you've read a small passage in my mother's medical records."

Mrs. Reynolds knew at once that her master's confidence denoted something serious, but when she read where he pointed, she grasped the full significance of his dark expression.

"Well, Mum?" Darcy prodded.

"I worked in Pemberley Village until you were one year old when Lady Anne installed me in the House. I can add nothing of value, Sir."

Darcy had forgotten this detail, but after a moment, he proceeded anyway. "Perhaps there were stories among staff that could indicate the physician's fallibility?"

She bit her lip and shook her head. As the day progressed, however, Sylvia Reynolds troubled exceedingly that she had not complied as fully as her master had requested.

Near nine o'clock that evening a note was delivered to Darcy.

> *Dear Sir,*
> *In regard to our earlier discussion, I only recall private glances between the then Housekeeper and Head Butler when guests exclaimed how advanced you were for your age. At one point, I queried another maid as to the meaning of said glances and was told it was not an issue for discussion. I regret I cannot help more.*
> *Sincerely, Mrs. Sylvia Reynolds*

The next morning, Darcy sat at the north hearth with his birth year from George's diaries. He utilized Elizabeth's key to interpret the ramblings: after listing the events as they occurred on each date, George had counted in seven or its multiples to the page where he detailed his sensibilities about one of those events. Darcy inserted slips of paper where each of the ramblings began, then counted backward from each slip, read the agenda entries and compared them to the nonsense paragraphs until he determined the context, which he noted in pencil at the start of the subject-less passage. He opened to September.

From her chaise, Elizabeth watched his expression change from confused, to unsettled, to a clenched jaw. "Is there a problem?" she asked.

"It is personal," he responded curtly and quit the pavilion.

She stared after him. He had raised "it is personal" as a barrier between them when she had trusted "personal" to be what connected them. You're far too sensitive, she scolded herself.

During the next days, Elizabeth met what were, in effect, two husbands: the delightful, teasing man who hammered on the tree house and the man who cloistered himself in his study except for meals. She appeared to weather their separation well, but beneath her equanimity, she suffered loneliness far worse than what had precipitated her ride to Monsal Dale, only now she couldn't ride a horse or even climb the stairs to prod their reconnection.

Having accepted that his birth date had been purposefully altered, Darcy was consumed to learn the context, which presented an unrivalled challenge to that gentleman's patience since he did not know the precise date of the facts he sought. After finding his answer, he despaired to have searched at all.

(Topic – "my friend")

24 December, 17 - -
My God, but for one night, I would not have known the purest joy and would have lived my entire life without the memory to which poets scribe their odes.

Darcy counted the weeks from 24 December to 16 September. Thirty-nine weeks. He counted again. And then again.

With exceeding self-control, he located the next rambling that fit his interest and its topic.

(Topic – "my friend")

2 January, 17 - -
"Fledgling daydreams are snuffed after learning of the betrothal to another to be announced on 1 April."

(Topic – "note from friend")

14 February, 17 - -
"Stomach illness compromises the last visit of my heart. Like a child, I weep for my loss, and like an adult, I worry for improved health. I despair."

(Topic – "friend's father visits Pemberley")

17 March, 17 - -
"From him, I learn the grounds for illness, albeit only hinted at, but I have counted from Christmas, and there can be no other explanation.
I am responsible. Dear God in Heaven, I am responsible! My father would disown me and my mother would succumb in shame, yet I calculate calmly: the distances, the documents and the best, final destination. I am not myself as history has hitherto defined me, but history's hold is loosed in the face of new reality. Nothing has prepared me for this and yet I embrace it as if I were my destiny."

Darcy's world deadened. His father had seduced Lady Anne, a fact that would have remained hidden but for their son's existence. George Darcy had set himself upon a girl young enough to be his daughter.

Locked in his bedchamber, Fitzwilliam Darcy's heart writhed in agony. Logic extrapolated that the man who seduced the daughter of a friend might well have been following a pattern of seduction more than a decade long. George's first wife had died twelve years before he had imposed himself on Lady Anne. Indeed, a man in his prime without a wife to satisfy nature's urgency would be hard pressed to maintain celibacy. The father, who Darcy had so admired and from whom he had so desired approval, had brought despicable shame on his son and family. George and Anne's later happiness could not atone for an action so salacious.

The clock's tick-tock rasped at Elizabeth's nerves; her husband had never missed their bedtime. In middle night, Darcy crossed the pavilion in stocking feet.

She called out in the darkness, "Will you tell me freely or must we argue before I learn it?"

"What?" he asked feigning confusion. He intended to burn the evidence on the morrow, having vowed never to divulge the humiliation his father had served his family.

"Don't play with me, William. I insist to learn what has stolen my husband from me."

"It is private, Wife." He creaked the bed ropes and pulled the covers over his shoulder.

"Precisely," she retorted. "'Private' is what you share with your wife." He lay silent. "William, something is troubling you and I insist to know it. Excepting our hours at the tree house, you are withdrawn from both me and the estate." Her heart reached out to him. "I need you, my love. My wellbeing is bound so tightly with yours that I am lost when you are." She found his shoulder in the dark. "If we must be lost, I will at least know the reason for it."

A hoot owl marked minutes of debate in Darcy's head: the son insisted to keep the blemish hid while the married man argued to share with his wife since given Elizabeth's tenacious prodding, maintaining a secret chanced to drive an irreparable wedge. He threw back the blankets, buttoned his breeches and disappeared. Elizabeth lit a lamp and waited. When he returned, his left hand gripped a volume of George's diaries with slips of paper poking out the top.

Abashed, Darcy revealed his unsettled feelings about the discrepancy of birthdates; a fact she had been convinced did not trouble him. Her surprise became dread when she apprehended the serious import he ascribed to her mistaken interpretation of religiosity. After explaining his penciled notations, Darcy turned away in mortification while she discovered for herself.

Elizabeth read, but despite every effort, she found nothing in George's words to support the undoing of her husband. "Forgive me, but I only see a couple who dabbled. Nothing more." She rubbed his back. "It's a surprise to learn one's parents did it, but such isn't grounds –"

"Dabble?" He turned on her, "'Dabbling' applies to a couple already betrothed, NOT a man twice the age of a friend's daughter, who he seduces."

"Seduce? Dear God, William, you can't think –" His look promised this was precisely his belief, and worse yet, he required every bit of control not to collapse in ignominy.

When he refused her logic to read the passages differently, Elizabeth sat still on her bed. She had grown to love the George Darcy she had met in diaries, loved him and appreciated the challenges he had struggled to accept at the hands of his parents. They had arranged his first marriage as they had his whole life and he had let them do it out of obligation. Elizabeth was as certain that

George ought not be condemned as she was that her presumption about a birth date had cost her husband his allegiance to the man he admired most. Though they lay in the same bed, each slept isolated in their separate purgatories.

The next morning, Elizabeth picked at her breakfast from a tray at bedside. Later, she sat under the great oak sharing only the length of the boards to be sawed and the position of the bolts to secure them in place, nothing more. Darcy rightly interpreted her distance as evidence of their disagreement about his father, but he didn't apprehend that she judged against herself as unforgivingly as he judged against his papa.

Chapter 51

The completion of the tree house was celebrated with a surprise organized by William. "Mrs. Darcy, your attention, please!" Darcy called from across the lawn where he led two columns of children from Pemberley Village. She watched the youngsters ranged smallest to tallest march behind their leader, and then queue in front of him at either side of the tree house ladder.

"You each understand the rules, do you not?" They nodded in unison, very solemn. "Good, then have at it, but take care for the safety of the little ones." He stood with hands on hips glancing his delight from wife to children, who clambered up, poked their heads out the windows and waved from the sturdy balustrade of the look-out platform on the roof. "If it can manage a dozen, Lizzy, it's certainly safe for two." She nodded. "When our children can make the climb, we'll establish weekly family picnics here. What say you to that, Wife?"

She asked, "Even in winter, Mr. Darcy?"

"Blankets and hot cocoa, Mrs. Darcy! Where there's a problem, there exists a solution!" He extended the children's play to stretch the minutes of Elizabeth's conversation, though such was limited only to single words and simple sentences, but they were more than she had shared in days. Until recently, he had forgotten his misery when she had withdrawn on Boxing Day, but on that day he could name her problem and this time he could not. When he prodded her directly, she changed the subject. He could have as well been living with a box, inside of which his Lizzy had sealed herself.

Elizabeth's only reprieve from self-imposed censure was Georgiana's daily visits, however on Tuesday a note arrived instead of her sister.

Cressbrook, 17 August, 18- -

Dear Elizabeth,

I write for Georgiana who at present is ill-disposed. She regrets missing her appointment with you and will write you herself when she can. She asked that I tell you she has nearly completed the art for your children's nursery.

Her love and mine, Henry

At Cressbrook, Matthew Simons sat heavily across from Henry. "She will recover. My concern is for her spirit not her physical health or the chance for future children."

"She fears she follows her mother's tendency to miscarry, Matthew."

"Only a living child will dissuade her of that."

Henry nodded, undone by the loss neither of them had considered. "Your advice?"

"For her health, abstain one month and assure there is no pregnancy before Christmas. For her spirit, mourn with her." Dr. Simons laid a hand on Henry's shoulder. "There are no words for my sorrow, my friend." He paused at the door. "I'll carry Margaret to Lambton to attend those waiting in my parlor. The change will do her good and permit your privacy."

Henry sat on the terrace above Water-cum-Jolly to recover enough to support his wife before he climbed the stairs to the master's suite. Panicked to find it empty, he rushed from room to room until discovering Georgiana rocking in the nursery she had only just begun to design.

"Dr. Simons admonished you to bed rest for two days at least."

She looked up with dry eyes hollowed by tears full spent. "I've ruined everything." Her voice was flat. "I didn't know to wait past three months before one can be assured. There's no way to take back the announcement of a fact that no longer is." For a young lady to turn woman and then mourning mother in the space of weeks was too much. "I wish I could die for what I've caused. No child… no brother… and you are blamed. All our happiness is snuffed."

He made a nest of cushions on the floor then coaxed her to join him. He held her close as he had done the night long and all morning until Matthew had arrived to confirm what they already knew. Henry whispered his only truth. "I hold my happiness in my arms, Princess."

She looked up to see tears slip down his cheeks. She had never seen a man weep which made his pain, for the moment, more tangible than hers.

"Please, don't turn away, Georgiana. Accept that we suffer the same and will help each other recover." He whispered a kiss across limp curls while she sat stiffly in the circle of his arms, her judgment fixed staunchly against herself. He continued. "Your youth feels the passion of life to its extreme, a passion I treasure for the energy and windows it opens to me. But for the moment, I ask you to take the years of your husband's experience for your own. Perspective will calm us, if we let it."

"I don't see how –"

"Listen… please. When you're happy, the world radiates your joy, and when you mourn, all is lost. They are extremes of emotion that tilt one's perception. There's a path between the extremes that lets one separate the true pain from the passion. For instance… are you listening? Good. For instance, together we mourn the end of a dream. Perhaps you're as astonished as I that a child we won't hold in our arms is as painful to release as if we'd felt the warmth of its breath on our cheek. We don't mourn there will not be any children, we mourn this one. Do you understand?" He held her chin to look at him. "Hear me, precious Princess. I married you because you are my partner, not to protect your virtue. I did rejoice to be a father, but father or no, you are my beloved. Do you understand?"

"You're too good."

"If I'm good, it's because you make me so. Accept it, Georgiana. I need you. When I denied my deepest attachment to you, I lost myself… the happy part that let me laugh at life and embrace the world with hope. It was your passion for the truth that supported me to choose my heart." He smiled through his tears. "You see, each of our aspects balances the other. I need you and … perhaps you need me as much?"

She answered by relaxing against him, her head on his shoulder and her hand slipped inside his shirt to feel his heart. "And my brother? If I'd known to wait, you wouldn't –"

He pressed his fingers gently to her lips. "See the facts as they are, Georgiana. Darcy's judgment isn't against a child-too-soon. He has never wholly accepted me to be the brother he professes. It is a fact I had preferred not to acknowledge. Our child provided him the convenience to impose judgment already taken, but which he previously couldn't justify." She sat astonished. "I'm sorry, Princess. I didn't fully accept my reality with Darcy until our recent events. I had hoped his ruse to condemn me would protect you from his fact: he doesn't love me." He stroked her cheek and bent to look into her eyes. "You bear no fault."

"If this is so, how can you forgive him?"

"Forgive him? Acceptance isn't forgiveness. Today, the balance sheet's been tallied on both sides and we each are left with naught. My concern is for you caught between us."

"What would you do if I weren't mixed in?"

Henry looked away.

"Honesty, Mr. Fitzwilliam!" Georgiana sat straight. "I'm your wife, not your ward."

"I wouldn't see him again."

She understood.

Chapter 52

On the day Georgiana Darcy was delivered, George balked to learn he had a daughter. An only child himself and the father of a ten-year-old son, life had ill-prepared him to raise a girl. It did not occur to him that the girl might raise him.

When Georgiana was three, she insisted her father take tea in the playroom; within weeks he managed proper conversations with the dolls sharing their table. When she was four, she wrote her papa "letters" formally delivered by a footman; George answered them in the same block print and little drawings for the big words she didn't know and soon he initiated letters to her on his own.

And when she was five, she arrived at his study with a story book under her arm and a determined look in her eye; her nanny didn't read it right. With her support, George learned the proper intonation for each character in her favorite story, and before long, he read so well that she gave him leave to read other tales while she leaned back on his lap and listened intently. He ordered children's books from publishers in Town, previewed them and selected those he judged as best. On the odd occasion when she disdained his choice, he stood his ground and read it anyway, which slowly revealed the father to the daughter.

George escaped with her into the stories until he could pretend as well as he could debate. As Georgiana grew, she understood the difference between papa with others publicly and papa with her in their special chair during story time. She loved him desperately and he loved her likewise so.

Since the night Elizabeth had blamed herself for her husband's revulsion against his father, Elizabeth conversed with herself in her diary when Darcy attended the estate. Except for Georgiana, the diary was her only vehicle of conversation.

Pemberley, 19 August, 18- -

Until two weeks ago, no matter William's and my trouble, one of us had been in a state of mind to help the other sort his issue. Perhaps we each had grown complacent to believe our balance board of moods would naturally compensate and always return us to equilibrium. Now that I am as stuck as he is, it's clear that something outside of our stalemate must intercede to help us both.

I've argued my case to William in regard to his condemnation of his father, but to no avail. And he has argued his case that I should return to my former self as if my pain to have opened a box he was not prepared to look into should simply evaporate. My guilt is too profound and his hurt and anger toward his papa is too fixed. I search

Elizabeth blotted her words and closed her diary at the sound of footsteps on the colonnade.

"This just arrived from Cressbrook, Mrs. Darcy." Mrs. Reynolds announced, a bit out of breath. "Would you like a pot of tea, Mum?" Though tea would cure nothing, it was all the Housekeeper had to offer the lady whose spirit remained a shadow of itself.

"Yes, thank you," Elizabeth smiled. "That would be nice." She broke the seal as the door closed behind the Housekeeper.

Cressbrook, 19 August, 18- -

My Dear Lizzy,

I have sad news to share that I'm only just now able to talk about. Henry and I suffered a miscarriage two days ago.

A gasp then a cry escaped. Elizabeth breathed deep and read on.

Please don't worry for us. We have wept together and help each other to recover. It was an awful shock; I didn't know one ought wait three months before one could take confidence. Though I fear telling you because I know you will be sorry for us and don't need an added burden at this time, you are my sister and the person I want tell first.

I also want to explain why I will henceforth converse with you in letters rather than in person. Because of the enmity between my brother and Henry, I cannot enjoy visiting Pemberley – at least not at present. You had the right, Lizzy; my first family is with my husband. He has not influenced me in this regard; I've made my own choice.

I do hope that as soon as you and your babies are able to travel you will visit Cressbrook. I don't know how we will manage our friendship in a family come apart, but I'm hopeful we'll discover a way to do it without difficulty for you.

I miss you so very much, Lizzy.

Your Sister, Georgiana

When Darcy arrived for luncheon, he saw Elizabeth in Mrs. Reynolds arms. His wife wept as if her heart had broken.

"Dear God, what is it?" he called, racing across the room. The Housekeeper raised her tear-stained face and whispered the sad news before leaving him to console his wife. Darcy held his wife and rocked her in his arms until she had calmed enough to hear him speak.

"I'll go to her, Lizzy," he said softly. "I'll go to her for both of us and carry the piano forte to her to distract her from her grief."

Elizabeth's eyes overflowed again. She could not bear to reveal the second part of his sister's letter. She couldn't say that half of the tears she wept were for him and his awful shock when he grasped the state of his family.

Darcy followed Castlegate Lane to Cressbrook. Though it was a much longer route than the New Road, he rationalized the flatter land traversed by the Lane would rattle the wagon less. When arrived at Bottom Hill Road, he still had no concept what he would say, despite that he had practiced speeches the entire way.

Mr. Hopewell admitted Darcy to the parlor where Henry had made his camp seven months previous. Georgiana had made it a proper home, a lovely home, in fact. Time shamed him; he had not stood inside the Hall since the issue with the crystal decanter.

"Darcy." Henry's voice sounded crisply from the doorway. He did not extend his hand. "Georgiana will be prepared to receive you momentarily." He then crossed the room and reached his cousin an envelope. "Your visit saves me dispatching a courier."

Darcy stared at the check inside then read the accompanying note. Agitated, he said, "But we agreed that Cressbrook was a gift, which you've more than repaid by re-establishing its viability. I won't accept this, Cousin."

"You have no choice," Henry stated curtly. "My wife and I are agreed that a gift is from the heart, but since there's so little heart left between us, what was a gift is made a business debt, which we *will* repay." He spoke as the stranger

Darcy had declared him to be. "You understand from the note that our checks will arrive regularly, though we cannot predict the amount each month. Be assured they will continue until the balance is paid with interest."

"You insult me."

"It's your choice how you take it. Our choice merely reflects the reality between us." Henry bowed and quit the room.

Georgiana sat pale on a chaise near the bowed windows in the master's suite. She rose when her brother entered. He kissed her cheek then sat in the chair opposite without invitation.

"We grieve with you, Sister," Darcy began.

"Thank you."

"Are you well, other than the mourning I mean."

"Yes. As well as can be expected."

"The piano forte I gave you last summer is at this moment being delivered to your drawing room. We hope it will provide you some solace."

She nodded and said, "Thank you."

Darcy searched for more words.

"How is Lizzy?" Georgiana asked.

"She suffers for you in the extreme, but otherwise is well. Mrs. Carroll has her walking several rounds of the pavilion morning and evening to strengthen her physically. She's due in three weeks."

"Henry and I had agreed on the name of our firstborn," Georgiana offered the topic to connect her brother with her loss and also present a possible point of reconnection with her brother in future.

Darcy smiled, "Only one name? No matter if it is male or female? What is it, pray?"

"I shall follow our mother's choice to use her maiden name as my first-born's given one."

"You can't mean you will call it 'Darcy'!" The master of Pemberley laughed out loud. "Come, Georgiana, think of the confusion, let alone the stares when the child is introduced."

"No more confusion than 'Fitzwilliam' introduced to our family," she stated firmly. "To minimize misunderstanding, we will call him or her 'D' when in its uncle's presence."

Darcy shifted uncomfortably. His silence spoke for him.

Though not surprised that he scoffed, Georgiana was disappointed. She offered another perspective to make the name more palatable.

"You might consider our 'Darcy' as less the usurpation of what is yours and more that we honor papa."

Darcy's eyes flashed. "Our father doesn't deserve such an honor." His sister sat stiff. "Forgive me. My prejudice is justified," he defended.

"You hate our father?" she asked, incredulous.

He fumbled, "Not 'hate' so much as 'have lost respect for.'"

She raised her chin and with a voice he had not heard before, she hurled back, "How dare you! My papa weeps that his first born and greatest pride abjures his memory. I –"

"Greatest pride, indeed!" Darcy interrupted. "Our father loved your husband better than his own son, but that's neither here nor there." He softened in conciliation, "Let us agree to our different views and put this behind us."

She stood. "Impossible. I love papa too dearly to ever accept your prejudice. Give Lizzy my best. I will not see you again."

He sat a few moments not comprehending the depth of her resolve, but when she waited in icy silence at the bedchamber's open door, he collected his pride and bowed, saying, "Georgiana," as he passed. She did not respond.

Darcy arrived late to dinner. His foul mood left no doubt as to his visit's outcome. He excused the servants and reported events to Elizabeth with the voice of a wronged man.

When he concluded, she said simply, "I'm very sorry, Fitzwilliam."

After dinner, she retired to her chaise with a book.

Wound tight as a bow string, Darcy exploded to decry her distance from him. He had naively presumed they had returned to "before" after he had consoled her grief for Georgiana. "You're being unfair, Lizzy!"

"How so?" she asked without looking up from her book. He pulled the book from her grasp, flung it on the floor and imposed himself on the edge of her chaise.

"Look at me!" he demanded. "You've withdrawn from me precisely when I need you most. By any definition, Mrs. Darcy, that is unfair."

Elizabeth had further sorted their issue in her diary that afternoon. She was clear as to her message. "No, my love," she said quietly, "what is unfair is that you married me."

Darcy sat still as if she had shot him through the heart.

"The truth is hard, William. I told you once that though I am outspoken, I don't wish to cause pain to others and especially not you. As a result of my mistake to query about familial religiosity, you are estranged from your father's memory and now from Georgiana. On Boxing Day, we both had fair warning that my nature could challenge you with hard choices, but neither of us conceived my potential to wreak such havoc in your life as I have now done. It is clear that 'Elizabeth un-reined' is a liability to your well-being, not an asset."

"You did nothing wrong, Lizzy."

She looked into his eyes. "A person's actions are judged by their effect, not her intentions. I stand indicted and convicted. Though I cannot change my nature, I can limit our interaction to protect you from my potential to cause you even more harm. Know that I also accept my part in the dissolution of your brotherhood with Henry. You lived twenty-three years in relative harmony with him until these past months when I prodded you to confront your ghosts. We must face the facts, my love. No matter our initial delight in our compatibility, my nature is a bad match with yours."

She prepared for bed, kissed his cheek and bade him "Sleep well."

Elizabeth's appraisal had dunked his head in a figurative barrel of icy water. Like a person stunned to hear that his beloved has suddenly perished, Darcy's head and heart sat numb. However, both fully comprehended her unwavering confidence in her analysis and the iron will of her resolve. Finally, he fell asleep, his head pillowed on arms folded on the dining table.

Darcy opened his eyes in pre-dawn darkness. Any hope that last night's reality had been but a nightmare conjured in sleep was dashed when he crossed the room and tripped on the book he had ripped from Elizabeth's hands. He picked it up, laid it on her chaise and stepped into the early chill through a French door.

After ten minutes, he found himself on the bench at lake side where he had first accepted he would not forfeit his fledgling connection with Elizabeth to his fear of sharing deeply. Certainly, he was no longer that man who had attempted to impose restrictions on her actions to assure his peace of mind, and yet his actions had ultimately caused her to deny herself the freedom to be Elizabeth. It was a grim irony.

A breeze ruffled the water. The first birdsong of early light interrupted the stillness. With hands clasped before him, Darcy accepted that their union would never be as it had been before he had learned of Dr. Ashworth's medical records; there was no going back once words were spoken and actions taken. Drawing on the lesson from the Boxing Day contract, he appreciated that stalemate could be resolved to "better than before," however, it required at least one of the parties to adjust his position. In that case, it had been he who had adjusted. And in this case, it must be him as well. He grasped their differences a bit more clearly. When he recoiled, it was often due to his myopic view of a matter, hence the possibility of change existed if he altered his perspective, whereas when Elizabeth recoiled, she had already tested the facts soundly and objectively, hence her judgment was absolute.

As the sun crested the horizon, he was sobered to realize that when his wife refused to forgive she only indicted herself while he usually cast aspersion on others.

At breakfast, Darcy was served the message that Mr. Fitzwilliam awaited him in the master's study. Elizabeth did not look up. Darcy left his half-eaten ham and eggs to meet the master of Cressbrook.

Henry had ordered tea, a presumption of comfort in a House denied to him. He returned cup to saucer when Darcy entered. "I come on business of clarification," he said matter-of-factly.

Darcy ordered a cup for himself. "What would you clarify, Cousin?" he asked, standing by his desk.

"Georgiana related to me her discussion with you. I've come to state that you have it wrong in regard to your father's preference for me over you. I don't expect you to accept my words, but in memory of George Darcy, who I hold very dear, I owe it to him to make the attempt."

Darcy nodded gratitude for the cup just arrived, but the topic distracted him and the cup sat steaming on the table. "Would that you could convince me, Henry," he said sincerely, "but the facts speak for themselves."

"What 'facts'?"

"Those I discovered in this very waste bin seven years ago." He gestured to the basket beside the desk. "Or perhaps it meant so little to you that you have forgotten when Father dispatched me to Derby so that he could discuss his will with the son he would have preferred." Darcy's misery collapsed him into a chair. After a few moments, he said softly, "I read the crumpled will, in which he designated you as Georgiana's sole guardian and executor of his estate. I grant that he later adjusted those wishes, but his initial intent was clear."

Henry laughed. "Dear God, Darcy, you can make an awful muddle of facts when you're emotionally distraught. I do understand how you could have mis-interpreted the discarded will, but you have it completely wrong."

"Do not insult me, Cousin!" Darcy bellowed, slamming his fist on the arm of his chair.

Henry sighed and shook his head. "You insult yourself, Fitzwilliam," he stated with finality. "If you hadn't hated me so much, you would have questioned how your devoted father might come to offer me sole guardianship and executor's rights. It's incongruous on the face of it unless one is already biased." Henry rose. "In honor of my Uncle, I shall relate the circumstances that caused him to worry for his children when he passed. Whether you hear it accurately is your choice." After laying out the details, the master of Cressbrook bowed and took his leave.

A half-hour later, Darcy drank cold tea and did not grimace to taste its awfulness.

Chapter 53

Georgiana's miscarriage affected Elizabeth deeply and was the topic of much reflection, not only for Georgiana's pain and disappointment or the clear break within their family, but also for the facts of life that a woman soon to give birth must confront. Elizabeth did not need a physician to tell her it would be days, not weeks, until delivery; her babies had quieted as if they prepared and their mama had best do as well.

Though still too emotional at times, she had been more herself than not for weeks, and as a rational person who was compelled to separate what she could control from what she could not, she was calm and deliberate in regard to what lay ahead. Resting on her chaise in late August, she had the facts at hand; two babies lived inside her with all indications of good health and she had gotten them close to her calendar's prediction. Once birthing began, there would be little in her power to alter nature's whims.

On one point, however, there was an action she could take and the more she considered it the more compulsion gripped her. There were but five scenarios post-delivery: all survived, one or the other child did not, neither child survived, the mama did not or all succumbed. As tragic as the loss of one or both would be, she was certain she would cope; Georgiana's daily letters demonstrated that no matter the heartache, the spirit was resilient and there was always the possibility of more children. The last two scenarios, however, would deny William his partner, and though she decried herself to be a poor one, they were each too vested in the other to cope well with the other's loss. Certain he would survive it better if she confronted the possibility with him, she accepted to share her feelings on this one subject and would prod him to prepare for all eventualities.

Sequestration in the pavilion during three consecutive days of rain served Darcy a small taste of confinement. That Elizabeth had endured more than four months of such restriction humbled any pride he had taken in his efforts to support her. On the fourth day, a tempest of thunder quaked the House as a bolt of lightning struck in the proximity of the great oak. When the worst was passed, Darcy stripped to shirt and breeches and set out with lantern in hand. He returned a happy, sodden mess to meet a wife set to address the possibility of her own demise.

"It still stands, Lizzy. I tested every part of our tree house and she's as sturdy as when we declared her done." He pulled a quilted throw from a chair to mop himself. "The lyme tree ten yards to the east was split clear to its roots. By rights it should have been the oak since it stands taller. It's a wonder the entire edge of the Park wasn't set alight." He sank to the carpet beside her chaise and rested his head on her bulge. "I would have built it again, but it would have cost me dearly." He smiled up with golden eyes. "The gods would not sacrifice our homage to our little ones." And then he considered, "I think we'll not wait until they can climb themselves. We'll winch them up in baskets to celebrate their first month with a picnic. What say you?"

After having accepted his responsibility for their impasse, Darcy had resolved to maintain a positive spirit with Elizabeth, no matter if she responded likewise or not. Until he could discover how to heal them, he would at least remind her how it used to be. His smile dimmed however when he saw Elizabeth focus on their blurred reflection in the glass. He read the signs; she had uncovered a problem and the set of her chin declared she would share it.

"Out with it, Lizzy! If you take exception to the baskets, we can –"

"I take exception that we have prepared for only one basket of expectation."

"A riddle?" His spirit buoyed again. He sensed an actual conversation.

"No, a difficult topic I am loath to broach and you will hate even more to hear."

Darcy watched the blur of them together in the glass doors until, sensing her direction, he erupted, "Say nothing more. I forbid it!"

"Just as you would have forbidden the loss of Georgiana's child?" Her voice was as tender as the topic was harsh.

He rose to escape.

"Sit, William! So help me I'll get up and follow you to assure this discussion."

Darcy halted, sank into a chair near her chaise and forced out words his heart cringed to hear. "If we lose either of them, we'll get through it, Lizzy."

"And if I'm the one who is lost? Sit and hear me out, Fitzwilliam Darcy! You can't escape that such could be the result!'"

He only half-heard her counsel; enough to know she reminded that his father had married twice and discovered his deepest happiness with his second wife. She did not require him to remarry only to know she would be glad for him to do it and glad for their children to know a mother. She had given him her blessing and he hated her for it. No, he hated that the blessing might be needed. Darcy sat like the limestone of White Peak. She continued as gently as possible. "You've endured so much during these last weeks and don't deserve more heaped on the rest, but if the worst occurs and I hadn't spoken, you'd be left without my support and that would be too much." She reached and grazed his cheek. "I think —"

"Be still. Let *me* think." He studied her then said, "Elizabeth, I expect full honesty. Do you promise?" She nodded. "Have you grounds for concern as to the outcome of delivery?"

"None but the usual," she said.

He paced. "If I could support your confidence, tell me how you'd have me do it."

"You?" She laughed a little. "Sit in the chapel and say a prayer, I suppose."

"A prayer would help you best?"

"A prayer is all a husband is permitted, Mr. Darcy, that and perhaps a bottle of Scotch."

He grimaced at her joke while he made space beside her to take careful measure of her expression. "If I sat with you during delivery, would it be better for you?"

"It's women's labor, William. Men do not attend."

"The fact for most need not be the fact for all," he postured.

She laughed. "Your pacing during hours of labor would only heighten my nerves and I'm certain I'll have nerves enough without adding yours to mine."

When he continued to press her to reconsider, she grasped the opportunity to confront his judgment against George. "William, your suggestion to attend at delivery is based on facts reinterpreted from a perspective not previously considered. It reminds me of a certain lady who thought she'd correctly gleaned the truth from facts that falsely indicted you and supported Mr. Wickham. You recall those days, do you not?" He nodded wary of where she was leading. "The difficulty, of course, was that I required more facts before the full truth could be appreciated."

His amiability turned defensive. "You refer to my father, I take it."

She nodded and let go the lesson.

On 24 August, Darcy presented his proposal to Dr. Simons and Mrs. Carroll; he would attend at his children's delivery. The midwife declared it inadvisable and the doctor concurred, but Darcy could not be dissuaded. He had seen the flicker of relief in Elizabeth's eyes before she had scoffed at his proposal.

Within earshot of the patient, the three negotiated Darcy's petition with animation. Mrs. Carroll laid out the general reasons why husbands were left out while Dr. Simons pointed to the complications caused by a distressed partner if problems arose. The two believed they had convinced their host when he sat back to study the mantle clock. Then of a sudden, he turned to his wife across the room. "Mrs. Darcy you've heard their reasoning. For my part, I would hold your hand throughout. What's your choice?"

Elizabeth's nerves had imagined enough on their own without the midwife's and physician's details. She locked eyes with Darcy, and with chin raised to midwife and physician, she declared, "My husband will attend so long as he can stomach it. I've witnessed him at his less than best. He deserves the same privilege in my regard."

Overruled, Simons and Carroll assigned Darcy three duties, which he insisted to practice by counting Elizabeth's pulse, holding a glass of water to her lips and laying cool cloths on her forehead. She extended her wrist without argument while he tested a variety of timepieces until identifying his piece of choice. She protested that every person could tip water to another's lips until he got her neck so wet that she instructed him personally in the art. As to the cool cloths, Elizabeth drew the line and told him to practice on himself. She giggled to watch him fold the cloth then wring it, then wring it followed by folding, until he fancied the best method before resting his head back on the settee to practice the cloth's positioning. Darcy took hope that their shared preparation began to reconnect them.

"I'm glad for your energy, William, but I wonder if you'll be sorry for the not so entertaining hours you will endure. Perhaps you'll reconsider?"

He sat up, catching the cloth in his hand, his eyes dark and piercing. "You miss the point, Mrs. Darcy. I attend to support my wife's courage and should that go missing, I will insert my own. I will not lose you, Lizzy."

"Losing Lizzy" weighed heavily on Darcy, but not because he feared she would succumb. The taste of their uninhibited exchanges had left him hungry for more, but after he had mastered his assigned duties, she had returned to polite murmurs.

On 25 August, Darcy collected his father's diaries, slips of paper and a pencil then settled in the Queen Anne by the north hearth. In this first stab to win back his wife's confidence, he dedicated himself to collecting facts. He began reading where he had left off in the year of his birth, and by day's end, he accepted that George Darcy sincerely loved his Anne, though this fact did not excuse the initial seduction. A number of diary passages had also recorded parental concern about Darcy's competition with Henry when George and Anne showed attention to their nephew. These entries had dated from the first months of Henry's arrival and continued through Darcy's tenth year when he closed the book to sleep.

The next morning, Darcy confided his renewed interest in his father's diaries to his wife. Elizabeth made no comment. He had not expected her to. Patience.

The day's reading on 26 August included his mother's illness. Darcy discovered his father had confided his suffering to these pages in order to maintain happy familial interaction for the benefit of his children and ailing wife. Such was his father's pain before his mother's death that Darcy braced to read the ramblings after her interment. Partway through those awful pages, his father's grief was interrupted by three sentences that did not fit. Darcy paused and reread them.

> *"I recommend the mastiff. It is my favorite breed. Refer to "Carter's Definitive Guide of English Breeds," plate 37, for an excellent representation of the beast."*

The mastiff was Darcy's favorite. His father preferred the sheepdog.

Darcy called to his wife, "This is strange, Lizzy."

With diary in hand, he crossed to her chaise with excitement, but when arrived he dropped the book. "It's begun, has it?" he asked. She held her great belly, her eyes focused to endure the first clutch of serious pain. She nodded with a grimace. He called to a footman to summon the midwife and dispatch a rider for Dr. Simons then he helped Elizabeth to her bed.

"I've felt the pains for three hours, William. I was surprised they weren't as bad as I'd imagined. Only…"

He timed the contraction then timed then the space between it and the next.

From where she washed her hands in the corner, Mrs. Carroll asked, "The times, Sir?" He reported.

Elizabeth finished her statement. "Only the pains got stronger much faster than I expected."

He whispered at her ear. "We agreed to do this together, Lizzy." He kissed her temple. "You've never broken your promise to me."

She watched him intently before squeezing her eyes shut. He timed the pain. Before the next one began she drew the hand holding hers to her lips and said, "I love you."

They were committed together. He prepared a cool cloth for her forehead to do his part.

After an hour, Darcy penned a note to Cressbrook.

> *Dear Family,*
>
> *Our Lizzy is in labor. She would want you to be here, both of you, if you can stomach being in my proximity. You need not speak to me or even look at me if it pains you too much, but for Elizabeth's sake come. Please."*
>
> *Fitzwilliam*

Chapter 54

Mrs. Carroll predicted that Mr. and Mrs. Darcy would hold two babies at tea time on the morrow. But luck is a relative thing. From William's view, the fourteen hours of labor had drained him of patience many times over, but he could have withstood more. From his lady's perspective, luck had forgotten her until Anne-Elizabeth slipped into the world, crying the loveliest announcement.

"She'll clean up nicely, Mrs. Darcy!" her husband beamed, noting their daughter arrived at four minutes before midnight on 26 August.

The intoxication of a living child with lungs implying excellent health let a mother carrying twins forget there was a second. The surprise of an intense, long pain froze celebration in her throat and only her excellent control took hold of panic to know she must do it again. Long since exhausted and wrung limp like one of William's cloths, tears wet her neck as if Darcy had forgotten how to tip the glass. Her pain evoked his calm, a balance of forces that made it better, if only a little.

"Easy, Lizzy. This will go quickly, remember? The second comes within minutes of the first." He glanced at the clock and began counting: less than eight minutes preferably, ten at the outside or there might be problems.

Elizabeth's labor had long since denied her husband any conversation, restricting him only to holding her hand, a hand that now threatened to bruise him for its sudden pressure. He glanced at the foot of the bed then at her. She appeared unaware that doctor and midwife had left their posts to whisper behind the screens. He willed himself to walk, not run then stood as spectator to intense discussion. Mrs. Carroll left to scrub her hands. Dr. Simons turned to Darcy.

"It is a son, sir. He is breech. He is caught by one arm and perhaps his chin. Mrs. Carroll will free him." Dr. Simons squeezed Darcy's shoulder to focus him. "She knows what she is about." Darcy's nod broke his terror. "Please step outside, Sir. We will summon you —"

"No!" Darcy shrugged free and nearly spat the words, "I stay! Do it and do it quickly!"

Dr. Simons said a prayer before rounding the screen.

Darcy bent to his wife's ear and explained the problem as he stroked her cheek.

Mrs. Carroll's voice soothed even as she rattled orders. "Did you understand your husband, Mum? Good. When you feel each pain start to ease say 'Now.' This will help me judge when I will help the lad. It will be a sharp pain, but will be very quick. You're doing well."

Darcy glanced at the mantle clock. His heart pounded. *Do it! Do it!* Elizabeth watched him with a steady look until, ashen-faced, she squeezed her eyes tight against pain born in hell.

Chapter 55

George Darcy led the hunt under a threatening sky. Fitzwilliam had counseled against the foray, but the old gentleman insisted and was glad for Henry's compromise that they could ride to the cottage above the Wye, where they would let the weather pace their plans.

On this particular afternoon, Darcy preferred riding at the rear and was relieved that Henry entertained his father in the lead. Papa got more stubborn with each birthday. One thought seeped to another. He and papa had not had smooth relations since losing mama, but their camaraderie had deteriorated even more since Darcy's graduation from university. It was as if they had exchanged places, father and son; as if, papa perceived his son's counsel as a challenge rather than well-judged insight, as if…

Darcy pulled up at the near side of the cottage where fat splats of rain danced in the dirt just as a bolt of lightning kissed the edge of the cliff above Hobbs House. The shock reared and twisted his father's mount. Papa lost grip of the reins.

"F – a – t – h – e – r!" Darcy's cry sounded in his father's ear just before the silvered head collided with a boulder. His blood washed away as quickly as it trickled over the ancient limestone.

The full way home Darcy raised up in the wagon on all fours with his back arched over his father to protect him from the pelting rain. The longest journey of his life let Darcy feel Papa more personally than he had touched the man in twenty-two years; he caressed Papa's cheek and felt between the layers of clothing for his heartbeat.

The nightmare lingered two weeks. "A strong, old gentleman," Dr. Simons had stated.

The master of Pemberley knew he would forever remember Elizabeth's look of becalmed trust become wide-eyed terror as she called out in mortal agony with a scream that shuddered staff throughout the House and slumped them to their knees in prayer. The Fitzwilliams, having arrived hours earlier, kept vigil in the breakfast room where Georgiana leapt from her chair when she heard her sister's cry and struggled against Henry's restraint.

"Wait, Georgiana. Let Matthew do his work."

Pemberley's clocks tic-tocked a conversation of seconds to fill the silence with time in a House that held its breath.

Instinctively, Darcy held Elizabeth's shoulders to the bed when her body rose up against the intrusion. He did not feel Dr. Simons' hands urge him to release. He did not respond to the doctor's words that he had done well and it was over. He did not hear his son's timorous cries that sounded as if he sensed his near brush with death, nor had Darcy held a watch to mark that James arrived two minutes into the new day. Elizabeth lay pallid and lifeless in her husband's hands.

"She sleeps, Mr. Darcy. It is common after labor and such pain as at the last. Here sir, feel her pulse." The physician freed one of Darcy's hands and pressed the gentleman's fingers to her wrist. "The maids have some tidying to attend, Sir. The nurses have carried the children to the nursery." Dr. Simons looked up at the sound of doors opening. "Henry, escort Mr. Darcy to the fresh air. Mrs. Darcy is resting."

Before that moment, Darcy had not known if the Fitzwilliams had responded to his invitation, and in a way, he still did not know as Henry took one arm and Georgiana the other. Too stunned to acknowledge them or respond to their gentle support, he walked stiff and mute between them along torch-lit garden paths. When he at last managed words, they were disconnected memories of fear and awful seconds stretched to feel like forever.

Georgiana's whisper of a voice soothed him to the present. "You are a father, Fitzwilliam. Come. Let us visit your children." She escorted him up two flights of stairs and down the long hallway to the nursery decorated in reds and blues.

Too numb to think what to expect, Darcy was undone to see his daughter in her cradle. Clean, swaddled and settled in cherubic sleep, she was a far cry from the glistening bit of wriggling skin he had witnessed born in the pavilion.

Anne-Elizabeth's nurse beamed, "She's the most beautiful child I've ever laid eyes on. Your pride and joy to be sure, Mr. Darcy."

Darcy nodded in a daze while Georgiana guided him to the Windsor rocker near the hearth and instructed him how to hold his daughter. Her brother did not respond. She asked the nurse to help him hold his arms properly then settled her niece with papa. He had never held a newborn and this doll-child, whose pink lips blew tiny bubbles as she slept, was smaller than any baby he had seen. Gently, Georgiana asked him to call her by name.

Barely audible, he whispered, "Hello, Little Anne-E."

She told him to kiss the baby's cheek.

Darcy felt the soft warmth of a rose petal in the sun against his lips and embraced magic that even his daydreams had not comprehended. From nothing, he now held a separate being.

Anne-Elizabeth's nurse returned the infant to her cradle while Georgiana fetched her nephew. Little James combined whimpers with tinny cries in a continuous drone of disquiet. His body, stiff in his distress, already began to evidence the discoloration of bruising along his left side from the intrusion of Mrs. Carroll's hand. Darcy was overcome to see his son and remember. Georgiana excused the nurses.

"I can't calm him, Brother. Perhaps he requires his papa to do it?" She thought she herself would weep to look into his tear-filled eyes too stuck in memories to respond. "Come, crook your arm as you did with Anne-Elizabeth."

Darcy watched the tiny stranger who looked nothing like his sister and then grazed his finger against the little cheek as warm and soft as Anne-E's.

"Oh my! Your rocking appears to calm him," Georgiana encouraged. "Sing to him. Perhaps the lullaby you sang to me when I was young?" Georgiana wondered if the lullaby did not serve her brother as well as little James. The child calmed, though he did not sleep.

Within two minutes, "papa" and "Darcy" merged as one. In a flurry of orders, he directed Georgiana to fetch Anne-E and called the nurses to supervise the transport of nursery essentials to the pavilion. His family would not be separated.

Clustered near the south hearth, the rocking chairs, cradles and two chests were arranged in a make-shift nursery. With his family united, Darcy's talent to master took control with the same devotion to detail he dedicated to his land. While Elizabeth remained in deep sleep, Darcy inserted himself as the attending parent and learned to support a newborn's head and even the art of folding and tucking a nappy securely in place. Then he mastered holding babies against his shoulder to elicit small burps and took exceeding pleasure in their joint accomplishment.

The next afternoon, the family sat numb. Dr. Simons whispered with the midwife behind the screens. The babies cried. The fire crackled. Mrs. Darcy had awakened with a fever, and though only slight, any fever after childbirth portended a problem.

Elizabeth insisted to nurse little James, who had refused the nurse hired to feed him. After each feeding Elizabeth closed her eyes to recover enough strength to do it again. Every fiber of her being focused to assure her son would live, hence she only sipped broth and tea then slept and nursed again; his stomach was too little to sustain him more than a few hours.

Georgiana did her best to distract her brother by assuring that one child or the other was always in its father's arms.

That evening, Darcy and Henry sat at opposite sides of the hearth; the former held Anne-E while latter held James. Darcy studied his cousin comforting the infant who still adjusted to the world with little whimpers now and then. He broke the silence. "I wish to apologize, Henry."

Georgiana glanced at her husband, dreading that her brother offered more of his hope to be followed by disappointment.

"No need, Darcy." Henry said tersely.

"There is need. Indeed, there is great need. When a man accepts he has acted like a child, he must acknowledge the injustice before he can move forward."

Both intrigued and circumspect, Henry studied Darcy. At last he asked, "Your meaning, Cousin?"

"I've read enough of my father's diaries to know it has been my jealousy that has challenged you over the years." Anne-Elizabeth shifted in her sleep. Darcy adjusted his arm for her comfort then continued, "While I'm chagrined to know my bad behavior, I'm also glad to realize my fault. I wouldn't wish to model such inconsistency to my children." He looked long at his cousin then said, "Of all the men of my acquaintance, you are the person I'd most like to emulate as the model of a good man. Hear me out. Please. You're as consistent as the stars in the sky, Cousin. You've always loved me no matter how I abused you; that is until I included the woman you love in that abuse. There is no excuse for my behavior. With diligent practice, I hope to learn at least a little of your devotion and dependable support. Such is the best recipe for raising happy and contented children, I think."

Henry considered then said simply, "Thank you, Darcy."

Georgiana watched her lap when her brother turned to her. "I can't think why you would want to name your child 'Darcy' after the reputation I've bequeathed to that name, but I'd be glad if you would do. A new 'Darcy' could reinvent the meaning to something better than I've given it. I'm sincerely sorry for the pain and distress I've caused you, Sister."

"Your words imply a change that is difficult to swallow, Fitzwilliam."

"On that, I have no doubt," he grimaced then included both in his gaze. "New facts cause me to reappraise what I had erroneously presumed to be the truth." He rose, settled Anne-E in her aunt's arms, kissed his sleeping wife and excused himself.

The Fitzwilliams sat silent watching each other. Georgiana was the first to move, and after returning both babies to their cradles, she sat close to her husband. "He appeared sincere."

"Indeed."

"He left so quickly. Should I follow to assure he is well?"

Henry pressed his lips. "Best to let him be. His consistency will reveal itself soon enough."

Chapter 56

D arcy had not intended to make a speech or even to apologize, but the words that had flowed from his heart felt liberating as he stretched his legs to his study's hearth-fire and reflected. No matter if Georgiana and Henry forgave him, he was clear that his path was forever altered. And though he had initially consigned the motivation for his reform to his children's benefit, he acknowledged that, in truth, he had done it for himself.

He ordered a sherry delivered to his study then carried a lamp to the library to locate *Carter's Definitive Guide to English Breeds*. He had at least learned his father well enough to know when George Darcy left a hidden message. Claiming Darcy's favorite breed for himself was too out of character, which meant the message had been written specifically for his son to interpret as instructions to inspect Plate 37.

Seated at his desk with the great volume of lithographs in hand, Darcy turned the pages with increasing anticipation.

Plate 37.

Only the artist's minuscule lines depicted a hunter with a leashed mastiff. There was no message even when he held a magnifying glass to study every line etched to make the image.

He laughed cynically to have sincerely believed there would be anything to discover. After gulping his sherry in one swallow, he set hat on head and walked the park.

When Darcy arrived at the pavilion, Henry and Georgiana had long since retired. His children slept and soon he did as well. Awaking in middle night when Elizabeth shifted her nursing son, he focused then reached a hand to her forehead and touched his with the other.

"Your fever might have reduced a little," he said. "How do you feel?"

"Weary."

"Is it costing you too much to feed James?"

"It would cost me more not to."

He fluffed his pillow and leaned back in his customary position to discuss.

"I met disappointment today, Lizzy."

"Mmm." She responded without expression.

"I thought my father conveyed a secret directive to me in his diary." He proceeded as if she took an interest. "I was so excited to learn it, Lizzy, so completely convinced that I had got it right." Darcy sighed. "There was nothing, of course. I can't tell you how silly I felt, sitting with that book like a lad caught with his pants down."

Darcy reached for James to burp him. "Let me do that," he said. "You rest." It felt good to pat the tiny back and feel his son adjust against his shoulder. Together they were a cocoon of interdependence.

"The clue?" Elizabeth's voice interrupted her husband's communion with their son.

"What?" he asked turning toward her. "Oh. It was a silly reference to a dog's picture in a particular volume."

"What made it a clue?"

"Because he said the mastiff was his favorite breed when in fact it's mine. And he wrote it in the midst of mourning mamma after her interment." Darcy had elicited one little burp and, deeming it enough, tucked James in his nearby cradle.

"Is there more than one edition of that book?" she asked.

Darcy stopped short as if struck by a bolt. In the next second, he grabbed his breeches and raced toward the doors, but before his bare feet reached the exit, he turned abruptly and ran to Elizabeth. "If you are correct, I'll forbid you to ever again judge against yourself in my regard."

"And if I am wrong?" she asked calmly.

"Then it is proof positive I need you to keep thinking for my benefit since my head accepts defeat too easily." He kissed her gently and thought she kissed him back, briefly.

With lamp in hand, a white-shirted Darcy raced up the stairs and along two hallways to the library. The night footman watched wide-eyed from his post in the entrance hall. The flapping tails of the approaching shirt looked like a ghost.

Darcy held his lamp along the shelves of gold-embossed, leather-bound titles. Nothing. He vowed to look again in the morning, but the feeling of foolishness already displaced expectation and he was again humbled by defeat.

On his return through the breakfast room, a fleeting thought of his wife's persistent advice to pursue a problem to its end steered Darcy up the children's stairs instead of down the garden ones. After climbing another flight, he knocked at Mr. Thomas' door. The boom of gongs and ringing of chimes declared it was four o'clock.

"Is there a problem, Sir?" the butler asked attempting a look of respectability in his nightshirt. Suddenly, alarm filled his eyes. "Dear God. Is it Mrs. Darcy?"

"No. No." Darcy felt silly, indeed. "I'm searching for a particular volume, which appears to be missing from the library."

Thomas nodded as if such a request were usual at that hour then pulled on trousers and jacket before leading their return to the library. After several minutes of perusing titles, Darcy's expanded explanation about the missing volume steered the pair downstairs to the basement.

"Perhaps you don't recall my letter three years ago, Sir. To make space for new editions, we moved the old ones here." He stood before a heavy wooden door and selected a key. While Thomas' lamplight disappeared into the cavernous room of books, Darcy vowed to devote as much time to learning his House as he did his land.

"I found it, Sir" the butler's voice called from the back of the vault. He approached quickly and reached the volume to his master, who bowed his thanks and hurried to his study.

"Say a prayer, Lizzy," Darcy whispered.

While turning the pages to Plate 37, he recalled this same leather binding he had held on his lap as a boy while papa had pointed out the characteristics of the breeds. Whether there was a secret to be discovered or not, this book felt right. He paused at Plate 36 and took a breath.

When he turned the page, he gasped. In the margin, scribed in his mother's hand,

> *"Go with your sister to the playroom and beneath the tallest tree you will find a special treasure."*

Darcy's finger caressed her words. The thought that his parents had conspired together surprised him, but when he left out the bias against his father, he admitted their united effort was in keeping with their public face of "best partners." It was all he could do to force his steps downstairs to the pavilion and not climb the stairs to the playroom. Mama had said to go with Georgiana. Darcy dug deep for patience to do it according to their mother's instruction.

Chapter 57

Too excited to keep his discovery to himself, Darcy woke Elizabeth to show her his father's diary message then Lady Anne's words in *Carter's Definitive Guide to English Breeds*. She complimented him, "You did well to spy out the clue, Mr. Darcy."

"*We* did well, Mrs. Darcy," he responded firmly then set both books on the floor. "I've cost you your sleep, Lizzy." He blew out the lamp. "Sweet dreams," he whispered.

Darcy rose at half-past-seven and hurriedly made his toilette in his bedchamber. He returned to the pavilion just as the Fitzwilliams sat down to breakfast.

Georgiana smiled to see him. "We think Lizzy begins to improve and Mrs. Carroll concurs."

"As do I," said Darcy, hovering at his sister's elbow. "Georgiana, would you mind very much to delay your breakfast?"

"For how long?"

"I don't know."

"To what end?"

"Ultimately, I don't know that either."

Georgiana was hungry. "It can't wait?"

"I'd prefer not."

Henry offered, "If I can be a service in Georgiana's stead, I'd be glad –"

"Thank you for your kindness," Darcy interrupted, "but I'm sorry. It must be my sister." Georgiana carried two pieces of toast with her as she hurried to keep up.

Lady Anne had created the playroom for her firstborn, but Georgiana had enjoyed it equally since the great room was made for imagining. The north wall was planted with a forest of painted trees while the south wall hosted a garden of the Lady's favorite flowers. The east wall connected the woods and gardens with a meadow whose rolling, green hills and cloud dappled sky sat opposite a village sporting shops, a church, and a village green along the south wall. On the floor, the Lady had painted a stone bridge crossing a brook that flowed from a little pond. There were shelves along the walls housing tired toys, a small carpet on which was arranged a child's chairs and table upon which sat the tea set papa had added and there were window seats with fat cushions below each window where one could curl with a favorite book.

Georgiana settled on a window seat and looked at her brother. "Well?" she asked.

Darcy sat in the pond near her feet and explained that in the process of learning his father better he had discovered his hint of a clue, and thereafter, their mother's message.

"The tallest tree is that one," Georgiana walked to the window above which a broad oak spread its branches across the ceiling. Seeing no visible treasure, she removed the window seat's cushion and opened the lid beneath. "Have a look, Fitzwilliam."

He pulled out a porcelain horse, two cracked leather ones, a doll with a very loose wig, and several rubber balls, also cracked and hard with age. Darcy inspected each one but found nothing remarkable. The siblings sat on the floor and studied the tree in silence.

"A treasure is buried," Georgiana's soft voice said at last.

Darcy looked inside the seat at the floor, and then at the floor on the outside. "There is no false bottom, Sister."

"Then it is the floor itself," Georgiana stated and reached inside to test the polished planks. "They are firmly set," she said at last, disheartened.

"Wait here," Darcy directed. He returned with his clutch of tools and selected a chisel and hammer. "It's tight in here," he declared after a moment.

"Shall I try?" she asked, kneeling beside him.

"You first and then me," he graciously allowed after having strained a shoulder muscle.

"Light a lamp to shine inside," she said. She managed to loosen the center board, but nothing more. Georgiana emerged from inside the seat with strands of hair slipped from the curls piled on her head. Her face was flushed and she sucked on a small finger-wound. "Have at it, Fitzwilliam."

Thinking better of again squeezing himself inside the box, Darcy attacked it from the outside. With the chisel to score the painted-over joints and the pry-bar to separate the pieces, he disassembled the window seat. It demanded some effort on Darcy's part, requiring that he remove his jacket and then his tie, which he later used to bind his shin after the pry-bar slipped, but in the end the job was done.

Georgiana immediately tapped on the floor: first where the window seat had been then on the playroom side. As she tapped, she said, "We ought to have done this before we –" A distinct difference in tone sobered them both to stare first at the floor and then at each other.

Darcy set the chisel on the joint of the loosened board and hit hard to free the peg holding it. The board sprang free so violently that it collided with his chin. Georgiana dabbed the blood with her clean handkerchief. "At this point, the wood appears to be winning," she teased.

Darcy smiled despite the pain. He soon noted that the peg was a false one, which implied the rest might also be. The glue holding them together had been time itself.

Inside the two by four foot cavity lay little leather volumes stacked in tidy rows.

"You look first, Georgiana," Darcy said huskily.

She selected one, rubbed the dust off on her petticoat, and opened the cover. Georgiana looked at her brother, her bluest of blue eyes brimming with tears. "They are Mama's diaries," she said softly. Emotion overwhelmed her. Darcy held her until she calmed.

While Georgiana emptied toys from a large basket in which to transport their treasure, Darcy spied a folded sheet beneath the nearest stack of books. After a cursory look, he slipped it in the breast pocket that protected Elizabeth's oval stone. Together, brother and sister carefully piled twenty-eight diaries into the basket, which Darcy carried to the pavilion.

"Shall we read them immediately or wait?" she asked en route.

"I think both we and mama have waited long enough," her brother answered.

Arrived at the pavilion, they found Henry's note; he would return from Cressbrook at tea time. Leaving Georgiana and basket by the north hearth,

Darcy slipped behind the screens to apprise his wife of their discovery. His heart pounded to see fevered perspiration glisten on Elizabeth's brow. She was very pale. He counted her pulse. It beat too fast. James cried. She opened her eyes, orienting herself before reaching for her son.

"Not now, Lizzy," Darcy said gently as he restrained her to her pillows. "You've accustomed him to suckling and nursed him past the crisis. Let him to his nurse for now."

"No." She sat up, unable to hide the pain that sudden movement caused. "He needs me."

"He needs you to live past a few days of feeding, Lizzy," her husband admonished gently. "They will lie beside you on the bed after their stomachs are full."

Too ill to argue, she closed her eyes.

When Darcy emerged from behind the screens, Georgiana was missing as were a number of their mother's diaries; he presumed she read elsewhere to permit their privacy. He summoned Mrs. Carroll, dispatched a rider to fetch Dr. Simons and ordered broth from the kitchen and a bowl of the coolest water. He next rearranged the screens for more space and then the furnishings at bedside to make room for an over-stuffed chair pulled close to Elizabeth.

Mrs. Carroll frowned to see her patient's condition. She touched the lady's forehead and neck to judge the extent of the fever then assessed whether the bleeding had increased. She said it was a good sign that it had not before quitting them to brew a special tea.

Darcy remained at his wife's side with one hand holding hers. And so he sat when the basin of fresh water arrived; he applied a fresh cloth every fifteen minutes. And so he sat when the midwife positioned herself on Darcy's side of the bed to coax Elizabeth to drink two cups of medicinal tea. And so he sat when Dr. Simons arrived, examined the lady and whispered the next twenty-four hours would be critical.

Georgiana ordered Henry's and her meals served in the breakfast room and had trays delivered to her brother. The trays returned untouched. Every three hours, Darcy awakened his wife to swallow a cup of special tea and one of broth while she watched her babies beside her.

The turn of events focused the Fitzwilliams on their familial dilemma. Behind the thick walls of Darcy's study, they troubled over the quasi-family/quasi-stranger relationship they had alternately showed their brother since the twins' delivery. They agreed that "sitting on the fence" was neither of their natures, and to be true to themselves, they must choose one side or the other. With trepidation for the further disappointment they might be inviting, they chose to follow their hearts. At nine o'clock, Georgiana crossed the pavilion's threshold and sat with her brother, her arm around his shoulder. Then Henry arrived, widened the circle of screens, and pulled in his own chair to hold vigil with them.

Chapter 58

A chair, no matter how comfortable, makes a poor bed; Darcy slept in short fits. Each time he woke, he glanced at his pocket watch on the nearby table before appraising Elizabeth's condition. He held "twenty-four hours" as a promise and took heart that only twelve hours remained. The mantel clock's tick-tock again lulled him to shallow sleep.

When the children cried, Elizabeth awoke, but she lay still without comment when their nurses carried them beyond her screens. She understood that life hung by a thread with no way to know how thick or strong the thread might be.

Daylight coalesced the clouds that had been accumulating for two days. Dark and heavy, they only drizzled at first, but by midday the heavens opened to flash lightening and crack thunder so powerful to awaken James. Elizabeth let her husband calm their son without one argument that she should do it.

She watched her babies nestled in her husband's arms. They were little people she could imagine to adulthood. Anne-Elizabeth's blond-brown hair evidenced curls like her papa, who had declared his daughter's gray eyes to be near the same color as his mother's. Elizabeth's baby girl was perfect; with fine-honed, delicate features, she would be a striking beauty. James, on the other hand, looked to be a work in progress, which pulled at his mother's heart. Two inches longer than his sister, he had no hair to speak of, though what one could see looked to be strawberry blond, a surprise to say the least. His eyes were dark and likely brown. Anne-E sucked her right thumb and James his left, each mimicking their mother and father's hand preferences. Lacking his sister's healthy plumpness, James was the child who would have done better to grow alone inside his mama.

Minutes of reflection between her naps accumulated to hours of understanding while Elizabeth lay flat, fearing any movement lest she shoot another pain through her gut. Despite that only a few days had passed since her children had taken their first breaths as two of England's newest subjects, the intensity of her attachment to them boggled her; she had hitherto counted her motherly instinct to be only average at best. Already, her babies demonstrated their individuality that teased her to wonder how they would grow and who they would make themselves to be. She watched William hold them, secure in his gentle mothering of them. His presence anchored her small world inside the screens. It was as he had said; when she could not manage alone, he would step in and do it for her.

That afternoon, Darcy demurred when Georgiana suggested she might sit with Elizabeth to let him bathe and change into more comfortable clothes. He nibbled at a sandwich when his sister insisted, but refused a second; his stomach too knotted to accept further intrusion. Later, he did slip on the fresh shirt and looser trousers Georgiana carried to him, but he did so inside the wall of screens, his eyes fixed on his wife. Twenty-four hours had passed, but her skin still burned and her heart still beat too fast.

That evening, Henry and Georgiana again held vigil with Darcy. At nine, they kissed Elizabeth and squeezed their brother's shoulder before they settled in the breakfast room with a clear view of the pavilion and close proximity to the stairs connecting them to their family. The Darcys deserved their privacy, but the Fitzwilliams were too concerned to sleep.

After the children finished their midnight feeding, Darcy arranged his wife's arms and nestled each baby inside them. He was startled to hear her whisper, "Thank you."

He bowed, "You're most welcome, Madam. Is there anything else you desire?"

She shook her head slightly to decline, but the movement slipped the cloth down over eyes. "Yes. Fix this, please," she amended. "I want to look at you."

He prepared a fresh cloth, positioned it carefully on her forehead then sat in his chair. "I fear I'm not much to look at, Wife. I see now I ought to have taken our sister's advice and freshened myself." He ran his free hand over three-day old stubble and was certain his face sagged to match his spirit, but he made his best effort to mimic a smile. "How do you feel?"

"Honestly?" Her eyes showed as much life as the limp hand he held. "I feel awful. Worse than awful." She swallowed. "I'm disappointed, William. I didn't expect to feel so weak or so tormented inside."

"Where is the pain?"

She nodded toward her stomach.

"No, lower," she directed when he moved his hand over the collapsed bulge where their children had grown. "Yes, there," she affirmed, feeling his light pressure on her knife pains. "Keep your hand there, if you can manage the stretch. It helps a little."

She watched him until her eyes closed. Thoughts chased each other in her head. How different they each were after nearly one year of marriage: she a spritely nymph now pained to move and staring mortality in the face and he a reserved yet self-confident master now wearing his heart on his sleeve and praying for the good outcome of a play that cared nothing for wealth and power.

When she did not awaken to her children's cries for their middle night meal, Darcy told himself it was because she slept more deeply, which must be good sign. And when he let go her hand long enough to feel her neck, he imagined she was not so warm as an hour before. Except for cool cloths and her nourishment, Darcy kept his right hand on her pain and his left hand wrapped around hers with one finger always stretched to gauge her pulse.

He awoke to the sound of gardeners trimming the hedges and digging to set blooming chrysanthemums in the beds beyond the French doors. His head had settled to sleep on the bedcover half-way between where one hand pressed and the other held hers. Their children had been returned to their cradles. Exhausted, he closed his eyes, acknowledging that neither of them had awakened to their children's cries.

Dr. Simons shook Darcy awake. "I recommend a bath and a hot meal, Sir."

Darcy looked quickly from the doctor to the midwife at his side, and then to Elizabeth. She slept. He could see her chest rise and fall. "I'd prefer to remain," he said.

"I understand, Sir, but at this point what is best for you and what is best for your wife are at odds. Mrs. Carroll will bathe her, after which I shall make my examination. Let us to our business, Mr. Darcy. I assure you she'll be here when you return."

Darcy rose suddenly and turned his temper on Simons. "Just as you said the worst would be passed yesterday?"

"Let me examine her, Mr. Darcy, then we shall discuss."

Georgiana waited outside the pavilion's doors and escorted him to the master's suite. Henry again spent his day at Cressbrook.

An hour later, Darcy took his meal at the pavilion's dining table with Georgiana ever at his side. When the physician and midwife emerged, Darcy insisted they dine with him, apologizing for his earlier outburst.

"No apology needed, Mr. Darcy," Dr. Simons assured him. "Were I in your place, I'd have said much more and done it louder."

"And my wife, Doctor?"

"We both believe she is stable," he nodded to include Mrs. Carroll, "and that is the best one could wish for."

"Stable?"

"Her fever, if anything, has decreased and the bleeding is negligible. We believe she suffers from childbed fever, a common illness during the first fortnight following childbirth." He paused, "It accounts for the majority of maternal mortality." Darcy did not flinch. Dr. Simons continued. "I wouldn't speak so forthrightly if I believed Mrs. Darcy in present danger."

"Present danger?"

"Nature cannot be predicted, but according to experience, she's past the worst."

Mrs. Carroll said, "It will be a long recovery, Mr. Darcy. I'll remain so long as you like."

Darcy said, "Thank you." He glanced at the screens. "Is she sleeping now?"

"Yes, Sir."

He swallowed before looking Matthew Simons in the eye. "Will she recover completely? I ask so that I'm better prepared to support her."

Dr. Simons pressed his lips and focused on his plate before responding. "There is a small possibility she might not conceive more children, Sir."

"That's all?" Darcy made no effort to hide his relief.

Georgiana, however, stared. "I think she'd take such news very badly."

"Yes. Most women do." He looked at Darcy. "I suggest you say nothing. She'll learn soon enough if there's a problem. If it is so, it is best she addresses it after she regains her strength."

Darcy nodded.

"We also recommend she resumes nursing. To not do so could invite breast infection."

Darcy nodded.

Behind the screens, Elizabeth stared at the ceiling and touched the bulge where her babies had lived, her eyes brimming with tears. The pain in her gut held no candle to that in her heart. The chance there might be no more children, no matter that she still suffered from bearing the first two, was a sorrow she dug deep to control.

The next morning Elizabeth awoke to a gold rimmed ivory-colored porcelain vase with an arrangement of yellow and white chrysanthemums on a small bureau at the foot of her bed. Every morning thereafter, Darcy welcomed her day with a fresh bouquet set by his own hand, though the gardener selected the blooms and tutored the master in the art of a balanced arrangement. Her husband's gift touched Elizabeth more deeply than spoken words.

Too much had happened since the babies' births to leave their mama unchanged. Accepting Mrs. Carroll's overheard-prediction that it would be a long recovery, Elizabeth did not press to imitate her former self too soon, and though she did not tempt disappointment with too much expectation, she knew she was getting better. The proud and independent Miss Bennet would not recognize her counterpart in Mrs. Darcy, who accepted dependence on others with a sincere smile of gratitude and who requested support when required. Elizabeth also acknowledged that her mistake regarding William's birth date had, indeed, been an art of prodding, and though the pain she had caused him had been profound, he now appeared to be more at ease with memories of his parents than since she had known him. She and William had settled into a calm routine divided between their children and each other.

Chapter 59

With the babies three weeks old and their mother recovered enough to host meals at the dining table and tend her children in the pavilion's makeshift nursery, Darcy celebrated life even better than before their babies' births. Next week, the Fitzwilliams would return to Cressbrook while Elizabeth and the children would move to the House-proper, though mother and babies would be restricted to the first level for another fortnight. With much polishing and ubiquitous smiles, the House anticipated the forgotten joy of holding children to its bosom.

During the days when Elizabeth had slept more than not, Darcy had sat at her bedside reading his mother's diaries, though he delayed opening the volume that might shed light on an issue he no longer deemed to be important. In fact, he felt no need to substantiate anything in regard to his father's actions except that papa deserved the formal vindication.

Wearing a simple morning gown sprigged with tiny pink and blue flowers, Elizabeth sat close to her husband near the north hearth. She rocked the cradles with her feet while he skimmed quickly and read out pertinent passages to learn Lady Anne together as they had agreed to do it.

19 November, 17 - -

It is done. Negotiations are completed. My betrothal will be announced at the commencement of the spring season. Mama has her wish. She has arranged for me to marry Lord Byron Titling in May. The announcement's delay is to let Mama prepare our house and wardrobes to impress the legions who will celebrate the coupling of one of the most powerful lords of the land with the Fitzwilliam family.

Lord Titling kissed my bare hand today. Dear God! His paper thin lips made my skin crawl. I cannot bear to think they will touch my lips soon enough. I have delayed the inevitable as long as I could.

"Did you know about this Lord Titling, William?"

"No." He studied the fire for a moment. "This explains much however. When that gentleman was introduced to me several years back, he was even ruder than his reputation implied should be expected. I daresay he recalled a betrothal gone awry."

"And to think you could have been a Titling instead of a Darcy."

Her husband grimaced and continued.

5 December, 17 - -

To my good fortune, papa commiserates that I shall be sacrificed for the benefit of mama's social standing. He has stood his ground that John and I should make a Christmas journey to Pemberley since I have not painted that lovely place during the holiday season. Of course as always, he made no mention of my art to her.

My life has devolved to a string of secrets beneath an ever more public persona. Not even my dear papa could guess what really draws me to Pemberley.

Elizabeth raised her brow and teased, "Can we guess what that allure might be?"

Relaxed, Darcy read on.

24 December, 17 - -

I must record this entry circumspectly, though my heart would rejoice to relive it in every detail on this page. Aware that this is likely my last visit to Pemberley before my betrothal is announced, feelings that I had not voiced, even to myself, were loosed.

He is everything wonderful, though admittedly I had no concept of "everything" let alone how wonderful "wonderful" could be. I did not think my love and admiration for this person could grow any greater until he acceded to my overtures and let me know him as a man. It is a memory that must last my entire life since I shall cringe when Lord Titling touches me. Though duty to Mother supersedes my wishes, I am so grateful for the courage to have followed my heart if only for a moment.

My only regret is that he compromised himself for me and this, I fear, will cause him severe personal hardship in future. I ought to feel more guilt for my selfishness, but his gift was too precious for me to despair too much. I pray he will eventually conclude the same.

Darcy rose and lay the book open where he had sat. He returned a half-hour later.

Elizabeth offered him a fresh cup of tea. "Where did you go?"

"To the park. I walked." He sat with head in his hands. "I apologized to him, to them both. I'm not sure a child should know his parents' secrets, and yet to know the secrets is to love them even more dearly."

"They weren't embarrassed for you to know. They agreed you should read the diaries." She smiled. "I wonder how many months were required before she convinced your father to share what his written habit preferred to keep hid."

"I doubt very many. He granted her most everything, I think."

25 January, 17 - -
I am one week late.

1 February, 17 - -
I am two weeks late.

8 February, 17 - -
I am three weeks late.

Elizabeth squeezed his hand. "I can feel her fear in those short sentences, William,"

He nodded.

10 February, 17 - -
I cannot guess how he managed to convince Papa, but my father has accepted another visit to Pemberley to include me! Papa announced it this morning at break-fast. Mama was all hysterics since our travel will disrupt the first fitting of my trousseau, but Papa had his way. I hope, no, I am certain this invitation has but one meaning: he cares for me as I do him. I rejoice to see him one last time.

"Despite everything, I think she intended to marry Lord Titling," Elizabeth said.

"It would seem so," her husband answered.

343

12 February, 17 - -

I am ill. There will be no Pemberley.

I shall send a note with papa to convey my regrets. It will be my last contact with him.

22 February, 17 - -

Mama begins to suspicion what I have feared since early in the month. She demanded to see my calendar this morning.

27 February, 17 - -

There is nothing to say. The betrothal is renounced, though mama had already whispered the marriage to enough of her friends that the scandal will entertain society for many weeks. She makes arrangements to transfer me to a convent for the duration. Papa is so distressed I worry for him. I discovered Catherine in my bedchamber last evening. Mama is intent to learn the name of my lover. I loosed a floorboard in my dressing closet and made a secret home for those volumes that reference Pemberley. I am more alone than ever in my life, yet not; I carry my love inside. My future is suddenly unscripted, yet not; I will not give up my child, which makes me unmarriageable. It is a double gift that I gave myself unawares at Christmas.

"Dear God in Heaven, what hell she must have endured," Elizabeth said softly. He husband nodded.

1 March, 17 - -

I am scheduled to depart for the nunnery at mid-month.

Today I received the fourth letter he has had smuggled to me since Papa last visited him. My fear that his concern derives from guilt and obligation are soothed by this letter, which lets me hope he feels for me, if only a little, as I do for him. I shall cling to hope.

He detailed a plan, which he beseeched me to I accept. On 5 March, I shall carry a hat box containing my most precious possessions, as if I visit the milliner, but instead I will board a mail coach to - - -, where he will meet me. To protect me while en route to him, my maid from Pemberley will be on the coach. I have already determined the contents of my hat box; my diaries fit, all but one, which I will secure on my person. There is the small problem of distracting my maid who will escort me to the milliner, but I shall escape her somehow.

"Your father's declaration to do what 'he did not think possible' makes sense now." Elizabeth pressed her husband's hand. "From the sound of it, he was a very clever man since his plan was obviously successful all around." She knew his silence bespoke sorrow to have presumed a conclusion before assuring he had all the facts. He read on.

7 March, 17 - -

We married yesterday. The vicar at - - -, George's long-standing friend, joined us, but not before his looks blamed me for having compromised George Darcy to a quick and clandestine wedding. Noting the vicar's look, George's wrath nearly compromised the ceremony.

Despite what others might think, we are shy with each other and suffer many small, daily misunderstandings. I am too sensitive about what I have foisted on him and he is too accustomed to life alone. Though my husband is the more staid and serious of us, it is he who begins to poke fun at the small crises we seem to meet at every turn. I had believed I could not love him more, but each day my admiration grows to humble that from the day before.

I am a burden on my beloved, though he claims not. My only solace is that I might present him an heir during the coming years. An heir would be small recompense for the sacrifice he makes for me.

"If I did not know better, Lizzy, their tryst was providential." Darcy said softly, "I hadn't considered that Pemberley remained heirless before my arrival."

Elizabeth smiled.

21 March, 17 - -

George and I were wed for a second time today. Since mama kept hid any mention of our elopement, society holds this as our wedding day. I agreed to this formal ceremony at Pemberley to let papa hold up his head at his club. He took such pride to walk with his daughter on his arm with his friends as witness. Mama's friends attended as well, though I held no care for them or her. That such a lovely and extravagant wedding could be arranged in only a fortnight is a tribute to our Pemberley.

As his gift to me, papa purloined the porcelain vase from Glenbrooke that mama had refused me. Dear papa. Had he known my intent for it, he would regret his effort, though perhaps not. Mama stated she and papa had not spoken since my elopement; she blames me for their rift.

Ever at my side, George permitted no look or innuendo to disparage me, not even from mama. He protected me so well that I overheard ladies bemoaning that they had not got the gallant and handsome George Darcy for themselves. When I told George of this later, he laughed and pulled me to his lap. "Those ladies could see only a solemn recluse when they looked at me. But you saw inside and goaded me to more," he said.

"Did you know your Grandmamma Fitzwilliam, Husband?"

"She visited on occasion, but I always regretted to learn she was coming and rejoiced when she departed. Papa adjusted his schedule to remain of House for the duration of her visits. I did not guess from my mother's demeanor when grandmamma visited that they were estranged. Unfortunately, Grandpapa died, God rest him, when I was too young to remember him, though from this I think I might have liked him."

19 September, 17 - -

A son was born to us three days ago. It was a difficult delivery. I called for George part-way through. That he held my hand until the end bespeaks a devotion, for which I dared not hope. He is my strength, my love and all of my happiness.

His arms are our son's cradle when I am not holding our little Fitzwilliam. I admit the name is an irony intended in part to connect our boy with the peerage he will not inherit at Pemberley and in part to goad mama that her family name will forever bespeak my emancipation from her. George laughed when he heard my wish for this name and said he had not guessed I harbor such a vindictive thread, but he understood and kissed his acceptance.

"The son appears to imitate the father during delivery, Mr. Darcy," Elizabeth joked.

Darcy smiled. "So it would appear, Mrs. Darcy."

10 December, 17 - -

We prepare our return to Pemberley after nine months from House. George insists to protect our son from gossip as best we can; hence the number of months between our departure and return as well as letters to Pemberley during the intervening months as if pregnancy revealed itself during our wedding trip. We will celebrate Fitzwilliam's first birthday on the day of his christening to further distance prying eyes from his facts in future. George believes that after only a few years none will think to count at all, and if anyone does, it is nine months from our wedding until Fitzwilliam's christening "birth date."

Perspective reveals George selected the perfect location for our months of seclusion at a place recommended by Dr. Ashworth, whose cousins invited us into their lives. This cottage in the far north is nothing like the homes, to which we are accustomed; first, there is no pretense, only comfortable necessities kept clean and tidy by our own hand; second, our addition of two more mouths at our hosts' table requires us to assist with daily tasks: George now chops wood with alacrity and I cook delicious stew and bake supremely light scones; and third, our hosts' loving partnership is the model denied us by our natural parents. We have learned so much from these dear friends that our financial contribution and their pleasure in our son is too small recompense. When Dr. Ashworth arrived to attend delivery, we suffered the extremes of emotion, both joy at the birth of our precious son and sorrow to know time was short with the couple we have come to love. That they won't return with us bespeaks their solid understanding of life; we each belong in different places despite our deep attachment.

And now George and I are set to write the next chapter of our lives together; our return to society, albeit the more gentle society of the Peak. We will introduce a child of three months as an infant one month old, a discrepancy that George will somehow make work as he does everything in my regard. I am a princess rescued by her prince who carries her to his realm of Pemberley.

Darcy closed the diary.

Elizabeth took his hand and pulled him toward the circle of screens. "Come," she said, "I want your arms around me."

Chapter 60

Despite the driving rain, twelve-year-old Georgiana could see the wagon approach and her brother's blood-soaked shirt wrapping papa's head. Henry had ridden ahead to fetch the doctor then returned to the House to prepare her. She sat stoically in her favorite chair until the House slept then tip-toed to papa's bedchamber. A single candle showed a fresh bandage of linen strips, but blood still seeped and made a dull red circle over his right temple. Georgiana sat on his bed and held his hand.

Unbeknownst to her, Fitzwilliam held vigil in a darkened corner. When his sister fell asleep, he carried her to her bed and pulled the covers to her chin.

After two nights of holding papa's hand in hers, she added songs to their communion. Each time, she asked, "Do you remember when we sang that, Papa?" And then she recounted memories to entice him from his sleep. Memories of pony rides, tea parties and fresh flowers for his desk. Memories of story-telling and silly letters, of walks in the Park and dancing lessons.

From the privacy of his chair, twenty-two-year-old Fitzwilliam learned about a personal world of sweetness between father and daughter. He did not begrudge his sister their papa's attention since such was what a parent should show a child, yet it haunted him that at Georgiana's age, he could not have filled one night with sweet memories that might lure papa from his sleep. When Darcy was Georgiana's age, his mother approached her own death.

D arcy did not recall the sheet of paper hid with his mother's diaries until breakfast the next morning.

"Lizzy, I have some business to attend, but only briefly." He looked at Georgiana. "Would you take an interest to help Elizabeth tend the children,

Sister?" Georgiana, her motherhood delayed, delighted at every opportunity to attend her niece and nephew.

Upstairs in the seclusion of his bedchamber, Darcy unfolded his father's words.

> *My dearest Fitzwilliam and Georgiana,*
>
> *We buried your mother last week, God rest her, though I know that a spirit such as hers cannot return to dust as if it never existed. She lives in me both as a torture, because I no longer hear her voice, and as a joy, because her voice enchanted me for thirteen years.*
>
> *As with all things between us, we each required adjustment to one another's needs; she desperately wanted to leave her thoughts for you to read and wrote her letters without my knowledge since I just as desperately refused to accept I must lose her. As you might now know, I did, at last, succumb to reality and am so grateful for our last months together. Initially, she intended to secret all of her letters behind one painting due to her physical weakness, but I convinced her to consign them to ten canvasses, making it ten times more likely they would be discovered. She was adamant they be kept safe and flat until you were of an appropriate age to read them and I was firm that the revelations in her diaries be read only by loving and compassionate eyes. To that end, she conceived that the clue to the diaries' location be included in my ramblings since only a mature and devoted child would trouble to decipher them.*
>
> *Your mother's letters are preserved behind eight landscapes executed by her hand, each of which is identified by A.D. 18 - - at the bottom right corner of the frames. The final two are behind our formal portraits. I myself placed the letters on the back of each canvas and refitted each dust cover with my own clumsy hand. She laughed at my awkwardness with tools then hugged me for my effort to accomplish what was difficult for me to do.*
>
> *I must say that I questioned the necessity for so much secrecy in regard to her letters, but I humored her wishes. Only after her death, God rest her, did I understand the grounds for the care she took. Twice I discovered her sister, Catherine, poking among your mother's things and your grandmamma confronted me directly that she should have possession of her daughter's diaries. I cannot explain such words or actions beyond that your grandmamma never forgave my wife for humiliating her publicly and perhaps feared your mama might reveal the charade invented to explain a broken betrothal.*

As for her diaries, your mother selected this location and detailed how I should set the floorboards so that you might uncover her gift more easily. You will note the excellent workmanship, which required these many days since her interment for me to accomplish. I have no doubt she designed this project as much to distract me from my grief during the first, most awful days as she did to keep her diaries from prying eyes.

Though this letter addresses your mother's treasures, I shall include my apology to you in this footnote. I regret with all my heart that the parent who remains to raise you is the least well-equipped to do it. Though I shall do all in my power to avoid disappointing you, I am certain that I will. Your mother imbued me with life as I had not imagined possible and her loss snuffs a part of me that even my deep and abiding devotion to you cannot rekindle.

Ironically, despite the gulf caused by her loss, too broad and deep to bridge, I pray that you will discover such love in your chosen partners as I have known with mine. When a man and woman complete each other, there is no greater joy, no deeper fulfillment of a human being and no more effective annulment of man's natural isolation. Please, do not waste sympathy on a man bereaved. I would not change one aspect of my life except that my partner could have lived so long as I.

You are the best gifts we gave each other, your mama and me.

Your Devoted Papa, George Darcy

Darcy wept like a child… wept in part out of guilt to have once condemned his father, but mostly he mourned that he had not known the man who had written this letter. Fitzwilliam Darcy had no doubt that knowing such a man would have changed his life. Despair took the upper hand while he watched the fire, but when Darcy considered his own children, he took control and was firm on his course of action. After dispatching a note to Elizabeth stating he would be delayed until tea time, he set to it.

He first made a list of the family memories still haunting him, and then wrote out each event in full detail absent his biased perspective. Written as if by an impartial observer, page after page exposed the jealousy and insecurity that had skewed his interpretation of the facts. He did shed tears intermittently, but each bout of despair spurred him to tackle the next memory on his list until his new-self grew confidence to accept the childish aspects he had put to rest and draw a line under what he could not change. When tea was announced, he lifted his parents' portraits from the nails above his mantle and carried them to the pavilion where Georgiana poured tea and Elizabeth prepared three plates. Henry would not return from Cressbrook until dinner.

Georgiana looked up to see the portraits her brother leaned against the server then glanced above the pavilion's mantle at the copies she had made. "Do you prefer these?" she asked, indicating the oils.

"Only for the gifts they protect," he said.

"What gifts?" She passed him his cup, and a plate of biscuits and sandwiches.

"I don't know precisely. I haven't seen them yet."

"More riddles, Fitzwilliam?" she asked, laughing.

Without conscious thought, Darcy invited, "Please, call me 'William.'" The formality of his given name no longer suited the friendship he wished to foster with his sister. He smiled at his wife, "You don't mind, do you, Lizzy?"

"Not at all," she laughed.

Darcy lay his father's letter in front of Georgiana then stood behind his seated wife. "The riddle is explained in that note from father," he said nodding at the sheet of paper.

Elizabeth watched in rapt attention. Georgiana's confusion turned to excitement to read her father's words, but after only a few lines, tears overflowed while she read the rest. She held the papa she knew in her hands and missed him as if her heart broke again to lose him. Her brother held her to weep on his shoulder. "You knew him better than I," he whispered, rubbing her back.

She sniffed and drew back to look at him. "Only because I was born a girl," she said with such conviction that Darcy stepped back in surprise.

He would have laughed, but her sincerity begged respect. "Forgive me, Georgiana, but I can't see how 'male' or 'female' can influence what is intrinsically an issue of personality. I don't blame you that he warmed to you more than me." He breathed deep to maintain composure. "I'm only sorry I didn't know him as you did. From that letter alone," he indicated the sheet on the table, "I know what I missed."

"My dear, dear Brother," his sister said, "you blame the wrong cause for what you missed. Please! Don't turn away, William," she said, forcing herself to use the name offered her. She held him to face her. "Papa had two duties in your regard. His love raised you as a person and his obligation to Pemberley raised you to be its master. As for me, love alone raised the daughter to whom he had no other obligation, which permitted me a clearer glimpse into the man himself."

Elizabeth sat straight. The simple explanation for the brother and sister's very different relationships with the same parent had escaped her as she had worked to make sense of William's conflicted feelings toward his father. She knew her husband and felt his shock at what obligation had cost him.

Darcy freed himself and crossed to the French doors, hands in pockets and eyes fixed on the autumn garden. He heard the swish of Georgiana's skirt then felt her arm as she slipped it around his.

"He rejoiced in each of us, Brother," her soft voice insisted, "but in the full balance of things, he was more glad for you because you continue his Pemberley." She patted his arm. "He was so very, very proud of you, William. He stood in awe of your natural talent to master, an obligation that his own nature struggled to do right. He admired you, Brother. He told me once that compared with those who came before he believed you would master Pemberley best of all." Georgiana rested her head on his arm and watched the garden with him. "I didn't understand until now," she continued, "that through you he took pride in himself." Darcy blinked to maintain his control. His sister concluded, "Though he would not have admitted it for fear of slighting me, his greatest pride and happiness was to call you 'son'."

She squeezed his arm, stood back and invited, "Let's open the portraits together."

Darcy wiped his eyes, got his composure and said huskily, "No. It was you who resurrected our mother." He pointed to the paintings. "You'll open their backs and read the letters first. I'd like a copy of each in your hand when it's convenient."

His sister reached up and kissed his cheek then spread a throw on the cleared end of the table and placed her mother's portrait face down. She loosened the tacks with a butter knife then lifted Love from where it had lain for sixteen years.

Next she freed the cover from papa's back and did the same with Courage.

Darcy stood behind his wife, his hands on her shoulders and watched. Elizabeth kissed the hands that held her for his courage in the face of too much.

After dinner that evening, Henry rose from the table and bowed with a sober expression.

"Darcy, I should like to meet with you in your study."

"We are among family, Henry. Whatever you wish to discuss we can do here."

"I realize this, Cousin, but I will speak only with you, hence my request."

"Oh. Yes, of course. We can go at once if you like."

Elizabeth watched with nerves for her husband. Henry led while Darcy followed. For her part, Georgiana continued conversation with her sister as if naught were awry.

After closing the study door, Henry pointed to a chair and asked, "May I sit?"

"Yes. You needn't ask, you know." Darcy sat in the chair opposite.

"Darcy, I am obliged to tell you that you have put Georgiana and me in a difficult spot."

"How so?"

"We had resolved to live our lives separate from Pemberley, but your recent actions and demeanor demand that we reconsider."

"That would be my dearest wish."

"However, my wife and I are agreed to insist on equal footing with Pemberley."

"This goes without saying."

"Very well," Henry rose, "then I must inquire if you have redeemed the check I gave you."

Darcy crossed to his desk and pulled the check from a drawer. "No, I didn't."

"Good. May I have it, please?"

Darcy handed it over and eyed his cousin. He sensed Henry was playing with him.

Henry tore it in half and dropped it in the waste bin. "Our meeting is concluded."

"Not quite," William said, planting himself in his cousin's path. "What was that just now?"

"Family does not repay a gift, Darcy. Such would be insulting."

The master of Pemberley studied the man who stood as tall as he and equally as proud. A smile lit his eyes then grew to a full laugh. He clapped Henry on the shoulder and would have embraced him, but sensitivity to his own previous bad behavior balked to presume too much. Henry, on the other hand, did the embracing for them both. At the last, he stood back and stated soberly, "I'm sorry to tell you this, Darcy, but you can no longer call me brother only when it suits you. We are brothers now, for better or worse."

The brothers carried their celebration to the pavilion where Elizabeth witnessed it from behind the screens. When her husband poked his head past the tapestry wall, his golden eyes confirmed the depth of his tranquility. "We are united again, Lizzy," he rejoiced and leaned across James to kiss his wife. "Join us soon, Lizzy," he said. She nodded and kissed him again. He lifted his lovely little doll from her cradle and stepped past the screens.

Elizabeth followed the sound of his step across the parquet floor and smiled to recall the taciturn man who had spurned her at a country soiree and compare him with William who took such joy in his babies a scant two years later. Of a sudden, her happy image connected with a tragic one to imagine William without more babies to delight in should Dr. Simons warning be true; the possibility tore at her heart. She composed herself, called William to burp James then claimed weariness and pulled the covers over her head; she must get control of the latent fear. Elizabeth's choice to seclude herself surprised her husband; it hadn't been so many minutes since her eyes and kiss had promised she would join them. The party with Henry and Georgiana felt less so without her at his side.

Later after the celebration had ended, Darcy sat at her bedside in his comfortable chair and reflected on one of the most remarkable days of his life. He and Elizabeth had not had time to discuss the day's events and he waited until she awoke to feed James to hear her thoughts. Anne-E stirred and he carried her to the nursery. When he returned, she already held James to her.

"I will hear your thoughts, Lizzy," as if they sat on their picnic quilt.

"About what?"

"About anything. About Georgiana and Henry. About my parents. About anything. I want to hear your thoughts."

"I can't say that I have any," she answered, her voice remote. Too distracted by her private burden, she had neither interest nor energy to discuss.

"Nonsense. You have thoughts about everything."

"Not tonight, my love," she said.

After sating James, she said, "Forgive me, Husband. I want to sleep" and closed her eyes.

Chapter 61

William endured a wakeful night. Elizabeth's recent easy conversation and sparkling smiles had left him unprepared to see she was troubled by some new issue, one significant enough that she preferred silence to sharing. Initially, his disappointment exposed a bit of anger and a touch of blame since, of late, it was certainly she who withdrew from him more than vice versa, but his recent education that first conclusions were not necessarily reliable waggled a finger in his face and prodded him to dig deeper.

He accepted that tallying her moods and comparing them to his own missed the point; marriage was not a balance sheet. From the beginning, each of their natures had prodded the other to meet personal needs, whose satisfaction, in turn, grew them together. He paused in surprise to realize that he had prodded as well as she.

In his mind, a husband and wife compared with the primary cogs in the machine of family. When their teeth meshed, honest communication flowed easily and they inevitably pulled each other in the same direction, but when disengaged, the family stalled. For her part, Elizabeth was most engaged when he withdrew and she did not stop prodding until they had regained their equanimity. Too often, however, Darcy had done the opposite as when he had kept his distance while she sorted the issues of a contract and when he had given rein to her moods in early pregnancy, and again, when he had waited too long to confront her isolation after a birth date revealed. At those times, he had believed he demonstrated respect when, in actuality, he had abrogated his marital responsibility.

As the clock ticked toward dawn, he lay beside her awash in memories wafting vignettes of their first year together. When strung end-to-end, they detailed the coming-out of Fitzwilliam Darcy, a fact less to be celebrated without his wife in full engagement. Darcy eased from their bed, lit a lamp on the dining table and dipped his pen.

The next morning Elizabeth saw a folded paper on her bedside table, on which "My Lizzy" was scribed in her husband's hand. Certain it confronted her distance the previous evening, she ignored it while swallowing breakfast, tending her babies' baths, feeding James, and pacifying Anne-E. But when all was done, Mrs. Darcy could shirk no longer. She broke the seal.

> *My Dearest,*
>
> *As I told you early on, I will sometimes require your prodding before I address what I need confront. Though I was naïve as to what I asked of you, you wisely understood what prodding might cost you. That you agreed to hold the stink of my stupidity under my nose bespeaks your devotion to a man who deserves much less, but who is thankful that you discern enough in him to entice your love.*

She had not anticipated he would focus on himself and continued with more curiosity than concern that he would challenge what she shrank to confront.

> *I have no doubt I would still disdain a fair understanding of my father were it not for my deepest attachment to you. Yes, I refused the insights you so patiently coaxed me to accept, but I could not ignore your detachment from me or the self-doubt my obstinacy caused you to suffer. Ultimately, dear Wife, I would endure my hell these past weeks again and again if such were required to hear my Lizzy laugh or feel her kiss me with her eyes.*

In three sentences, he had summarized weeks of torment for them both. Again, she marveled at his gift to distill facts to their essence, admiration that further disarmed her worry he would press her to share what words could not convey.

> *There have been so many lessons during recent weeks, but the most salient to my wife and children is that I accept past failures in regard to my father, as well as to Henry and myself. But rather than wallow in guilt, I am committed to assure that Anne-E and James will not suffer as I have from poor communication with their papa.*

His insights bespoke a man she did not wholly know, though they went far to explain his unruffled equanimity of late. Of a sudden, Elizabeth understood that the inordinate sleep required during recovery had cost her more than a few days of social interaction; her William had reinvented himself without her and Mrs. Darcy hated to be left out.

> *Before last night, I believed we had returned to our open and honest partnership until you retreated behind the veil of weariness. I heard our separation in your tone and felt it when I lay beside you. If I have caused you some other disappointment I will hear it. If you still fear to trust in our compatibility, I will learn it. If it is some other problem, tell me. The worst part for me is not to know your thoughts. Talk to me, Lizzy. I pray that you will talk with me.*
> *Your desperately enamored husband,*
> *William*

She refolded his letter, laid it on her bedside table and watched the circle of screens.

Fitzwilliam Darcy was slow to admit his disappointment. During four hours, he had accomplished next to nothing at his desk since every sound outside his study door had raised his hope for a note inviting him to discuss. When the clock announced luncheon, he prepared for confrontation.

Arrived at the pavilion, he stopped short on the threshold to find a darkened room with curtains drawn across the walls of windows. The dining table sat bare but for the gold-rimmed vase of white chrysanthemums. There were no servants.

"Over here, Mr. Darcy," Elizabeth's voice called from among the furnishings clustered at the north hearth.

Intrigued, he stepped toward her then paused and scrutinized the chamber. "Where are the children?"

"In the nursery with their nurses."

A slow smile teased the corners of Darcy's mouth. Arrived at the carpet anchoring the sitting area's furnishings, he met his wife relaxed among cushions on their picnic quilt, beside which their lunch waited under silver domes. He pulled her to her feet and rejoiced in the reconnection of her embrace.

"I had anticipated an argument," he confided.

"You might still get one," she responded in a half-tease. "I only got this far," she indicated their special quilt, "and can't predict what lies ahead."

"Then let's have at it, Wife."

After pulling off his boots and jacket, Darcy leaned back in their private world. He preferred wine to tea; she had anticipated his choice. He selected meat sandwiches. She ate stew. Despite his invitation to "have at it," they initially put off words of any import.

With their glasses refilled and their stomachs sated, Elizabeth adjusted to sit at his side, facing him, hugging her knees with her back to the fire. "My trouble last evening is a problem without resolution, William," she began. "It is a small issue over which we have no control."

"A 'small issue' wouldn't withdraw you in weariness, Lizzy."

"I suppose not," she granted. Wishing very much to put this behind her, she took a breath and began. "Three weeks ago, I overheard Dr. Simons' caution that I might bear no more children." He sat straight; tense in his concern for her. She continued. "I had thought I'd come to terms with the possibility, but yesterday when I watched you carry Anne-E to the party, my heart broke for what barrenness would cost you." Her soft brown eyes admired him. "I doubt there is any man more enamored of his babies than you, William. Watching you with them is to witness pure joy in your look and your touch."

Darcy reached to hold her, but she backed away. "There can be no consolation, my love. No matter how passionately you deny it, I know you would long for what I might not be able to give you." She sat stoic in silent declaration that the topic had been closed to discussion.

Unprepared to be dismissed, Darcy sat stunned until frustration and anger raised him to his feet. "You'll let this sit between us, will you?" he demanded.

Taken aback, she bristled and stood to meet him at the edge of their quilt. "There's no reason it should come between us. You requested to know my problem and I shared it."

"What you 'shared' was *your* perspective, Elizabeth, after which you announced that *mine* counts for naught." He turned his back, stuffed his hands in his britches' pockets and wandered the chamber in stocking feet.

Movement adjusted Darcy's perspective to shed light on a discussion turned sour. As historic aspects of Elizabeth slipped into place, he believed to grasp why she had forfeited their partnership and assumed unilateral control, an anomaly explained by her opposites. She was, on the one hand, a woman fully engaged in the moment, yet when confronted by disappointment she could not remedy, she locked it in a metaphorical box with part of herself as well. Darcy hesitated to confront such a deep-seated aspect of his wife then accepted his duty to engage.

He glanced at Elizabeth bent to return bits of their picnic to the tray; she appeared as despondent as he felt. In keeping with their exceptional natures, they had managed not only an argument, but an impasse, and on this occasion, Darcy was certain he was not the party obliged to do the adjusting.

Elizabeth prepared to fold their special quilt when he returned to the sitting area. "Spread it again, please," he requested then sat where he could lean against the sofa frame, before he patted the place beside him. "I'd like it if you would sit with me, Lizzy." She did, but with the separation he anticipated.

"Given our opinionated natures, I have no doubt we shall enjoy more misunderstandings in future, Elizabeth," he began as he focused on his hands clasped on his knees, "but I wish them to be honest differences of our own opinions, not ghosts pulling one party's strings." He tossed her a smile. "We have had enough issues with my ghosts to haunt two lifetimes, have we not?"

She smiled a little, but sobered immediately to insist, "Please get to the point, Fitzwilliam. I take it I am the party under discussion?"

He bowed and proceeded. "It would seem my feelings are like an object you have held in your hand and examined so as to choose which you will accept and which you will not."

Elizabeth stared with mouth agape to hear the confidence shared in November be used against her. Too hurt and angry to respect the source and consider his message, she scrambled to her feet and would have escaped had he not grasped her arm.

"Sit, Lizzy, or you'll land on my lap and I doubt that's not where you want to be at present." She sat as a supremely controlled, icy version of his wife. He adjusted to face her. "I spoke directly just now to distract you from a mindset, which earlier refused to hear me. Elizabeth," he intoned for emphasis, "your observations this afternoon were not spoken by my partner. Instead, they were uttered from inside a box, the thing in which you hide the pain and disappointment you fear you cannot bear.

"I shall confront it directly, Wife. By its nature, your box is a closed, private affair, which means the woman I love isolates herself from me, and thereby denies me my part in her healing. If a box serves you better than I am able, I will be left alone, which will invite my peevishness witnessed earlier. I note it only so you are forewarned, my love." Then his voice lowered as if in prayer. "It is your choice, Lizzy, and it is my dearest hope you will choose for me."

While he spoke, he watched her fury give way to discomfort then self-consciousness, until Darcy saw his wonderful wife sink into herself and watch her lap.

He judged he had elaborated enough on the negative, and rather than heaping salt in the wound, he adjusted his topic. "Let me tell you how I love you, Mrs. Darcy," he said.

Startled, she looked up and met the embrace of his golden eyes. Elizabeth sat mesmerized to learn bits of his changes she had missed to witness during her illness.

"My love makes me naked in your presence." He spoke his heart so sincerely that his words flowed like miniature love poems. "I am a soul bared only to your eyes." He grazed his finger along her cheek. "I thrive in you, Mrs. Darcy, not just 'with' you, but 'in' you. I fear nothing so long as we are connected."

He watched her like the steady flow of the River Wye. "My love for you rejoices in itself. I live it, Lizzy. It is the air I breathe… the blood pulsing through my body."

"This is your gift to me, Elizabeth. My self, as I sit before you, would not exist, but for my devotion to you. You coaxed me to trust… wholly and completely with the unguarded innocence of a child. It is trust, which deepens love and binds partners, wonderful wife."

He moved close and slipped his arm around her shoulders. Though ridged, she did not pull away. "Would that my wife hears her husband's heart that having only two babies to nurture would be enough, because we would do it together. Would that she promises we will always, without equivocation, share openly, immediately, honestly." And then he bent to her ear and whispered. "Trust me, Lizzy, we can survive anything, if we hold each other close."

Elizabeth felt his words alive inside… felt them course through her as if carried by her blood to every corner of her being. The man who shared her bed sat open before her, his feelings hung on a line in full-sun with no care that a ghost might taunt him and no interest to conceal himself behind careful words. Pa-pum. Pa-pum. Elizabeth's heart pulsed his promise through her head. Pa-pum. Pa-pum. William prodded the last of her boxes into oblivion.

"Hold me," she said and locked her arms around him.

www.ingramcontent.com/pod-product-compliance
Lightning Source LLC
Chambersburg PA
CBHW071225250626
47163CB00001B/100